HUGE

"Credible and engaging, [with] a hero who assumes the most eye-catching characteristics of Holden Caulfield, Philip Marlowe, and Nick Twisp . . . Fuerst pulls off the same trick as the 2005 film *Brick* in making his protagonist's suburban surroundings and mundane foes seem as hard-boiled and corrupt as those in the Chandler novels Huge treasures, [while] capturing the pathos of adolescence without talking down to the audience. There are few challenges greater than voicing a smart, tough kid."

—*Kirkus Reviews*

"A picaresque romp around suburban New Jersey . . . full of nostalgia, humor, candor, and emotions that all readers can relate to."

—*Publishers Weekly*

"A coming-of-age tour de force that borrows some of the tone and attitude of hard-boiled detective fiction while giving its first-person narrator an irresistibly noirish, wise-guy voice. . . . His search for whodunit, which turns into a search for self and sense in a world that's smaller than it should be, is always engrossing."

P9-CCV-228

—*Booklist*

"Funny, rude, and tender all at once, *Huge* is terrific. Hard-boiled and half-baked, Eugene Smalls is a bristling undersized hero for all of us who have felt the furious, desperate need to make life matter, or get splattered trying."

—Sean Stewart, author of the *New York Times* bestsellers *Cathy's Book* and *Perfect Circle*

"An evocative black comedy of manners . . . Imagine Philip Marlowe as a troubled tweener in suburban New Jersey, add a touch of Thoreau's *Walden*, and you have Huge Smalls, the protagonist of Fuerst's debut, who effortlessly lures you into his hard-boiled imagination and completely dysfunctional life."

—Keith Donohue, author of the *New York Times* bestseller *The Stolen Child*

"Huge Smalls is my new favorite fictional character: hilariously potty-mouthed, but also sweetly innocent (well, mostly anyway). He is an utterly original creation. Join him on his cruiser as he tries to solve crimes and misdemeanors in his hometown and somehow ends up with the girl of his dreams—I can guarantee you'll enjoy the ride."

—Alicia Erian, author of the bestselling *New York Times* Notable Book *Towelhead*

HUGE

HUGE

a novel

James W. Fuerst

THREE RIVERS PRESS
NEW YORK

Copyright © 2009 by James W. Fuerst

Published in the United States by Three Rivers Press, an imprint of the Crown Publishing Group, a division of Random House, Inc., New York.
www.crownpublishing.com

Three Rivers Press and the Tugboat design are registered trademarks of Random House, Inc.

Library of Congress Cataloging-in-Publication Data

Fuerst, James.
Huge / James Fuerst. —1st ed.
p. cm.
[1. Interpersonal relations—Fiction.   2. Self-actualization (Psychology)—Fiction.
3. Books and reading—Fiction.   4. Family life—New Jersey—Fiction.   5. Old
age—Fiction.   6. New Jersey—Fiction.   7. Mystery and detective stories.]   I. Title.
PZ7.F948Hug 2009
[Fic]—dc22   2008051190

ISBN 978-0-307-45249-8

Printed in the United States of America

Design by Maria Elias

10   9   8   7   6   5   4   3   2   1

First Edition

A mi abuelita

—often the richest freight will be discharged upon a
Jersey shore;—

—Henry David Thoreau, *Walden*

HUGE

ONE

It was one of those lurid August days, all haze and steam, the sun hidden and stewing like a shameful lust. I dropped the kickstand, locked the Cruiser to the NO PARKING sign, and wiped the glaze of sweat off my face and neck. Thrash was at my side (I'd doubled him along), and we shared a quiet look before heading in.

As we stepped through the glass front doors, the chill from the air-conditioning slapped me like I'd mouthed off. But that was good. It gave me a jolt, woke me up. There wasn't anyone at the front desk, so we hung a left and tiptoed down the pale gray corridor, sticking close to the wall. The Oakshade Retirement Home bragged about cleanliness in its brochures, and to back it up they made sure every inch of the place always reeked of rubbing alcohol and used rubber gloves. Some of the janitors said that if you stayed there long enough, the smell alone could make you sick, or even kill you. Not me, though. I loved that goddamn smell.

We slipped past a few cocked and shadowed heads lolling on the backs of Naugahyde furniture in the TV room, and then double-timed it through a quick Z-shaped turn on the left. I knew the way.

I'd been there plenty of times before, enough to know to keep the sneaker-squeaks to a minimum, to pass open doorways without looking in, and never to stop to talk to anyone for anything, even if someone cried out for help. If I did, I'd be spotted, ambushed, corralled, a mob of them materializing out of nowhere, shuffling through the half-lit halls like zombies, penning me in. And then I'd be stuck getting pawed and petted and pinched for who knew how long.

Sure, it was risky, and even riskier with two of us instead of just one. But I wasn't worried that Thrash would give us away. He was the quiet type, the heavy; the brawn in the background who never seemed to move or make a sound except when damage needed to be done. He wasn't very big or much to look at, but he was expert at laying low, blending in, and holing up somewhere just out of sight until the time was right to strike. Not that I'd ever turn him loose on the bags of bones clattering around this joint—that just wouldn't be fair. No, right now Thrash knew he was just along for the ride, and I'd do all the talking.

We turned at the last room on the left. I rapped once on the door, opened it, and was greeted by two expectant eyes staring back at me. Her wheelchair was on the far side of the bed, in the corner by the window, and she was in it. Her wig was putty-colored and mangled and tilted too far to the right, and she'd forgotten to pencil an eyebrow over her left eye. The whole effect was like her head was sliding off to one side. She looked smaller than usual, crooked. But at least she had her teeth in.

"Genie!" she cried, smiling, opening her arms to me.

"It's Eug," I corrected her, pronouncing it "Huge," because that's what I called myself.

"Huge? What's wrong with Genie? It's a perfectly good—"

"Can it, sweetheart, you got no eyebrow," I leveled.

"Oh." She frowned. "See my purse?" She pointed. "When you hand it to me, you can give your Toots some sugar."

The woman had a one-track mind; she always wanted her sugar. I grabbed the red leather bag hanging on the closet doorknob, dropped it in her lap, and laid one on her. Her skin was cool, dry, and loose against my lips. Thrash was slouched over in the wooden chair on the opposite side of the bed, near the door, and out of the corner of my eye I caught that smirk of his. But I didn't mind giving her what she wanted, and I didn't give a damn who saw.

"There, that's better," she cooed, her knobby hands trembling as she held up a compact and drew a thin arch over her left brow. She seemed so pleased with the result that I didn't have the heart to tell her the pink over her left eye didn't match the purple over her right. "So . . ." She turned her eyes back to me. "How are you getting along?"

"I'm getting along as best I can," I said, and swallowed hard at the truth of it.

"I mean, how's your summer?"

"It's had its moments." I shrugged. "But it'll all be over soon."

"That's life, Genie," she sighed, "what'd you expect?"

"It's Huge."

"What? Okay, all right, have it your way . . . Huge," she said as she placed her bag on the floor beside her. She went quiet, peering over her shoulder toward the window and then down at her white orthopedic sneakers. Not a good start: she was either drifting or upset. I took a seat on the bed and made myself comfortable, because I knew it could take a while for her to snap to.

"Do you want a sweet?" she asked.

Shit, that was quicker than usual, and I should've yelled no or made a break for the door, but it was too late. She'd already reached into the plastic dish on the nightstand and pulled out this shiny green nugget.

"Here, it's lime." She wrapped my fingers around it and motioned for me to eat.

I froze. My lips tightened and my stomach whined, but she was nodding and smiling and there was nothing I could do. I took a deep breath and popped it into my mouth. It tasted like sweat from the crack of a dockworker's ass. Not that I'd ever sampled any, but I felt like spewing and then gargling with bleach all the same. She was watching me, though, so I had no choice but to choke the damn thing back.

"Good, isn't it?"

I didn't say anything, but that didn't keep Thrash from smiling.

"Now, don't tell your mother that I gave you candy." She winked. "It'll be our secret."

It was sad, really. Because if she thought this was candy, then she was much further gone than everybody said.

She talked about my mother and her new boyfriend, Craig, how it was good for mom to have a man around the house and good for my sister, Neecey, and me, too, but how it meant that mom had less time for her. I didn't have any problem with Craig, because he wasn't around as often as she thought and he never gave me trouble when he was. The dig about mom not stopping by as often wasn't true, but I didn't argue the point.

Then it was the usual stuff about the activities they'd done last week (a day trip to the horse races at Monmouth Park) and what was scheduled for next week (a day trip down to the casinos in Atlantic City). And she said, "With all the gambling they expose us to, you'd think we're swimming in cash. But Margaret in sixteen can barely afford her medication, and she's not the only one. Now, tell me, where's the sense in that?"

I told her there wasn't any, but that they had to do something.

"You may be right, Genie," she sighed, flattening her dress across her lap so the flowers weren't wrinkled, "but sometimes it seems that old age brings nothing but one petty insult after another."

Great. Two gripes and then right into the old-age shtick. That could only mean one thing: she was upset about something, and I'd have to hear it.

"To watch the sun go down with a little bit of dignity," she went on, "is *that* too much to ask?"

I knew better than to answer that.

"Speaking of which," she said, her cloudy brown eyes flaring with annoyance, "did you see what they did to our sign?"

"No," I said, because I hadn't. I'd taken the back way instead of the front. "What'd they do?"

"They *vandalized* it," she hissed, glaring and shaking her head.

Maybe that's why she was so cranky. "Vandalized it? Who? How?"

"There, over there." She pointed with her left hand as she turned her wheelchair to face the window with her right. "See for yourself."

I followed the direction of her finger, over the air vents along the windowsill, through the parted green curtains, across the parking lot pavement shivering from the heat, to an island of withered grass near the four-lane highway that ran along the front of the home. In the center of the island were a dirt mound, a few mangy weeds, a high, thick hedge that bordered the roadway, and a tall wooden sign, which ordinarily read OAKSHADE RETIREMENT HOME. But the "irement" was covered over in black paint, and the sign now read OAKSHADE RETARTED HOME.

Retarted?! Jesus Christ, what kind of bullshit was that?

I didn't know what made me angrier: the fact that it was a cheap shot at harmless seniors and their families, that it was the kind of put-down only a moron would use, or that it'd been slapped up there by the kind of moron who didn't even have enough sense to check his goddamn spelling. That must've been what was bothering her, and now I was bothered, too. Suddenly I was livid. The tips of my fingers quivered and curled, and I started counting backward from ten in my head—*ten . . . nine . . . eight*—but I wasn't quite sure what would happen when I reached one: would I cool down or blast off? I looked over at Thrash. He had that expression on his face again.

"It's disgraceful. There's no respect for anything anymore," she sighed, wearily this time. "And because it's kids, nobody will lift a finger to do a thing about it. That's why I've always told you to mind your manners, keep your nose clean, and be careful, because kids today—are you listening to me, Genie?"

Six . . . five . . . four. Yeah, I was listening. I'd heard the "be careful" speech a million times, and was as receptive now as all the others. *Three . . . two . . . one.* "Fucking monkey fuckers!"

"Genie!" she snapped. "You'd better wise up, young man. They won't tolerate that filth of yours in junior high."

I didn't give a shit if they would or wouldn't. Whether I skipped another grade or was left back again, there was one thing I could count on as far as other people were concerned, although I couldn't remember what it was at the moment because I was too busy trying to compose myself—you know, act like a gentleman, watch my mouth in front of a lady and shit. "Sorry," I grumbled, but didn't mean it.

She looked at me sternly, the bluish blobs on her brown eyes filling with light. I thought she was gonna let me have it and got ready to swallow the next load of crap she dished my way. But she only flashed me this scheming, sideways smile, leaned forward, and reached for her purse.

Suddenly I didn't feel angry anymore; I felt excited. This was how it usually happened for Marlowe—Philip Marlowe, the most badass private detective the world had ever seen. He'd go to the mansion of some wheezy old geezer propped up in a wheelchair, or the wood-walled study of some crabby battle-ax, everything always smelling of eucalyptus and sandalwood, and after a couple of stiff drinks and a few minutes of chitchat, he'd walk out with a new client, a case to solve, and a substantial advance in his pocket.

But I wasn't getting my hopes up just yet. Thing was, I'd only been on one case before, and I'd taken that up on my own initiative. I'd never had a real client, never been paid for my efforts, so as far as my status as a detective went, I guess you could say I was still an amateur.

Maybe that was about to change. After all, she's the one who'd dumped a wheelbarrow of yellowed and musty detective books on me in fifth grade—all the Marlowes and Sherlock Holmeses and a Sam Spade one, too—and I'd been through each of them dozens of times since then. They'd been my grandfather's books, but I hadn't started reading them because I'd gotten all sissy and sentimental about the relics of a man I'd never met, or because I'd been duped into thinking that reading was fundamental like the commercial said. Nah, I'd read them for a simpler reason: because she'd stood over me and forced me to. She'd had to watch me at the time and said that being out of school (which I was then) was no excuse for letting my brain go to rot. She'd sit me down at the kitchen table, pour me a glass of milk, stack a few cookies on a napkin, stand behind me or pull up a chair, and read along, line by line, page after page, annoying the crap out of me, cracking the whip and mushing me onward like a Husky into an avalanche, until she trusted that I'd read them on my own. That didn't take long, because it turned out the books were good, really good, and they taught you everything you needed to know about crime, detection, the world, and more—the exact opposite of what I would've been learning in school. Besides, back then I didn't have a damn thing else to do, so why not save myself more headaches and make the old lady happy? The Encyclopedia Brown, Hardy Boys, and Nancy Drew she gave me all bit the big one, but I didn't see the point of throwing that in her face when we talked about what I'd read, which we always did, because more than anything else, that's what she said books were for.

Now she laid her bag on her lap, stooped over it, thrust both hands inside, and began clawing and sifting its contents like a miner panning for gold. I scooted my butt to the edge of the bed, eager for her to cut to the chase. That smile of hers had tipped me off. I'd seen it more times than you could count on an abacus, and it always meant the same thing: she had an idea, something sneaky or secret; she was up to something, and any second I'd be up to something right along with her. That's how she'd always been with me. She knew I got into trouble more often than most people got out of bed, and she usually took a minute or two to remind me all about it when we were alone. But that never stopped her from egging me on, coming up with pranks or stunts I could pull just for the hell of it, convincing me to do them. She told me boys had to have some mischief in them or they might as well wear dresses and party socks and play with dolls, and just because I'd taken a running leap way over the line in fifth grade, it didn't mean I'd lost the right to mix it up and have some fun. Yeah, I guess that's why I liked her so much. Even at her age, she was still a bit crafty, a bit sly, and it made me think she must have been a handful when she was young and pretty and had all her marbles.

But she was taking forever. My elbows fidgeted, my knees bounced, and my impatience finally got the better of me. Then again, it never took much. I sighed far too loudly and said, "If you haven't found it by now, doll face, chances are you won't. Just what are you looking for anyway?" It all came out too harshly, but at least I didn't curse.

She looked up and pursed her lips. "Oh, now, how does that go again?" She paused, rubbing the tip of her chin. "'A man who is not himself mean, who is neither . . .' ah, this memory of mine." She winced and tapped her forehead. "What's the rest?"

Somewhere in the back of my mind, I could've sworn I heard a whip crack. But I knew the rest of the quote, so I said, "'A man who is not himself mean, who is neither tarnished nor afraid.'"

"That's it. You're so smart, Genie."

My heart surged. It was a line from an essay by this guy named Chandler, the guy who wrote the Marlowe books. The part I'd recited was where Chandler describes what a detective's supposed to be like, and if anybody knew what a detective was supposed to be like, Chandler sure as hell did. I'd chanced upon the essay in a pile of bound periodicals at the public library about six months ago, coughed up the fifty cents to Xerox it, stapled it in the corner, and given it to her as a present. You know, a little tit for tat, a token of gratitude to butter her up and keep myself in her good graces, just in case I needed them somewhere down the road, like I usually did. Anyway, cheap and crappy as it was, she was knocked silly by the gesture and gushed over my "resourcefulness." She either couldn't remember the essay all that well or pretended not to (sometimes it was hard to tell with her, like the way she insisted on having a wheelchair when she could walk just fine), but we'd read it and talked about it so many times that I knew most of the damn thing by heart without wanting to or trying.

Sure, I realized I didn't exactly fit the bill, because most people around here would tell you that I was meaner than a short-order cook and more tarnished than all the girls in Catholic school. So I had two strikes against me from the jump. But I had one thing in my favor: I wasn't afraid of a goddamn thing. More than that, I knew how her mind worked, so I knew what she was getting at. She was looking for a detective, and that meant me.

"Aha, here it is," she said, straightening the crumpled ten-dollar bill she'd pulled from her purse.

Pay dirt! "What's that?" I asked, leaning forward, showing some teeth.

"This is to retain your services. I'd like to hire you to find out what happened to our sign and give me a full report."

I'd never considered how much I'd charge for my fee, but ten dollars wasn't anything to sniff at, so I gladly reached for the cash.

"Ah," she said, pulling it back, "but you have to promise to control yourself. No tantrums, no fighting, and if you find out who did it, you are to do nothing more than tell me, and I'll handle it from there. I mean, don't let anybody push you around, but you understand, don't you?"

I leaned back on the bed. I wasn't supposed to fight *or* get pushed around. Yeah, I understood, because I understood a contradiction when I heard one, just like everybody else.

"Stop frowning, Genie, it makes you look simple." She was serious again. "You're going to have to learn to control yourself sometime or another, and I'm giving you a reason to try. You're always telling me how much you want to be a detective—well, here's your chance to get started."

A classic example of pot and kettle—she talked about it just as much as I did, if not more. Shit, it was practically *her* idea.

"Of course," she said shrugging her shoulders, "if you can't give me your word that you'll act like a professional and conduct yourself like a gentleman, then maybe you're not ready yet."

I was ready all right. Ready to act like a professional, to be a gentleman, ready to hop up and down on one foot, to sit, heel, roll over, shake hands, play dead—whatever it took to keep her from putting the cash away, because that's what she was doing. Just before she did, I said, "Okay, Toots, you got yourself a deal. I'm on it."

She yanked the bill backward again. "Promise—"

"Christ, lady, you win, I promise." I removed the loot from her fingers. "But let's get one thing straight: the name's Huge."

She started to laugh but covered her mouth. "I beg your pardon, Huge. As for our arrangement, can I trust you to carry it out in the strictest confidence?"

She knew she could, because that was like a law all detectives obeyed—never rat out your clients—and since I had a client now, I'd have to obey it, too. But I didn't want her to think that she could give me the business without getting some back. I tucked the ten in my pocket and said, "You got no choice but to trust me—you already paid."

I guess you could say we talked awhile longer, but her mind had wandered off, and no matter how hard I tried to follow her, nothing she said made any sense. She swung back and forth like that, sometimes there, sometimes not, and when she'd first started doing it a couple of years ago, I couldn't stand it, couldn't even look at her, and had to get away from her fast. Since then I'd learned to ride it out, because she'd usually come back sooner or later, and because if you had enough time you could get used to anything. Right now, though, I wanted to get started on the case. Thrash looked antsy to leave, too.

I leaned over and stroked the back of her hand until her eyes locked on mine. "I'm gonna get going. I have things to take care of."

"Oh, so soon?" She was back, just like that, and she let a nice block of silence settle in, hurt. "Well, I guess you don't have to visit me three times a week when you should be out having fun. That's what being young is for. But do me a tiny favor before you leave."

"What?" I asked, although I knew what it was, always the same routine.

"Give an old woman a thrill and tell your grandmother that you love her."

I did and was gone.

Kathy was a tall, stacked blonde who studied physical therapy at the local community college and adorned the front desk of the retirement home. As the receptionist, it was her job to sit at the desk, greet people, answer calls, take messages, and crap like that, but she spent most of her time roaming the hallways, pushing people in their chairs, helping them with their walkers, stopping in their rooms to visit, bringing them extra blankets, fluffing pillows, or changing the channels in the TV room. She had a warm, easy smile, was kind and cheerful, and brought lots of life to a place that never seemed to have enough to go around. Even the cranks and fusspots constantly sought her out for updates of all the new complaints and gossip they'd dreamed up in their spare time. And they had a lot of spare time. So if anyone had heard what the people who lived or worked in the home knew about the sign, Kathy would have.

I walked up to the front desk to ask her a few questions and was treated to the side view of her bent over the desktop in all her summer finery: open-toed sandals; firm, sun-kissed legs that came up to my chest; short-shorts; tight waist; two skimpy tank tops with thin shoulder straps that warped and curved around her breasts like they were reflected in a fun-house mirror; narrow shoulders; and poufy bangs. Damn, Kathy was so fine it actually hurt—just a single glimpse of her could break a full-grown man down to weeping or despair. I didn't know how they let her dress for work like that with all the old-timers around, or how come more didn't drop dead because of it. But at least you'd go with a smile on your face.

She was a sweetheart, too, as if she had no clue how scorching she was, which only made it worse. When she'd started working at the home last fall, it was like trying to watch an eclipse—I *wanted* to see it, but knew it was too dangerous to gaze directly. Once I'd realized that I wouldn't melt down to a puddle just from looking at her, though, it'd gotten easier to stutter something back when she said hello. No, I'd never been much of a talker to begin with, and even less of one with the ladies, but Kathy was such a total honey that you felt ashamed not to try. So I did, and after I got the hang of it, I started using our chats to polish up my game, to get myself ready for the chicks I might actually have a chance with.

Kathy saw us and waved. I straightened up as tall as I could, smiled, and played it extra smooth.

"Hey, cutie," she said. "Hey, Thrash."

"Hey," I said. Thrash just looked at her. "You go to the beach this weekend?"

"Yeah. Why? Am I tan?"

"Totally."

"Well," she led me, "how do I look?" She stepped back from the desk and spun in a circle with her arms outstretched.

I gulped back a groan just in time. "Like butterscotch with blue eyes," I said.

"Aw, you're sooo sweet!"

"Melt in your mouth."

She laughed. "You're totally funny. If you were ten years older I'd marry you."

Yeah, and if I had ten minutes alone with her, there'd be no telling what I'd do. But I didn't say that. I said, "Wait for me, then."

"Okay, but hurry up." She looked at her watch and winked. Kathy was a great flirt, the best.

"Kath."

"Yeah, honey?"

"Did you see what they did to the sign?"

"Yeah," she sighed, and shook her head. "It's like so mean, isn't it?"

"When did it happen?"

"Late Saturday, I think. Irma said she saw it on Sunday morning when she came in, but Bryan said everything was fine when he left on Saturday night."

"Old Pencil Neck, eh?"

"You shouldn't call him that," Kathy giggled and whispered at the same time, moving her eyes from side to side. "Bryan can be really sweet, you just need to know him better."

No, I didn't. Bryan was the manager of the home, and I knew first-hand how he treated the captives, so I knew what a fucking creep he was. But Kathy was too good-hearted to see through his act—the way he was always sucking up to her, flattering her, tailing her like a duckling, begging her to go out on a date—or she was just too nice to tell him to screw off, or maybe afraid to because he was her boss. Whatever. That worm was slithering up on her almost every time I came around, and I hated to see it because I knew she'd probably cave in at some point, if only to keep from hurting his feelings. Then Bryan, this pasty noodle of a guy with a pencil neck, gold chains, and spiked hair, would be out with Kathy, who was so far out of his league they were playing different sports. He'd pick her up in that massive IROC Z-28 of his, with him so tiny behind the wheel that it looked like someone dropped a GI Joe action figure in the middle of the driver's seat, and she'd get in anyway and then he'd drive her around, park somewhere, climb a stepladder into her lap, and try to feel her up or something, taking advantage, milking it for all it was worth, until he got what he wanted. Nah, I didn't want to know any of that.

"I'm just jealous," I said.

"Don't be, honey. He's not my boyfriend or anything."

Maybe there was hope after all. But Thrash was getting bored by all the small talk, so I had to get to the point. "Hey, Kath?"

"Yeah, honey?"

"About the sign. Anybody see anything?"

"No, hon, nobody saw anything. Not even Cuth."

Cuthbert Stansted—ninety-three, former accountant, always dressed in a black wool three-piece suit and tie, smaller and grayer than an eighteen-year-old Scotch terrier, insomniac, and the home's self-appointed night watchman.

"Not even Cuth?" I asked.

"Is that my grandchild?" came a shaky voice from my right. She was hunched, with badly balding silver hair, limp spotty arms dangling out of what looked like a green burlap sack with a neck and armholes cut into it, and one hand against the cinder-block wall to steady herself.

"No, Livia," Kathy answered. "This isn't your granddaughter, this is Toots's grandson."

"Oh," Livia said, frowning. "But you'll call me the second they get here . . . uh—"

"Yes, sweetie. Kathy will call you as soon as they get here."

Livia smiled, the most hopeful smile I'd ever seen, and then inched along on her way, as if the laces of her shoes were tied to each other.

Kathy dropped her eyes and sighed. "Poor thing, her family moved to Maryland nine months ago and we haven't heard from them since."

And some stupid fuck thought Livia deserved to be called *retarded* because of that. Sure, I already knew the world was sick, but now it was my job to cure it.

"Kath, you guys call the police?"

"Yeah, hon."

"And?"

"Nothing, so far."

"Think they'll catch who did it?"

"They're probably not even looking, sweetie. It's like if nobody saw anything—and nobody did, not here anyway—then what do they have to go on? Besides, you know the police around here . . ." She trailed off, leaning over the desk with her head down to look at some papers.

"Yeah," I said. I knew the police all right, and what was worse, the police knew me. But if they weren't looking into the case, then that cleared the way for my investigation, and that was good news. Since it was right there, I took a quick peek down the front of Kathy's top. It was sweet, real sweet, all soft and cozy and snug, like one of those forts you made out of pillows and quilts and curled up in on stormy nights. But I had to be careful not to stare too long, or things could get awkward.

"Uh, sweetie?" Kathy asked.

"Yeah, Kath?"

"I'm up here," she said, straightening her back and pouting her lips out at me.

Oh, shit—busted. I had to smooth it over fast. "Sorry, Kath," I shrugged. "I, uh, I get confused sometimes. Don't be mad, though, okay? I don't know any better—I'm just a kid." I grinned so hard that my cheeks hurt.

Kathy shook her head and laughed.

T W O

Anybody who wasn't still watching the Smurfs
knew that Darren and the crew had been tagging just about everything within reach of hand, arm, ladder, or rope all summer. They hit
bridges and underpasses, stores, billboards, offices, the high school,
the police station, parked cars, kiddie pools left out overnight—
nothing was safe. Sure, there had always been graffiti before, but this
year it seemed worse, bigger, as if they'd suddenly realized that the
only way they were ever gonna make a mark in this world was by
wrecking other people's stuff, whether those people deserved it or
not. But the crew all lived by the reservoir, and unless they got caught
in the act or were stupid enough to hide their kits under their beds,
nothing ever happened to them. They were bored, had money, and
plenty of time to spend it.

I knew just where to find them.

The town I lived in had only two claims to fame: the Circle and
the mall. The Circle was one of the biggest traffic junctions in the
state: it looped three different highways together, everybody knew it
by name, and it was a major reference point whenever anybody gave

or got directions to anywhere within twenty-five miles of it. It was conveniently located, too, because it was right next to the mall. Or maybe it was the other way around. Whatever. The latter was "Central Jersey's Largest Indoor Shopping Mall," according to the billboards on the highways. I didn't know if that was true or not, but the parking lot was about a mile across at its longest point, just to give you some idea of how the joint stacked up. Then again, it was the only mall I'd ever been to, so I was in no position to judge. But I was sure about one thing: like every other mall on the planet, it was a magnet for misdirected youth, so I aimed the Cruiser there.

The arcade was in a small, one-story building of shops and offices right outside the main complex, at arm's length from the real action, like the kids' table at Thanksgiving. I parked around the corner, and Thrash and I decided he would take a position near the Cruiser, lay low, and watch the front, in case something went down and I needed backup. At the far rear corner of the mall parking lot there was a trail that ran through the woods to the reservoir, so we were close to the crew's turf now, and we couldn't be too careful.

Inside, it was as dark as a boarded-up bomb shelter, and the cold, stiff air filled my snout with a paste of sugar, machine grease, and sweat. The A/C was cranked up high, and long rows of video screens flickered seductively through the dimness. I slapped the chill off the back of my neck, jammed my hands into my pockets, and stopped myself short. I wasn't here to play games. I was here on business.

Darren was a creature of habit—he always hogged the Defender machine in the far right corner. As soon as my eyes adjusted to the dark, I saw the back of his sun-damaged hair, yellow T-shirt, and blue-and-white Jams bouncing from side to side, dodging the alien invasion. I didn't see any of the other crew members with him, so I slid up behind and watched as he tried to evade the fate an enemy missile was sending his way. He couldn't do it. Then again, none of us could.

"Hey, little dude, what's up," he said, slapping the fire-button to mount his counterattack.

"Nothing." I watched for a few minutes in silence, until a group of mutant landers surrounded his ship and ended his game. He was rattled, and I knew it.

"Fu-u-uck!" he yelled, his fist making a loud *plap* against the screen.

A booming "HEY" sounded behind us, and we turned to see the manager's milky forearm rising above the guitar magazine concealing his face, directing our eyes to the sign above his head: YOU HIT THE MACHINES YOU HIT THE ROAD.

"Ah-ight, dude, chill," Darren called to the magazine cover. "What's up with that guy?"

"D, you know the sign—"

"I fully know the sign, little dude," Darren cut me off, chuckling. "I've like seen it before." He smiled down at me and rolled his slow brown eyes, after flipping his orange bangs out of the way. "But that doesn't mean I'm gonna like obey it and shit."

"Nah, D," I tried to redirect him, "not *that* sign."

"Dude," he insisted, "that's like the only one in here."

Christ. I should've known we'd have to two-step before we tangoed. It wasn't that Darren was the space cadet he pretended to be, though. It was more like he'd been playing dumb so goddamn long that he'd just forgotten he was playing. I wouldn't be surprised if his parents had to pull him aside, douse him with ice water, shake him by the shoulders, and remind him that he was in the top five of his class at the beginning of each school year. Just so he'd know.

"Nah, dude," I kept at it, "I'm talking about a different sign."

"Little dude, you're like totally confounding me, and that's way harshing on my buzz." He stopped before feeding another quarter into the slot, and suddenly looked over his right shoulder, toward the wall. He stayed that way—frozen, staring, fingering his pukka bead choker, a black rubber bracelet rolling down his tanned forearm—for about ten or fifteen seconds before he snapped out of it and shook his head. "Whoa," he declared.

"So you don't know anything about *other* kinds of signs"—I took my time saying the rest—"like the signs of old age?" It took him a second to make the connection, but when he did, I saw the panic spread across his face. It was beautiful.

"Let's talk outside," he whispered. He tried to put his arm around my shoulder, but I pulled it back. I never let anybody put a hand on me without returning the favor, and that went double for wannabe punk surfers who were balling my sister on the sly.

Darren was moving quickly and made a left out the door. I was following behind him, but something made me check out the couple whispering to each other to the right of the exit, leaning against the Grand Prix racing machine. I hadn't seen them when I'd come in. The chick's back was turned to me, but I saw that she had on black Converse high-tops with folded-down white socks, about thirty black rubber anklets dangling over each sock, and a cryptic trail of pen marks zigzagging up the length of her smooth, taut thighs. Her denim cutoffs were faded, frayed, and wedged so deeply into the crack of her ass that about a quarter of each cheek was showing.

I'd seen that ass thousands of times. Ever since she'd moved to town two years ago, I'd been keeping vigil over it from a distance, and sitting behind her in every class last year had practically tattooed those cheeks onto my brain. Shit, I would've known them anywhere, in any light, from any angle, under any conditions, just like I knew they belonged to Stacy Sanders, who'd been an army brat at the military base until her parents broke up the summer before fifth grade and then moved with her mother to Sunnybrook apartments and transferred to our school that September. If Chris Singleton hadn't moved to Arizona, I never would've gotten my ringside seat by all the action, because his last name came before mine in the alphabet. Good old Chris Singleton; I knew that kid about as well as I knew any of the other dweebs at school, which was hardly at all, but if I ever saw him again, I might just kiss him out of sheer gratitude.

Stacy was wearing a sleeveless, fluorescent-orange T-shirt knotted at the waist so her stomach was showing, four or five bangle and rubber bracelets on each wrist, and two earrings in each of her ears. The extra piercings were new. Her hair was the same, though—a short black bob, shaved in the back, with long slanted bangs that hung over one eye to her chin. She had squinty hazel eyes that tapered at the corners, a short, thin nose, high cheekbones, broad lips, and a wide mouth that jutted out a little too much. Okay, she wasn't exactly pretty, but then again, she didn't have to be. She had that *thing* that some chicks just had, and for chicks who had it, it didn't matter if they also had hunched backs, bald heads, two teeth, one of those withered arms, clubbed feet, or acne all over their bodies like a poison ivy rash. I didn't know what that thing was or where it came from or what to call it, but I knew it when I saw it and I knew that Stacy had it and that it made me feel like I'd just finished going all-out for half an hour on a Sit 'N Spin.

My head was a little light and my stomach cramped. But I fought it off. I was a detective now.

The guy said, "What the fuck you lookin' at, dick cheese?"

I shifted my eyes to the tall, angular goon standing next to Stacy, the one whose voice was cracking but sounded like it meant business anyway. I knew who he was—everybody did. He was Ray "the Razor" Tuffalo, last year's junior-high quarterback, nicknamed for the way he sliced through opposing defenses, a guy who'd punch you in the back of the neck or stick his knee in your gut as casually as most people said "hey" or "what's up"—especially if you were younger and smaller and his teammate Tommy Sharpe was around to watch. Yeah, quality guy. He had a flattop crew cut, a pinched face, a snarled mouth with cruddy braces, and was wearing a red Joe Montana football jersey with the sleeves rolled up over his shoulders, probably to show everyone how long his arms were, because there wasn't a shadow of muscle on him. Nah, the kid was all bone; thick, stupid bone, just like his head.

I was giving up more than a foot and close to sixty pounds. But I held my ground and acted like he wasn't there.

"Hey, ass-stain, why don't you draw yourself a photograph, it'll last longer."

Jesus Christ. For a second I considered explaining to him that a picture was drawn, while a photo wasn't, but it seemed like a waste of knowledge, time, and breath, so I turned to go.

"That's what I thought." Razor smirked.

No, it wasn't the healthiest idea, but I turned around to face him.

"Leave him alone, Razor," Stacy whispered. She was chewing her lip; she looked worried or anxious about something.

I didn't like any of it. I didn't like the fact that over the past half-year eighth-, ninth-, and tenth-grade guys had taken to circling Stacy like vultures; I didn't like the idea of her talking to Razor; and I liked the sight of them together a shitload less. But I had to get outside before Darren forgot he was supposed to be talking to me and wandered off. As I walked to the door, Razor called, "Yeah, peel out, skid mark," at my back. I clenched my fists, bit my tongue, and let it go. I had bigger fish to fry.

Outside, it was still sweltering, and I was doing my best to forgive Stacy for hanging with that knob. I couldn't blame her for not knowing what she wanted, because there was no way she'd know until I worked up the nerve to talk to her. So that was my own goddamn fault. But it was different with Razor. He had one coming, and sometimes I fell asleep at night dreaming that I'd be the one to oblige him.

Right now, however, I had to get all of that crap off my mind and concentrate on Darren and the case. I took a deep breath, turned the corner, and saw him eyeing the Cruiser. Thrash was tucked away close enough to land a shot if needed, but Darren hadn't seen him. We had the advantage.

He looked over his shoulder at me and said, "You get lost or what?"

"Something like that."

"No worries." He shrugged. "It happens." He turned back to the Cruiser. "By the way, totally bitchin' ride, little dude."

"Lay off it," I warned.

"No way that's the same bike I stole from you."

"No, it isn't." It wasn't.

"Thought not. Like check out that banana seat, and those chopper handlebars are *so* rippin'."

The concept of looking but not touching apparently held no meaning for him.

"Sting-Ray?" he asked.

I nodded.

"Full-on classic, my man." He nodded back. "Where'd you pick it up? They go for like major ducats."

"I didn't pick it up. I built it."

Darren pulled his head back and stared at me skeptically. "No way."

"Way."

"Get the fuck outta here. Seriously?"

"Seriously." He seemed to be having trouble processing the information, but it was true. I'd built the Cruiser this past spring out of spare parts from the junkyard. I got some of the money from trading in the bike he'd stolen from me, because I'd promised myself I wouldn't ride the damn thing ever again after that, and I hadn't.

"Shee-it, mini man, you got some radical skills. You're like a bike-building black belt—waa-saah," Darren yelped, and threw what I guessed were karate chops at the air. When he pulled himself back together, he said, "Congrats, little dude, your ride's rocking, you're styling and smiling."

He raised his hand for a high five and I was able to count very slowly to four before he put it down again. I didn't need a poser like him to tell me the Cruiser was styling, because I already knew it. Besides, he hadn't said anything about the sixteen-inch front wheel and the larger, twenty-inch back wheel, which gave it that tricked-out look, the whitewall tires, the chrome front and back fenders, the high-gloss blood-red paint job, or the original crossbar stick shift that everybody knew had been outlawed like more than a decade ago. So how was I supposed to feel complimented when he'd overlooked most of the coolest parts?

"C'mon, Scrappy Doo," Darren said, tilting his head to the side, "you can't go on being all sore at me forever. I said I was sorry when I gave the other one back, remember?"

Yeah, I remembered all right. But he didn't say he was sorry, not to me anyway, so I could stay sore as long as I damn well felt like it.

"Besides," he went on, "I wouldn't have lifted it if I knew you were Neecey's little bro."

That was such bullshit and we both knew it, but he couldn't lay off it; he just had to bring it up. That's why things would always be tense between Darren and me, a kind of frozen war.

"So what's she up to tonight?" he asked, fishing around in his pockets.

"Dude, the sign." I thought it best to remind him of the business at hand, because if Darren got talking, we could grow old together, and there was nothing I wanted less.

"Yea-ahp," he gulped, sparking a roach and nodding his head. He held his breath and started to offer it to me, but then seemed to realize what he was doing and pulled it back. I wouldn't have taken it anyway. First of all, people said pot stunted your growth, and at fifty-six inches tall and barely ninety pounds with a full head of hair and a pair of work boots on, I took that kind of warning very seriously. Second of all, I wasn't crazy about eggs, so I didn't want my brain turning into one—fried, scrambled, or otherwise. Darren exhaled and took another hit before speaking.

"Fucking cops came to my house on Sunday morning to ask me about it. My pops freaked."

"So?"

"So? Dude, he almost grounded me."

I could see it was serious.

"He was talking much smack about canceling his trip with my mom this week, because he couldn't like trust me. As if. He chilled, though." Darren paused, then went on, "What do you know about it?"

I shrugged.

"You see, dude, you see"—he pointed at me and then at his forehead, the first rush of weed kicking in—"*you're* prob'ly the one who sicced the cops on me, 'cause you're still all pissed and shit."

He was getting tight already; I had to cut him off before the idea got hold of him, or he wouldn't let it go.

"You got it all wrong, D. I know you didn't do it," I conned him. "That's why I'm here."

"That's right," he agreed. "That's what I told the fucking cops." He paused, swimming between thoughts. "How'd you know I didn't do it?"

"Your signature."

"Aw-haw-haw, mee-yan," he laughed, smoke twisting out of his grinning maw, "you know my signature? That's sooo cool."

"Yeah," I said, playing to his vanity, the weakness of every artist, "and yours wasn't there."

"But that don't mean shit, little dude." He stubbed the roach out on the bottom of his flip-flop and returned it to his pocket. "What?" he asked.

"You said it didn't mean shit that your signature wasn't there."
Keeping Darren focused was always a little more trouble than it was
worth.

"Yeah." He remembered. "I tag lots of things without signing."

"Like what?"

He started to plateau and looked like he wanted to talk. His eyes
were small and glossy. A devilish smile darkened his lips. "Can you
keep a secret, dude?"

I nodded.

"I didn't hit that sign because I rounded up most of the crew on
Saturday night and tagged the church."

"The church?" That surprised me, not because I went to church,
but because I hadn't heard.

"Yeah, dude." He looked around before he continued, whispering,
"You know Sticky, right?"

I nodded. Sticky was the oldest of his crew, a dark-haired beanpole
with a problem resisting five-finger discounts, even though his family was probably the richest around.

"Well, Sticky said his little bro told him that Father Paul was
touching him way up on the thighs and patting him on the butt and
shit for like the past two months. So we loaded up, went down there,
and painted 'pervert' and 'molester' and 'homo' all over the church
wall and rectory. Full-on payback. I heard the people at the seven
o'clock Mass the next morning were all like wigging and shit, but
they painted over it before the nine and told everyone to keep it
quiet."

"No shit?" That explained why I hadn't heard about it, that and the
fact that I'd taken the Cruiser down the Shore yesterday for some R
and R and hadn't been around. But everybody knew Father Paul was
the kind of priest whose hands needed something more than hym-
nals and the Holy Eucharist to keep them busy, and if I didn't already
know Darren and his buds, even I would have been impressed by the
boldness of the deed.

"No shit," he boasted, "but we didn't sign that."

Yeah, I could see why not—there'd be hell to pay.

"All right," I said. "But if you didn't hit the sign at the retirement home, and both of us know you didn't, then who did?" I made sure to speak slowly so he wouldn't get lost.

"If the cops couldn't get anything out of me, little dude, what makes you think you can?"

"Dude, my grandmother?"

"Shit, yeah." He looked down and then away, as if he'd just forgotten or remembered something. For him there probably wasn't much difference. "That's right. Shit. So you're like totally vengeful or what?"

"Let's just say I'm curious to know who's responsible."

Darren flipped his hair back and wiped his hands down the front of his T-shirt as he considered for a moment. "Sorry, no dice, little dude." He tried to appear decided, but I could tell he was wavering.

"I just want to know who did it, D," I reassured him. "I promise I won't—"

"Look, Genie," he interrupted. "It's complicated. It's like totally fucked up." He stopped short, like everyone with a big mouth, struggling not to say more. "Even if I knew who did it, and I'm totally not saying I do, I wouldn't tell you. It's too bogus a deal for a little dude. You could wind up getting majorly jawed or whatever, so just lay off it."

"The name's Huge," I corrected him, but he was definitely worried about something because he'd never called me by name before.

"Huge?" He laughed. "That's a righteous handle, bro."

"What? You don't think I can back it up or something?" As if I fucking cared what he thought.

"No, dude, it ain't like that," he retreated. "Your sis made me promise to keep an eye out for you is all—"

That bitch. She was always butting into my business and I was getting sick of it. I didn't hear the middle part of what he said.

"—sorry about your grandma, though. Earnestly. I'm like bumming, too, but no dice." He shrugged his shoulders and reached up for his choker as he turned to go. But instead of going, he stopped and turned back to me. "Hey, if it makes you feel any better, little dude, the hit on the old folks' home was wank anyway. Total amateur bullshit."

I didn't know what the hell he was saying or why the hell he was saying it, but I was interested to hear more.

"Wank?" I asked.

"Yeah, man, tag talk—you know, pro lingo?"

"But what is it?"

"Dude, don't tell me you don't know what 'wank' is."

I shook my head.

Darren sighed. "It's a hit with no spray, no stencils, no style, no signature, just paint can, brush, fucked-up letters and lines and shit. That, my man, is *wank*."

I had the feeling he meant something more, so I pressed further. "But why's it called wank?"

"Du-uu-ude," he groaned, almost in disbelief. "Wank, you know?" He pumped his fist rapidly back and forth in front of his crotch. "Wank"—he drove it home—"*hand* painted, *hand* job? It's a fucking hand job, dude. Like I said, total amateur bullshit."

"Oh," I said. But Darren wasn't paying attention, because he was inspecting the Cruiser again, closely this time.

"Dude, is that—"

Oh, shit, Thrash's cover was blown.

He turned to me gravely and said, "Little dude, word of advice. That Ninja Turtle in your backpack? It's time to ditch it."

"He's a *frog*." What a fucking moron. Thrash didn't look anything like a Ninja Turtle.

"Whatever. Ditch it. Junior high is seriously rough, bro. You want everybody calling you a fag?"

Instantly, I was hot. I stepped forward and leaned toward him, sticking my chest out, cocking my elbows back near my sides, rolling my fingers into fists. I was measuring him and I wanted him to know it. I'd learned all about prejudice in social studies; it was all the same, and I wasn't gonna take it. First they called you names, then they made you use separate bathrooms, and then they crammed you into the bottom of a slave ship headed for the concentration camp. I'd be damned if that happened on my watch.

"So what if they call me a fag?" I growled.

"Dude, steady, okay? I'm just trying to help you out."

"And you think calling me a fag helps?"

"Like ease off, all right? You know I wasn't saying that. Shit, dude, I'm on your side."

"Then our team's gonna lose."

"Whatever," Darren sighed, shaking his head. He took a few steps but turned back again. "Why you gotta be so fucking strange?" he asked, and walked off.

Shit, even if I knew the answer, I wouldn't tell *him*.

THREE

The skies were darker, angrier as I drove the Cruiser along the abandoned railroad tracks skirting the athletic fields behind the junior high. I'd dropped Thrash off so he could sort through what we'd gathered so far and work on a list of suspects. We knew we were looking for someone a little older, maybe someone who was linked to Darren in some way. Plus, we knew we were looking for someone who was not only stupid enough to risk exposure by hand-painting *retarted* on a sign next to a busy highway, but also stupid enough to misspell it. No, probably not a master criminal, but this was the suburbs, so it could be just about anyone.

That's why I left it to Thrash. He never said too much, but he was always thinking, figuring things out. I'd never been sure why he was always so pensive. But there was a lot going on inside that little green body of his that I didn't understand, and when I thought about it, I probably didn't want to.

When my first counselor gave him to me a couple of months into third grade, my sessions were still voluntary, and she said it was to help me actualize, because I was too alone and locked up inside myself. I didn't have a single friend, and she said that not being able to actualize or express what I was feeling to anyone was probably what was causing me to go all ballistic from time to time. So she handed me this dorky-looking frog and told me to take him home and try to relate to him in the way that came most naturally. I took it as the insult and attempt to baby me that it was, so I beat the shit out of him. After two days, mom had to Krazy Glue one of his eyes back on. When I saw my counselor the following week, she could tell I'd been wailing on him, but she didn't mention it right off. Instead, she asked me if I'd given him a name. I said, Yeah, Thrash, because that's what I did to him; it was the way of relating that seemed most appropriate. She let that slide, too, but pointed out that *thrash* was a verb, and that I had this tendency to name things after verbs, which was a symptom of my deeper problem with actualization.

That was the first time I'd thought she wasn't just dropping buttbombs on me, because I used to wonder if there was a connection between the way my brain worked and what I said, or what I didn't say, because I didn't say much. Shit, I barely talked at all, except for when I was already too far gone and laying into somebody. But my mind was always running; it was like my thoughts kept racing and spinning but they couldn't figure out where to go or what to do. So I started listening to her a bit more after that, and when she said Thrash might be good for something other than an excuse for violence, I decided to give him a try.

I had to give it to her; she was right on that, too. Thrash and I hit it off, and I started telling him things, about what I was thinking or feeling, or how I was so sick with rage all the time, and pretty soon he started answering me back. Okay, I knew he wasn't actually answering me back; he couldn't, he was a stuffed animal you could buy at a toy store for less than ten bucks. But when I told him things, I started to hear all these new ideas inside my head, and they came to me in a voice different from my own—kind of slow and croaky, like that kid made in *The Shining*, only deeper—so I gave Thrash credit for them. I didn't know where he got his ideas or why I was the only one who could hear them or why almost everything he said was so fucking twisted. Then again, I didn't really care, because after I got used to talking to him, I realized that having him around settled me down some and helped me to think.

And one of the first things I thought was that people were making a grave mistake by underestimating him or mocking the shit out of us the way they did. Behind his wide plastic eyes, surprised expression, open-mouthed grin, and the goofy pink tongue hanging out, there lurked a cunning, almost evil intelligence that knew neither failure nor fear. Thrash had a predator's planning and patience, a frightening temper, and a long memory, so he wasn't the sort you wanted to cross. I'd never had to sweat him, though; we were a team, and I was cool with that because he was the baddest and meanest partner any detective ever had. Made Watson look like a bitch.

Thrash didn't care much for football, though, and since I was on my way to the second round of tryouts for the junior-high team, there was no point in dragging him along. There wouldn't be much to watch anyway. For the first round, all we'd had to do was bring our signed permission slips, turn our heads and cough, and then run some sprints and drills. The slowest runners met the assistant coach, the fastest ones were introduced to the head coach, and everybody in between kind of wandered up behind their friends in one group or the other. Then they lobbed some balls at us to see who could catch and who would get hit in the face. That was it. Today would be a little different because we were going to do more or less the same thing in helmets and shoulder pads. No, it wasn't the most rigorous process, but if you couldn't make the junior-high football team in this town, then the rest of your life wouldn't be too promising anyway.

The equipment was laid out on the side of the field when I got there: one pile of helmets, one of shoulder pads, and another of red mesh jerseys. A lot of the guys were scrambling to get their stuff because there weren't enough helmets to go around, so some would have to share, and those who did would have to sit out for part of try-outs. Nobody wanted that because this was our chance to impress, and you couldn't impress if you were standing on the sidelines with no helmet on, digging the wedgie out of your ass. But I took my time. I knew there'd be only one set of equipment sized extra small and I'd be the only one who could use it. That's the way it'd been last year in peewee league, so I couldn't see how things would be any different now.

I got my stuff, no problems, and went off to the side to suit up. I fitted the jersey over the shoulder pads before I put them on, like draping a shirt on a hanger, because if you did it the other way, you couldn't get the jersey over the shoulder pads without asking someone to help you, and I already knew that no one was gonna help me, because the other guys didn't want me there. Yeah, I was on my own and I knew it, but all it really meant was that I had to plan ahead. I could handle that. I laced up the cleats that were in my backpack, slid the shoulder pads on, made sure they were tight across the front, and fixed the straps under my arms. I wedged the helmet down on my head, started adjusting the chin strap, and was looking around to see if Orlando was there when I heard Coach Rose calling me.

"Smalls! Front and center, on the double!"

Coach Rose, the head coach, was the sort of guy who was born to be in the military but somehow wasn't bright enough to find his way to the recruitment office. Not that missing out on his destiny had ever stopped him from wearing a crew cut and a whistle, barking orders, telling time the army way, and making everybody call him sir.

"Smalls," he grunted as I hustled over to him, "are you squared away on the parameters of today's exercises?"

I could see the beads of sweat on his upper lip, and warped versions of myself reflected in the lenses of his mirrored sunglasses.

"Smalls! You have a problem, son? Don't you know to sound off when I ask you something?"

I didn't know which question he wanted me to answer—if I had a problem or knew to sound off—so I didn't say anything.

"All right, Smalls, let's take this slow," he said through clenched teeth. "Are you . . . squared a-way . . . on the pa-ra-meters—"

"Yeah," I cut him off. I hated it when people treated me like I was suffering from imbecility instead of rage.

"Yeah what?"

"Yeah, I know there's no contact, so I can't run around laying into people."

"Can't run around laying into people what?"

"You know, like hitting them and tackling them and stuff."

He shook his head in disgust. "Smalls, what do I look like to you?"

The word *penis* came to mind.

"Do I look like some kind of pansy school counselor or one of your imaginary friends?"

"No," I said.

"No, he says," Coach Rose exclaimed to no one in particular. "So you're not brain-dead. And if you're not brain-dead, then you must know what you're supposed to call me."

"Coach?" I asked. I couldn't help myself.

He let out this agonized groan, as if he'd swallowed his whistle and was trying to hock it back up. "Smalls," he whispered, his teeth flashing in front of my face mask, "I don't give two shits if you're the fastest kid in the seventh grade or the whole damned school, you will call me sir or you'll be watching this season from the bleachers. Do I make myself clear?"

"Yeah," I said, but made him wait a few seconds before adding the rest.

"That's better. Now remember, no contact. Well, what are you waiting for? Get out of my face."

What a cock. Of all the nose pickers and wussies farting around on the field, he had to single me out, and I was one of the few who could actually play the game. But ever since the end of peewee league last year, I'd gotten a bad rep, and he was acting on it. I'd spent most of that season on the bench; the coaches wouldn't play me because I was so small that I had to stuff rolls of quarters in my jock-strap each week at weigh-in to make the official minimum weight, and they used that as an excuse to keep me off the field. That was, until the third-to-last game, when we were getting blown out by Red Bank, 37–0. They put me in with about two minutes left, just so they could tell all the parents at the annual team dinner that everybody had seen playing time. Whatever. I'd never gotten my uniform dirty and I was rabid to get in and hit somebody—hard. Luckily, they put me in on defense, at safety. Of course, at safety, I was furthest back from the action, so they probably put me there hoping I wouldn't get any. But I had other ideas. The first play Red Bank ran was a sweep to our right, and I'd taken off in that direction with the snap. I wasn't even looking for the ball, just the biggest guy on their team I could get a clear shot at. Somehow that guy turned out to be their halfback, ball in hand. I turned my legs loose, and while it seemed to cause Coach Rose some kind of moral crisis, he was right, I was fast, really fast, and I met the halfback in a dead sprint, top speed, head-on, as he turned up the field. Blam! I guess he dropped his head just as I hit him, because I got up and he didn't and there was the ball, lying on the field about three yards away. I scooped it up and ran it in and we lost 37–6 instead of 37–0. It felt great.

They started me on defense for the last two games, but other play-ers and coaches complained because it seemed that every time I tack-led somebody, they got carted off the field. It happened in practice, too, with my own teammates, and that's how I got pegged as some kind of maniac. But it was all bullshit. In football, you either hit somebody or got hit. Period. And it wasn't my fault that a lot of kids still cringed at the first hint of contact. It just meant I was going to have to listen to Coach Rose talk to me like an idiot all season. But at least he didn't call me Genie.

We did some warm-ups, ran agility drills, got timed in sprints, and then the veteran players who hadn't graduated joined us at the end of their practice to run some plays so the coaches could get a feel of who was who and what was what.

That's when I finally spotted Orlando, although it was probably easier to miss an aircraft carrier in a duck pond. He'd been almost six feet tall in sixth grade, and now, going into eighth, he had to be at least three inches taller, maybe fifteen pounds heavier, and was starting to get buffed all over. In the midst of the others, he looked like the only Doberman at a Chihuahua convention, and it almost didn't seem fair—he was too good for a bunch of saps to try out against. Shit, he was probably too good even to practice against, unless what you really needed was practice getting knocked on your ass.

It wasn't easy picturing Orlando as some kind of superstar athlete, because he couldn't have been further from one when we'd met outside the counselor's office in fifth grade. That was the year I got left back, but it was before the shit really hit the fan, so I was still in voluntary counseling. My sessions came right after his, and we saw each other coming and going at the office all the time, and after a while, we stopped feeling like freaks enough to say "hey" to each other. Shortly after that we started having lunch together, just facing each other across the cafeteria table, eating our sandwiches and snack cakes, not saying anything beyond "hey" and "later."

It took some getting used to at first, because Orlando always had his head down and whispered rather than spoke—like the last thing he wanted was for you to actually hear him—and because we were such opposites. His family lived by the reservoir, in a big house with huge lawns and a pool, and although there were plenty of black families in our area, his was the only one that lived there. I thought that's what made him so shy, always standing out like that, because he wasn't just the only black kid who lived by people like Darren and Sticky and Razor, he was also one of the biggest kids around.

And he dressed funny. Well, not funny, but sort of fancy. He always had on sweaters with collared shirts and ties, dress pants, really shiny leather shoes, and he carried this brown leather briefcase with his initials on it. His eyeglasses were the coolest ones in style, but the lenses were pretty thick, and because he kept his head down all the time, it looked like they were too much weight for his neck to support. We were opposites in that way too, I guess, because I was dressed like everybody else and was the sort of kid nobody seemed to notice, unless they were looking for trouble.

Anyway, after about a week or so of grunting and nodding, Orlando and I started talking. I don't remember who talked first or what we said, but after breaking the ice, we always looked for each other, ate our lunch together, and then walked around during recess before we went back to class. Once I'd learned that Orlando didn't fit in anywhere either, I could see it was kind of natural for us to fit together the way we did. Orlando kept to himself as much as possible, just like me, but other kids took that to mean something else, like they always did with everything. The white kids who lived by him told him he should go hang out with his "own kind" if he was too good for them, but his "own kind," the other black kids at school, told him he wasn't one of them, because of the way he dressed and where he lived and because he didn't hang out in their part of town, or go to church or dances with them. So he got it coming and going, all the time.

Orlando said the one time he'd tried to tell the other black kids it wasn't his fault that his parents were really strict and wouldn't let him hang out in their part of town, it only got worse because they pulled out all these insults that black people reserved for themselves. I didn't know there were such things; I thought insults were insults and all the same. But Orlando told me they started calling him "sellout" and "incog-negro," which was their way of saying he wasn't black enough. That confused the shit out of me because Orlando had to be the darkest person I'd ever seen outside of *National Geographic,* and I told him if he wasn't black enough for them, then I couldn't imagine who would be. He told me that sometimes being black had nothing to do with how dark you were, but with how you acted, and if you were different, like he was, then some black people would always say you were acting white, which was the worst thing to be.

I already knew a hell of a lot about people telling me what I was or wasn't, so I thought I understood what he was going through. But what I couldn't understand was why it didn't drive him mad and crazy, like it did to me. I'd seen a group of four or five kids standing around him as he waited for the bus after school one day, and they were laying into him something awful, taunting him, mocking him, throwing his briefcase on the ground, pushing him—even a couple of girls were getting in on it. But he just stood there and took it, and he was a head taller than all of them and could've beaten the snot out of every single one, all at the same time. I got so mad that I was heading over to jump into the teeth of it; I didn't care how many there were, I wasn't afraid, and it was the first time I'd ever thought all the nastiness I had inside me might be useful for something. But the bus got there before I did, and Orlando just picked up his briefcase, got on, and rode off, like nothing happened.

The next day at lunch, I told him what I'd seen and how nuts it made me, and I asked him why he never stood up for himself. He said when people picked on him, it hurt his feelings, but he didn't feel it like I did; it didn't make him angry, just really sad and afraid, like he was falling deeper and deeper into a pit he could never get out of. The only thing he wanted to do was cry, and he knew he couldn't do that in front of them, so he didn't do anything. That's why the counselors said he was depressive, because he felt like most everything was pointless, or his fault, and because of that, he didn't even try to actualize, although it was pretty obvious he could do all kinds of things, both good and bad, if he wanted to. I told him it was the other way with me, that I was more or less okay until I wanted to do something but realized I couldn't, and then I'd be stuck wanting it more and more and grinding my gears until all that energy and friction burst in this wild explosion.

We talked a lot about stuff like that and stuck pretty close, so I guess you could say we were friends. He'd even invited me over to his house one time and gave me a birthday present (a book, actually), and no other kid had ever done anything like that before or since, so that had to count for something. But it didn't last long. After I got suspended, Orlando's mom wouldn't let him talk to me anymore, and when I got left back, we stopped being in the same grade together. Shit, we'd hardly said a word to each other in more than two and a half years.

Once I made the team, though, I figured we'd finally be able to pick up where we left off. I got into football and would've wanted to play anyway, but I didn't see how Orlando's mom could keep us from speaking to each other if we were teammates, even if she told the coaches to make sure we didn't, because teammates had to communicate to be successful. And if she tried to make Orlando quit on my account, then Coach Rose would probably kill himself on their front lawn in protest, and I was pretty damn sure she wouldn't want to clean up a mess like that.

There was one final ace up my sleeve. I knew football was part of Orlando's therapy, just like it was part of mine, so there was no way in hell his mom was gonna make him quit. Like I said, we couldn't have been more different, but that didn't matter to our counselors. Since Orlando's family didn't trust the new pills some kids were getting and my family couldn't afford them, we both got the same fall-back prescription: sports—to bring him out of his shell and give him some confidence, and to provide me with some nondisruptive, non-criminal outlet for all that violence. Shit, our counselors had to make it look like they were doing something to collect their pay, and they probably figured that if slamming into people didn't straighten us out, then nothing would.

We walked through some offensive and defensive formations, whistles blowing now and then, and Wally, this fat kid who loved to talk tough, got bumped into, swung his arms in slow, giant circles, fell backward onto his ass, and started to cry. After everybody finished laughing, we lined up for special teams, punt coverage. Coach Rose told me to return it, wanted to see what I was made of. Fuck him. Greg, the punter, was supposed to be this awesome Dungeon Master, but that didn't make his kicking leg any stronger, so I lined up about twenty-five yards from the line of scrimmage in the defensive backfield. It took a while for the coaches to get everybody into place and explain to them what a punt was all about: snap the ball to the punter, block the man in front of you, wait for the punter to kick it away, and then break your ass down to the guy who catches it (me) and drill him.

I was visualizing catching the ball—punts could be tricky—when I saw Orlando lining up at the end position on my left-hand side, his sports goggles making him look like Eric Dickerson without all that slimy Jheri curl. That could be good, I thought. Unlike the other players on the punt team, the ends released with the snap, running downfield as fast as they could to cream the guy fielding the punt as soon as he caught it. That's why they were called headhunters, because their only mission was to get to the guy returning the ball first and knock his block off. It was good because I was every bit as fast as Orlando, maybe a little faster now, and if I caught the punt, gave him a juke, and dusted him, then I'd be practically guaranteed a starting position.

After about five minutes of the coaches explaining and yelling, we were set to go. I looked at Orlando just before the ball was snapped and nodded at him. He saw me but didn't nod back. That should've told me something was wrong. But the ball was already in play, and the next thing I knew it was in the air, a low, wobbly duck drifting to the left. If I wanted to catch it on the fly, I had to get moving. I had plenty of wheels to cover the ground, all I wanted and more, but I had to be careful. Even when I thought it wasn't possible to run any faster, I always had something in reserve, like a few more horses or an extra gear. The final burst into that higher register of motion felt like ripping through a barrier, or taking flight, but I couldn't control it for more than a step or two. Every time I hit it, it was like I outran myself, lost the rhythm, and crashed to the ground. Someday I might learn the trick of toeing that line between velocity and disaster, but I couldn't risk it now. The ball was sinking fast, so I leaned down into my sprint, pumped my knees, not up but forward and back, staying low to the ground, my eyes fixed on the ball. I got there just before it hit the turf, stuck my hands out, and snared it about six inches above the grass.

I didn't even hear him coming.

I wasn't afraid. Then again, there was nothing to be afraid of. There was only darkness, as if this dense black curtain had suddenly snapped down and blocked everything out, covering my whole brain and the rest of me with it. It was so dark and silent and numb that I couldn't feel a thing, and I guess I probably could've stayed that way forever without knowing it or caring. But as soon as that darkness began to break, I started to feel again. I didn't feel fear, though. I felt pain, lots and lots of pain, and this sadness like my heart was dying. It seemed like something was really wrong with the world lighting up around me, as if it were more sinister somehow, or less complete.

I'd walked right into a trap and I knew it as soon as my eyes finally blinked open. Although the rain had started to fall and was stinging my face as I lay there on my back, I saw Orlando standing over me. It took a few seconds for me to recover consciousness, focus, and draw a bead on his face, but as things started to sharpen I could see his mouth was all twisted and that there were tears welling up behind his goggles. Shit, I knew exactly how he felt.

"What in holy hell was that!" Coach Rose bellowed as he dashed over blowing his whistle. "Goddamn it, Orlando! Bump and wrap! *Bump and wrap!* Goddamn it! You tryin' to kill somebody? Goddamn it!"

Coach Rose ran up and grabbed Orlando by the shoulder pads and started shaking him, screaming in his face and slapping the sides of his helmet. The words came out of his mouth so loud and so fast and I was still so woozy that I didn't get most of it, but he was laying into Orlando like he'd knocked Coach's mom out instead of some kid he didn't give a wet fart about anyway. The only part I caught was "gonna run till you puke," and then he pushed Orlando away. Before he started off on the torture that was supposed to teach him a lesson, Orlando leaned over to me.

"I . . . I'm sorry, G," he whispered, his voice thick and breaking. "I didn't . . . I mean, I wouldn't . . ."

There was a sound like distant waves crashing in my head and my thoughts were patchy and loose, but somehow I knew what he was going to say. "No, I know you wouldn't," I stammered, trying to prop myself up on my elbows. "So who made you do it?"

Orlando's teary eyes grew tense and frightened.

"Who put you up to it, O?"

"Orlando!" roared Coach Rose from halfway across the field. "Why in the hell aren't you running? You want twenty *more* laps? Answer me, boy!"

43

"No, sir."

"Then get your ass moving this second!"

"Just a name," I asked as Orlando stepped back nervously, "that's all I need."

"I'm sorry, G . . . I can't." He turned and sprinted off.

Yeah, it was just what I'd thought. Somebody had gotten to him, forced him to send a message, and this was it. I'd only just started and already I was too close.

Coach Rose sent the trainer over to have a look at me, and he must've trusted the diagnosis completely, because he never checked on me himself.

F O U R

By the time I got home, I was soaked. The heavy
slates of green-gray sky had cracked and burst, tossing streaks of light
and biblical floods down on the Cruiser and me. My head was
pounding, and all I wanted was a shower, dry clothes, something to
eat, and a little time in front of the tube to clear my thoughts before
Thrash and I got back to work. But as the old man told me before he
split, the less you wanted, the harder it was to get. And the way
things had gone so far, I should've known I was in for another
surprise.

My mom, sister, and I lived in a two-story, three-bedroom house
with meager lawns in front and back. Slapdash construction, aluminum siding, neighbors right up in your face, close to the trailer
park, the Circle, and the crappy strip mall. In other words, a place
cheap enough for my mother to afford on the tips she made waiting
tables at the diner in the day and tending bar at night. It wasn't the
best part of town, but it wasn't the worst either, and it sure as hell
wasn't a dump like some people said. It was home, and I was lucky
enough to have one, so I wasn't complaining.

As I pulled up out front, I couldn't help noticing the moped parked in the back, a red Puch that looked brand-new. My first thought was, What kind of jerk-off would leave a brand-new moped out in a downpour like this? But I didn't have to wonder about it for long. I hopped off the Cruiser and started walking it toward the back of the house when the jerk-off came rushing out, helmet on, visor down. He jumped on, cranked the pedals, revved the engine, and drove off. Ray "the Razor" Tuffalo had just been at my house, and the way he avoided looking at me made me fear the worst about what he'd been doing there. I chained the Cruiser underneath the sheet of tin hanging over the concrete slab that we called the back porch and went inside to see if I was right.

Like I'd thought, the water was running in the upstairs bathroom and Led Zeppelin was rumbling the walls. Neecey was so predictable it was almost funny. Whenever she got laid, she'd crank "Kashmir" on the stereo and jump in the shower, like punching a clock after work. I should've been used to it by now, but it still annoyed the shit out of me. Even though her boyfriend Gary hadn't been around for a while and Darren only came over now and then, that song was starting to feel played out. Not that I had anything against Zeppelin; they rocked all ass and I had a patch with their logo on my backpack to prove it. But I was worried about my sister and what people might say, and although she was playing "Fool in the Rain" now and not "Kashmir," so I couldn't be sure about what, if anything, she'd done with Razor, it still bothered me, not only because it was a Cro-Magnon like Razor, but because I didn't know how much Zeppelin was too much.

I went upstairs, tossed my backpack in my bedroom closet, and then banged on the bathroom door.

"I'm in the shower," Neecey called.

"I need to get in," I shouted back, though I knew it was pointless.

"What?" she replied. "I can't hear you."

Typical. "I said I have to get in there." I yelled that time.

"Whadyasay? I can't hear you. Just open the door."

I hated this fucking game. Whenever she was in the shower, she pretended she couldn't hear me through the door, even though I knew she could. If I wanted to tell her something or ask her a question, I either had to wait until she got out, which could take forever, or I had to go in. She wouldn't just let me open the door a crack and talk through it, I had to step all the way inside, so I had to turn my head or keep my eyes down to avoid seeing her through the clear plastic shower curtain. And if that wasn't bad enough, she'd gotten the timing down so perfect that no matter how long I was in there, even if it was just a second or two, she'd already be finished, have the water turned off, and her hand out waiting for a towel. Then she'd keep talking to me as she dried off behind the curtain, real casual, taking her time.

The point of this fucking farce was to force me to be in the room with her while she was naked, and she'd started doing it a little over two years ago when she started filling out. She wasn't quite fourteen at the time, and mom said that while Neecey had been slow to get going, she was quick to catch up. In a few months she'd gone from being a flat, ugly stick that guys didn't notice to the kind of teenage girl that made men and boys mutter curses beneath their breath. She had long brown hair, glossy and straight, huge, sad eyes so dark brown they were practically black, a wide, pouting mouth with full lips, curves all up and down her figure, and breasts that would've been totally killer if they'd been on someone else.

Yeah, I knew it was completely twisted that I'd seen her naked or half-naked as much as I had, and I was worried that it was just a matter of time before I turned into a pervert. But that's why she made me come into the bathroom, or called me into her room from time to time when she was wearing only a bra and underwear, which she said was no different from a bikini. I never really said anything to her about it, but she must've realized it made me feel weird and gross, because she told me she didn't want me to feel embarrassed or ashamed about nudity the way she had when she was my age, and that if we couldn't be comfortable in front of each other, then how would we ever be comfortable in front of anyone else? Even though Neecey got that kind of crap from all the books on puberty, self-esteem, and sex she read, it still sounded flimsy to me. I thought it was just another way of torturing her younger brother, of showing me how grown up she was and making me aware that there were some things in this world I wasn't ready to handle. As if I needed to be reminded that she was hot, or that she probably didn't put up much of a fight for the few guys she'd liked. Shit, I knew that. And even if the whole town found out and started saying my sister was a slut, I still wouldn't want it rubbed in my face all the fucking time.

I stepped into the bathroom and said, "I just got back from football. It's pouring. I'm soaked. I need a shower. Get out."

"Why didn't you say so? Jump in," she said.

"Neecey, I'm not in the mood for your crap, really."

"Don't be such a fairy. Like I'd let you shower with me, you little perv. There, I'm done anyway, hand me a towel," she said, turning off the water and sticking out her hand.

I handed her the towel but kept my eyes on the floor.

"Look, Genie, I have something to show you."

"No," I said. I wasn't going to fall for that one again.

"Come on, sissy, I had my bikini line done, check it out."

"Jesus Christ, Neecey!" She was un-fucking-believable. "I don't give a shit what you do with your bikini line, and I sure as hell don't wanna see it."

"Chill out, Genie, I totally wouldn't show you anyway. And stop being such a wuss, okay," she went on, "because it's not like you've never seen a *vagina* before." She sang the word like it was part of a witch's spell instead of the female body. "I bet you wouldn't be such a chicken if Cynthia was here and you were in my closet."

Cynthia was Neecey's best friend—she was every bit as smoking as Neecey, and because she didn't have a boyfriend, there were lots of rumors about her. Everybody called them the Twins because they looked so much alike—same color hair, same height, similar facial features, same kind of figure—and it freaked me out a little, actually. Anyway, they were always together, so Cynthia was at our place all the time and slept over a lot. About a year ago, Cynthia was spending the night and they had an argument, a nasty one. To get back at her, Neecey hid me in her closet while Cynthia was in the shower and told me to stay there until Cynthia returned, and then jump out and scare her. Neecey's closet door had horizontal wood slats, and if you were inside with the door shut, you could see out, but nobody could see in. Well, Cynthia came in all right—shiny-wet, soapy-smelling, wearing only a towel—and I could definitely see her strolling back and forth between the bed and the vanity, drying her hair, inspecting herself, but as I was about to make my move, her towel hit the floor. Everything went from PG to *Porky's* so goddamn fast that I didn't know where the hell I was or what was going on, but I couldn't jump out because Cynthia was completely naked just a few feet away and I suddenly felt kind of warm and rigid all over. All I could do was wait for her to get dressed and try to make the best of it until she did. After Cynthia went downstairs, Neecey came in to see why I didn't frighten her, and I told her what happened—most of it anyway. She smiled at me, gave me a hug, said she was sorry, and told me to for-get about it. But after that I couldn't look at Cynthia or be in the same room with her. It was like I knew something about her that I wasn't supposed to know, and if I looked at her, she'd be able to tell and then she'd crack me one.

When Neecey noticed how I was avoiding Cynthia, she pulled me aside and said what happened wasn't my fault and that I had to stop feeling bad about it, and the only way to stop feeling bad about it was to do it again. She'd read that in one of her books, too. So the next time Cynthia slept over, Neecey hid me in the closet when she was in the shower, and told me it didn't matter if I jumped out to frighten her or not, I just had to try to relax so I wouldn't be freaked or act all weird around Cynthia anymore. Cynthia came in, and I watched her change. No, I didn't jump out, but it wasn't because I was caught off guard, like the first time. Maybe knowing what to expect made the situation easier to handle, because I sure as hell handled it.

The next day, Neecey asked me if I was still freaked, and I said no, and she asked me why didn't I jump out, then. I didn't answer her. She smiled and said it was fine if I liked it; it was perfectly natural for me to want to look at Cynthia, who was totally gorgeous. She said my liking it was probably the only normal thing about me, and I should feel good about being normal in something, and that it would be our secret. After that, when I was having problems in school or feeling really down, Neecey tried to cheer me up with some closet time. We called it Manning the Lookout because that's what I did: I looked out. For a few months, I guessed Cynthia didn't know anything about it, but I supposed she must have found out the time I was Manning the Lookout and mom came home early from work, because Neecey rushed into the room and made Cynthia get dressed real fast and go downstairs, and pushed me into my room while Cynthia was still in the stairwell. I was convinced she'd seen me, and I was totally embarrassed and couldn't talk to her or look at her or be in the same room with her again, and everything stopped for a few weeks. But about two months ago, Cynthia was staying over and mom was working at the bar and Neecey said it was all clear to Man the Lookout again, if I wanted to. Since then, I'd been doing it pretty regularly, about once a week, all through the summer, and the only thing different was that Neecey had started teasing me about it, and I'd started to wonder if Cynthia knew.

"*Cynthia's not my* fucking sister," I pointed out.

"No duh, dipshit. But you're not such a total horn dog that you can't see me in a towel without getting all freaky, are you? Because that's like way gross."

"No," I said.

"Then what's your damage?"

My damage was I didn't know if she was right or wrong about any of these things, and I was starting to resent being the guinea pig in her experiments. Plus, I'd had a rough day and felt like she was really riding me for some reason, and I wanted her off my back. So I broke the silence I'd always kept about her business, because I usually didn't want any part of it. "Why don't you get Razor back in here and make him look at it? Or has he seen it already?"

That got her. Her face went flush. She wrapped the towel tighter around herself and said, "So, you saw him leaving?"

"Yeah," I said. "Why? You thought you could hide it from me? Fat fucking chance," I added, realizing I was suddenly much angrier than I'd thought, maybe because thinking of Neecey and Razor reminded me of seeing him with Stacy earlier. "So, tell me Neecey, did you show him your snatch? How'd Razor like playing ball on a field with fresh-cut grass?"

"Stop it, Genie," she said calmly. "You're getting all worked up over nothing."

"Or did he trim it for you? Is that it? And then you thanked him by banging him silly on my bed, right?" My face was hot and my hands were shaking.

"Calm down, Genie," she soothed. "You're scary when you get like this."

"Oh, so now who's scared? Who's the fucking chicken now?" The anger was running on its own steam, racing forward, and there was nothing I could do to stop it. "I'll show you who's the fucking chicken!" I pulled my shorts down to my ankles and whipped off my shirt.

Neecey let out a shriek, jumped back, and covered her eyes. "Jesus

Christ, Genie!" she barked. "Put your shorts back on right now and like get a grip!"

Yeah, sometimes I had problems with self-control. I bent over and quickly hiked up my shorts. "They're on," I mumbled.

"You are so majorly deranged sometimes, it's like, I don't even know what."

As I stood back up, my heart was still racing, but my wits were coming back; they were telling me I should feel like an idiot. My cheeks reddened and my chin drooped toward my chest. "Neecey, I . . ." I began, but didn't finish.

She sighed loudly, calming herself. "Seriously, Genie? Don't *ever* do any shit like that again, I totally mean it."

I couldn't look at her, so I nodded at the floor.

"Let's just like forget it now, okay?"

I nodded again.

"Except . . ."

"Except?" I asked.

"Except," she snickered.

"Except *what*?" I cringed, panting, edgy like a madman.

"Except those big-ass balls of yours! Holy shit, Genie!" she said, and burst out laughing.

"Shut up, Neecey. They're not so big."

"Shit, yeah, they are. They're like sideshow big, and you're not even thirteen yet."

"Two more months," I said.

"And you'll still be a dork." Her laughter trailed off and she shook her head. "But you never know, you could have a decent little pecker when you get older, so maybe you won't always be like a total waste of humanity."

"You think?" I'd never thought about that before, that when I got bigger I'd get bigger all over.

"I hate to say it, but yeah. It reminds me of Murray's. Remember Murray? He moved like two years ago?"

"You mind sparing me the details, Neece?"

"God, you're like such a little priss sometimes, Genie. Get over it already." She flipped her hair back over her shoulders. She was starting to relax again, and all of a sudden she was excited, clapping her hands together and bouncing up and down. "Ohmigod. I *so* can't wait to tell Cynthia! She thinks you're totally cute. Weird as shit, but cute. That's why she keeps letting you Man the Lookout even though she knows about it. You know that, right?"

"I kind of figured that."

"Oh, yeah, right. Anyway, she totally knows. She was kind of mad at first, because she's like scared of boys, and that's why she doesn't have a boyfriend. She's totally curious and won't ever stop talking about it, but she's like, I don't know. Whatever. Anyway, I told her she shouldn't be mad because it happened by mistake, but you got really excited seeing her, and it was like one of the only things that made you happy, with you being a miniature Holden Caulfield and all."

"Who?"

"This guy in one of our summer reading books last year. He's totally lame and hates everything and has a nervous breakdown."

"Thanks, Neecey, that's really encouraging."

"Don't have a baby, Genie, I'm just busting on you. Besides, you're like *way* more evil. Anyway, Cynthia started asking me all these questions about you and what was wrong with you that you didn't think she was heinously fat and ugly, because she has like this really weird thing about being a total sled dog, even though she's a complete babe and everybody always tells her so."

"Cynthia thinks she's heinous?" It was impossible for me to imagine that.

"You've seen her family. She's like the only non-lard-ass of the whole lot, and she thinks it's in her genes or something. I mean, she totally eats, and doesn't scarf and barf or anything like that, but she's got it in her head that she's gonna swell up any minute like it's the ghost of Christmas future and shit."

"That's so bogus."

"For sure. But like I was saying, she started getting all curious about you Manning the Lookout, and she was like, well, your brother's really sweet, and if it makes him totally happy, what could it hurt?"

"No way."

"Yeah way," Neecey assured me. "But the thing is, I think she likes doing it because it makes her feel sexy, you know, and even though it's kind of strange, it's totally safe." She paused. "When I tell her you got that little monkey pecker down there, she's gonna totally shit herself."

"Okay, Neecey, that's enough." I didn't think the Lookout's stature was any of Cynthia's business, or an appropriate topic for them to dish about. I knew Neecey was only trying to get my mind off what I'd just done, like she usually did when I went off the deep end, but I couldn't tell if she was teasing me or bullshitting me or if she was really going to tell Cynthia or what. More than that, the whole situation suddenly struck me as so fucking weird that I couldn't figure out what the weirdest part was—the fact that I knew it was weird or the fact that it didn't feel as weird as it should have. I didn't know what to do. So I just looked back at Neecey, keeping my eyes on hers, and we both smiled, but I didn't know why.

She turned to leave.

"Neecey," I said before she got through the door, "are you a slut?" For some reason, I felt like I had to know.

She stopped and looked back over her shoulder at me. "Why? Did somebody say something?"

"No," I said, "I just want to know."

"No, Genie, I'm not a slut. I've only been with two guys, Gary and Darren, and I wouldn't do it with just anyone, because that's like gross and pathetic. Besides," she continued, "even if I was a slut, whose business would it be but mine?"

I didn't know, so I shrugged my shoulders, and she left.

I turned on the water, took off my sneakers and shorts, and stepped into the shower. The hot water felt good—so good that I didn't think about the case, or who was out to get me, or how screwy my sister was, or whether or not I was going to jail for incest because of what just happened. After a couple of minutes my mind had cleared out and began to fill up with images of Kathy and Cynthia and Stacy, and I soon realized the Lookout had already manned his post and was on the alert, standing at attention.

FIVE

Once I'd dried off, I hid the ten-dollar bill under a box of Magic Markers in the top drawer of my desk, threw on some cutoffs and the WHO FARTED? T-shirt Neecey had bought me a couple of months ago, and went downstairs. I had a couple of pointed questions I wanted to ask her about what Razor had been doing at our house, but when I got down to the living room, she'd already cleared out. And since it was her job to watch me while mom was at work, that meant mom would be home any minute, because if there was one thing I was *not* allowed to be, it was home alone at night with nobody watching. Someday I would be, sure, like in two months when I was fully self-sufficient. But until then, waiting for "someday" felt a lot like being strung along by a marathon of movie previews when all you really wanted was for the show to start.

I went into the kitchen, opened the refrigerator, and saw my dining options were limited to a bucket of cold fried chicken, milk, lettuce, half a grapefruit, onions, soda, pickles, Kraft cheese slices, economy-sized ketchup and mayo, or the four beers left in a six-pack. I'd tried beer before, and I guess you could say it was pretty good—that was, if you liked flat club soda that was sour and stale on your tongue and burned your throat. I grabbed the bucket of chicken instead.

I'd just finished dusting off two drumsticks, a thigh, and three wings when Mom came home with her arms full of groceries. Her hair was slicked down wet, her cheeks were moist and shiny, and the white button-down blouse of her waitress uniform was turning see-through at the shoulders from the rainstorm outside. The grocery bags were sopping and starting to give, so I hustled over to the front door to lend her a hand.

After we unpacked the groceries, mom and I had a little face time. I knew my counselors were always reminding her that she needed to take an active interest in me on a regular basis, but I also knew that she didn't need to be reminded. Almost nothing I'd ever done had slipped her notice, and if it were up to me, I'd reward her with some well-deserved time off.

But right now she just wanted to chew the fat and have some company after a long day of work, which I was more than happy to supply. She asked if I was hungry and how grandma was doing and how my day went. I told her I wasn't really hungry because I'd just eaten six pieces of chicken in less than three minutes, and then I told her about football tryouts and getting plastered on my ass, but not about being knocked out. She wouldn't have taken that well, and I didn't want to spend the rest of the night sitting around in the emergency room, waiting for them to tell us that I'd probably live. I didn't mention the case, my client, or her identity, either, because real detectives never revealed that kind of thing unless they were swapping it to a source for an important piece of the puzzle in return, or unless the coppers forced them to.

Mom gave me her worried look when I told her about tryouts and asked me if I was hurt. I told her the trainer had checked me out and said I was okay, but my head ached a little and my neck and shoulders were stiffening up. They were. The effects of the hot shower were wearing off and the soreness of the thumping was settling in. Mom gave me a glass of water and two aspirin, and pressed her palm on my forehead. She said she'd hoped we'd spend some time together this evening, maybe watch TV or play a board game or just sit and read together in the living room like we sometimes did, but if I wasn't feeling well, I should probably lie down and rest. Normally I would've taken her up on the offer to play a game, because we were pretty evenly matched at Scrabble and it was always a close game, right to the end. But I really wasn't feeling up to it and I needed what energy I had left to try to do some work on the case. I told her I was sorry and I'd give her a rain check if that was okay, and she said it was, she understood, and that I should go up and rest.

I closed the door to my bedroom, slapped the light switch, and heard rain ticking loudly against the roof, windowpanes, and sides of the house. I picked Thrash up from my bed, tossed him on my wooden desk chair, and clicked on the fan to circulate the air. Then I unlocked the side drawer of my desk, pulled out my journal, and made some notes about the case. I took my time, trying to remember everything I'd learned so far and doing my best to record the witness testimony verbatim, because you never knew when you'd have to throw their own words back in their face, and it was better to get them right when you did. But since I hadn't found out all that much yet, it didn't take very long, so I put my journal aside to confer with Thrash.

He was already ticked off—like he was every time I picked up my journal or a book. He'd always thought that writing in my journal was a waste of time, and that if I wanted to get something off my chest, I'd be better off actually *doing* something about it, instead of just sitting around playing hide-and-seek with myself on a piece of paper. Yeah, sometimes Thrash was worse than the mad scientist in a bad movie: he had crazy theories about everything. And according to him, reading and writing were timid and bloodless; the only thing they'd do was wind up dulling my instincts and making me weak, which at my size was the one thing I could *not* afford to be. He might've had a point in there somewhere, but I'd heard his tirade a thousand times before and told him I still wasn't in the mood for it.

I changed the subject and asked him what he thought about the case. He said that since Darren was a liar, he *had* to be lying—he either knew who'd done it and wasn't saying or had done it himself—and that we should stick to him like green sludge on stagnant water until we had enough evidence to nail him. But I wasn't so sure yet. Thing was, Thrash had his own reasons for wanting to see Darren take the rap—he'd never forgiven him for stealing my old bike—and that might've been affecting his judgment. Okay, I hadn't forgiven Darren, either, but I couldn't charge him with this crime just because I knew he was guilty of the other one. That wasn't the way detectives worked.

As for who was responsible for what'd happened at tryouts—who the message was from and what it meant—well, Thrash got all worked up at first and carried on about how Orlando was a low-down dirty rat and had to pay, but then I told him Orlando had apologized and told me somebody else had made him do it, and because I knew Orlando was depressive and felt guilty about everything, it wasn't the sort of thing he'd do on his own or be able to lie about. Thrash had always been jealous of Orlando, so I knew he wanted him to get some payback the same way he wanted Darren to. But the explanation I gave him seemed to calm him down just enough for him to think about it some more.

We sat there for a few minutes, not saying anything, and then came the surprise. Thrash thought *Razor* was behind it, and when I asked him why, he had his reasons all lined up. One, Razor and Orlando had some history between them because they both lived down by the reservoir and had been starters on the junior-high team last year. Two, everybody knew Razor was the kind of guy that pushed around and roughed up anyone younger, smaller, or that he could get some leverage on. Three, Orlando was a prime target to get leveraged. Although Orlando was bigger than Razor now, all Razor had to do was blackmail him: he probably threatened to lie to Orlando's mom, telling her he'd seen Orlando and me hanging out, if Orlando didn't rattle my skull at tryouts and keep his mouth shut about it. And with the prospect of his mom's wrath in the mix, Orlando would have to do it—he'd have no choice. Four, there was the timing. I'd seen Razor at the arcade and then left right after I'd questioned Darren, which must've been between quarter after three and three-thirty, because tryouts had started at four. A half hour to forty-five minutes was more than enough time for Razor to track down Orlando, whether at home or at practice, and put the squeeze on him, especially since we now knew Razor had a moped to get around quickly if he needed to look in both places.

It sounded pretty convincing, and I was willing to buy it, at least until a better theory or more evidence came along. But if I wanted to know *why* Razor had set me up for a shellacking at tryouts, then I knew better than to ask Thrash. He didn't give a shit *why* people did what they did, only who'd done what to whom—action, reaction; crime, punishment—because he said a failure to respond with a show of strength meant certain death in the wild. And if a show of strength meant sucker punches, eye gouging, kicking, scratching, biting, ambushing people, luring them into traps, or slowly ripping them to pieces, then that's what had to be done.

So I didn't bother asking him. I already knew what his answer would be, and that he didn't really understand the question anyway. Yeah, there were lots of things Thrash didn't really understand, which meant there were lots of things I couldn't talk to him about, even when I wanted to, because he just didn't get them. Like chicks. Sure, Thrash was killer on questions of conspiracy and revenge, but he just wasn't built to handle the allure of the female half of the species. Literally. Thrash's round, featureless underbelly didn't have the necessary equipment, and that gap in his plumbing was why he was never interested in talking to Kathy, and why I never told him about Cynthia or the Lookout, or how Stacy made me feel like someone was burning popcorn in my stomach. He knew about Neecey prancing around like she did because he'd seen her, but he never understood why it weirded me out so much. Then again, that's the way it was with Thrash—there were some things he had in spades, and there were some things he just lacked, and that's the way he'd always be.

I'd always supposed that first week of beatings had made him hard and cruel, but I couldn't be sure because I never got beat like that. I mean, I got into fights with other kids and took some lumps when I wasn't giving them, but my parents never hit me and neither did Neecey. That's what eventually made me suspicious of my first counselor and caused me to ditch her—she was always trying to get me to say that I'd been abused. But I couldn't say it, and never would, because I hadn't been, and I didn't think I'd ever get better if I blamed my parents or my family or anybody else for shit I *knew* they hadn't done. I was a little fucked up; that's all there was to it, there didn't have to be a reason or a cause. But my counselor kept trying to squeeze the easiest answer out of me, like to prove herself right or something. So I started lying to her, making shit up to keep her in check. After a couple of months she said I was "unresponsive" and passed me along to another counselor, where things went more or less the same way. By the time I got to counselor number five at the beginning of sixth grade—the one who suggested I start a private journal to try to write about what I thought and felt and to keep track of my urges and "episodes" and everything—I was officially branded a problem. But by then I didn't give a shit. All I had to do was keep my mouth shut and my hands to myself during school and there wasn't anything they could do to me.

Then again, they'd already done it. After I hit Ms. Witherspoon they suspended me for three months and then held me back, so I had to do fifth grade all over again. Yeah, that was a real treat. Fifth grade had been so easy the first time that I couldn't remember learning a single thing, and as I sat there day after day with nothing to do the second time, I could actually feel myself getting dumber. If I hadn't brought the detective books to school to keep me busy, the ones grandma had given me and talked with me about during my suspension—so I'd have something to do besides stare out the window all goddamn day, pining for lost freedom like a convict in maximum security—then I probably wouldn't have made it. Scratch that, no *probably* about it; I wouldn't have made it. Period.

Not that my teachers gave a shit about whether I made it or not. During my suspension, it was up to them to decide whether they would send me my assignments or let me make them up. Some of them did, most of them didn't, simple as that. And because most of them were happier to pad their roll books with zeroes by my name than to give me a fair shake, there was no way in hell I could pass, not even with summer school, and because my "reprehensible" marks in conduct had just about cinched the case anyway.

I didn't get that at first. It wasn't like they enjoyed my company so much that they couldn't bear the idea of going on without me. Shit, I thought they would've been happy to get me out of their hair. That wasn't what they did, though, so I knew I had to be missing something. So I started watching people—teachers, kids, a few of the other parents, the cleaning staff—observing them closely, paying attention to details, trying to size them up at a glance like Sherlock Holmes, or to predict their moves two steps ahead like Sam Spade and Philip Marlowe, applying what I learned. Not that I gave a shit about any of them—most of them were so dull and stupid it hurt to be in the same room with them. But I was a marked man by then, with nothing going for me and nothing to do, except to work out the bigger picture, so that's what I did.

I'd already skipped a grade, second grade actually, after I was given some tests to figure out why I wasn't integrating socially with my classmates. I didn't speak to other kids and didn't respond when my teachers called on me in class, so the higher-ups probably wanted to see if I was "special," meaning retarded. Truth was, I just couldn't do it. Every time I was called on, I knew the answer right away, but my mind would start going so fast—spinning round and round, wanting to say not just the answer but everything I was thinking all at once—that I couldn't figure out what to say first or how to say it, and even though it'd be something really simple like "seven" or "noun" and right on the tip of my tongue, I'd draw a blank and say nothing.

So they gave me these tests to see if there was anything up in the old attic at all. I didn't score through the roof, but I did score damn well near the rafters, and they figured that I hadn't integrated with my peers because they weren't really my peers—I was already at a much higher level than they were. The tests had proved I was "special," just not in the way anyone was expecting. Not that that made me feel any better. But being "special" in this way meant I was moving on to third grade instead of second, with a group of kids I didn't know from shit. And because my birthday was in October, after the cut-off date, so I'd started kindergarten just before I'd turned six, I went from being the oldest kid in my class to the youngest, and all of a sudden everybody else was much bigger than I was.

My new teachers in third grade knew all about those test scores, so they wouldn't let it go when they called on me and I couldn't answer them. They said crap like, "That's an easy one, you have to know it," or "You certainly don't act like the smartest kid in class," or they pulled me aside and told me I shouldn't be afraid to share my "gifts" with everyone else, like I was being stubborn or selfish or something. Shit, they should've just taped signs to my forehead and back that said KICK MY ASS and saved all of us a lot of time. The kids I would've been in second grade with had already started getting used to me because most of us had been in the same class together since kindergarten; I didn't talk to them and they didn't talk to me, but at least they'd left me alone. But my new classmates didn't know me and I didn't know them any better, and the way our teachers carried on basically handed them a cause to rally around.

And since I wasn't exactly the most humongous guy you'd ever seen, having a name like Eugene Smalls didn't help. Shit, it was the kind of name that practically got down on its knees and begged kids to fuck with me. It wasn't great for Neecey either, I suppose, whose real name was Eunice, although Neecey was a much better nickname than Genie, so she'd come out way ahead in that bargain. About our names, she used to say that first our parents screwed each other and then they screwed us, and that the old man had gone one better and didn't just screw mom, but all of us by leaving.

Neecey blamed the old man, I guess, but I didn't. No matter what you wanted, if it wasn't at the mall, then you wouldn't find it here— nowhere New Jersey, close to the Shore, in a town that only existed so you could make a few purchases on your way to somewhere else— and I wasn't mad at him for leaving, because I understood that. I understood it because I listened to a lot of Bruce Springsteen like everybody else, and just about every song the Boss ever wrote was either about leaving where he was from or how disappointing it was to stay, and that was just a couple of towns over.

So I wasn't having problems because of the old man or because of mom either. She broke her back to keep us afloat, and I knew that food and houses didn't grow on trees and that it was better to have sneakers bought on blue-light special at Kmart than to have none at all, no matter what the other kids said. And I especially knew I shouldn't pay attention when my new classmates started calling me "Genie the Teeny Wienie," or danced around me singing the theme song from *I Dream of Jeannie,* or dared me to do some magic, because they didn't know dick, so it didn't matter what they said.

No, it didn't matter, but it got to me anyway, and when I was called on in class and couldn't answer, or kids kept riding me after school when it would've been much easier for them to leave me alone, I started to feel that mayhem hatching in my heart. I was lucky to get Thrash around then. He understood what I felt without much explanation. Then again, Thrash was an amphibian, and amphibians were cold-blooded, so all he wanted was revenge. He told me people had to be taught that they couldn't fuck with me, but for people to learn anything, they had to get hurt, maimed, or disfigured in some way. That was the only way they'd remember what they'd done for the rest of their days.

Sure, Thrash was pretty sick, but his schemes for revenge didn't always work out like they were supposed to. That time Keith Montgomery was shooting spitballs at me in the cafeteria, I pretended to ignore him at first, then I circled behind him real casual, as if I were leaving, and then I swung my lunch tray with both hands and whacked him in the back of the head as hard as I could. But Keith's head didn't go flying off like Thrash had said it would; the lightweight plastic just made a loud *thunk* against his skull, and I got two weeks' detention. When we took that field trip to see the lighthouse in Sandy Hook, I brought a roll of duct tape in my backpack, got a seat on the bus right behind Andrew Barnes (who'd thrown my Yankees cap down the sewer two days before), slapped a big piece of tape on the back of his neck, and ripped it off before he knew what was happening. It didn't tear his skin off down to the bone like it was supposed to, though; it just pulled out a few of his neck hairs, made him scream, got me two weeks' detention, and no more field trips for the rest of third grade. I didn't get caught the time in fourth grade when I kicked the chair out from under Ricky Leland (who'd pegged me in the cheek with a rock after school one day), because I made it look like I'd tripped on the chair leg and that it'd come out from underneath him on accident. But his spine didn't shatter when he hit the floor and paralyze him like Thrash promised it would; Ricky just bruised his butt-bone and got a week off from school. So, after a few misfires like that, I thought it might not be such a bad idea to actually think about what Thrash told me to do instead of just doing it, because if it was only gonna get me my own private Breakfast Club, I wanted it to be worth it.

Of course, carrying Thrash everywhere and talking to him out loud like he was a person only added fuel to everyone else's fire. But when I felt things unraveling, I could look over at him or whisper in his ear, and he'd come up with some kind of vicious payback that I'd have to consider, and that usually brought me back down pretty fast. When I finally went berserk in fifth-grade art class, it was partly because I'd been late for the bus that morning and left Thrash at home by accident, so there was nowhere for me to turn and nothing to hold me back.

And it was all so fucking stupid really. Ms. Witherspoon obviously hadn't planned anything for us to do, so she pulled out some macaroni, gave us some paper and glue, and told us to make a picture. That pissed me off. We were in fifth grade, not first grade or kindergarten, and she was treating us like babies because she hadn't bothered to do something as simple as her fucking job. Plus, she gave us a kind of macaroni that looked exactly like the ready-mix packages of macaroni and cheese that Neecey made me for dinner when mom was at work, so I was pissed about having to make a picture out of my goddamn dinner, and there was everybody else, tossing the shit around the room, like it wasn't food, like it was nothing. I tried to play along, though, because I didn't want to be singled out again, not without Thrash. So I started pounding the macaroni into small pieces, using one of my big textbooks, not slamming it, but pushing it down to grind it, because the macaronis were small and hard to break. My plan was to make a picture of the beach, because I liked the beach (always had since I could remember), and I was gonna use the ground-up macaroni as sand. Something about the texture of it seemed right to me. But when Ms. Witherspoon saw what I was doing, she came over and started yelling at me for making a mess. I wasn't making a mess, I was being really careful, and I tried to explain to her what I was doing, but she wasn't having it. She said making a picture of the beach wasn't the assignment, because it was December, and I was supposed to be making a holiday scene; and then, totally out of nowhere, she added, "You see, everyone, just because you're a genius doesn't make you an artist." That was so out of the blue and so goddamn wrong that something inside me broke.

First of all, I wasn't a genius and never said I was. To be a genius you had to score 140 or better on the tests, and I scored 133, which was pretty good, but not genius. I didn't play chess or any musical instruments, and although I kicked ass at math, I thought it was boring. So what was the point of calling me a genius if the tests said I wasn't and I wasn't a prodigy in anything, except not fitting in? Didn't you have to *do* something to be a genius? I'd always thought so, and that's why I'd always thought everybody was making a big deal out of nothing, especially my teachers. Not that that stopped them. They just kept after it, about how I was supposed to be so smart but didn't show it, like I thought I was too good for everyone or had some kind of fiendish plan or whatever. The other kids hated me for all of it—for being complimented like that by our teachers (because they thought it was a compliment to be singled out for false praise), for spending most of my time huddled up with Thrash, and most of all because they couldn't stand the idea that "Genie the Teeny Wienie" might be better than they were at anything, instead of just some total freakish loser. They'd been making my life hell for two years, all of them, and there was Ms. Witherspoon, ragging on me in front of everyone, having a nice big laugh about shit she didn't know anything about, and she was supposed to be my goddamn art teacher.

I lost it. I really lost it. I was so busted with rage that I don't remember half of what happened, but I'd cleared that room out faster than the lunch bell and trashed most of it within a couple of minutes.

I remembered hearing the screams of the other kids out in the hall, but that didn't turn me back. Somewhere along the line, probably when that chair found its way through the window, Ms. Witherspoon must have thought she should come back in and try to stop me, instead of just letting me run out of steam, which I was doing when she snuck up behind me and grabbed me by the shoulders. Big mistake. There was nothing left in the room to save ($573 worth of damage), she hadn't announced herself or warned me that she was coming, and I didn't hear her, so she startled me, bad. I felt myself being grabbed, turned real fast, and before I could think of anything or stop myself, I threw a punch, *blam*, right into Ms. Witherspoon's jaw. She went down, hard, and the next thing I knew, Mr. Randle was holding my wrists behind my back with one hand and pushing my face into the floor with the other, his knee wedged into the small of my back. The police came and took me to the station in one of those "scared straight" moves they loved to pull on kids, because kids were stupid enough to fall for it. I didn't fall for it, but then again, I didn't need it. I didn't give a shit how badass you thought you were, when you knocked a teacher out cold as a fifth grader, you knew that you'd crossed a line, and beyond that line wasn't freedom but danger, lots and lots of danger, and because you found yourself on one side of that line instead of the other, things were never gonna be the same for you again.

Mom was crying when she came to get me, and the principal threatened to expel me. But mom couldn't afford to send me to private school, so if they expelled me it would mean that we'd either have to move to another school district, which we also couldn't afford, or my educational career would be over, and mom would have to deal with the law for that as well. So they struck a deal: they made her set up a payment plan to cover the damage and suspended me for three months, which led to me being left back, and when I came back to school they sent me to mandatory counseling during the period I was supposed to be in art class.

And the bigger picture I'd realized as I was rotting away in fifth grade all over again was that the people running my school didn't know what the hell they were doing, but that didn't stop them from doing whatever the fuck they wanted, as long as they never had to admit they'd made a mistake. They couldn't figure out what my problem was or how to help me, so they made me pay instead. Period. They pushed me up a grade and held me back, sent me to one counselor after another, jerked me around like a goddamn puppet, but always found a way to shift the blame to me, or my family, when things went wrong. They flunked me to show all the other kids who was really in charge, so everyone would know that being "special" didn't mean a goddamn thing when it came to falling in line. Even though I hadn't meant to do it, I'd taken aim at one of theirs, and they'd taken aim back, simple as that.

After that incident, though, I wasn't "special" anymore; I was "different," which was a nice way of saying I was a problem. When I realized what was happening, I tried to tell my counselors I thought some of my problems were more institutional than familial (which were words they used), but they couldn't or didn't want to hear that. They were part of the institution, so they were the good guys. And I was just one of those kids who was fucking it up for everybody else. It was total bullshit, all of it, and, yeah, I lost interest in school after that.

I glanced at the clock on my nightstand and saw Spider-Man's hands forming what looked like a "greater than" symbol from math. It was after ten-thirty, less than half an hour till lights-out in the summer, but I wasn't gonna wait for it. I felt tired, spent. I looked down at my journal, saw nothing but blankness on the page before me, and realized I'd been too preoccupied with yesterday's headlines to write anything more than the notes on my case. I closed my journal, put it back in the side drawer of my desk, locked the side drawer with the key, and then hid the key in the top drawer—under the ten-dollar bill that was beneath my box of Magic Markers—for safekeeping.

Thrash looked spent, too. He'd been sitting in that hard wooden desk chair for the past couple of hours and it was starting to take its toll: his shoulders were slouched forward, his head was drooping a little, his tongue was hanging down, and although his eyes were as wide open as ever, it seemed like he was fighting to keep them that way. The sandman was mopping the floor with his ass, so I scooped him up, laid him on his side of the bed, took off my shorts and T-shirt, turned off the light, and slipped under the sheets.

But as soon as my head hit the pillow, my mind started racing, and I wondered if Razor really had set me up for the plant job I'd gotten at tryouts, then what the hell was behind it? I wondered if it had something to do with my investigation, or the sign at grandma's home getting tagged. It seemed like they might be connected because the MO's were the same: they were both just forms of bullying, one of them aimed at me and the other aimed at old people, most of whom were really sick or practically out of their minds, like grandma; and as if waiting around for the big sleep weren't torture enough, they had to get mocked by some idiot kids who couldn't even spell *retarded*.

That was bullshit, too, but I couldn't let myself think about that now or my mind would just keep on going and I'd never get any rest. I rolled over onto my side and pictured Orlando moping around that cavernous bedroom of his, surrounded by books, being all depressive about what happened and feeling like total shit. Christ, sometimes I wished there was a switch I could throw to shut off my brain, make it all go quiet and dark. I rolled over the other way, pulled the pillow over my head, and tried to get some sleep.

SIX

You had to have guns if you wanted to go to war.
So when my alarm clock woke me up the next morning, I made sure
I wasn't suffering any lingering damage from yesterday (which I
wasn't) and then jumped out of bed for my daily regimen of push-ups
and sit-ups. I did fifty of each every morning, alternating every other
day between push-ups and pull-ups, the latter of which I did in the
doorway to my room on an extension bar that I kept in the closet. I
used nothing but my own body weight for resistance, because that's
what Herschel Walker had done on the farm in Georgia when he
was young, and it'd made him into the star running back for the New
Jersey Generals. Okay, this wasn't exactly a farm, and I'd never been
as far south as Delaware, let alone Georgia. But if you didn't switch
exercises like that, you'd develop unevenly, and that just looked stupid, no matter where you lived.

When I was done, I saw a note on my desk paper-clipped to an
envelope. It was from mom. It said that grandma had come up short
again and told me to take the money in the envelope over to the
retirement home this morning, first thing.

73

That figured. No matter how far the buck got passed, it always landed on me. Every two weeks grandma had to write a check for $275 to pay for the luxury and splendor of confinement in the retirement home. But along with a good portion of her memory and her grip on reality, she'd somehow lost the ability to distinguish between 20 and 70 and had been handing over checks for $225 instead of $275 at least once a month. Or maybe she was just screwing it up on purpose: I wouldn't put it past her. Whatever. Pencil-necked Bryan did the books at the home, because he'd probably gotten a mail-order degree in penny-pinching or something, the twerp, so he'd gone to talk to her about it the first time it'd happened. I wished I'd been there, because grandma'd had one of her moments, not remembering or denying everything, but then Bryan showed her the check, and she accused him of altering it after cashing it and trying to swindle a defenseless old woman. She must have totally reamed him, because he was still shaken up when he'd talked to mom and told her what the problem was. Anyway, that's what mom had told me, and that's why he called us every time it'd happened since, so he didn't have to deal with grandma anymore—because he couldn't—but so he could still extort the difference from mom anyway. Fucking weasel.

Well, at least I'd get to check out what Kathy wasn't wearing and give my client an update on the case. I went into the bathroom, washed my face, brushed my teeth, and gelled up my hair. I wore it spiky on top and clipped on the sides and back, except for the rattail in the center of my neckline, about four inches long, braided and fastened with a rubber band. Neecey usually braided it for me, but every time she did, she told me it looked like trash, same as mom, and they were always squawking about how I should cut it off. Either that, or they teased me that I was the mailman's son, because my hair was dirty blond and not dark like theirs.

When I came out of the bathroom, Neecey's bedroom door was closed, so I knocked to see if she was there. No answer. I knocked again. More of the same. She must've spent the night at Cynthia's. I still had questions for her, especially about Razor, but I was starting to wonder if she'd ever be here long enough for me to ask them. Shit, she'd been absent from the premises so often this summer you'd think she was the landlord instead of a tenant.

I went into my room, pulled out a pair of knock-off Jams with orange and yellow flowers that mom had bought on sale at the Bradlees in Hazlet and a yellow T-shirt with HULKAMANIA across the front in bold red letters. I turned the T-shirt inside out before I put it on, though, because professional wrestling was so fucking fake that it made me sick to watch it. But the T-shirt matched my shorts, and that's why I was wearing it. I skipped the socks, slipped on my white canvas sneakers, and checked myself in the mirror on the closet door. My clothes were cheaper than a toothless prostitute's, but the bright colors brought out the tan I'd gotten at the beach on Sunday, and the tan brought out my eyes. They weren't dark brown like mom's and Neecey's, but gray-blue—translucent, icy—and my face wasn't rounded and soft like theirs either, but lean, even, and slanted slightly down in V's from my eyebrows to my chin. Even my ears and smile were kind of V-shaped, so much so that while Marlowe had been my favorite from page one, I'd always thought I looked more like a young Sam Spade: I was a blond Satan just like he was. The only real difference was that I was a tanned, gutter-mouthed, bike-riding beach rat of a dirty-blond Satan who roamed and patrolled the pocket-lint streets of a shit town close to the Shore, instead of someplace cool like San Francisco. And every once in a while it made me think I must've been adopted.

The bus they used for day trips was parked in front of the home when I pulled up. You could tell it was an old school bus because all they'd done was slap some green paint on it and write OAKSHADE RETIREMENT HOME in white lettering on the sides. Other than that, it was the same kind that used to shuttle me to school every damn day, until I'd started taking the Cruiser instead. Then again, the retirement home itself used to be the town's elementary school way back when, and it still looked every bit of it. It was one of those sprawling, one-story, U-shaped brick jobs, with tall glass windows, a long concrete overhang leading to the front entrance, and a large parking lot in front. When the town coughed up the dough for a new school, the old one was bought up by investors who must've figured that since the building already had offices and a cafeteria, all they'd have to do was divide the classrooms into bedrooms, add a tiny bathroom to each, hang some Sheetrock around so it didn't look exactly like a detention center, pack it to the rafters with the weak and weary, and keep the linoleum floors in the hallways for that institutional touch. I didn't know how much they'd forked over for the property itself, but I was positive that they hadn't spared a penny on the renovations. Nah, they'd spent all three.

As I got closer, I saw about twenty of the inmates lined up alongside the bus on the front walk: old men in golf shorts, leather sandals, and dark socks over lumpy, blue-veined calves, elderly women in plaid elastic-waist pants or shapeless dresses, pale white skin glowing in the cloud-laden light, everyone in jarring colors and wraparound sunglasses, some wearing heavy sweaters although it was already eighty degrees, plastic tote bags and fanny packs, umbrellas and fishing hats, handheld radios with earpieces, walkers, canes, each one of them complaining about something different, but all of them jockeying for position, trying to get on board. Irma was standing at the front of the bus, wearing a green blazer and a white blouse, smiling her chubby, patient smile, clipboard in hand, nodding her head, writing down names as the old-timers climbed onto the coach, assuring them that there was plenty of room, reminding others to use the can first, asking some if they'd remembered their pills, and generally working the crowd, telling them how much fun they were going to have, like they were kids.

I saw grandma's head in one of the bus windows, barely high

enough to notice, all giggles and anticipation, like a kindergartener on her first trip to the petting zoo. She waved at me and blew a kiss and I waved back, but I didn't go over. I couldn't. The whole scene was so goddamn depressing that it practically gave off a smell. There they were, all worked up, raring to go, like flea markets and outdoor auctions, slot machines and casino buffets, horse races and early-bird specials were worth looking forward to, when everybody knew they were just ways of wasting time and money until it was all over. It made you wonder what was the point of living a life if that's what it came down to in the end. Then again, it wasn't like the alternative to living was a hell of a lot better.

I chained the Cruiser to the NO PARKING sign out front, went inside, shook the goose bumps from the A/C off my arms, and saw Bryan behind the front desk. Damn, his ears were big. I took the envelope out of my backpack and slapped it down on the desktop. As usual, he didn't look up.

"Where are they off to?" I asked.

"Hey, squirt," he said, because he had a really endearing way with people. "They're going to the auction in Collingwood. They'll be back this afternoon. Is this the money you owe me?"

He was wearing a pink short-sleeved collar shirt with one of those gay little alligators on it, like four gold chains of varying length and thickness, white wristbands on both forearms, and diamond studs in his ears. You could tell he had no idea what he was supposed to be— guido, preppy, or andro—so he just threw together whatever he had in his closet to see what came out. The result was total lameness.

"The name's Huge."

"As if."

What a douche. "Where's Kathy?"

"She starts at nine." He looked at the wall clock. "In like two minutes. So don't cream yourself, okay?"

This guy was really asking for it. He opened the envelope, removed two twenties and a ten, and held each of them up to the light, like he was checking to see if they were counterfeit. Then he looked toward me, somewhere slightly above my head, and said, "Well? Shouldn't you be out terrorizing the neighborhood? No, wait, wait, don't you have *two dollars* to collect?"

He turned his back and snorted, apparently cracking himself up. I'd seen *Better Off Dead*, too, and while the movie was funny, his reference to it wasn't. But it gave me an idea.

"No, I'm waiting," I said, and after a long, casual pause I added, "for my receipt."

Bryan stopped and turned around. "Receipt?"

"Yeah, you know," I said, "a little piece of paper that proves we gave you money?"

"I know what one is, runt," he said, staring down at my neck, "but what do you need that for?"

Runt? He was about five inches taller than I was and he was like thirty. But I let it slide. "Just what I said," I said. "We pay you in cash, so how do I know you're not putting that money in your own pocket?"

"Who are you, the junior division of the IRS?" He snorted again, because he seemed to think he was hilarious. "Look, I'm doing you guys a favor by calling you in the first place. You know why? Because failure to make biweekly payment in full without prior approval through submission of a waiver form"—he shook a piece of paper at me—"is grounds for contract review and possibly dismissal from residency in the Oakshade Retirement Home. Check the fine print, Mighty Mouse."

He made a wheezing sound when he laughed, like a whoopie cushion with a leak.

"Wanna guess how many of these your grandmother's filled out? Right, zero. And instead of making a major production out of it and forcing her to do paperwork, I just get the money from your mother and put it toward her bill. I'm taking care of you guys, so don't give me any more static."

Like that noodle could force grandma to do anything.

"I won't," I said, "as long as you give me a receipt."

"You don't get it, do you?" he heaved, fixing his eyes on what I guessed was my ear. "If I give you a receipt, I have to enter the fact that I gave you a receipt in this book here, and if I enter it in this book here, then I have to record it in that book over there, the red one, see? Then, all of a sudden, there's a record that your grandmother's checks come up fifty dollars short from time to time, because an additional cash payment will be logged in the ledger, and if that happens, then the head accountant will ask me about it during our quarterly review, because that guy is suspicious as hell and doesn't miss anything." He was breathing so hard I thought he might faint. "And you know what that means, Einstein? That means he may decide to pull your grandmother's contract for review, because the very first thing he's gonna think is that she can't afford to live here, because that's what he's *paid* to think. And believe me, you don't want that guy on your case."

"No," I said, "I don't. I want a receipt."

Bryan's face turned a delicate shade of pink, like his shirt. The symmetry was lovely to behold.

"Are you dense or something?" His voice was shaking. "This is a business, Tiny Tim, not a charity, and the owner, Mr. Silver, is a real bastard when it comes to money. Receipts that point to a history of short payments are exactly the kind of excuse he's always looking for to kick someone out and charge the next person in line that much more. So I *can't* give you a receipt, get it? In fact, you should be *thanking* me for taking care of your grandmother and saving you guys a lot of hassle. So do *me* a favor for once. Just take your dolly, get on your Big Wheel, and pedal off. Quit busting my chops."

"All right, you can't give me a receipt. Fine, I get it," I said. "Just mail it to us, then."

"Mail it?!" He curled his skinny fingers into fists.

Up to that point, I'd never realized how high-strung Bryan was.

It almost made my plan too easy—to pester him with a phony request, keep peppering him with jabs, pushing his buttons, just long enough for Kathy to arrive and catch him in the act of yelling at me. Then she'd let him have it, or at least see for herself what kind of prick he could be. Grandma would've been proud of me, and it'd keep Bryan out of Kathy's pants, at least for a few more days.

But when Kathy walked in—all lickable legs, swishy hips, and bubbly, bouncing boobs—she was intercepted near the door by Cuthbert Stansted, dressed neat and tidy as ever in his three-piece suit, who had his arm around poor old Livia. Cuthbert was a good twenty years older, but they were both short and small and bowed and hoary as all hell with age, and the way they were clinging to each other made it look like if one moved away too quickly, the other would collapse. Not that there was any danger of either one moving too quickly, but still. They said something to Kathy, she gestured *just a second* to them with her hand, and then she walked over to the front desk.

I realized Bryan had still been talking at me when the buzzing in my ear finally went quiet, but he never had anything important to say, so it didn't matter that I'd missed it. As soon as Kathy got to the desk, he switched off of me completely, like I'd vanished.

"So what are those two up to?" Bryan grinned.

"Livia says something is missing from her room," Kathy whispered, looking down.

"It's more like there's something missing from somewhere else." He dragged an index finger very subtly down the side of his temple.

Kathy frowned at him. "That's not nice, Bryan, even if it is true. And Cuth says he can verify it, so don't you think we should go check it out?"

"Oh, Jesus, here we go," Bryan huffed. "All right, lead the way."

As Kathy turned, I saw Bryan palm one of the twenties I'd just brought and pocket it. I can't say I was completely surprised. I'd always wondered how he afforded that souped-up IROC of his, and maybe now I was finding out. Kathy led Bryan over to the other two, and since nobody was paying attention to me, I hung back a few steps and followed.

Livia's room was in one of the back corners of the building, like grandma's, only it was in the other prong of the U. It took a long time to get there because Livia took the tiniest steps and drag-shuffled her feet when she walked, as if she were making sure the bottom of her shoes touched every square inch of flooring on the way there. She had Cuthbert on one arm and Kathy on the other, and she kept telling them, "It's gone," "Someone broke in," and "They steal from me" over and over again. Cuthbert tried to commiserate, saying how awful it was and that he knew it to be true because he was a witness, while Kathy reassured her that they were going to get to the bottom of it. Bryan seemed in a hurry, because he'd gone up ahead and was out of sight. As for me, well, whatever was gone from Livia's room or whether anything was missing at all, it didn't really matter. The whole thing just made me feel sorry for her.

Once the others caught up, Bryan pulled a key chain out of his pocket, opened the door, and they all went in, while I waited down the hall for about a minute or so before creeping to the threshold to have a peek. Inside there was a small dresser, a sitting chair with a matching footrest, a single bed, a nightstand, and a couple of lamps. Pretty much standard issue at the home, only Livia's furniture looked about thirty or forty years more out of date than everyone else's and gave off that dull sheen of too much wear and tear. There was a framed photograph on the dresser of a man, a woman, and a little girl who must've been her family, although it was anybody's guess because she wasn't in the picture with them. Everything else was old tabloids and gossip magazines, dust and doilies, and metallic centrally cooled air.

Cuthbert was pointing at the nightstand under the window, with Bryan standing right behind him. Kathy and Livia were on the other side of the bed, closest to the door.

"There, right there," Cuthbert said. "I escorted Livia from the television room last night, after our program had ended, and I noticed it resting on the corner as I bid her good evening from the doorway."

"But it's not there now?" Bryan asked.

"Apparently not. Nor, however, was it there when Livia awoke this morning." Cuthbert put his hands on his hips when he'd finished, as if to say, *Deal with that, sonny*.

"Is that true, Livia?" Bryan asked.

"Yes, Bernie." She nodded sadly. "It's gone. Someone broke in and stole it."

Bryan winced but didn't correct her. "All right, all right. Let's not jump to any conclusions. Let's all just look around and see if we can find it first. Cuthbert, will you please check around the dresser? Kathy, Livia, will you two please look on the floor around the bed where you are?"

Everyone started searching, and Bryan knelt down in front of the nightstand, sliding his hand in his pants pocket as he did so. There were twenty good reasons for my eyes to be on him, so I saw him do it. Then he ducked down under the nightstand, like he was reaching back to the corner behind it, and as the others started calling out that they'd come up empty, Bryan said, "Aha! Found it." Livia, Kathy, and Cuthbert crowded around him and he held up the loot. Then he told them that everything was fine, no one had broken in and nothing had been stolen, the money had just fallen behind the nightstand where Cuthbert and Livia couldn't see it.

I didn't know whether to applaud him or to scream out that he was a liar, a fake, and a thief and sound the alarm. I knew I wasn't supposed to be there and that my opinion wouldn't be welcomed, but I couldn't let some bullshit like that pass without comment. "Wow, it's really lucky you found the money, Bryan," I said, sneering.

He looked across the room at my shoulder and said, "We're having grown-up talk in here, if you don't mind. Why don't you run along and play?"

"I do mind. My grandmother lives here, too, and I just want to make sure the place is secure."

"Well, as you can see, it is. Thanks for your view, though."

"It is? Really? Did you check to make sure that the window next to the nightstand was locked, or that the screen behind it hasn't been moved or tampered with?"

Bryan froze.

"You know something," Cuthbert said, reaching up to finger the top of the windowpane, "the young man does have a point. The window is not locked."

Bryan spun around and locked the window, almost knocking Cuthbert over as he did. "Well, it's locked now. Problem solved. Anything else?"

"No, you're right. Problem solved. Except . . ."

"Except what?" The color was rising in Bryan's cheeks again.

"Well, except for the corner of the nightstand." I stepped into Livia's room, toward the dresser on the left, and ran my finger along the top. "See how everything else is covered with dust? The corner of the nightstand isn't. So how come the corner of the nightstand, the place where the money was, you know, right next to the unlocked window and all, has no dust on it? Why is that the *only* spot that looks like it's been wiped clean?"

Kathy, Cuthbert, and Livia all glanced around them and then turned their eyes on Bryan.

Bryan forced out a laugh. "Ha! That was a good one. Really. You almost had me. For a second I thought you were *serious*."

"I am serious."

"No, you're not," Bryan beamed. "Because you don't know what you're talking about. That's where Livia *always* puts her money, isn't it, Livia? So, naturally, there wouldn't be any dust there. And since we already found the *money* that was *supposed* to be *stolen*, maybe you should admit that the case is closed. I'm sure we all appreciate your *concern*."

Lying, patronizing asshole. Worse still, I was already losing the others, even Kathy, and I knew it. The money in hand was too much for them to ignore, and as for how it actually got there, it would be his word against mine. But I wasn't done just yet.

"Yeah, well, I *am* concerned. I'm concerned that money goes missing from Livia's room only to miraculously reappear, and I'm concerned that the front sign was vandalized and you guys haven't done anything about it. How about *that*? Have you even *tried* to figure out who did it? What if the one has something to do with the other? What if the vandal and the burglar are the same person, or working in cahoots? Why aren't *you* concerned about *that*?"

"We are, honey—" Kathy started before Bryan interrupted.

"We *are* concerned, all of us." He swung his arm outward, as if to include the others. "And we've already called the police, so we *are* doing something about it. But that still doesn't make this any of *your* business."

"Oh, yeah, Bryan? I got *twenty dollars* says it *is* my business." I knew Kathy, Livia, and Cuth wouldn't have the slightest idea what the hell that meant, but I wanted Bryan to know that I knew where things stood.

He faked a helpless shrug and asked Kathy to make sure everything was all right with the others before motioning me down the hall. We stopped about a dozen feet from the doorway and he whispered angrily, his beady eyes glaring at my chin.

"What are you trying to do, Buttinsky, start a panic?"

"What are *you* trying to do," I shot back, "cover up a crime?"

"Come off it, already. Nobody knows if that money was stolen or not. Jesus, this is the fourth time in the past month she's pulled the *same* thing—somebody broke into her room and stole twenty dollars. But the sad truth of the matter is that her family doesn't send her much extra cash, and at this point she isn't sure if she ever *had* twenty dollars or not, and Cuthbert is blind as a bat, so *he* doesn't know it either."

"But that still doesn't—"

Bryan cut me off, his temper kicking in. "Can't you see all you're doing is encouraging them to believe that someone broke in and stole from them? Do you know what that'll do to them? *Do you?* Do you have any idea what it's like to be old and alone, far from your family? There isn't a lot for them to do but gossip and complain and worry themselves sick over the tiniest little things. And if they start thinking the home is under siege by criminals, well, Jesus, that'll *really* set them off. This place will be a madhouse by morning. Is that what you *want?* For them to think they aren't safe, that someone's after them, just because *you* said so? Is that what you want *your grandmother* thinking when she tries to go to sleep at night? Well, let me tell you something, kid, it's my job to keep the peace around here and that's what I'm doing. You may not like it, but it *works,* so unless you have a smoking gun to hand over to the police, you should *keep your mouth shut.*"

Sheriff Shit for Brains keeping the peace. Now I'd seen everything. "No criminals around, you say?" I asked calm and slow because I wanted it to sink in. "Then what about the sign? And *what the hell are you doing with my twenty dollars?*"

"Christ," he spat out, reaching in his back pocket. "Is *that* what you're worried about?" He opened his wallet and pulled out a bill, shaking it at me. "*Here.* Here's your twenty dollars. I just grabbed the one that was closest, because when Livia needs a new one, it *always* comes from me."

Bryan's hand was trembling, and for the first time ever he looked me dead in the eyes. I recognized that look, I knew it inside and out—he was shot through with rage. Kathy closed the door behind her and slipped into the hallway before we could go any further, though, so Bryan bottled it up fast, smiled, and played it as false and slimy and two-faced as he could be.

Kathy told him that Cuthbert and Livia were fine, and Bryan pretended to give a shit as the two of them started down the hall. I let them walk up ahead, took the nearest side exit out into the soggy heat, and made a beeline for Livia's window. If Bryan couldn't be trusted to check it, then it was up to me.

There were small, flowerless bushes bordering the wall beneath the windowsill and gray waterlogged wood chips on the ground, which had probably been, in the distant past, some kind of mulch. The decorative shrubbery had definitely seen better days, but it didn't appear that its sorry state had been caused by human trampling. I checked the screen for fingerprints and signs of being moved up or down, but I didn't see anything telling. What struck me, though, as I peered through the window, toward the nightstand, and further into the now-empty room, was that it would've been easy as pie to lift the screen and the unlocked window from where I was standing, slip a hand in, swipe whatever was on the nightstand, and break away fast, clean, and unseen in about ten seconds or less, even if someone was sleeping in the bed just beyond. It would've been so easy that almost anyone could've done it without getting caught.

What I couldn't be sure of, though, was what was bothering me more—the very real possibility that the home had become the target of ongoing criminal activity, or that the guy who was supposed to be in charge was doing everything he could to make it look like it wasn't. Maybe the sign had only been the tip of the iceberg. Maybe the case was a lot bigger than I'd thought.

As we approached the front sidewalk where the Cruiser was parked, Thrash started ragging on me, and I told him to shove it, but he was right. I hadn't inspected the scene of the crime when I'd been here yesterday. That was the very first thing a detective was supposed to do, and I hadn't done it. I didn't know how I could've forgotten. But there was no time like the present, so we headed across the parking lot to check it out.

When we got to the island where the sign was, I could've slapped myself. There were clumps of crabgrass, a few tattered dandelions, tangles of browning weeds clinging to the soil, and a tall hedge dividing the island from the shoulder of the highway. Otherwise there was only limp yellowed grass and dirt, dirt that had been rained on practically all night, which meant that it wasn't dirt anymore, but mud. If there'd been any tracks or footprints in the area, they were long gone now, all washed away, and I'd missed my chance to inspect them. No, it was not the finest moment in the history of private detection. But at least Thrash was in my backpack, so I didn't have to see that look on his face.

I stood there with my thumb up my ass for a few minutes, listening to the cars rush past on the highway, filling my lungs with exhaust fumes, trying to think redeeming thoughts. Then I looked up at the sign and noticed that they hadn't repainted it yet. That burned me up. It still said OAKSHADE RETARTED HOME, same as yesterday, only now the smudge of paint over the "irement" was like a thick black tongue sticking out at me. I closed my eyes, inhaled deeply, and shifted my feet to calm down, thinking I'd probably have to paint the damn thing myself if I wanted it fixed, just like I'd had to rake the leaves off the tiny patch of lawn outside grandma's window last fall.

After a few seconds, I opened my eyes again, and that's when it hit me—an icy pinprick in the back of my brain that grew and widened like some Antarctic flower. *There were two perpetrators.* The height of the sign gave it away, which I hadn't thought about yesterday, seeing it from the window in grandma's room. The wood placard itself was about three feet tall and five feet wide, but it hung from the top of wood posts that had to be ten feet tall at their highest point. The bottom of the placard was a good seven feet off the ground, and the word *Retirement,* the one that was painted over, was more like eight and a half feet high, because it was right in the middle.

The point was, you'd need to stand on something, like a stepstool or a short ladder, to reach it, unless you were like six-foot-six or taller, and nobody around here was six-foot-six, not even Orlando. So there had to be two people, because there was no way one person could carry a paint can, paintbrush, and a stepladder while trying to make a run for it, and in the dark and seamy world of graffiti, it almost always came down to a footrace to safety, and everybody knew that, so whoever did it must've factored that in. Either that or they were totally brain dead.

I decided to look around the island more closely before I left, just in case. Henry David Thoreau, the guy who wrote the book Orlando had given me, said he could tell not only when someone had been at his cabin in the woods while he'd been out, either by bent twigs, footprints, or some other bit of forest, but also what age and sex they were by some trace they'd left behind, like a plucked flower, discarded blades of grass, or the faint smell of cigar or pipe smoke. I guess that's because he studied nature and knew what to look for, but I didn't, and for a second I wished I had a magnifying glass to help me out, like Sherlock Holmes. But I got over it. If you didn't know what you were looking for, it wouldn't matter if you saw it close up or far away, so a magnifying glass wouldn't have done me a damn bit of good. Thrash told me I should set him down and let him have a go at it, because he'd been born and bred through millions of years of evolution to master the lower terrains and was better equipped for the job. He was probably right, but the last time I got him muddy, mom said she wouldn't wash him for me anymore, so I told him I'd handle it.

I searched the bottom of the hedge and found three crushed beer cans, a waterlogged book of matches, and a crunchy old sock stuffed back into the leaves. It seemed like they'd been there forever, and I wondered when was the last time the home had had a landscaper in, other than me, to tend the place, because it looked like an old man's sweaty armpit. It made you wonder what the hell they were doing with all the money they got if Bryan wasn't actually skimming it, because they sure as hell didn't step sharp when it came to fixing anything. If I wanted the island cleaned up, I'd probably have to do that, too, along with repainting the sign. What else was new.

There was nothing else to find, so I turned back toward the sign and bent over to pull up a weed. I wanted to see how long the job might take, because even if I had to do it, I didn't want to make a goddamn day out of it. And just as I reached down for the weed, I saw it lying in the grass—a thin black rubber ring, about three inches in diameter, the kind of band used as a seal inside plastic drain pipes and that most everyone was wearing as bracelets these days, guys and girls alike. A low belch of thunder sounded in the distance. I was so stunned that I held the bracelet up and stared at it, like I'd never seen one before or didn't know what it was. But once I snapped out of it, I knew exactly what it was—my first real clue.

SEVEN

I stood on the pedals and leaned forward as I cranked the Cruiser northbound on a tree-lined lane of drab homes in the residential area just behind the retirement home. I was on the west side of town, where all the streets looked the same: they all had the same grayish asphalt on the roadway, the same narrow sidewalks that wedged violently upward in places thanks to the tree roots growing beneath, the same moderate-sized yards and paved driveways, the same wood-paneled ranches, or brick-and-wood split-levels with garages and basketball hoops, the same plastic trash cans lined up on the curb, and the same red metal arms on all the mailboxes. You'd think a few people might refuse to cut their lawns, just to spice things up a bit. But no—even the grass was the same damn height. Sure, everything was more or less tidy and in pretty decent shape, but I guess that's why Thoreau was dead set against conformity: it just made everything look tired and bored.

Not that the town center was any better, because that was the crappy part, and like most others in the county, it wasn't in the center of town at all, but to the north and east. It had the police station, the fire department, the mayor's office, the chamber of commerce, two fast-food restaurants, a bank with drive-through tellers, the post office, a ninety-nine-cent store, the public library, and not much else. All of it was crammed together on one measly avenue that ran east to west and was only remarkable for its ability to look rundown and barren in both directions. At the western end a T-junction fed into a small north-south highway, one of those dinky four-laners that criss-crossed the whole state—with jug handles for left turns, traffic signals every half-mile or so, and lights that were carefully timed to stop you at every one—and it split the town in two, right down the middle, just about all the way through. On it were the appliance store, the hardware store, the gas station, a used-car dealership, the supermarket, a Carvel ice cream shop, a roller skating rink, the grimiest diner on the planet, a packaged-goods store, which meant they sold liquor after hours, and a juice bar, which meant that you had to bring your own because the chicks dancing inside were *all* nude, *all* the time, and if I ever got caught within a hundred yards of it, mom would poke my eyes out long before I was legal to go in. A little further south was the convenience store and the strip mall (which, among other things, had a hairdresser, a toy store, and the only decent pizza parlor in town), while across the highway, directly to the east, was the street I lived on. The Circle and the mall were just south of our place (they were dead center of town in terms of actual geography), and southeast of them were the reservoir and the wealthy developments surrounding it. And below that was nothing; literally nothing for four and a half miles but woods and proposed highways all the way down to industrial road, which had no industry of any kind and nothing to it at all, except being the southernmost boundary. Just north of our place was the trailer park (also on the east side of the highway), and above that was the mess of apartment complexes, boarded-up houses, abandoned lots, and random, ramshackle huts unfit for dogs that encircled the town center. Like I said, the crappy part.

That's exactly where I was going, and I was running through the town's layout in my mind to narrow down the options for my next move. The way I saw it, I either needed to scour every single house, trailer, apartment, and workplace for a stepladder, stool, or crate bearing soil samples from the retirement home, which I'd have no way of testing or matching, or devise some way of tracking down the owner of a kind of bracelet that was hanging from just about every ankle and wrist in town, including mine. Those were my options, and I knew they weren't good ones. In the trade, we called it having a clue but no leads. Outside the trade, we called it not having shit.

I needed something better to go on, something more direct, and I needed it quickly. Between the mesh of leaves arching above and the colorless sky beyond, a low ceiling of ashen clouds was descending from the west like the sole of a giant boot. From the looks of things, it wouldn't be too long before that boot came splashing down. But I wasn't all that worried about how long I had before the weather turned against me; I was much more anxious about the questions I wanted answered, and who I planned to ask.

I realized that a little more time to prepare myself probably wouldn't kill me, so instead of going straight, I took a right at McDonald's and crossed over the T-junction to the town center. I hung another right off the main street onto a smaller one that started south for a few blocks before hooking around to the northeast. Then it split off and curved northward behind Carvel's, jogged through a small, misplaced patch of woods, and then cut between two sandlots, one on either side, with the rusted hull of an El Camino on cinder blocks in one, a Dodge Charger in the other, clotheslines with crusty shirts and faded underwear, busted gates, and rusted tools scattered about both, and sorry clapboard shacks at the back of each that made plots at the trailer park look like country estates. I didn't know who lived there, but I somehow got the feeling that they didn't want company, so I did my best to respect their wishes. Just beyond, the road went up a short hill and then rolled down the other side into

Sunnybrook, an apartment complex of twenty-five to thirty buildings, all of them long, narrow, red-bricked, with shingled A-roofs, like a barracks grid of two-story warehouses and numbered parking spaces.

Yeah, it sucked, but I never said I came for the scenery. I came for the view. There was a swimming pool in the center of Sunnybrook— a big one, maybe a hundred feet long and twenty feet wide—with two diving boards, a large concrete sunbathing area, plastic tables and chairs, a snack bar, and a ten-foot chain-link fence guarding the perimeter. Admission was members only, restricted to residents like Neecey's friend Cynthia and their guests, so my perch this summer had always been confined to the gate, on the outside looking in.

As I pulled up to the fence now, there wasn't anything to see. The lifeguard, a tall, bronzed Q-Tip in baggy red shorts, was setting up tables and chairs to the tinny sounds of a transistor radio, but otherwise the place was deserted, the threat of rain keeping people at bay. The pool's flat surface looked glossy and cold in the dampened light, as if it were sulking over the lack of swimmers and sunbathers, and while the emptiness of the place made everything seem gloomy and sullen, I actually felt kind of relieved.

I felt relieved because Stacy Sanders wasn't there, which meant I'd dodged the bullet of having my first conversation with her be an interrogation of what she'd been doing with Razor at the arcade yesterday. I wanted to know that and how long they'd been there because it might help me with the case, or at least ease my mind about a few things.

Not that it would've been a goddamn cinch to just roll up and ask her. I'd had about a million chances to break the ice with Stacy over the past couple of years, but I'd clutched up and choked every time. She was the reason I'd been staking out the pool this summer: whenever it was sunny, she'd lie out on a lounge chair that she pulled to the front right corner, away from everyone else, listening to her Walkman and wearing a pink string bikini that clung to her like colored

Saran wrap. She never did anything out of the ordinary, just reclined on her back with her eyes closed, sat up and scribbled in her notebook, rubbed suntan oil on her stomach and legs while sucking on a long strand of bangs or stretching her gum—you know, usual stuff like that. But at some point she'd turn over onto her stomach and start pedaling her feet. Her butt cheeks would spring out dense and curved from the small of her back and wiggle like balls of cotton candy in a stiff, swirling breeze. That alone was worth the price of admission, but it also had this way of hindering my ability to speak.

It was the way that Stacy didn't seem fazed by anything that tripped me out the most. In class or out, it was the same with her: she was always a bit removed from everyone else, wrapped up in her own business, as if there were this tiny bubble around her that only she could fit into. I had a similar kind of thing, I guess, except it was more like a safety cage. Whatever. Stacy seemed pretty happy in her bubble, as if she wanted nothing more than to be by herself with her head bent over one of the notebooks she was always writing in. She must've gone through thirty of them last year, each one a different color. I was curious as hell about what she did in them, but you could bet your lunch money *and* your allowance that it wasn't schoolwork, not even if she was in class. She was one of the worst students in sixth grade, straight D's, but when she got called out by one of our teachers for paying more attention to her notebooks than to what we were supposed to be learning, she just shrugged her shoulders, smiled a little, said okay, and went back to doing what she was doing. That was cool. But what really impressed me was that when she got detention or sent to the principal's office for not listening, she did the same thing—she shrugged, said okay in this really cheerful way, and then either went about her business again, or packed up her stuff and left.

That chick was a mystery all on her own, one I'd been itching to solve for nearly two years. The best part was that it was natural, totally natural; she didn't act all coy or teasing like other girls in school, and it wasn't some put-on or front. It was like Stacy knew what she was all about and just did her thing and didn't let anything else bother her, and that was that. She wasn't nasty or bitchy about it either. When kids talked to her, she'd talk back, and not phony, oh-my-God-like-why-are-you-in-my-face talk, but all involved and animated, making her eyes real wide, tilting her head so her bangs covered one side of her face, scrunching up her nose a bit when she laughed, and showing that tiny gap between her front teeth. Like I said, she wasn't all that pretty, and when she made that face she looked kind of slow, but it still drove me nuts. There was just something about her, and she could've gotten away with being a snotty, stuck-up priss if she'd wanted to, but she wasn't. She just went with it, like whatever she was doing right then, or whoever she was talking to at that moment, was perfectly fine, and she was good to go with it. Shit, I'd even seen her talking to Doug Le Fleur by the water fountain a couple of times, and hardly anybody talked to him, because he was the smelly kid—every school had one, he was ours, and, to be honest, he had a gift for it.

Yeah, I realized I'd wasted far too much time running surveillance detail on Stacy this summer, and because she wasn't at the pool, I was just wasting more now. But I also realized that if someone like Doug Le Fleur could talk to her, then I shouldn't have any problems doing the same, and the only reason I still hadn't was that I'd been flooding my engines and stalling out over nothing like I always did. Big fucking surprise. I knew my time would come, though, and to make the most of it, I'd taken steps to prepare myself. I'd been practicing my rap on Kathy at the home for the past few months, trying to come up with a smooth line or two, and the more I talked to her, the easier it got, so I figured I was almost ready.

My only worry now was that I'd have to get in the game sooner than I'd wanted to. Lots of older guys had taken an interest in Stacy over the past few months, crawling out of the woodwork and pushing up on her with all the subtlety and good intentions of sharks in a feeding frenzy. Guys like Razor and his pal Tommy Sharpe, center for the junior-high team last year and the grim, doughy Hardy to the other's screeching Laurel. Both had cool names but were total dicks. Then there was Lou Patterson, a freshman who'd had vocational school stamped across his oversized forehead since the fourth grade; Hubert Donovan, a sophomore metalhead with a soft chin, a lint mustache, and a one-man garage band with no fans; Michael Corey, this ghostly nonentity of a freshman who was dark-haired and shifty-eyed and just way too fucking creepy to stand a real chance with anyone; and a few others who weren't worth mentioning. Yeah, real winners. It was getting to the point where if I wanted to talk to Stacy, I'd have to take a number and stand in line like the deli counter in the supermarket.

But I wasn't sweating it too much. Everybody knew that chicks totally lost it over bad boys—real ones, not slaphappy jocks, dirtbags, or fakers—and as far as bad boys went, I was the worst one around. And sooner or later that had to start working in my favor.

My trip to the pool had been a dead end and clocks were ticking all over the damn place. The trail of the crime was growing cold while I still had practically nothing to go on, and any day now Stacy could be swept off her feet by an older guy who wasn't a total sleazebag. All of a sudden it felt like I had too many things on my plate, each one leading in a different direction, and I knew if I thought too long or too hard about which to do first, I'd just get flustered and hamstrung and wind up doing nothing. Same shit, different day.

So I jammed the Cruiser's stick shift into third, eased back on the banana seat, and stepped on it, but I'd only gone a short distance from the pool's entrance when I saw a browning shrub rustling next to one of the apartment buildings about thirty feet away. I looked more closely in that direction and spotted a small, thin girl with long black bangs, a pink bikini top, and a towel under her arm poorly hidden behind the bushes. She was looking at me, watching. My heart pounded, our eyes locked, and I couldn't look away, my head turning on a swivel as the Cruiser coasted forward. The shock of it hit home: *Stacy Sanders was looking at me.* And then the unthinkable happened: *she lifted her free hand and waved!*

I felt excited and panicked, but I tried to be cool and wave back anyway. I loosened the grip of my right hand from the handlebars and shot a quick glance in front of me to make sure the way was clear. It wasn't. The Cruiser was drifting over to the left, toward a car parked at the curb, and it was coming on fast. Suddenly all I could think about was how badly the Cruiser would be scratched, dented, and maybe even busted if I hit that car. I slapped my right hand back down on the handgrip, veered hard left, bunny-hopped the curb, and found myself headed straight for a tree at the edge of a grassy area just beyond the sidewalk.

There was no time to go around it and nothing else to do. I had to lay the Cruiser down or plow headfirst into the tree trunk. I leaned back, threw all my weight hard to the left, and yanked the handlebars into my chest as I did so. I hit the ground with my shoulder, hip, and knee and bounced and slid through the wet grass while the Cruiser's back tire whipped forward in a semicircle, the bottom of the rubber tire whacking hard, but safely, against the tree roots. I didn't take any time to collect myself. I knew I'd saved the Cruiser from serious damage, but I'd also made a total drooling jackass out of myself in front of Stacy Sanders.

I got up, jumped back on, and got the hell out of there.

EIGHT

I was mad at myself. But I was kind of mad at Stacy, too. Why the hell did she have to pick such a goddamn awkward moment to acknowledge my existence? Sure, she'd caught me staring at her like, well, pretty much all the time in class, but it never seemed to have any effect on her before, and she never did or said anything about it. Then again, Stacy didn't seem to mind much to begin with, and that's partly what drew me to her. Okay, she also had an ass so tight that you couldn't pull a strand of dental floss down the middle, and the way she'd started dressing this spring made *Playboy* center-folds look bashful and withdrawn. But still, didn't she know you weren't supposed to distract people while they were driving? That was one of the most basic principles of road safety, and a good way to get someone killed. And what the hell was she doing behind the bushes anyway, lurking like that? The thought made me nervous, mostly because it led to others. How long had she been watching me? Had she seen me outside the pool before? Had she figured out why I'd been going there?

As I turned onto the street that led home, my stomach felt

unsettled. *I* was supposed to be the one watching *her,* and somehow the idea that it could go the other way, too, didn't sit so well with me. I didn't like the idea of being dirty all day from wiping out in the grass either, so I wheeled the Cruiser to the back porch and used the hose out there to clean myself off. There was a clump of soil clinging to the edge of the left pedal, so I rinsed that off, too, then I locked the Cruiser up and went in.

I dropped my backpack on a chair in the kitchen, dried my arms and legs off with a wad of paper towels, and heard the TV well before I went into the living room. I found Neecey curled up on the couch watching MTV in a red top and jean shorts.

"Well, well, well, look what the cat dragged in," I said.

"What?" Neecey asked, using the remote to kick up the volume on the TV with one hand while taking a sip from a can of beer with the other.

I'd seen Neecey drink a beer before when her friends were around, but never alone and never so early. "What are you doing?" I asked.

"What does it look like I'm doing?"

It looked like she was taking the first steps down a slippery slope to tragedy, just like we'd learned in health class, because after beer and cigarettes came rotgut alcohol and pot, then whippits, glue sniffing, and acid, and then the really hard stuff like cocaine, heroin, turpentine, Sterno, and bottles of vanilla extract stolen from the houses she'd have to break into to support her habit and survive her miserable life on the streets.

Yeah, it made me a little bit worried, but I wanted some information from her, so I couldn't let myself get distracted with giving her a lecture on the perils of peer pressure and teenaged drinking. She'd taken one of Craig's beers, so I limited myself to telling her that.

"It's like no big deal, Genie. It's just one beer, and it's summer vacation and all. Besides, there's way more in the cooler on the porch."

She didn't take the hint, so I had to let it go. I sat down next to her on the sofa and pretended to watch videos for a few minutes, while she pretended I wasn't there. That didn't bother me. What bothered me was that a metal-mouthed pantywaist like Razor had been alone in our house with my sister, while Page and Plant had set the mood, and I still didn't know what the hell they'd been doing, or why he'd even been here. I wanted some answers, but I realized that I needed to stay a bit calmer than I had last night in the bathroom and use some tact.

"Neecey."

"Yeah?"

"Can I ask you a question?"

"For sure, monkey nuts."

Great. Now I was gonna have to hear about that for the rest of my life, too.

"So, what's the deal with Razor?"

"What do you mean, 'deal'?" She slid a few inches to the left.

"Well, he was over here, wasn't he?" I couldn't have been sweeter if I was coated in honey, and it was making me feel sticky and sick.

"So? Lots of people come over."

"But he's a guy."

"Yeah, and?"

I ran my palms up and down my thighs to steady myself. Neecey wasn't one to withhold information. She usually gave straight answers that included all the rank and sweaty details she could think of—even about her time of the month—until I fled the room screaming. I tried again. "Well, the only other guys who've been here alone with you are Gary and Darren."

"And you and Craig," she said, piling her hair like spaghetti on the top of her head.

"C'mon, Neecey, you know what I mean."

Neecey stopped what she was doing and glared at me. "So you want to know if I balled him, right?"

The image of Razor's bony hips pumping in midair made my skin retch. "No, it's just—"

"It's just what? Jesus Christ, Genie. Like, what do you think I am anyway?"

A year ago, a question like that never would've come up between us. But things had changed a lot since then, or maybe only she had, and I guess that's partly what I was trying to figure out. I made my voice level and soothing. "I just want to know—"

"Whatever you want to know, it's not what you think. So like don't even worry about it, okay?"

"How the hell do *you* know what I think? You're not letting me finish."

She wriggled into the corner of the sofa and squared her shoulders to me. "Well, I already told you last night that I'm not a slut and that there's like no deal with Razor, so what else is there to know? C'mon, Genie, you're the *genius* around here, you tell me."

If she was trying to wind me up, it was a stupid move on her part, but it was working. "What else? Okay, well, for starters, how about *what the fuck was an assmunch like that doing here in the first place?*" So much for tact.

"Why? Are you *jealous?*"

She knew I hated that question more than Care Bears, Cabbage Patch Kids, and the Ice Capades all rolled into one, so she made sure to ask it each time she started seeing someone new. It was *not* the answer I was looking for.

"No, I'm not fucking jealous," I said. "But Gary and Darren might be when I tell them."

"As if," she scoffed. "Besides, Gary's way too busy delivering pizzas and saving money to go off to college to care about anything else, and you can like go ahead and tell Darren whatever the hell you want. He'll just get high and forget all about it. So like sit back down and mellow yourself out or I'll have to call mom."

Empty threat, just like mine. She'd never made that call or told on me in her entire life, but I sat back down anyway. I was getting nowhere. I took a breath, regrouped, then plunged in. "So you didn't ball him?" I asked.

"God, Genie, why can't you ever trust me when I tell you something?"

"Not a hummer, either?"

"Ee-ew!"

"Didn't even shake hands with the president, then?"

"Could you like do me a favor and obsess *more*?"

I could, but I'd already exhausted my list of dirty deeds, and she'd danced around all of them. The only thing I'd gathered so far was that the moment I'd been fearing had finally arrived. Grilling my sister about her sex life only made it official. Yeah, I was a pervert. But I was already a Peeping Tom and a chicken-choker, so it wasn't like this great leap or anything.

"You see," Neecey went on, "this is why I told you not to worry about it. You never listen to anyone; you just believe like whatever you want to believe and then throw a total conniption. And that's like completely beat, Genie, because there are all these things I *could* tell you and *want* to tell you, but don't, because I know there isn't a snowball's chance you could handle them."

Blah, blah, blah; she sounded exactly like mom. "I know." I yawned. "Everything's always my fault. But if you and mom stopped treating me like a soft-ass sissy fucking baby all the time and didn't keep me in the dark about every goddamn thing, then maybe you'd both find out I can handle a hell of a lot more than you think."

Neecey frowned at me for a few seconds, as if I'd just insisted, in all seriousness, that I could fly. "Ohmigod, you're like so right on cue," she said. "You probably don't even listen to *yourself*, do you?" She sat up straight and folded her arms across her chest. "Let's just drop it, okay? Sure, Razor was over here, you saw him yourself, big fucking whoop, but that's between him and me. It's got nothing to do with you."

Funny, I never said it did. She was clamming up, though, and if I wanted to get anything out of her, I'd have to change tactics—soften her up, hit her from a different direction—the kind of crap my counselors always tried to pull with me. "Know what, Neecey? You're right. It's none of my business. I'll drop it." Oh yeah, they also taught me how to lie.

"Cool, thanks, Genie," she said, flicking through the channels with the remote.

It was working. I tilted my head to the side, made my eyes all puppy dog, and said, "It's just, I guess I got upset because I had a few words with Razor at the arcade yesterday, not too long after I'd been at grandma's and saw what'd happened to the sign, so I wasn't in the greatest mood when I bumped into him. Then I had a pretty rough time at tryouts and they sent me home early and, bam, he was here when I got back." Saying it out loud made me realize that Thrash had been right on the money—the timing of it was perfect. "It's not like I don't trust you, Neecey," I went on, "I do. But you see how that could piss me off, right?"

"What do you mean, 'a few words'?"

"Nothing, the same punk bullshit he tries to lay down on everyone under fourteen. Nothing I can't handle."

"But he was alone, right? I mean, Tommy wasn't with him or anything?"

"Not that I saw," I said. "But it wasn't like I was gonna wait around to ask them for their autographs either."

Neecey snickered. It was funny all right, but not ha-ha funny. She'd completely skipped my mention of the sign, as if she hadn't heard me, or as if it wasn't her grandmother, too. Something seemed off, and I was suddenly glad I hadn't told her more.

"There's no need to get your panties in a bunch, though," I said. "I'm not afraid of those chumps."

"Well, they're gonna be freshmen in September, and they're definitely not afraid of you. So just stay away from them."

"No worries . . . as long as they stay away from me."

"No joke, Genie, don't even talk to them, you know how they are." Neecey took another mouthful of beer, flipped her hair back, and folded her legs beneath her. "Okay," she sighed. "I mean, since you told me what was bothering you, and because it's like no big deal anyway, I might as well tell you. Can you keep a secret?"

Bingo. We were back on track. I nodded.

"You know Razor's thinking about quitting football?"

"Bullshit." I wasn't expecting her to say that, and I wasn't sure I believed it. The kid was too stupid to qualify for wood shop, sure. But why the hell would he quit the *only thing* he was good at?

"Seriously," she insisted, "because of Chuck and Easy."

Chuck Freel was the high-school team's starting quarterback; he was first-team All-County last year as a junior and looked primed to be All-Universe this year as a senior. Ezekiel "Easy" Hightower was Chuck's go-to receiver and second-team All-County last year as a sophomore, but everybody knew Easy was the best athlete in town by a mile, which accounted for his nickname—it was how he made everything look on the field, easy—and the fact that he was the second-string quarterback. With Chuck and Easy ahead of him, Razor was looking at holding the clipboard at least this year and maybe next.

"So he's thinking about quitting instead of riding the pine?"

Neecey nodded. "He said he doesn't want to be a jock anymore now that he's gonna be in high school, but all his friends are jocks and it isn't gonna be easy on him if he quits."

What a fucking baby. I didn't give a shit if Razor led a happy and well-adjusted life, but if I wanted her to keep talking, I had to play along. "Is that why he came over, then?"

"Kind of, yeah. I mean, I don't know. It's complicated, Genie. It's like all fucked up."

That's *exactly* what Darren had said yesterday, not about Razor, though, but about the sign. "C'mon, Neecey. How complicated can it be? Why doesn't he just get some new friends?"

"It's not that simple, Genie," Neecey replied. "You of all people should know that."

"It's different with me," I said. "People don't like me because I scare them, and I don't like them back because of it. Don't ask me why, but people seem to like Razor, so it's different."

"Yeah, maybe," she said, "but not everybody in high school likes Razor. He's kind of a dick and he's picked on way too many of their little brothers and sisters. Besides, at least a couple people like you. You just need to make more of an effort."

"Oh, yeah?" The same old crap to boost my self-esteem. "Who likes me?"

"Well, Cynthia likes you, and Darren likes you. He's always saying what a little wild man you are and that you'd be really cool if you could just chill out some. And he's like old enough and popular enough that he could make your life total cake, but you don't ever give him a chance."

"He only *pretends* to like me because of you, Neecey, and by the way, I don't need him looking out for me."

"God," she sighed, "he just can't keep that mouth of his shut when he's high, can he?"

"No, I guess he can't," I said, deciding to cast one out there to see if I caught anything. "And if Razor's anything like Darren, you could find yourself in a fat, hairy mess."

Neecey slowly raised an eyebrow and said, "What the *hell* are you talking about? They don't even hang out."

Actually, I didn't know what the hell I was talking about. It was as if there were two different conversations going on at the same time and I wasn't up to speed on either one.

"Nothing," I said, "I was just saying."

"Well, don't worry, it doesn't have anything to do with Darren either."

It didn't have anything to do with Darren, it didn't have anything to do with me, and it didn't have anything to do with what she either did or didn't do with Razor. In fact, it didn't seem to have anything to do with anything at all, except Neecey wasn't leveling with me, and that sure as hell didn't add up. I was at a loss, and if I so much as hinted that Razor had set me up for a clock-cleaning at tryouts, Neecey would flip out and I'd never find out all the things this didn't have a damn thing to do with.

"I wasn't saying that, Neecey." I hit the soft-talk again, hamming it up. "Shit, I don't know what I was saying. What happened at the home is still sort of weighing on my mind. You know about that, right?"

"Huh? No. What happened?"

Her answer didn't make sense. "Darren didn't tell you that the cops came by his house on Sunday morning to ask about the sign at the retirement home getting tagged?"

"No, he must've like forgotten or something." Neecey pinched her fingers to her lips and rolled her eyes. "But it was tagged? For real? Ohmigod, that's like so lame!"

It wasn't lame, it was *retarded*, and I was almost positive she already knew it.

"Yeah, grandma was upset and shit, so I had to hear all about it, you know how she is." I was conning Neecey so well that I was actually getting into it. "Then, like later on, I stopped by the arcade and ran into Darren. I'm surprised he didn't say anything to you—that's weird."

"Why's it weird?"

"No reason, just you guys see each other practically every day and he has a big mouth and all. Whatever." I shrugged. It was all so easy; there was nothing I could do to blow it. "And like when I saw Razor with Stacy . . ." Aw, shit. Except for that.

Neecey cut me off instantly. "Oh, you saw Stacy there, too?" She paused. "She's the one you have the hots for, right?"

Now, *that* definitely didn't make any goddamn sense. I'd never told anyone about Stacy—not Thrash, not mom, not *her*, not anybody. I couldn't put my finger on it, but all of a sudden everything seemed more confused and tangled up than I'd expected. I'd missed something, I must have, and whatever advantage I'd thought I was playing was gone.

Neecey smiled, a big aha kind of smile. "Oh, *now* I get it. *That's* what this is about, right? You totally have the hots for Stacy, and because you saw her with Razor, it made you feel all jealous and inadequate and everything, so you're like taking it out on me because he was here."

I didn't dignify that with a response.

"Jesus, Genie. Why didn't you just say so?" She perked up now, like she knew she had me and couldn't wait to finish me off. "This one book calls it affirmation, and says that guys need it because they're totally insecure about how their little squirts stack up. But don't worry, except for those massive gunions of yours, you're like normal for your age."

Just who the fuck was she supposed to be, anyway? My sister? My sex-ed teacher? My goddamn social worker? I honestly couldn't tell anymore.

"Sure, Razor's older and bigger and all, but that doesn't mean his pecker is. You can *so* trust me on that."

I was prone on the ground, bleeding, and she was twisting the knife. I had one move left. "You never answered my question," I said.

"What?"

"What did Razor come over for?"

Neecey hesitated, as if considering whether or not it was safe to tell me. Then she said, "Razor came over to like ask me to do something for him, but I wouldn't, so he left. Got that? Good, because that's all you're getting. End of story."

Yeah, I got it, but it wasn't all I was getting. And it wasn't the end of the story; it was only some of it. I dashed out of the living room, into the kitchen, grabbed my backpack, and slammed the back door as hard as I could on the way out. Then I jumped on the Cruiser and set off, so Thrash and I could go somewhere to piece together the rest.

NINE

I rode around for a while, going nowhere in partic-
ular, trying to figure out why Neecey was giving me the runaround
and if her doing so had something to do with the case. I guess
driving in circles was the best I could do about it. I wasn't quite sure
where to go or what to do, but that pretty much told me what the
next move was, because if you didn't know what to do around here,
then there was really only one place to go. I took the back road by the
trailer park to the Circle, hopped off the Cruiser when I got there,
and went through the chore of walking it halfway around. Then I
jumped back on, off-roaded through about twenty-five yards of landscaping, and pedaled the whole of the mall's perimeter, casing the
sidewalks slowly as I went, keeping my eyes peeled for the signs of a
red Puch. If another ambush was heading my way, I wouldn't mind
knowing in advance. I didn't see anything, though, so I locked the
Cruiser to the bike rack by Abraham and Straus, which had an overhang in case of rain. Then Thrash and I went in.

I snaked through ladies' fashions, conquered the urge to examine
the skimpy lingerie in the underwear department, and then held my

breath like a magician in a water-torture chamber as I raced by the perfume counter and out into the mall. All together I had two floors and a mezzanine to cover, "more than seventy stores," if you believed the directory in the main hall—all of it faux-marble floors, sparkling display windows, and a continuous loop of Muzak that wouldn't have annoyed you at all if you were either deaf or dead.

I took the escalator to the bottom floor and passed by Osh Kosh, Kay-Bee's, and a pottery store on my way to Giorgio's, an Italian restaurant with full-service dining in the back and a pizza counter in front. I avoided eating there whenever I could, because their dough tasted like it was special-ordered from a Styrofoam factory in China. But lots of other kids couldn't get enough of the stuff and were always clustered around. And that's what I was after—a few stoolies to lean on, a couple leads to work over. At any rate, it wouldn't hurt to try. I wasn't quite sure who I was looking for or how I'd approach them, but on a cloudy Tuesday afternoon in the summer, chances were I'd have my pick of opportunities.

I rolled up to Giorgio's and saw the waiters inside crowded around a table in the back, stuffing their faces in the lull between the lunch and dinner rushes. All it did was remind me that I hadn't eaten lunch. There were a few skinny kids dressed in oversized shorts and T-shirts loafing around the front, but they were only fourth-grade video-game addicts, jonesing for a quick pizza fix before their next half-day session of Dragon's Lair. I already knew they couldn't tell me squat, except how to save the maiden or how many quarters they'd swiped from their parents today, so I didn't waste my time.

I kept going, past the Gap, Spencer's, and Chess King, until I reached the fountain near the escalator bank at the center. The fountain—a two-foot-deep concrete pool with a statue of a fat, naked baby spitting water into it—was situated between the escalators, had a clear view of who was coming and going in all directions, and served as the mall's unofficial meet-up point. In other words, it drew kids like flies and sucked up loose change. It wasn't doing much of either right now, though, because there were two teenaged couples sitting on the fountain's edge, grabbing and pulling and purring at each other and mashing their mouths together and grossing everyone else out so they all stayed away.

Thrash and I took a seat on the opposite edge of the fountain, our backs turned to the French-kissing four. With all their slurping and the fountain's gurgling in the background, I started to realize how difficult the case actually was. It was only graffiti, sure, but with no eyewitnesses, no hard forensic trail, I'd either have to catch the perpetrators in the act (too late for that), get someone to rat, force the culprits to confess, or I might never smoke them out. And even if I somehow got lucky enough to discover who they were, a single rubber bracelet didn't seem like enough evidence to make the charges stick. Worse still, the sources I'd questioned so far were obviously hostile, so the information I'd gotten from them wasn't totally certain. I had no leads, a few vague hunches, and no one to grill. It was enough to stump anyone.

Thrash was swatting as many flies on what to do next as I was, so I stood up from the edge of the fountain and walked to the front window of the bookstore on the right. It was called Waldenbooks, named for the book Orlando had given me, and there was a placard just inside the store's entrance to spell it all out for you, in case you didn't know. What the placard didn't tell you was that *Walden* wasn't just the title of the book, it was also the name of the pond in Concord, Massachusetts, where Thoreau had gone to live for two years and two months, all alone in a cabin he'd built by himself. He'd named his book after the pond because that's where he'd written it, and the pond was named Walden because, at some point or another, that's what it had been—*walled in*. Thoreau had pieced that one together all on his own, just like a detective, and I knew he had because I'd read it.

Orlando and his books, shit. There'd been all this crap about how I was supposed to be the smartest kid in school, but I'd always thought Orlando was way smarter than me. It was like he'd read and remembered everything. He also had this weird thing where he knew the birthdays of all these famous authors by heart, which I found out the time he'd asked me over to his house on my birthday. Even though I had junior peewee practice after school that day and knew mom was getting off work early to take us out to dinner, I said okay anyway, but that I couldn't stay long.

His house was awesome. It had like six or seven bedrooms, a finished basement with a sauna, this crazy office with bay windows, a glass den with high ceilings and a concrete wall and a real fireplace, all this new and modern furniture, paintings and sculptures everywhere, and a pool out back that was made to look like a lagoon with a waterfall. I told him his place looked like an art museum from the twenty-first century, and he said that's what his parents wanted, because they were both architects, and took me upstairs to his room. It was bigger than Neecey's and mine combined, and it had all this pocked concrete and metal and skylights in the ceiling, which made it look like part Fortress of Solitude, part library, because all the walls were lined with books.

Orlando knew it was my birthday because I'd told him a couple of weeks before, and he said I was lucky because there were a lot of famous authors born on that day—this guy named Nietzsche, a poet named Virgil, and some other ones, too—so it was a great day to be born. Then Orlando walked over to one of the shelves, pulled out a book, and handed it to me. He said the guy who'd written it was born in July, and that it was one of his favorites, so he was giving it to me as a present. I tried to pronounce the name but mauled it, and Orlando laughed that high-pitched laugh of his and said, no, it's pronounced *Thuh-row,* and that I was really gonna like it.

I felt weird and kind of embarrassed. I'd never been invited to somebody's house before, or talked about writers or books with someone my age, or gotten a birthday present from another kid, and I realized I was out of my depth. But I was game to play along, so I asked Orlando why he thought I'd like it. He said I'd have to read it for myself and then I could tell him. He warned me it'd be hard at first, but since I was already a genius, I'd figure it out sooner or later. That was the first and only time he ever mentioned anything about that, and although I knew he was busting on me, there wasn't any spite in it, and we both cracked up laughing.

I didn't know what to say, so I said thanks, and asked him when his birthday was. He said in early January, but it wasn't as good as mine, because the only writer born on that day that he knew of was this Italian guy who wrote a detective story about a monastery, but he'd only just become famous in the past few years. I told Orlando he was luckier than I was, because my birthday seemed crowded, but his was practically empty, and that he should write a book, become famous, and even our birthdays out a bit, or at least get off his ass and actualize for a change. He shook his head, sighed, and said that sounded an awful lot like selling out to whitey, and we both cracked up again.

That's how I'd gotten *Walden* in the first place, all the way back in fifth grade part one, and by now I'd read the book four times, cover to cover. And Orlando was right; it was hard. In fact, it had like no plot at all, so it was even hard to describe. But if I had to say what it was about, I'd say it was the story of some guy holing up in the woods for a couple of years, more than a mile from his nearest neighbor, kind of like a hermit, only he spent most of his time writing about what he did and what he thought was essential for like a deeper and more meaningful life. The moral of the book was self-reliance. Well, it was about nonconformity, too, but you couldn't be nonconformist if you weren't already self-reliant (I read that in the editor's introduction), and Thoreau went to live in the woods to conduct an experiment to see if he was. *Walden* never told you straight out if Thoreau was self-reliant or not, but I figured he must've been, otherwise he would've died alone in the woods and never would've been able to write about any of it.

Thoreau didn't die in the woods, though, and he somehow managed to write down just about every single thing he thought and did while he was there. He built a cabin, dug and stocked its storage cellar, made a chimney to warm the place in the winter, planted and sowed a bean field and other crops, and he told you how he did all of those things down to the smallest details, even how much they cost him. Shit, that guy actualized his ass off all the time and was *never* at a loss for anything. Then again, he couldn't afford to be. I'd read the biography about Thoreau at the public library, too, and it said that a lot of the people who'd known him either didn't like him or said or wrote all this nasty stuff behind his back, like how short and ugly and confrontational he was, as if he'd been some kind of jerk in real life, or the kind of person who was really tough to warm up to. So it made sense how a guy like that would write about being self-reliant, because if nobody really liked him, then he pretty much had to be.

But the rest of his book had all this other stuff about economics and railroads and how to observe and study nature and the proper names for things and transcendental philosophy that I was sure I didn't get. Worse still, all that other stuff sometimes made me think I didn't understand the book at all. For instance, *Walden* was supposed to teach you about being self-reliant. Fine, that was pretty clear. But if being self-reliant was the best thing you could possibly be and every bit as great as Thoreau kept saying it was, then I could never understand why he eventually *left* his cabin in the woods and moved back to town with everyone else, like he did. You know, why didn't he just *stay* there? Maybe self-reliance wasn't really the moral of the story, or maybe I wasn't reading it right, but that didn't make a hell of a lot of sense to me.

It also didn't make a hell of a lot of sense for me to be standing in front of the bookstore's entrance, scouring the tops of bookshelves for the young, dark-skinned giant who clearly wasn't there, when I had more legwork to do. So I snapped myself out of it, turned around, and headed to the cheap jewelry and accessories kiosk on my left. The salesclerk was this big disheveled teddy bear of a woman who was seated on a wooden stool, had her nose buried in a paperback, and looked like she could bake the hell out of a cake. I slid up to the scrunchies, hair clips, and earrings, and ran my eyes over the bangles, spiked wristbands, and beaded friendship bracelets hanging on the rack until I found what I was looking for. I took the rubber bracelet from the retirement home out of my pocket, held it up to the ones for sale, and saw that they were practically identical. I'd expected as much, but detectives had to verify whatever facts they had as best they could, even the really obvious ones. That way you could be sure of what you knew before tackling what you didn't.

"Can I help you?" asked the saleswoman.

"No, thanks, I was just checking something," I said all cheery and polite as I pocketed the bracelet and turned to go.

"Um, excuse me," she called, standing up.

I turned back, saw her pointing at the $1.50 sign by the bracelets, and knew what she was getting at.

"This is mine. I brought it with me," I said.

"How do I know that?" She smiled. "Can you prove it?"

"It's got dirt on it—look." I showed her the bracelet, pointing to a little brown smudge on the side.

"Okay, sorry." She smiled again. "Just making sure."

"Is there a problem over here?" a gruff male voice sounded from behind.

I peeked over my shoulder and saw the tan uniform, thick belt, and child-molester mustache of a mall security guard closing in from out of nowhere.

"No, no problem, my mistake." The saleslady waved him off, sweet as could be.

"No problem, then, you say?" He kept advancing.

I wondered what the hell was wrong with some people—you gave them walkie-talkies, pepper spray, and a beat to walk and it made them hard of hearing. The saleslady reassured him again that nothing was wrong, and our little party broke up: she got back on her stool, the security guard walked one way, and I went the other. I realized I had to be more careful. Not because I might get ejected from the mall by a rent-a-cop with nothing to do, but because I'd been set up for a hit yesterday and I hadn't been watching my back. And if a slow-footed, beer-bellied mouth-breather like that could sneak up on me, then just about anyone could, so I had to stay on my guard.

I took the escalator up to the mezzanine, hung a right in front of what used to be Bamberger's, and made for the exit at the far end. There were a couple of pay phones right before the glass doors leading to the parking lot and wooden benches just outside, so you could usually find some kids making prank calls or ducking out to sneak a smoke. That end of the mall was pretty vacant, like they hadn't finished it yet or couldn't rent all the space, and I could see nobody was clogging up the exit well before I'd gotten near the pay phones. I poked my head out the exit doors and checked the benches anyway, and saw a freckled Yeti with a shock of red hair relieving himself against the wall to the right of the benches. His back was to me, but I knew instantly it was Tommy Sharpe, even though he looked a lot different from the last time I'd seen him at the beginning of summer. He used to be fat, but over the past couple of months he'd lost all his flab and gut and had replaced them with shoulders the size of bowling balls, a neck just slightly thinner than a fire hydrant, and patches of swollen zits so peaked and red across his hulking arms that they must've been visible from outer space.

For a second I caught myself wondering what in the hell you'd feed a kid to grow him so goddamn big, and more important, where I could get my hands on some. But I got over it fast, backed up silently the way I'd come, and spun around quickly to check my rear flank, because if Tommy Sharpe was at the mall, then dimes to doughnuts Razor was with him, and that spelled hard times for any preteen who wandered aimlessly into their path. Razor was nowhere to be seen in the long, vacant corridor ahead of me, but I knew I wasn't safe out in the open where I was, because that end of the mall was the perfect place to corner a kid and spring a trap.

I darted into the small hardware store near the pay phones as fast as I could, hustling toward the back. I passed an aisle with handsaws, jigsaws, and hacksaws; another with hammers, screwdrivers, and pliers; and shortly arrived at the end of the line—the paint section. There were plenty of colors to choose from, and that struck me as a damn good thing. Not because I had anything I wanted to paint, but because the shelves were tall and wide and easy to hide behind. All I had to do was wait a few minutes, make sure the hall was clear, and then I'd be on my way again. In the meantime, though, I had to make it look like I was mulling over a purchase or the salesclerks might escort me out the door to certain doom. So I got busy.

As I pretended to read the label on a gallon of latex indoor paint, it finally occurred to me where I was, and it gave me an idea. I walked into the far right corner, pulled out the smallest can of black paint they had, went to the hammer aisle, picked up a tape measure, and made a mental note: a small can of black paint was about three inches tall, three and a half inches in diameter, and cost exactly $2.49. Back in the paint section, I found out that a paintbrush with bristles small enough to fit into that size can came in two different lengths—a four-inch model and a six-inch—but no matter which you preferred, you could still get it for under a dollar. Add a small screwdriver from the screwdriver aisle to pry open the lid, and you were looking at less than five bucks to get yourself started in a life of crime.

A salesman came over and asked if I needed any help as I was putting everything back, and I fed him the same line I'd used at the jewelry kiosk—nope, I was just checking something. He raised an eyebrow at me, nodded his head, and left me alone. Yeah, it worked like a charm, but it was also true. I *was* checking something: I was reconstructing how the crime had been committed, building a picture of it in my head, so I could keep running through the image in my mind, studying it from different angles until a new or overlooked detail popped up and gave me a better lead, like the height of the sign had earlier. Because in detective work it was just like Holmes and Thoreau were always saying: it wasn't always *what* you saw but *how* you saw it that mattered.

Right now I could see that a small can of paint, a paintbrush, and a screwdriver meant something to carry them in, because only extra-large clown pants would have pockets big enough, so my next stop was the sporting goods store in the middle of the mall. Sure, to get there I'd have to run the risk of strolling right into the not-so-welcoming arms of two knucklescrapers, but running risks was what detectives were supposed to do.

I edged to the front of the hardware store and peered out, first one way, then the other. All was clear. I stepped out, sliding along close to the wall, speeding up like a racewalker as I crossed store windows and slowing down to below Livia's speed as I passed each entrance, just in case I had to duck in. My body tensed up as I went, and the way I kept shifting gears and looking in every direction, ready to break for it at a moment's notice, made me feel like I was in the final round of the first annual Musical Chairs Championship. I got back safely to the main corridor, passed Orange Julius and the pretzel place without incident, and shortly after that the escalators in the center of the mall came into view.

There were a few standing plants and bushy, potted trees to the right of the escalators, while the sporting goods store was across on the left. At about thirty feet away, I dropped the pedal and sprinted all out until I'd reached the escalators, where I dipped into the foliage for cover. I crouched behind one of the biggest, bushiest planters and took a glance toward the sporting goods store opposite me—just in time to see Razor and Tommy coming out of it. Jesus, that was close. But I'd made it. I could tell they hadn't seen me, because they were too busy pulling the price tags off the matching Jets jerseys they'd either just bought or shoplifted. There was nothing for me to do but stay where I was and wait for them to leave, which was exactly what I was doing when the hair on the back of my neck sprang up. It was a strange as hell kind of feeling, like I was being watched. I panned my eyes slowly to the left, turning my head to see over my shoulder, and found myself staring a security guard dead in the eyes. He was a different security guard from the earlier one, much younger, maybe eighteen or nineteen, with a long, gangly frame, a massive Adam's apple, and the most ridiculous mullet you'd ever seen—like there was a porcupine with a foot-long beaver tail nested on the top of his head. Worse still, he was about eight or nine yards away and had obviously been staring at me for a while, watching me hiding in the bushes and acting suspicious. Then again, I was wearing enough red, yellow, and orange to be about as camouflaged behind all that greenery as a flaming banana in a bowlful of spinach. And I'd just turned my head and made eye contact.

Shit. Any second I knew he'd walk over with his tan uniform and bad mess of hair and blow my cover, and Razor and Tommy would see all of it and tail me outside and give me a primer on the finer points of pain. All of a sudden I was in a tight spot, and I had to think of something fast. Still looking the security guard in the eye, I raised my index finger to my lips and tilted my head twice, quick and sharp, in the direction of the sporting goods store. He stood his ground for a second, not moving, then knelt down to tie his shoe, lowering his head as he did, and then gave me a wink and a slight nod on his way back up. It worked, just like in the detective books. I'd given him the signal for undercover surveillance and he'd bought it.

Maybe he'd seen Razor and Tommy taking the tags off the shirts they'd worn out of the store, or maybe he thought we were all playing a game of Manhunt in the mall. Whatever. I couldn't be bothered to give a shit. As he sidled up to them, and they fumbled around in their pockets to show him receipts, I flew out from behind the planter, booked up the escalator steps, and slipped away.

I triple-timed it toward JC Penney's, seeing a few girls with moms or college-aged sisters getting a head start on their back-to-school shopping and some nerdy-looking teenagers acting, well, nerdy, in front of Radio Shack, but not much of anything else as I whizzed by. Once I was in the store, I took refuge behind a group of mannequins to see if anyone was hot on my heels, and although I didn't see anyone coming, I realized that checking to make sure I wasn't being followed only made me feel like I was. Since JC Penney's had a sporting goods section in addition to hardware, appliances, clothes, and whatever else, it hit me that I could finish what I was doing in one stop, and then scram. And because nobody ever went into JC Penney's except parents dragging their unwilling kids and old people so old they didn't even like bingo anymore, I knew I'd be safe.

I grabbed a shopping basket, filled it with painting supplies in hardware, and weaved my way in and out of lawn care, patio furniture, and seasonal, through electronics and lighting, and over to sporting goods. Standing in front of an entire aisle of backpacks, rucksacks, gym bags, tote bags, and duffel bags of all sizes, colors, and styles, it took me about half a second to figure out that just about all of them were more than big enough for the contraband I was lugging. The backpack I had on was big enough, too, and Thrash said I could've just used that as a gauge. I told him I agreed, but it hadn't seemed thorough enough.

And I had to be thorough, so I dropped the basket in sporting goods, went to house and kitchen wares, and was glad I did when I got there. Right away I saw that stepstools or short ladders were a problem; even the smallest fold-ups that extended high enough to reach the middle of the sign were too bulky or too heavy or too awkward to carry easily, while the really small ones wouldn't get you anywhere near the correct height. My picture of the crime was off, but it was good to know how, because the perpetrators still must've stood on something.

I kept searching the store and saw that a metal trash can turned upside down would do the trick but was too conspicuous; a flipped-over laundry basket was too low; and a large cardboard box with someone on top would collapse under the weight. I noticed some plastic containers the same shape, size, and construction as milk crates near the back-to-school stuff, so I picked one up, felt how light it was, stacked two together, one on top of the other, and saw that they would work. That was just it, though: you needed at least *two* of them, and even if one criminal carried one and the other criminal carried the other, Perry Mason could still hawk them down without breaking much of a sweat.

I was drawing a blank, ready to head out, and noticed a male cashier and the old lady beside him staring right at me. It made me feel uneasy, like I was the only one who'd forgotten to wear pants, so I turned quickly to go and almost smacked face-first into the special-offer display directly in front of me. It was an entire pyramid of lightweight ten-foot, roll-up plastic rope, home fire-escape ladders, complete with hooks at the top to hold the sill of a second-story window. I stopped short just before I crashed into the display, but I almost fell over anyway. *That was it*. It *had* to be. Rolled up, one of those ladders could fit into a large backpack or duffel bag. You could sling it over your shoulders like a quiver of arrows, get it out of the bag fast, throw the hooks over the top of the sign from the ground, do your business, pack it up quick, and still have free hands to pump like crazy as you fled. And you could do all that for just $19.99.

It was a bit pricey, sure, but I bet plenty of families around here already had ladders like that, especially families by the reservoir. Light, portable, a cinch to use—shit, I sounded like a commercial—but most important, it fit. My picture of the crime was complete: a small can of black paint, a paintbrush, a screwdriver, a roll-up ladder, and two bags or backpacks, one for each culprit, to split up the load. I knew *how* it'd been done; now all I had to find out was *who'd* done it.

I rode the escalator inside JC Penney's to the ground floor, just to be safe, and was cautious going out into the mall. It took me all of about three steps to wish I'd been even more cautious, though, because that's when I felt that meaty mitt slap down on my shoulder. I craned my neck back to see who it was but still only managed to take in a small fraction of Tommy Sharpe's colossal upper body.

"Hey, Razor," he called out, "look what I found."

All of a sudden Razor was trotting toward me from out of nowhere, kind of like Pepé Le Pew, only he was taller and warming his knuckles.

Shit. The trap was closing and I only had a split second before the lid snapped shut. I took a quick lunge step away from Tommy, to get the arm holding me fully extended, then spun back toward him as hard and fast as I could, into his thumb, so he couldn't clamp his grip all the way. If he did, I'd be tenderized, seasoned, and cooked for sure: dinner for two. But he couldn't tighten his grip with my shoulder pushing his thumb back—his wrist folded up and his hand loosened. I jammed my arms out, shoved him in the chest to make some space, and floored it for all I was worth.

"You are *so* dead, shit dick!" Razor yelled from behind.

Funny, I didn't feel dead, but I knew I could be if I was stupid enough to let them catch me. I chugged hard toward the escalator, shortening my strides and cutting left, right, left, right to avoid the late-afternoon shoppers. Razor's cursing was getting softer behind me; I was putting some distance between us. All I had to do was make it up the escalator and I'd be gone. But as I got close, a lady with a baby carriage wheeled in front, taking her sweet time making a half-circle to back it up the parading steps.

Fucking baby carriages. I couldn't get past her; there wasn't enough room. I hit the brakes, spun on my heels, and came to a full stop with Razor and Tommy, all green-and-white jerseys, red cheeks, long arms, and blazing eyes, thundering full bore at me. I didn't think; I didn't have time to. I just squatted down low like a catcher to cover up, and both of them swung high, hit air, and blew right by me. But that's what happened when you only played offense; you weren't taught you had to breakdown before you tackled your man.

Fucking idiots. I gassed it, dropping the accelerator to the floorboard. Well, almost. They were after me again and I was tempted to light it up for real and leave a molten lava of fake marble floors in my wake. But I'd just had the narrowest of escapes and probably wouldn't be lucky enough to make another if I outran myself and took a tumble. So I popped it into as close to all out as I could control, and let them sample some of my dust.

In a few seconds, I was pulling away from them. Only thing was, I was running the wrong way: Abraham and Straus was at the *other* end of the mall. But I also knew it was dumber than hell to lead them there, because with them on my tail I'd never be able to get the Cruiser unlocked in time to ride off. And Razor had a moped, so it might not make any difference if I got to the Cruiser anyway. Shit. Even worse: Sam Goody's, end of the corridor, was dead ahead. I was cornered. There was nothing for it—I'd have to turn around, face them, and run the gauntlet again.

I stopped and turned. This time Razor and Tommy were ready. They'd chopped their steps, slowed down, and fanned out. There were only two of them, but they were so big and broad, it looked like a whole mob of angry teens was headed my way. Tommy was on the left and Razor was on the right, and they were close enough to me that I could hear the profanities and promises of violence through their panting breaths. Razor was the faster of the two—that was obvious—so I inhaled deeply and ran right at him, about two-thirds full speed. Not right at him, actually, but wide to my right, his left, so he had to step laterally and cross his feet to cut me off. When he was within range, maybe a yard or two from contact, I played it like a kick return, stopped short, made a three-quarter reverse spin, and busted all ass far, far left, to get around Tommy, who was cruising over to mop up the carnage. Tommy was caught off guard by my cutback, tried to stop, grunted, swiped a hand out at me, grabbed the collar of my shirt, and tore it clean off just before Razor, quickly reversing his field, slammed into him. I heard what sounded like the dull *plonk* of their heads whacking together, and wanted more than anything to stand around pointing and laughing at them till I puked.

But it wasn't time to celebrate just yet; they'd recover soon and be back on the chase. They were well behind me now, though, so all I had to do was make it up the escalator in the center of the mall, out the nearest exit, and then take the sidewalk outside to the entrance of A&S, where the Cruiser was. And if I got out the exit quickly enough, by the time they'd reached the escalators and looked around for me, I'd just be gone. I pushed forward again, breathing evenly, keeping my upper body relaxed as I pumped my arms, gobbling up the distance between the escalators and me like Pac-Man after a hunger strike. The fountain up ahead seemed as if it were racing toward me on a conveyor belt, and I saw that I was in luck, because the escalator was clear.

I looked left and right to see if anyone was moving toward the escalator, crossing into my path before I got there, but all I noticed was the shiny-black skin and low-top fade of a really tall kid disappearing behind one of the shelves in the bookstore. I didn't have a chance to look again because I was hopping up the escalator steps two and three at a time, but I was positive it was Orlando. Nobody else in town looked anything like him, unless he'd gone out and found himself a twin. I wondered if he'd seen me, and I wondered more if he knew that Razor and Tommy were there. Then I just felt worried.

But there was nothing much I could do about it, so I burst through the exit doors and kept motoring along the sidewalk to

A&S. I unlocked the Cruiser, jumped on the seat, and heard a loud metallic thud directly beneath me. I scanned the entrance and the surrounding sidewalks, my heart hammering and my stomach spiraling down to my feet. Somebody had let the air out of *both* my goddamn tires! I got off the Cruiser and started running with it across the parking lot. I had to get out of sight in a serious goddamn hurry, or Razor and Tommy might pick up my trail. And that would mean curtains.

It occurred to me that maybe they'd seen me send the security guard after them in front of the sporting goods store and wanted to pay me back for it. That could be why they were after me, and, as they were scouring the mall, they'd gone outside, seen the Cruiser, and flattened the tires so I couldn't get away. But I knew Razor already had it in for me for some other reason, so it was more likely that all of this was tied to the case in some way.

Well, either that or *someone else* was after me, too.

TEN

The side street I'd taken from the mall parking lot was small and sleepy and well enough off the beaten track that I wasn't too worried about being followed. But it angled northwest and didn't have any turnoffs, so it left only one route to my next destination—the long one. I knew it'd be even longer than usual, too, because walking with a bike was much slower than regular hoofing, and I was looking at a serious trek ahead.

Pushing the Cruiser almost two miles to the gas station gave me more than an hour to get angry, and the sudden cloudburst on the way there made sure that I was. So it was getting late and I was wet and tired and starving and completely ticked off when I wheeled around to the air pump in the back, filled my tires, and just happened to look at the gas station bathroom before I rode off. It was like all gas station bathrooms—cinder-block walls, gray metal door with rust spots, shit stains in the corners and hinges, a thick ribbon of gnats and flies gyrating in front of it, and a stench like an open cauldron of manure over a low, steady flame. I was a good ten feet away but still felt like scrubbing myself with Pine-Sol, and if I were one inch closer to that cesspit than I already was, I'd have to get home and bathe within fifteen minutes or less, or I could just skip everything else and head straight for the morgue.

But someone I knew had gotten closer, a lot closer. To the right of the door, there was a big white skull with yellow lightning bolts in the place of crossbones carefully spray-painted on the wall. It kind of looked like the Grateful Dead symbol, only the expression on the skull's face was meaner, more menacing. It almost killed me to admit it, but as far as graffiti went, it was top-notch work: the outer lines were smooth and unbroken, there were no gaps or missed spots in the interiors, and the finished product was solid and crisp. It was obviously the effort of someone who knew what he was doing; someone who wanted other people to know who he was. So, at the bottom, in a fluid scrawl of darkest red, it said DINK. The skull and cross bolts, the three colors—white, yellow, red—and the DINK were a signature, as identifiable as a fingerprint, and they all pointed to the same hand: Darren's. Apparently, the crew had already marked so much of the town as their territory that Darren felt safe to piss here, too.

Fucking Darren and his fucking crew. Those dickweeds broke a different law practically every goddamn day, left evidence of it everywhere, but never got caught, while I couldn't so much as break a little wind without counselors, teachers, coaches, and cops calling a series of emergency meetings up my ass. All right, nobody ever said life was fair, and it wasn't like anybody in the crew had ever started with me, because they weren't that kind of gang. But when Darren stole my old bike, I got my first real glimpse of what their program was all about, and it'd been chafing my sphincter ever since.

I was at the arcade with Thrash one day last February playing Frogger. I remember that because I'd gone to play Track and Field, but Thrash wouldn't quit pestering me until he got his way and we played the other one instead. He was like that sometimes, especially when it came to Frogger, because he just lost his shit over that game. He got so into it—yelling, grunting, telling me when to go, when to stop, moaning and carrying on when the frog got flattened by a car or eaten by an alligator—that you'd think he was rooting for a close relative to cross the river or highway instead of some stupid, pretend video-game frog he didn't even know. Then again, every once in a while, it *was* pretty fun.

Anyway, after I'd blown half my allowance without breaking the high score, I went outside and discovered that my bike was gone. Just gone—no tire tracks, no witnesses, no clues, no nothing. Okay, I didn't have a lock back then, so maybe I'd been asking for trouble, but my old bike was such a piece of crap—one of those tiny three-speeds with wrap-down handlebars designed to look like a mini ten-speed racer, but really looked like a bike for thumb-suckers and bed-wetters—that I'd never needed a lock before. That was part of the reason I'd held on to it, not because it was the very first bike without training wheels I'd ever owned all to myself, without having to share with Neecey, or because I'd had it since I was eight, but because the whole point of having a really shitty bike was that you never had to worry about somebody stealing it. So when I found it gone, I wasn't expecting it to be gone, and that pissed me off, and I stood there cursing and boiling over and not knowing what to do.

Then it hit me, kind of all in a rush. My bike had been stolen, a *crime* had been committed, which meant I had a *mystery* on my hands, and since I was standing in the middle of the crime scene, it was the perfect opportunity for me to put my detective skills to use for real. Suddenly, I wasn't angry anymore, but all keyed up and raring to go. I was on my first real case, with myself as client and detective.

There still weren't any clues, of course, just an empty space in the bike rack where my ride should've been and a lack of witnesses to press for leads. So I settled myself down and made a few deductions to try to figure out what kind of maggot would steal my piece-of-shit bike, because if I could figure out what kind of kid had done it, then I'd have a better idea of where to find him. And it came to me pretty quickly. Since nobody could possibly want a bike like that, the only kind of lowlife that would actually steal it was either the kind that couldn't afford anything else, or that would attract too much attention by riding something better. That meant a kid who was poorer than I was, so I set my course northeast, toward the town center, to track down a thief.

It turned out I was tracking that thief for a while—hours, actually—in the stinging wind and needling mist of a frigid February evening, making a systematic search of the roughest part of town. I didn't find anything, and sooner than I knew it, it was well after dark and I realized I'd been out on foot for ages. It'd gotten a hell of a lot colder, too, and as I walked I got the kind of chill that grabbed you down at the base of your spine and worked its way outward, that inside-out chill where you felt like you'd never get warm again, and I was late for my curfew, so I was more than ready to pack it in and try again the next day. The only problem was that I'd lost my bearings a little. I'd gone so far north and east that I was practically in the next town; in fact, I was so far from everything that the kids who lived there didn't even go to our schools. So I was way out of my territory and had no other choice but to take my best guess toward home.

I wandered for a while and eventually turned down a dim side street, where I came across a shabby duplex with four guys playing hoops in the driveway under floodlights, with four bikes piled on top of one another over to the side. One of the bikes looked like mine. My blood went up in a hurry, but I was cool about it, and just sort of ambled over, as if I were mesmerized by the way they kept bricking lay-ups. I inched closer and saw that the bike was the same make as mine and about as old, but it was black or looked black in the downward glare and shadows, while mine had been blue. It was similar enough that it *could've* been my bike, but I would've had to get even closer than I was to tell for sure, and that seemed like an unhealthy idea at the time, so I just figured I'd crapped out and turned to go.

As I did, however, I felt this dense object thumping me in the chest and my arms shooting up and catching it of their own volition. I realized pretty much instantly that it would've been better to let it drop. The guys were around me in a flash—all four of them older and athletic looking—asking me what the fuck I was doing trying to steal their rock. It was the oldest trick in the book for picking a fight; I was in trouble, Thrash was croaking *retreat* from inside my backpack, but I was cold and tired and taken by surprise, so I didn't move right away. When that first fist cracked me sharp in the ribs, I snapped out of it, whipping the ball at one kid's face with my right hand and pitching a reckless hook at some other kid's throat with my left. That gave me just enough space to bolt, but I took a few more body-shots as I hit the accelerator and hot-footed it the hell out of there. I sprinted my ass all the way home, where mom was already waiting for me in the living room because she didn't have to work at the bar that night. I was more than two hours late and she was pissed as hell, and the only thing that saved me from the riot act and a week in solitary was the fever I'd come down with.

I didn't have to go to school the next day, but I was sick, bruised up, and practically dying on the sofa for most of it, when who should appear on our doorstep for the very first time that afternoon but fucking Darren—wheeling my goddamn bike, turning himself in, and trying to make amends. He made such a major production of explaining himself—saying he'd been high at the time, got stuck on how funny it'd be to ride such a tiny bike home from the mall, but that he hadn't meant anything by it, how totally beat it was, and all this other crap—and tried so hard to be convincing and sincere that the whole thing seemed rehearsed.

Sure, it was a nice act for all the bullshit, I guessed, but it wasn't for me. Literally. Darren didn't look at me *once* the whole time he was there. But he didn't have any problem keeping both eyes on Neecey.

That was because everything he said and did was for *her*, all of it, like he was only there to prove that he was bad enough to take whatever the hell he felt like taking, but also big enough to own up to it and give something back if he wanted to, like some kind of stoner bandit with a heart of gold. As if. I'd taken a beating because that dildo had felt like amusing himself, and worse than that, by returning my bike he'd cheated me out of solving my first case. And as if that weren't enough to make me want to swear a blood feud on Darren and all his present and future kin, it was all just a bad joke to him.

I failed to see the goddamn hilarity in it. I felt mad, stupid, and swindled, but right then I saw what Darren was up to. He'd used me and my old bike to get close to Neecey, so that when she broke up with Gary, who was a senior last year and would be leaving for college practically any day now, Darren would be first in line to succeed. Worse still, she fucking fell for it, because she started seeing him on the sly about a month and a half later.

That's when I had my first serious reservations about Neecey's intelligence and loyalties, because she didn't just flap her gums about Darren so goddamn much that I felt like ripping my own ears off, she actually took *his* fucking side about my bike. Christ, at least Judas got thirty pieces of silver; but not Neecey, she worked for free. When I asked her a couple of days later why Darren had apologized to *her* instead of me, not even glancing my way although I was lying right there, she told me he'd felt like such a tool for taking my bike that he was already all hangdog on the way over to our place, and when he saw I'd gotten sick because I'd been out looking for it in the cold, it just made him feel ten times worse, so he felt too guilty to face me at the time. Yeah, right, like he even knew I had a face then. Anyway, she also said he'd explained everything again the next day—that it was just a simple mistake and he was totally remorseful—and he told her to tell me that when I came around and warmed up to him a little, he'd make it up to me, because he owed me one. I got the message all right: my sister was turning into a pothead's parrot. And then she went on about how different Darren was when he wasn't with his buds, how smart he was, how cool, how much fun to talk to, how awesome the paintings and sketches he'd made were, how he planned to go to art school instead of college, how much I was going to like him, and all this other crap that I wasn't listening to because I'd already heard more than I'd wanted to hear without liking the gist of it a single goddamn bit.

And here I was, staring at Darren's graffiti and Darren's signature on the gas station shitter, like he owned the whole fucking town and everything in it. And what did *I* have? Nothing, that's what I had, not a single goddamn thing. I was first in my sixth-grade class and had the best grades by a mile, but I didn't win so much as *one* of the subject awards they gave out at the end of the year. I had to sit through the assembly on the last day of school and listen to little Stevie Thurgood's name being called time and again, and watch him go up to the stage to get one award after the other, because he was the teachers' pet and I was the psycho and that was that. Seeing Stevie Thurgood walk away with the prizes that should've gone to me made me do something I regretted, but I left school that day the way I left everything else—the same way I was right now—empty-fucking-handed.

Well, I had Thrash, but he couldn't be bothered to talk about any of this shit, because it didn't matter to him. He always had the same answer for everything: if Darren or Stevie or anybody else was giving me trouble, then I should break them down at the knees and gut them like fish; or if I couldn't do that, then I should hop my ass under a rock and hide out until everything blew over. That's the way it was in the wild. Period. No, Thrash wasn't always as helpful as he could've been.

And I had the Cruiser, too, so I saddled up. I made a left out of the gas station's back exit and aimed homeward. I would've loved to nail

Darren and the crew almost as much as I would've loved Seven Minutes in Heaven with Stacy, but just because I wanted it didn't mean I was gonna get it. Besides, I was a detective, and a detective needed evidence before he went off half-cocked accusing people of shit. And as far as evidence went, I didn't have any. Well, I knew how the crime had been committed and I had a rubber bracelet that had been dropped at the scene of the crime by one of the two perpetrators. Other than that, I didn't have jack.

Worse still, what little evidence I did have didn't seem to point to Darren. For instance, if Darren had hit the sign at grandma's home, he would've done a much better job; the tag I'd just seen reminded me of that. More than that, although there was some danger in tagging a sign in open view of a highway, it wasn't enough danger to impress anybody, and if it wouldn't impress anybody, then you could bet your ass Darren wouldn't consider doing it. He'd gotten way too big to sweat small shit like that; plus, he had the crew's reputation to think about, which he could only maintain at this point by sticking his neck out every once in a while to pull something ballsy.

So it seemed to make sense that Darren had dragged the crew down to the church on Saturday night, like he'd said, because that was a high-risk job, and kids were sure to talk it up once they'd heard about it. It made even more sense, now that I thought about it, that Darren had *told* me they'd done it, because if the people at the church had painted over the tag and hushed it up early Sunday morning, then other kids might not know that the crew had even hit it. And if other kids didn't know about it, then they definitely wouldn't talk about it, and that defeated the purpose of doing it in the first place.

I made a left turn behind the strip mall, sped up, gave the Italian salute to the brown Datsun hatchback that honked at me, grabbed the handlebars again, and jumped the curb as a tailwind hit my back. I caught some sweet air, and as I floated gently back to earth, my mood began to change. I finally felt like I was getting somewhere, partly because I'd just realized something that I hadn't thought of before. Although the clues I had weren't leading me to anyone in particular, I still might be able to crack the case by working in the *opposite* direction. In other words, if I could eliminate people from the list of possible suspects, then I'd have fewer to choose from, which meant I'd stand a better chance of apprehending the culprits. And since two perpetrators and a rubber bracelet pointed to almost every possible pairing of teens and preteens in the whole damn town, I could do a hell of a lot worse than to narrow the field a little.

So I set my mind to the cheerful task of eliminating Darren—at least as a suspect. The biggest problem was easy to see, and I saw it right off: it didn't seem like Darren had a motive to hit the sign. But while he might not've had any motive I could easily discern, the fact that *both* he and Neecey had lied to me in connection with the sign, independently of each other, made me think there had to be something rotten as all hell in DINKmark. She'd lied to me by saying she hadn't heard about it, and Darren had lied to me when he'd said he didn't know who did it.

Neecey could be lying to cover for Darren again, like she'd done with my bike, but that still didn't necessarily mean he'd done it, because there was always the chance that Darren had lied to *both* of us to cover for somebody else. But if that's what he was doing, then the question was, for whom? Well, that was pretty simple: he'd be covering for someone in the crew. Maybe *that* was why he wouldn't say whether he knew who did it or not, but tried to warn me off the case anyway.

Fair enough. If I were Darren, I'd be afraid for their sake, too. But that instantly shrank the field of suspects down to less than the number of starters on a Little League team, because beyond Darren there were only six other members of the crew, and I knew the names and addresses of every single one of them. There was Sticky, who was six feet tall and weighed a hundred and a quarter wearing a full suit of armor. He'd be a senior this year, so that made him the oldest. Then there were the juniors: Squat, who had light hair, a medium build, the height to go with it, and was named for what he knew; Burger, a goofy, almost likable guy who got his nickname because he was kind of round and because his favorite food was hot dogs; Roni, pronounced with a long *o*, as in maca-*roni* and cheese, but meaning cheese, because everything he said was really fucking corny; and Lyle, who was another pipe cleaner like Sticky, but didn't have a nickname, because Lyle was his real one, and I guessed they figured that was bad enough. Finally, there was Johnny Scatto, who was going to be a sophomore this year, like Neecey and Cynthia, and whose nickname was Chakha, not after the singer, but because he was short and square-shaped and had thick hair *all* over his body, so he reminded you of the prehistoric ape-boy in that old TV show *The Land of the Lost*. He was the youngest, and once he'd started high school last year, the crew had closed their ranks and hadn't admitted any new members since. Not like that was a surprise. They'd all been friends since the beginning of elementary school and they'd only been waiting for Chakha to start his freshman year to go exclusive anyway. And now they were.

I cut behind the convenience store, stuck out my right leg, and kicked one of the plastic milk cartons by the Dumpster a good four or five feet. When I got to the driveway at the far end of the lot, I dismounted the Cruiser. I was getting close to home, but that also meant I was close to the Circle again. There was so much traffic on it during the morning and evening rush hours that it backed cars all the way up to the Garden State Parkway, and people tried to outrun the bottlenecks by drag racing from light to light on the highway so goddamn fast that just thinking about crossing on your bike could get you killed. So I waited for an opening, sprinted the Cruiser across all four lanes, and hopped on again without breaking stride. For some reason it struck me that the Circle and the mall worked in tandem: the traffic jams of the one detoured people toward the other, which simply lay in wait to pick their pockets. I'd never realized it before, but it was a perfect setup, and it was goddamn obvious.

I was around the corner from my house, but the word had stuck with me—*obvious*. If I added a "the" to it, that's what I'd been over-looking. Nobody in the crew ever did *anything* without Darren's say-so—he was the leader, it was *his* crew—and that meant if a pair of them had done it, then at the very least he'd known in advance or had even ordered it. And to me, that was the same damn thing as doing it himself, maybe worse. But that's what being a crime kingpin was all about: you got your minions to do the dirty work for you. I started to think I'd been on the right track from the start. I should've pushed Darren harder yesterday when I'd questioned him, and after I got home, had a quick bite to eat, and changed my torn shirt, I'd see if I couldn't track him down and push him some on his motives in the hour and a half or so that remained until dark.

I leaned forward and cranked it, eager to get back to work. But as I rode up to our place, I saw a light blue Chevy Nova parked by the curb and knew that my day was done. It was Pauline's car, the babysitter—an interstate pileup of a woman with a wispy Fu Manchu beard and a hairy mole on the side of her neck so grotesque that you couldn't look away from it. Neecey and mom were out for the night, while I'd be locked in. *Goddamn it*. All I had to look forward to was a plate of grub, a shower, writing in my journal, and maybe some reading later on in my room. Everything else would have to wait for the morning.

ELEVEN

*The sound of mom's voice woke me up. She was sit-*ting on the edge of the bed in the white blouse and black skirt of her waitress uniform, with her hair pulled back, her lips pressed into a smile, stroking the side of my face, humming the same song she'd been waking me up with for years. She seemed tired around the eyes and could've used a day or two in the sun but was otherwise holding up well in the looks department. Yeah, mom had always been easy on the eyes, and it was weird to think that one day her head would shrink, her skin would wrinkle, her eyebrows would fall out, her mouth would pucker, and she'd turn into grandma, the way Neecey was turning into mom, like a series of before, after, and way-the-hell-after photos. You couldn't really see it yet, because mom looked more like twenty-eight than thirty-eight, but it was bound to happen. Just like if I hung around long enough, I'd turn into I didn't know what, because the only thing left to compare me to was a cardboard box of old junk and photos that we'd tossed on the curb years ago.

I yawned and said good morning, but she didn't answer because she'd decided that today was one of those days when it was better to sing the song's chorus than hum it. I would've preferred that she hadn't, because it made me think her life had to be pretty goddamn dreary if I was supposed to be the sunshine in it.

"Good morning, yourself," she finished, planting a wet one on my forehead. "You boys awake?"

As if anyone could sleep with her carrying on like that.

"How are you feeling this morning? Any nightmares?"

"Not that I can remember," I said. "What time is it?"

"That's good." She smiled, brushing my cheek. "It's a little after seven."

"What's wrong?" I asked, sitting up in bed, rubbing the crud out of my eyes. Something had to be wrong if she was getting me up this early on my vacation.

"Nothing's wrong. Lana has an appointment at the orthodontist this morning, so I'm covering her shift."

If anybody needed some quality time with an orthodontist, Lana did. Shit, I'd seen barracudas with better grillwork. Come to think of it, she could've used some time with a dermatologist and a dietician, too, but I didn't like the idea of mom having to wake up at the crack of dawn so Lana the teenage duckling could work at becoming a swan, and I told her so.

"It's no big deal, Genie. She's a sweet girl and she's covered for me lots of times when I've had to leave early for the bar, so I owe her a few. Besides, we could always use the extra money. Speaking of, did you take the envelope I left to the home yesterday?"

"Yeah, I took it," I said, thinking that we might just as well have flushed it down the goddamn toilet with Bryan there calling the shots. "But I told you, you should let me do grandma's checks from now on so we don't have to go through this shit every two weeks."

"That's not such a bad idea, but it's a little early for that gutter mouth, don't you think?"

"That way we can be sure they're not double-dipping into grandma's pocket," I added for good measure.

"C'mon, Genie, they're a little tight-fisted, sure, but they're not crooks."

"No? Then how can Bryan afford that cherry IROC of his, did you ever ponder that?"

"Ponder?" She laughed. "Bryan's no embezzler, he's a jittery little mouse. Besides, I hear they practically give those cars away on lease now."

"You can't go believing everything you hear," I said.

"And *you* can't go believing everything you read." She smiled, tousling my hair. "Those crime novels are making you cynical."

If knowing how to smell a rat was being cynical, then I was goddamn glad to be it. But I didn't push the point.

"Maybe you're right, though," she went on. "It'd be a lot less hectic on our budget if I didn't get surprise requests for fifty dollars every two-odd weeks." She shifted her weary brown eyes over to Thrash and tugged softly on his leg. I could tell it tickled him by the way he was smiling. Mom moved her hand back to her lap and said, "And, you know, you're almost a teenager now, so maybe you're ready for more responsibility."

My heart stopped. I'd been hoping for the you're-a-teenager-now speech for so long that it didn't seem real. Mom had been dancing around it all summer, dropping hints, cutting me more slack, like letting me take the Cruiser to the Shore on my own and not making me call her every two hours at work to check in, and I'd been toeing a strict line since the end of school to help her around to my way of thinking. It seemed like she'd finally arrived. But there had to be a catch. For a second I expected her to reach up to her face and tear the skin away, leaving in its place the dead, mechanical stare of one of those Fembots from *The Six Million Dollar Man*. But she didn't. She said, "Only if you continue to behave yourself."

There it was, the catch, the price tag stitched in the collar. But freedom always came at a price. "Piece of cake," I assured her. "I'm a model citizen."

"Well, there's no denying you've been great all summer and I'm really proud of you. So I'll think about letting you be in charge of grandma's bills. You're better at math than I am anyway. I'll let you know. For now, though, I'm going to give you a reward—"

"What?" Suddenly, I was wide awake.

"A trial run, I guess you might call it."

"What?" She was killing me with all the preamble.

"Well, Neecey's staying at Cynthia's tonight, but . . ." She paused, letting the suspense burrow into my stomach. "I'm not gonna call Pauline to come and watch you. I'm gonna let you watch yourself. How does that sound?"

I could've hugged her. A night home alone, the house to myself—it was like a dream come true. No Neecey and handing her towels, no having to listen to her squealing on the phone with her friends or them running in and out, slamming the back door, blasting MTV or Led Zeppelin while I was trying to read, no Gary renting a video and her not letting me watch, bossing me around, making me get this or that, sending me up to my room; and no lonely Pauline camping out on the sofa so there was no room to sit, with about nine bags of potato chips and sour-cream-and-onion dip, cramming them in her mouth, guzzling Tab by the bucketful to wash it all down, stinking the house up with junk food but not sharing, watching *The Cosby Show* or *Cheers* or some other sitcom, slapping her jiggly thigh, her booming laugh scarifying the walls, calling to me, *Genie, you missed it, Norm just told Cliff whatever,* but ruining all the jokes in a way that made you wish the world would end. No, not tonight. Tonight I'd be on my own, left to my own devices—*free*. It was enough to make you want to weep for joy.

"Sounds all right," I said.

Mom smiled; sometimes she could tell when I was shitting her. "I know this is a major step for us, but don't get your hopes up. It's just a test run, one night only. There are still two months until you turn thirteen and you should plan on having a sitter at least till then, and maybe longer if you can't handle being on your own. It's all up to you."

"No worries, mom, I'm all over it."

"I hope so, honey." She kissed me on the cheek and stood up. "I need to be able to trust you. I need you to show me you've put that other stuff behind you for good."

That was a low blow, but I should've seen it coming, because moms were all the same. The tiniest suspicion that their kids might get hurt and they never stopped wetting themselves over it.

"Mom, don't worry," I assured her.

"I'll *never* stop worrying about you, remember that," she said, pouring on the guilt. She moved toward the doorway but stopped and said, "Oh, there's one other thing."

"I know," I cut in, "I'll straighten up in here as soon as I get back." I had to throw her a bone for the good turn.

"No, not that," she said, "although this room could always stand a little less disaster. Something else."

"What?" It was like Guess My Secret with her this morning.

She narrowed her eyes, pulled her shoulders back, and lowered her chin, making her face all serious. "I know about the sign at the retirement home."

I hadn't been expecting that, and didn't especially care for her tone.

"Sucks, doesn't it?" I shrugged.

"I suppose it does." She stood there quietly, arms folded across her chest, staring at me, for like three days.

"What?" I asked.

"You were asking questions about it yesterday."

What the fuck?! That was it; it was out of my hands. Neecey had to get whacked.

"Are you listening to me?" she asked.

"You're gonna be late for work," I reminded her.

"Let me worry about that—"

"All right, but I'm just saying—"

"Drop it."

"Hey, if you want to be late—"

"Don't try to change the subject, Eugene." Shit, now I'd done it. "I said drop it. I know what you're up to, and I'm telling you right now that you're only asking for trouble. Haven't we had more than enough trouble around here? Can't we make it through one summer without you getting into some kind of mess?"

Those were rhetorical questions, so I didn't need to answer them.

"You forget, she's *my* mother. I know what she's like. Look at me when I'm speaking to you. She had me thinking I was Nancy Drew until I was sixteen years old."

"For real?" That was news to me.

"Yes. And you know what happened? I broke into my high school one night and went through all the lockers to find out who stole Kelly McGovern's English paper."

"No way." My mom, breaking and entering. This was getting good.

"Yes way. But I was caught and I got myself into a world of trouble."

"Were you suspended?"

"For a week."

The plot thickened. "You never told me that before."

"Because it's nothing to be proud of and I'm only telling you now because this sign business has your grandmother written all over it."

I wasn't gonna touch that. "But you found out who stole Kelly what's-her-head's paper, right?"

"No, Genie, and that's the thing. Nobody stole it. Kelly McGovern lied about her paper being stolen because she'd never written it in the first place, and she was suspended, too."

Wow, what a crappy story. But what else could you expect from Nancy Drew?

"Do you see my point?"

"Not really," I said, because I didn't. "Are you saying that some-body's lying about the sign being painted? Because it sure as hell looked painted to me."

"Don't get cute with me, young man," she huffed. "That's not the point. The point is, this isn't the first time your grandmother has pulled something like this, because she used to do it with me. It never really worked with Neecey because she's always had lots of friends, even before she became a knockout."

Yeah, sure, Benedict Arnold with boobs.

"You're more like I was," she continued. "I was very susceptible to your grandmother's schemes because I was an only child—"

"And I'm susceptible, too, because I'm a lonely one, right?"

"Oh, Genie." The tightness in her mouth dropped and her eyes widened. It looked like she was gonna step forward and smother me with sympathy like she was supposed to, but she wasn't finished lec-turing, so she couldn't. "It won't be that way forever, honey, I prom-ise."

Whatever. I wasn't holding my breath.

"Where was I?"

"The fruitcake falling close to the tree."

"You know your grandmother, everything's always secrecy and intrigue with her, and it's all very tempting when you've got no one else to play with. Believe me, I know. But you're not like I was, Genie, you're much more impressionable and far more destructive." She let that one suck the air out of the room for a second, and then continued. "Can't you see how dangerous this could be for you? I mean, have you stopped to think what's gonna happen if you find out who did it?"

I knew the answer to that one, but it was top secret.

"Do you think I'm fool enough to believe you'll control yourself, knowing how much you adore your grandmother?"

Through the waxy green leaves outside my bedroom window, I saw that the sky was gray again. Looked like rain was on the way.

Mom took a deep breath and shook her head, but her voice was softer when she spoke. "Look, Genie. You're starting a new school in September, junior high. You'll have a clean slate, a chance to start fresh, make new friends, and move on to something better for yourself. Do you really want to throw that away by getting a reputation as a snitch before the first day?"

"I don't give a sh—" I stopped myself just in time—the eyebrow of doom was rising on her forehead like a cobra set to strike. "It doesn't matter what they think, they won't like me anyway."

"Spare me, okay? You seem dead set on giving other kids all the ammunition they need to single you out, and you've got to stop doing that."

She was talking nonsense and it was time to call her on it. "So what? I'm not supposed to do the right thing because a bunch of pimply geeks won't like me for it? Jesus Christ, mom. Am I supposed to be a coward so I can be one of *them*?"

"No, Genie, that's not it. You should always do the right thing, when it's *yours* to do. As soon as you know the difference, then you can call yourself a man. Believe me, you've got a hell of a long way to go yet, buster."

I had to admit it, I liked it when mom talked tough.

"And that's where I come in. This sign business isn't for you. Do you know why? Because nothing good can come of it. If you don't find out who did it, you'll be disappointed, and we both know how you handle disappointment."

Like a grenade without the pin.

"But I'm not so concerned about that, because I know how smart you are, and if you're determined to get to the bottom of it, you probably will."

She finally said something I agreed with.

"But what then? If you go to the police, you'll only make problems for yourself with the other kids at school, problems that you don't need and haven't even thought about because you've already written them off. And that would be bad enough. But I'm not most concerned about that, because I know you, Genie. And *that's* what worries me."

"Yeah, but—"

"Excuse me. I'm talking, which means you are . . ."

"Listening."

"Thank you. Because I know you, both of you"—she looked at Thrash, and he flashed this innocent, who-me look—"there's only one option. You two are just out for payback. So you're gonna track down whoever did it and pick a fight. Now, you already know that you're not supposed to fight anymore, but the thing that scares me to death is that this time you might meet up with someone, maybe even a group of kids, just like you, angry and out of control, only bigger, older, stronger, and who won't think twice about putting you in the hospital when you charge at them, which you will, because when you get upset you just fly off the handle without ever stopping to think. Does any of this sound familiar?"

I pled the Fifth.

"Do you understand what I'm saying? Or do you actually like coming home with bloody noses and black eyes all the time? Because if that's what you really want, to hurt yourself, there are easier ways of going about it. But you already know that, don't you, because *you* know everything." Her upper lip was twitching; she was worked up now. "Well, you don't know everything, you only think you do, and that makes you your own worst enemy. Neecey and I can't be there to protect you from yourself all the time anymore. You're getting too old for that. I'm sorry, Genie, I really am, but that's the way it is. So you have to start helping us out. God knows I've begged your grandmother, begged her, not to encourage you to play detective, but your grandmother, she doesn't . . . she can't—" mom's voice cracked and she stopped. She raised the tips of her index fingers under her eyelashes and held them there. "Shit, if this mascara runs, then I'm really gonna be late."

"Mom, sewer mouth." Someone had to lighten the mood, because it'd gotten too damn heavy all of a sudden.

"Oh," she sniffled, faking a laugh, "you're right. Sorry." She looked at her watch. "Crap. I have to run." She cleared her throat, looked me in the eye, and said, "Promise me you'll drop it."

Now, that was a pickle.

"Stop frowning, Genie, it makes you look simple. Well, are you gonna promise or do I have to get on the phone with Pauline?"

And that was just good, old-fashioned hardball. The whole thing had been a setup from the start, and I'd bought every bit of it. It made me wonder how much of what she'd told me was true, because I already knew that people would say just about anything to get what they wanted, especially moms. But I had to give her credit—true or not, she'd suckered me good.

"All right." She turned to leave. "If that's your decision, I'll get on the phone right now. I can always tell them I was late because I had trouble finding a sitter."

"Wait," I said.

"Yes?" She raised her eyebrows and looked surprised, like she didn't know what I was gonna say. I hated that crap.

"All right. You win."

"What did I win?"

Christ, now she was making me work for it. "You know."

"No, I don't. Unless you say, 'I promise to drop the case,' I don't know what we're talking about."

I pronounced the words.

"That's great, Genie, I'm relieved to hear it. But now that you've promised, I'm gonna hold you to it." Mom straightened her shoulders and smoothed her hair. "Look, I know she probably gave you some money. Shh, I know, I know, she told you to keep it a secret. She always did that with me, too. It made it more fun. Don't worry. I'm not going to ask you any more about it. Keep the money. I'm sure it's not a lot. Think of it as a reward for a lesson well-learned."

"And then what?" I only asked because if she wanted to wreck my plan for the day, then she should at least have the courtesy to offer me a new one.

"I don't know. You're the one on vacation. Go to the mall, see a movie, take your bike down the Shore."

Just what I thought—nothing. "It looks like it's gonna be crappy," I said.

"Genie, you have a brain most people would kill for. I'm sure you can figure out something that doesn't involve trouble or getting hurt. Try using your head."

I nodded.

"Remember, you're gonna be in the house on your own tonight, so no going out after dark and no funny business, okay? I mean it. There's money for pizza on the counter. I'll call you later." She kissed me and smiled. "I'm trusting you to do the right thing."

"I know."

"That's my little man. I love you."

I wasn't in the habit of making promises to my mother that I had no intention of keeping, and that put me in a bad situation. But she'd left me no choice: I'd already given my word to grandma, who was higher up the chain of command than mom and had fronted the dough to make sure I delivered the goods. I knew all kinds of vandalism and suspicious bullshit were going on at the retirement home and that nobody was sticking up for grandma or any of the other old-timers, so that's what I had to do. Besides, Marlowe, Spade, and Holmes always had to work around the authorities and run the risk of getting into trouble themselves in order to get to the bottom of things—it was just part of the job. But I had to be careful. If mom found out what I was up to, I wouldn't have to contemplate the trouble my future might bring, because I wouldn't have one. Period. But she'd said the whole business scared her to death anyway, and since I didn't want to worry her, it was better to keep her in the dark, at least for her own protection. As for her lecture on the right thing to do, I already knew what it was. I had to break this fucking case wide open.

I got out of bed, did my exercises, and tried to figure out the exact moment that Neecey had switched teams, which she must've done, because she'd *never* sunk this low before. In the past year, she and mom had been ganging up on me more and more about all kinds of things—making an effort with other kids, avoiding fights, staying out of trouble—but Neecey ratting me out about the sign was by far the most extreme of her connivance. Sure, she'd always entertained herself at my expense, like putting dresses and makeup on me when I was little or telling me that eating dirt would make me grow or making me hand her towels or Manning the Lookout or that time she convinced me to lick one of the metal posts holding up the back porch in the wintertime. Being treated like her pet monkey drove me crazy sometimes, and a lot more lately, but it was just the usual sister-brother sort of crap, at least for us. Telling on me wasn't. We'd never done that. *Never*. Even the time I'd punched out the front window, we'd both sworn it was broken when we'd gotten home from school and that I'd cut my hand making a sandwich. I didn't think mom really believed us, but there wasn't anything she could do, because we'd stuck together.

But all that was over and done with now, and those days were gone forever. Not only had Neecey held out on me about what Razor had been doing here and lied to me about the sign, which Darren had definitely told her about, but she'd also dropped dime to get me banned from the case. I couldn't be sure what she was playing at, or with whom, but whatever it was, that shit just wasn't gonna float. Whether she was in cahoots with mom to mold me into someone more to their liking, or whether she thought her stupid friends and boyfriends were more important than her own grandmother, Neecey had gone too fucking far this time. She'd crossed over to the dark side, and while watching her go down in flames wasn't my idea of a great time, there wasn't much I could do to stop it now.

After I brushed my teeth, washed my face, and spiked my hair, I pulled out a pair of white shorts and a light blue T-shirt and got dressed. Then I grabbed Thrash and my backpack and went downstairs. I was in a Marlowe state of mind, ready to take care of business, but I had to eat first. Marlowe's breakfast of choice was soft-boiled or scrambled eggs, toast, and strong coffee. He made it himself in the morning because he was a bachelor and lived alone, but if he had a dame over who'd spent the night, he'd sometimes make it for her, too. Me, I didn't like eggs, wasn't allowed to touch coffee yet (except as ice cream), and was prohibited absolutely from cooking anything on the stove or in the oven without adult supervision. But I knew how to make crispy bacon in the microwave between sheets of paper towels, how to put chocolate syrup in milk so it sort of looked like a cup of joe, and I could burn toast with the best of them. After I'd eaten a couple bacon-toast-and-cheese sandwiches and polished off about a quart of milk, I cleaned up in the kitchen and headed out.

Stepping outside felt like being wrapped head-to-toe in a steaming quilt, and the haze was so thick that it seemed like I was looking at the world through a pane of frosted glass. I was only three or four blocks from home and already I was practically soaked with sweat. It couldn't go on like this. The weather would have to break soon, and when it did, it would sure as hell be something to see, but not anything you'd want to get caught out in.

I wanted to speed up but knew that doing so could lead to heat stroke or dehydration or plain old spontaneous combustion, so I settled back on the banana seat and took it easy. The church wasn't that far anyway, and that's what I was going to check out, to see what there was to see. Thrash had been right from the start—about

Darren lying because he was a liar—and I needed to step back a little, reconstruct *all* of the events of Saturday night as best I could, and then use them to build my case. There might be nothing where I was going; in fact, if the crew had hit the church on Saturday night, then there *should* be nothing, except maybe signs of a fresh coat of paint on the church wall and rectory. But there was no reason for me to believe Darren or anybody else; they were all lying or scheming or holding out in some way, and that meant I had to go check everything for myself if I wanted to get anywhere near the truth. And then, piece by piece, I'd figure this damn thing out.

I drove through the parking lot of what used to be the parochial school, but was now a school for K-through-6 kids with special needs who rode the short bus, then hung a left at the back of their freestanding gymnasium—which had a full-sized basketball court *and* an indoor pool—before coming up on the rectory. It was a three-story Colonial with wide steps, white columns on the porch, white wood siding, and stained glass in all the front windows. The windows were closed and there were no A/C units anywhere to be seen, which meant there was probably just enough left in the collection plate each week to foot for central air. Then again, without air-conditioning, Father Paul might be too exhausted from the heat to chase altar boys in the summer months, and that just wouldn't be fair.

Directly to the right of the rectory was the back of the church. The building itself was ultra-modern in style: the kind of architecture that was supposed to look like it'd come from the future when they'd built it about twenty years ago. Luckily for us, it was a future that decided not to bother showing up when it saw what it would have to look like. Most of the building was brick and most of the rest was tall stained glass in stainless-steel frames, but what threw it off completely were the three short gabled roofs in the front. One spread out wide in the center over the entryway and the other two were recessed from that on the sides. Taken together they looked like wings—three seagulls in dive-bomb formation or maybe a space ship that didn't have enough thrust to get off the ground. Either way, the whole thing looked more like something you'd see in *The Jetsons* or get beamed up to than a place you'd go to pray.

Then again, I didn't go there and I didn't pray, so I really didn't care what the hell it looked like. All I cared about was the right wall of the rectory, the back of the church, and the footpath in between. I got off the Cruiser, walked it between the two buildings, and then dropped the kickstand to have a look. All the wood siding on the rectory was white, but anyone could see that there was a large patch, maybe five feet by six, that was whiter than the rest, as if it'd just been painted. I turned around and stepped over to the back of the church. There was a heavy cross-and-Bible door leading in the back way and about four feet of brick on either side, creating a small mudroom or vestibule at the rear entrance. As I got closer, I could tell that the door had recently gotten a couple of coats of white, whether for the first time or as a touch-up, because there was hardly any dust or pollen or dirt streaks on it, which should've been the case given the time of year and all the humidity and rain we'd been having lately. Wide swaths of the bricking on both sides of the door were slightly off-color and faded, too, as if someone had gone out there with turpentine and a hard-bristle brush and gotten to work in a hurry.

That cinched it. Either Darren and the crew had actually hit the church on Saturday night and the tag had been covered up in a rush the next morning, or the church needed to think about hiring a new handyman because the one they had sucked. If the first conclusion was the true one, then it seemed that Darren hadn't lied to me, because the crew couldn't have vandalized the sign at the retirement home if they'd been here instead. Then again, they could've done it sometime before or after, or since there were seven of them, they could've easily broken themselves up into teams to pull two separate jobs at the same time if they'd wanted to. All of that was possible. The only problem was that none of it was certain.

If the crew had hit *both* the church *and* the retirement home on the same night, though, I'd have some new questions to mull over. Like, why would they go to all the trouble of coordinating hits at different places across town from each other on the same night? And why, if that's what they'd done, would one of the tags be so piss-poor awful? Because they'd almost gotten nabbed at the home and been forced to rush it was one answer. Another was that maybe there was something more than just graffiti going on—maybe something else was at stake.

I jumped on the Cruiser, popped the kickstand, and had a tickly sensation in the base of my brain, like I was getting close. Close to what, I couldn't say yet, but closer than I'd been so far, that much was sure. Just then I thought I saw a flash of movement in the rectory window on the left. I looked up to see a balding head, wire-rimmed glasses, and a pale, jowly face staring down at me from behind a parted curtain. It was Father Paul. His mouth arched downward at the corners, he wasn't wearing his collar, and he had a telephone pressed against his ear.

Even though there was a wall separating us, being that near to him made me feel a little bit wary, kind of like the first time you tried to go in the ocean after seeing *Jaws*. But then the rest of it hit me like a shot. *The criminal always returns to the scene of the crime*—and there *I* was, inspecting the location of a tag that Father Paul and the people at the church probably thought *nobody* knew about. I could see it all too clearly: on the other end of the line was someone in a dark blue uniform, pen in hand, copying down the suspect description Father Paul was giving them—*my description*.

I'd already checked my calendar earlier this morning, and playing the fall guy wasn't on it. I spun out of there, fast, staying away from the main roads and zigzagging randomly down one side street after another until I'd put enough crooked distance between me and the church that I felt certain I couldn't have been tailed. The effort took its toll. I was gushing sweat from every pore, my legs were like heavy rubber, and my throat was aching from thirst. I had to sit down somewhere and take a break for a few minutes or I'd overheat. I slid back on the seat and coasted as far as I could without using the pedals, then turned them over a few times to maintain my forward momentum, and coasted again, saving my energy and catching my breath.

I passed an empty, fenced-in lot where the Stewart's Drive-In used to be and a mom-and-pop liquor store with a comatose-looking German shepherd collapsed in a heap on the front walk. A little farther on there was an asphalt park with a rusted swing set, monkey bars, and a dented-up slide next to a macadam basketball court with no nets on the rims. I knew without looking up at the street signs that I'd crossed over to the part of town where most of the black people lived.

They called it the Woods, like almost everybody else did, because all the streets in the area were named after trees: Maple, Spruce, Pine, Oak, Walnut, Elm. There were mostly ranch-style houses throughout the neighborhood, but the few two-story homes popping up here and there were just like mine, only they seemed older in some way, or just more weathered. The blocks themselves were smaller than where I lived, which meant most of the places had front porches and larger front yards because the backyards only had enough room for a view of the rear wall of someone else's house. Both new cars and old cars were parked in driveways and along the curbs; some houses had nice gardens and landscaping and porch furniture and some didn't; and there were mailboxes and trash cans and flagpoles and the occasional fire hydrant like you'd see anywhere else. What I didn't see was anything that made this part of town any different or worse or more frightening than any other, and I knew that the handful of sub-morons I'd heard call it the Jungle instead of the Woods had probably never even seen the place, and most definitely didn't live there, so what they called it didn't amount to the stink off shit.

You could tell that the people who did live here had plenty of common sense, though, because the streets were practically empty.

Everyone was probably inside in the air-conditioning or sitting in front of a fan with an ice-cold drink instead of roasting their chestnuts off in the punishing heat like I was. But I was in luck; I saw a couple of benches under some tall trees about a block ahead, so I glided over and took a load off. I mopped the sticky, hair-gelled sweat off my forehead and face, wiped it on my shorts, and wished I'd shoved a canteen of lemonade in my backpack instead of Thrash. He heard that and started to go off on one of his rants, but I was too busy looking at the building across the street to pay him much mind.

If someone had asked me what the chance was that I'd visit *two* churches in one day, I would've said zero before they'd finished the question. But since I was sitting across from the second church this morning, I guess I would've been wrong. This one was a much simpler affair than the last one; in fact, it looked almost exactly like the rectory at the other church, except that this building was taller, the front steps and porch were much narrower, the stained-glass windows on the sides went all the way up to the roof, and there was a small belfry with a steeple toward the back.

The only reason it caught my attention at all was that there were three people standing to the side of the building, looking up and pointing. There was a tall, caramel-skinned man in a black suit; a short, stout, dark woman in a floral blouse and beige skirt; and a younger, barrel-chested guy with workman's jeans, T-shirt, chiseled arms, and a copper-colored Afro. I traced the direction of their upturned faces and fingers toward the church and saw what they were looking at: a massive star-shaped hole in the top half of one of the stained-glass windows, a good thirty feet or more above their heads. I looked back at the trio and saw that the man in the black suit was holding a baseball-sized rock in his right hand, tossing and catching it, as if he were measuring the kind of throw it would take to send that rock up and through the stained-glass window the way someone else had already done.

From the way he and the others were studying it, they had to be thinking what I was thinking: the size and weight of the rock, the height of the top of the window—it would have to be a damn good throw by someone with a strong, accurate arm to do that amount of damage. Before I'd even finished the thought, the name of a prime suspect popped into my head. He had a strong, accurate arm, didn't seem to give much of a shit about anyone but himself and his chum Tommy Sharpe, was a punk-ass bully, had set me up at football try-outs, and nearly cornered me twice in the mall. I didn't know if Razor was a bigot, too, the kind to destroy the property of the only black church in town, but that was for someone else to find out. All I was gonna do was walk across the street and give the man in the black suit a free tip, a lead that would take him, and the cops, I hoped, down to the reservoir, to the front door of the Tuffalo residence.

I stood up realizing how angry I was. Breaking the window at the black church was just totally fucked up and wrong, and even though it seemed similar, it wasn't the same thing as Darren and the crew tagging the other church, not by a long shot. Every kid in town knew about Father Paul, even if none of the grown-ups were aware or had tried to do anything about it, and Darren and the crew had only paid him back a little for all the nasty shit he'd done. Eye for an eye, that's all that was. But, as far as I knew, nobody in the black church had done anything to anyone, so their window had gotten smashed not for something they'd done, but most likely for who and what they were. That was some low-down, dirty bullshit, and in some ways, it reminded me of the retirement home. No one there had done anything to anyone either; shit, they were so old and so weak they practically couldn't do anything at all. But their place had been van-dalized, too, and what's more, it seemed they were subject to an ongoing series of burglaries and thefts, while nobody seemed to give a damn. I guessed the home and the black church were the same in that way; to the depraved criminal mind they were targets, and that's all they were.

I grabbed the Cruiser by the handlebars and walked it toward the curb. Under ordinary circumstances I wasn't a squealer or a rat, but I'd be delighted to make an exception this one time so the people across the street could have a leg up in nailing the scumbag who'd broken their window. I stopped at the curb and looked both ways before crossing. A blue Ford pickup sped by from the right, followed by a green Honda, and then a white squad car drove up on the left. I glued my eyes to it, to make sure it kept going, only to see the brake lights flash red as it rolled to a stop. The driver didn't jam on the brakes, the car didn't skid, and the lights and siren remained dormant. Maybe they'd stopped because they'd seen the same three people on the side of the church that I'd seen and were getting out to find out what was going on.

I stayed where I was, relaxed and nonchalant, just watching the cop car. The people across the street turned to look at it, too. I was thinking that maybe Father Paul hadn't been on the phone with the cops or hadn't gotten a good look at me or hadn't been able to give them an accurate description, because almost a minute had gone by and the roller just sat there. It occurred to me that Father Paul might not have been able to describe me very well, but the Cruiser, well, the Cruiser was unmistakable. It was the only bike of its kind in town and easy as all hell to pick out. So when the reverse lights finally lit up, the vehicle started backing toward me, and the three people beside the church peered across in my direction, I took all of it as a polite way of saying I should make myself scarce, which I did.

TWELVE

*I'd never lammed it from the cops before, but I fig-*ured now was the time to learn how. It wasn't so hard. They were in a car, so they had to go around street blocks while I could ride through them, and after some quick turns, a few cut corners, and a couple counts of trespassing through fenceless backyards, they were nowhere to be seen. No sweat. The difficult part was getting home *after* I'd ditched them, because since the cops were nowhere to be seen, I had no clue *where* they might be.

That meant being extra careful, making a lot of unnecessary turns, stopping every once in a while behind a parked truck or a hedge and peeking out from behind to take the lay of the land, and more back-tracking than anyone who wasn't actually lost should ever admit to doing. It wasn't that I was afraid of getting picked up and questioned by the cops—I'd been through it before and knew the routine, and as far as Saturday night was concerned, I had a rock-solid alibi by the name of Pauline. No, my motives for bolting were nobler than that. If the public pork hauled me down to the station house for a session with a klieg light and a rubber hose, sooner or later they'd have to call mom, and after the warning she'd given me this morning, that would pretty much ruin not only her mood and her day, but also the rest of my summer. So it seemed wiser to avoid them and spare her the unneeded trouble.

When I finally got home, I chained the Cruiser to the back porch, quietly though, and gave the outside of the house a thorough inspection—staying low, peeking through the windows, keeping my ears open for the slightest sound—because I still wasn't too stoked to meet up with Neecey the Narc if she was home. I circled the house twice, once in each direction, and found the coast was clear. She was out—big fucking surprise—so I went inside and headed for my room.

I needed to check a couple of facts in my journal. More specifically, I thought I remembered Darren saying that he'd been with *most* of the crew on Saturday night, instead of *all* of the crew, or just the crew, when we'd spoken on Monday. And that's what I was after, confirmation, something small but concrete to let me know I was on the right track. It wouldn't exactly blow the case wide open, but if Darren *had* said it, it would at least strengthen my theory of what had actually gone down.

I sat Thrash on my wooden desk chair, put my backpack in the closet, shut the door, and stepped back over to my desk. I was just about to open the top drawer when I caught the smug grin darkening Thrash's face. Yeah, I'd seen that look before, plenty of times, but I'd never found it very appealing. It was the face he saved for when he thought he knew something that I didn't, or when he was calling me out for trying to pull his leg, or just about anytime I reached for my journal or a book. I didn't have a clue what had crawled up his tiny plush ass this time, though, and that made me nervous. My skin went clammy, my breath shortened, and I felt a sticky sweat on the back of my neck. Okay, sure, it was a little fucked up to have an imaginary friend at my age, but the idea of an imaginary friend that could turn on you was some pretty sick shit, even for me.

I took a couple deep breaths and slapped my cheeks a few times to snap out of it, but my hand wasn't as steady as it could've been when I pulled open the top drawer to my desk. Right away I noticed something was off. My Magic Markers were gone—and the key to the side drawer, where I locked up my journal, was *on top* of the ten-dollar bill grandma had given me, instead of underneath, where I'd hidden it Monday night. My cheeks flushed, my scalp stood up, and I was covered with goose bumps so pointy and sharp that I felt like a blowfish. I had this flash of being ice cold and burning hot all at once, like a Steak-Umm going from the freezer to the frying pan. It took a couple more seconds for the rest to sink in, but when it did, the pressure started building, fast.

So *that* was how Neecey had found out about Stacy; *she'd been reading my journal!* Jesus Christ, that was a new fucking low, even for her. That journal was *private*, only for *me*; the only reason I had it was so I could practice expressing what I was thinking or feeling without having to worry about people slapping the cuffs on me, and that meant *nobody else could read it*. But I couldn't even have that anymore, not so much as a single thought to myself, without some goddamn head-shrinker or two-faced hench-daughter trying to wring it out of me. That was serious bullshit, because Neecey wasn't just stealing my stuff, or lying to me, or trying to screw me up on the case. She was messing with my brain now, and there was no way in hell I could just sit there and take it.

My fingers twitched, my face snarled. Maybe this was it, maybe I finally had to break with Neecey once and for all—*and tell mom*. I didn't want to do it, because, like I said, I might've been a lot of things, but a rat had never been one of them. As soon as I'd thought that, I wished I hadn't, because all of a sudden mom's lecture from earlier came shrieking back to me, all that talk of snitching and doing the right thing. I'd thought it'd seemed fishy then, but it stunk to high heaven now. Was it just coincidence, or had mom been telling me something without meaning to, just by the way she'd run things together? But if mom had been hinting at something, then maybe it wasn't just Neecey; maybe Neecey . . . Jesus, maybe Neecey had been acting on *orders*!

My chest and back felt hot, itchy, and tight, as if a heavy wool sweater, two sizes too small and fresh out of the dryer, had been yanked down over my shoulders. Hadn't mom and Neecey started ganging up and really putting the screws to me right about the time I'd started my journal? Couldn't I see they'd begun acting that way because they *knew* what was in it? Was my newest counselor in on it, too? That made sense; the journal had been *his* idea in the first place, and I'd never once suspected that it might be a scam to get me to give up information I wouldn't have told him or anybody else. Mom, Neecey, my counselor—were they *all* in on it together?

I heard dry, uneven breath rattling in my lungs and my head felt steamy and light. *Of course* they were in it together. *Shit*. What did I think they were talking about during those closed-door portions of my monthly progress meetings, when mom and Neecey went in to talk to my counselor while I waited outside? Did I actually think they were all patting themselves on the back about what a swell kid I was, or how nicely I was coming along? What an *idiot* I'd been! All that time they'd been scheming, plotting the mind games and espionage they'd use to keep me down, right under my goddamn nose, playing me like a chump.

I wanted to hurt someone, bad, and I would have, but no one was around. I must've figured that smashing something was the next best thing, because before I knew it, I heard the door to Neecey's room clattering open and I was standing next to her closet. I had to destroy something, something good, something it'd hurt her to lose, because she hadn't just ignored the KEEP OUT sign on my door and gone into my desk and read my journal, but she'd torn what little privacy I had to shreds, and I could never put it back together again, not with all the rubber cement in the world.

I was fuming, but it came to me: I'd burn one of her scrapbooks—

those sissy, construction-paper albums that she filled with stickers, doodles, sayings, magazine photos, pressed flowers, and pictures of her and her friends that they all wrote in and signed. She'd been making them since about fourth grade, and she kept a pile stashed in the back of her closet, tucked safely away. One of those would do nicely; they had all her memories, crushes, roller-skating parties, fair-weather friends—you name it, it was in there. If I couldn't have any thoughts to myself, then neither could she, and if I destroyed one of those, it'd blast a big fat hole in Neecey's world the way she'd blown the bottom out of mine.

I went to turn the doorknob, foaming at the mouth, growling, wanting nothing more than to open that door and exact my revenge, but my hand froze up, wouldn't budge. I tried to push the thought out of my mind, focus on the task before me, but I couldn't. My chest heaved, my ears pounded, and my muscles clenched so hard I thought they'd snap off the bone, but I just stood there, strangling the doorknob to death, not moving.

I was thinking about Cynthia, about hiding in the closet, Manning the Lookout, and my shoulders slouched forward and my chin fell to my chest and I felt weak and queasy, like I'd collapse if the doorknob weren't holding me up. If I ransacked Neecey's closet now, she'd never let me *near* it again, let alone *inside*. I'd either have to give up on vengeance or on Manning the Lookout, and no matter which way I played it, I only stood to lose.

I should've been able to whip that door open and wreak a whirl-wind of havoc without batting an eyelid, but I felt torn in half and realized there was more to it than just forfeiting my private peepshows. Neecey reading my journal behind my back was the same thing as me watching Cynthia naked without her permission; you could argue that shit till you were blue in the face, but there was no getting around it. And wrecking something of Neecey's to settle the score—on purpose, knowing it was wrong—would make me *exactly* the same kind of bottom-feeder as Neecey, mom, my counselor, and whoever the hell else was involved in the town-wide conspiracy to break me down to nothing.

My hand slipped off the knob and fell limply by my side. I dragged myself back into my room, closed the door, and flopped facedown onto my bed. I was pissed off and shaking and thwarted and felt humiliated and guilty and betrayed, and if I didn't know any better, I would've said that, for the first time in my life, I even felt *ashamed*. Not for having seen Cynthia naked, I guess, but for how I'd gone about it. If you wanted to show something private to someone, you had to invite them to see it, simple as that. And even if Cynthia had found out that I was Manning the Lookout and was okay with it after the fact, she'd still never invited me to do it and probably never would, so I'd only been fooling myself to think it was all right. The same went for Neecey. I'd never told her she could look at my journal, but she'd taken it upon herself to do so. And she'd have to answer for that. I didn't know when she'd answer for it, but I hoped it'd come sometime sooner than the apology I knew I owed Cynthia—the one she'd never get.

After a few more minutes of doing the dead man's float on my mattress, I lifted my face out of the pillow, picked myself up, and moved Thrash over to the bed so I could sit in the chair. But I didn't look at him. He was in one of his I-told-you-so moods and it was better not to get him started, especially when he was right. I'd never stopped to think my journal wasn't just for me to express myself and work my way up to actualizing, but that it was also a record of what was going on in my head, *evidence* that people could use against me if they ever got hold of it. I guessed Thrash had either known or suspected it all along and that's why he'd always been dead set against it. But that didn't mean I had to let him chew my ear off now.

I reached into my desk, put the key to my desk drawer on my key chain to prevent further breaches of security, stood up, and looked out my bedroom window. Just beyond the window fan and the small maple tree right outside, the sky was a smear of dark blue and charcoal, like a smudged finger painting. The nearby maple leaves hissed in the wind, the bough-tips swayed and shook, and I thought about all those nights I'd squirmed through the window and hunkered down in the crux of its branches. I wasn't allowed out after dark, but I sometimes let myself out on my own recognizance anyway, to get some air, watch the stars, read with a flashlight, or just to take a break, especially when I'd had all I could stomach of Pauline's noisy grazing and guffawing and talking out loud to keep herself company. Sometimes I just felt like I had to get out or I'd crack, and the tree outside my window was the closest and easiest place to sneak out for a breather when I needed one.

That's what I needed now, because I felt nervous and tense all over. I tucked Thrash under my arm and went downstairs to the kitchen, where I grabbed some cleaning products from under the sink, a roll of paper towels from the counter, and then stepped outside to the back porch. I'd been on the Cruiser in the rain twice within the past couple of days without wiping it down, and I knew for a fact that someone else's grubby hands had been all over it, and the thought of that made me sick. I probably could've waited until later to clean it, because more rain was coming, but working on the Cruiser had a way of relaxing me, and since it was mine, I enjoyed taking care of it.

I plopped Thrash down on the lawn chair next to the beer cooler, drenched a paper towel with window cleaner, and set to work on the front wheel. I did the wheels first, because cleaning along and between every individual spoke was the kind of drag that I usually wanted to get out of the way as fast as I could, and once I'd finished them I'd do the rims, the rest of the chrome, and then the frame. That's how mom's new boyfriend, Craig, had taught me to clean it, and he was a mechanic, so he knew about those things. He'd also given me some pointers and an old manual on bicycle repair he'd had lying around his shop while I'd been building the Cruiser in the spring, but I'd collected all the parts from the junkyard and put them together myself.

I couldn't really describe how it felt—having built my own bike from nothing, making a masterpiece out of other people's garbage—but it didn't take long for me to figure out what it meant. I'd actualized like a madman for a month and a half; I wasn't tied to the same four or five crummy blocks between the trailer park and the strip mall anymore; I could wake up in the morning and get to and from school without having to worry about what kind of bullshit was waiting for me at the bus stop twice a day; I could go further from home than I'd ever been before; and no matter where I went, I kept my chin up a little, because I was traveling in style. To anybody else the Cruiser probably just looked like a totally sweet ride (which it was, easily one of the sweetest rides in town), but to me it was more than that. To me the Cruiser was like a new way of life.

It didn't change much with the kids at school; they just gave me all these confused and jealous looks, as if seeing a kid like me on a ride like that was some kind of riddle or paradox. But I'd expected as much from them. It was different at the beach this summer, though. There the Cruiser was a conversation starter; kids would come up and ask me about it, where I got it, how much it cost, if they could try it out, and I'd tell them about how I built it myself and lie about how easy it'd been, although I restrained myself so I didn't brag too much. When I broke it to them that nobody was allowed to ride the Cruiser except me, they usually took it pretty well and didn't pester me too badly, and they asked me to play Frisbee or Nerf football anyway, so I generally wound up hanging out and goofing off with other kids for most of the day, which was something I never did around here.

I'd been thinking about that a lot more lately—how far out of my way I had to go to feel like a normal kid. Most of the kids I met at

the beach were tourists or day-trippers from the city, so they didn't
know anything about me or what people said I was supposed to be
like, and since the beach was in a different town from the one I lived
in, there was no way for them to find out. They didn't know I had
emotional problems, a past, and a bad reputation, so they didn't treat
me like I did, and they didn't have any reason to stare or back away
like I was a total nutjob either, because Thrash wasn't there to clue
them in. No, I didn't take Thrash to the beach, but it wasn't like I'd
planned to leave him behind or anything, because I hadn't. There just
wasn't enough room in my backpack for a big beach towel, sunscreen,
a packed lunch, and him, so when I went to the beach, I went alone.

Maybe I'd gotten lucky. Maybe I'd needed a break from Thrash,
too, without knowing it, just like having the Cruiser and going down
the Shore had given me a break from everything else. I didn't know
and really couldn't say. All I knew was that everything seemed different, felt different, when I was down the Shore on my own, like some
weight had been lifted from my shoulders and everything kind of
rolled off. In fact, I hadn't been in an argument or a fight all summer
long. Go figure.

But I wasn't dense enough to think that it had changed me in
some way, or that all of a sudden everything else would be chill and
easy like that, or that it would last, because I knew it wasn't real.
Well, the Cruiser was real, but everything else wasn't. It was only
vacation, just a few hours amongst strangers where I felt like someone else, and at the end of each day, I had to come back home.

THIRTEEN

It was still hotter than a cookout in hell, but the Cruiser was all spruced up and I figured I'd give it a quick lube while I was at it. I wheeled it around to the side of the house, under the kitchen-sink window, next to the big metal cube of the heating and cooling unit. I had to lube the Cruiser over there because WD-40 stained concrete when it dripped, and mom didn't want the back porch to get all ruined. She said it was murder on weeds, too, and since we had a few at the base of the house on that side, she told me to do it there, kill two birds with one stone, and keep everybody happy. Yeah, sometimes it seemed that mom was too on top of things just to wait tables or tend bar and that she could do something else, but those were the cards she'd been dealt and she was only playing them. It couldn't have been the easiest hand in the world, or the most fun, but that's probably what made her so good at stacking the deck against me.

That got me wondering. What if mom had let me take the Cruiser down the Shore on my own this summer not as a reward for straight A's and good behavior like she'd said, but to get me out of the house long enough and often enough for Neecey or her to snoop around in my journal? What if they'd been doing it for months without me catching on? What if mom knew *everything* I'd written in it, too? Everything I had to say about teachers, classmates, counselors, what Thrash and I shared between ourselves, the way I'd started looking at girls in the past year, tailing Stacy down the road to full-on ass-obsession, or me hunched over myself in a closet giving the Lookout one hell of an Indian burn while I watched my sister's best friend getting undressed through the slats like a sex offender? Jesus, that was just too goddamn humiliating to contemplate. I'd never be able to look mom in the eye again. Worse still, how would I ever be able to trust her?

Screw that shit, I couldn't think about it, I already had enough on my mind. I set Thrash on the heating unit, leaned the Cruiser against the wall, squatted down, and sprayed the chain in short, quick bursts. I did the handbrakes after the chain, put the cap on the WD-40, and sat on my butt under the kitchen window with my back against the wall.

Just as I started to get comfortable and clear my head, I heard the front door open and close. Fucking Neecey. I could hear her inside, going up and down the stairs, opening doors, moving through the house, and I knew what she was doing—she was making sure I wasn't home.

Sure, we used to have good times together, look out for each other, stay up past curfew together when mom was at work, build pillow forts and tell ghost stories with flashlights under our chins or make Jiffy Pop and watch *Saturday Night Live,* drink too much soda and rock out with the stereo cranked up, or just screw around and laugh our asses off at nothing, and I'd thought we were close. Shit, I even used to look up to her, because she was pretty and popular and had so many friends and was good at school and always busy with this, that, or the other thing, but still found time for me, and made all of it look so goddamn easy. But she'd changed, and I barely knew her anymore.

She was turning into this phony, two-faced, social-climbing snitch who knew she was hot and flaunted it everywhere, even in front of her own brother. She put on airs and was hardly ever around and didn't know what the hell was going on in my life because she never bothered to ask anymore and told on me to mom and hung out with the cool rich crowd and was too good for us now and didn't give a rat's shaved nut about me.

I suddenly had a feeling for Neecey that I'd never had before, one far more disturbing than anger, and if I saw her, I knew I'd do something I'd never come anywhere near doing in my life, and that was punch her dead in the face. Yeah, I was as close to the bottom as I'd ever been, but I got the feeling I could still sink a little lower. So I stayed right where I was, the way I was, trying not to move or think, only breathe, with my head down and my wrists tucked under my armpits, so she wouldn't see me. I stayed that way even when I heard her come downstairs, into the kitchen, open the back door, step out onto the back porch, and then go back in and close the door.

The sky above was gray like a stone, and that's exactly what I was, a cold, mute stone leaning against the side of the house, with no sense, no emotion, easy to overlook, and that's the way I wanted it. I heard her puttering around inside, opening the refrigerator, pouring something in a glass, and then closing the door. Just knowing she was in the vicinity was making me boil over. But all I had to do was keep myself balled up tight, stay quiet, remember to breathe, and wait it out, either for Neecey to leave or go upstairs, and then I could make a break for it on the Cruiser.

If I'd had a long stick, a bandanna to tie my stuff in, and my ten-dollar bill, I could've hit the road right now and never looked back, "Born to Run" style, just like the Boss, or the old man. I'd ride the Cruiser as far away from here as I could, maybe go to the city and run out of money in four seconds and have to pawn my ride and fall in with junkies and dirtbags and then wind up in a gutter somewhere, with my teeth all broken and brown, half my head caved in, and a hypodermic needle hanging out of my arm, or I'd get taken in by some pimp with rings on all his fingers, who'd dress me up in mesh T-shirts and spandex shorts and slap me around and rent me out to wealthy middle-aged degenerates, male and female alike, who'd give anything for a few minutes alone with a ripe young boy, because those were things that happened to runaways and everybody knew it because crap like that was always on TV. No, it wasn't as appealing as Tom Sawyer laying low in a cave with that Becky chick, or moving to a cabin by a pond far off in the woods, but it'd almost be worth going through all of it to see mom and Neecey freaking out when they'd realized I was gone: worrying, crying, pulling their hair out, calling the cops, putting my picture on milk cartons, losing sleep, fearing the worst, blaming themselves for all they'd done wrong, and wishing for one last chance to apologize and make it up to me and have me come home again—which was the one thing I'd make sure they never got.

But my ten-spot was upstairs and Neecey was inside, so I couldn't get to it, and there was no way in hell I was gonna run away from home with a stuffed frog and no backpack and empty pockets on top of it all, because that was just suicide. Besides, that money had come from my client, and I hadn't finished the job she'd paid me to do, so if I just took off without finishing it, that'd be like stealing, which I guess I wouldn't have minded so much if my client wasn't also my grandma, because you'd have to be a hot runny piece of shit to steal from your own grandmother, and that's all there was to it. But I'd never steal from her, and I'd never run out on her either, because she didn't run out on us. No fucking way. She'd jumped right into the breach when the old man split, picked up all the slack, practically moved in, so there were still four people in the house pretty much all the time instead of just mom, Neecey, and me sitting around, scratching our heads, trying to figure out what the hell was missing from the picture.

When the old man up and split, Grandma was already retired and lived in this small apartment about half an hour away on her Social

Security checks and the pension she got from working in that factory all those years, and she was supposed to be kicking back, taking it easy, learning to knit or whatever, and enjoying her golden years. But she tossed all that aside, stayed over three or four nights in a row, and looked after us when mom was at work, because mom had to quit her night classes and take a second job tending bar to pay the bills. So grandma took care of the house and cooked and cleaned and stayed up late to talk to mom when she was down and hugged all of us a lot. She was small and stern and shrewd and full of energy and more fun than having one of those inflatable bouncy chambers in your very own bedroom. She let us stay up to watch *Fantasy Island* and always had candy in her pockets (good candy, not that poison she tried to feed us now) and made pudding or baked cookies or cupcakes from scratch and tickled us and taught us how to dance like they did in the old days before good music was invented and showed us how to cheat at cards and told us secrets and read us fairy tales or *Where the Wild Things Are,* which was my favorite then, because Max was a bad little fucker and I always respected that.

And when I got suspended a few years later, she came over every day to watch me and didn't keep her distance as if I were toxic waste, like everybody else did, and never gave up on me and brought me the detective books to read so I'd have something to do besides feel how empty and meaningless time could be, and she talked to me about them, quizzed me on them, showed me how to pick up the clues as I read and how to think things through, and made me grilled cheese sandwiches and tomato soup for lunch and played practical jokes on me so I'd feel normal, like putting her teeth in my glass when I wasn't looking so I'd almost drink them or hiding Thrash so I couldn't find him or sneaking up behind me and kissing me loud on the ear or making me hide our neighbors' newspaper under the bushes because she didn't like them, and she was always telling me that I was her special little man, no matter what anyone said, I was just a handful like my grandfather, that was all, or timing how fast I could run from our house to the corner or seeing if I could jump up to touch that tree branch or that one, hugging me whether I could or couldn't, and forcing me to tell her that I loved her.

But then she started dressing funny, like her shoes wouldn't match or she'd have on one knee-high but not the other, or she'd talk to people who weren't there, in a language that wasn't really language, and she'd get confused a lot and leave the iron on or the oven on or the car running, so that she almost killed herself or us ten times, and couldn't find her way back from the store or called the cops at two A.M. because some prowler had stolen the dentures that were still in her mouth, or she sat up all night on the sofa with a lit candle in her hand, saying they were coming, and we had to put her away, although all of us together could barely afford it. Since then she'd steadied a little, but was in and out more and more and was clearly getting worse, so it was only a matter of time, and mom could hardly talk about it without breaking up and someday soon we'd lose her, either the lights would be on but nobody would answer the door or the lights would go out and that would be that.

But until that happened I'd never run out on grandma or give up on her, and I'd visit her two or three times a week like I always did and look after her the best I could, because who else was gonna do it, fucking pencil-necked Bryan? Bullshit. Grandma was a bigger man right now in her wasted state than he could ever hope to be. Fuck that, if anybody was going to take care of her, I was gonna do it. She was *my* grandma. I was claiming her, even if nobody else would. And if somebody thought that was fucking *retarded* or that she was fucking *retarded* or that anybody else was fucking *retarded* just because they had problems or couldn't answer when they were called on in class or because they were old and their brains were dying, then they shouldn't sneak around misspelling it on the front sign under cover of night like fugitives from special-ed, but have the balls to come up and say it to my face, so I could relieve them of their lips and teeth.

No, I wasn't gonna run from this; there was too much riding on it.

I was gonna stay right where I was, see it through till the end, and make goddamn sure that somebody paid.

I was still crouched down on the side of the house when I heard Neecey turn on the water in the kitchen sink and rinse out her glass. I was just on the other side of the wall, maybe three or four feet away, directly beneath the window where she couldn't see me, and it took about a thousand years for her to clean that glass, or at least that's the way it seemed, because it was absolute murder to keep myself still. My insides were taut, jumpy, and drawn, like the spring-loaded arm of a pinball machine pulled all the way back, ready to blast forward. I heard the window lock above me shift and the panes scrape upward. The aluminum siding felt like a cheese grater against my back. Mom was right about one thing—I'd need deodorant soon, because I could smell myself a little, and it wasn't the fresh, clean scent of Irish Spring. The doorknob to the back door turned and the door squeaked open. *Fuck.* Neecey was coming out to check around the sides of the house; I just knew it. Any second now she'd turn the corner and see me and then I didn't know what would happen, but whatever it was, it wouldn't be good. If I were younger, I would've covered my face, thinking that if I couldn't see Neecey, then she couldn't see me. But I was too old for that shit. So I just took a deep breath, lowered my head, and closed my eyes.

The seconds ached by like hours, but nothing happened. Then Neecey said, "Hey, Mrs. Murdock," and while the sound of her voice was like metal fingernails raked across a chalkboard, what she said was oddly soothing. Mrs. Murdock was Cynthia's mom—that's who she was calling. Neecey hadn't seen me, she hadn't come out to check the side of the house; she'd just opened the window and the back door to get the cross breeze because it was always stuffy in the kitchen in the summer. Everything loosened up, and I suddenly felt so relaxed that I could've fallen asleep. But I wasn't in the clear just yet.

"Hey, babe," Neecey chirped. "Yeah, I just got back."

Great, this was just what I needed. I was trapped into hearing one of Neecey and Cynthia's girlie gossip sessions, and the way they went at it, I could be here all day.

"Okay, I guess. It's like we both knew it would happen sooner or later, with him going off to college and everything."

It sounded like they were talking about Gary, and my only hope was that he'd dropped her like a water balloon off the Empire State Building.

"By the way, I totally told you he was seeing Jessica Whitmore. Yeah, he told me, but like who couldn't figure it out with all the pizza deliveries she's been getting lately?"

Nice one, Gary—giving Neecey a taste of her own medicine. All of a sudden I was almost sorry to see that wood post go.

"*Meat lovers!*" Neecey screamed and laughed. "Ohmigod, Cyn, you're a total slut!"

As far as I knew, Cynthia had never even held hands with a guy, so if she was a slut, then I was the pope.

"Darren? Uh-huh, I told him, but he already knew. Not really. He said he'd started hooking up with Jessica about the same time, so he didn't think it would be fair to like have a canary on me, or hold me back from finding someone new, because he was totally leaving anyway. I know, right? That's what I'll miss about him most, I guess. He's just, I don't know, he's always been like so *decent.*"

If you asked me, Gary letting Neecey run around with Darren wasn't decent—it was stupid.

"Yeah, we talked for a while, said what we had to say and all, promised we'd still be friends, and that was like it."

Fucking Gary. He'd had a chance to twist the knife as they called it quits but punked out instead.

"No, hon, I feel totally fine, seriously. I'm not like melancholy or anything. It's like I'll miss him, but it was time, you know? Yeah, I hope so. He was my first, Cyn, and he was totally gentle and he always did everything he could to make things easy for me and I'll always be completely grateful for that, because a lot of guys are total selfish pricks and he could've been that way, too, but he wasn't."

I wondered what that was worth—the gratitude of a two-timing fink.

"Totally. Uh-huh. Maybe I was lucky, because he's like older, more experienced, and way laid-back and all. But your first is always special, ask anybody, even if he's like this grodie skeezer, and once you've had yours, you'll completely know what I mean. Which reminds me . . ." Neecey's voice faded, and I couldn't hear her. She had a habit of walking in and out of the kitchen while she was on the phone, twisting herself in circles so that the cord wrapped around her waist, which was probably what she was doing.

After a few seconds, she was back in the kitchen. "Hook up tonight?" she laughed. "Who? You? Cynthia Murdock? Hook up? Ohmigod, you are *so* full of shit. With who?" I could hear Neecey screaming "eeiew" and "no" and giggling like a Munchkin from the living room. "Aw, c'mon, honey, I'm just busting on you. If you think he's cute, then you should totally go for it, and I'll still love you, no matter what. Just remember, guys don't understand 'no' unless you say it like fifteen times and totally shove them around when you do."

Gratitude for Gary, undying love for Cynthia—was there anyone outside our family that Neecey didn't care about *more* than she cared about us?

"I was like *completely* skeeved, Cyn; ohmigod, you don't *even* know. Nuh-uh, not the foggiest. But it's like, who can really say what's going on in somebody else's head, right? Especially a helmet head like his. Yeah, he *so* totally does, but I'm sure he wouldn't know it, not even if someone took the time to like explain it to him."

I wondered if she was talking about Razor, or someone else. Then Neecey said "all kinds of thorny" or "horny" and then "last night" or "the other night," but I couldn't be sure about any of it, because she'd walked into the living room again. But that figured. The only part of the conversation I wanted to listen to and I couldn't hear it.

Thrash suggested that I get a little closer, so I edged up the wall until my head was just under the window and craned my neck to hear better. It didn't really help, but at least I wasn't just sitting on my ass in a puddle of my own sweat doing nothing anymore. Neecey was well into the living room and her voice was low, so I couldn't catch anything, and then it was quiet, as if she were listening to Cynthia— or something else.

For a second I thought maybe Neecey had heard me and I was about to slide down the wall again, when she came back into the kitchen. I froze where I was and tried to breathe as little and as quietly as I could.

"Yeah, I totally wish they'd quit, too, before they go any further and get completely busted. I know. Then what would we do? No, it's not the worst thing in the world, I guess. But there are like so many other ways to get your kicks."

It sounded like she was talking about Darren and the crew, and either the tags they dropped or the weed they smoked.

"Did I get the stuff? C'mon, Cyn, you *know* I got *the stuff*. Darren would have a total seizure if I didn't. He'd be all, 'Dude'"—Neecey made her voice gravelly and slow—"'this is so not a righteous party without the stuff.' Omigod," Neecey laughed, "I'd be *so* cut off."

I had to admit it, she did a pretty good impersonation of Darren. But what it seemed to mean sent air-raid sirens off in my head.

"Not a clue, I don't think," she went on. "But I'm still kind of worried. He can be a serious brainiac when he's not going all Cujo and everything. Ohmigod, don't *say* that. You've never seen him go off, but I have, so like trust me, okay? Total fucking shitstorm."

If I *had* to guess, I'd say that Neecey could've been talking about me.

"What-ev. Let's talk about it when I come over. I want to outtie before he gets home."

Bingo.

"Me? No. I totally know how to handle him. It's just he's been act-ing all suspicious and slick lately and I so don't want to be around him when he's like that because, sooner or later, it's like this switch goes off and he totally loses his shit. No, why? *Follow me?* C'mon, Cyn, get real. Even if he tried to, *he'd have to be home before dark.*"

Neecey cackled at her own cheap shot. And suddenly, putting a tail on her didn't seem like a half-bad idea.

"Pool? Hel-lo? Have you looked outside? The weather's totally beat. Oh, I know! Maybe we can go tanning. C'mon, Cyn, wha-dayasay? Please? Cynnie-Cyn-Cyn? Yea! Cool. Around eight, so we can deliver the stuff and help set up—you know how the guys are. I don't know. I'll wear something of yours. All right, love you, too, cutie. Kisses, bye."

Neecey hung up the phone, closed the back door, shut and locked the kitchen window, and went upstairs. And I just slid down the wall onto my butt again to let it all sink in.

FOURTEEN

I'd always heard there were moments in life when things you didn't understand suddenly lined up and came together— all the different pieces gravitated mysteriously into place like the last few Cheerios at the bottom of the cereal bowl—and then, *bam,* everything that confused you made sense, the lights came on, the fog lifted, you could see things for what they were, and everything was clear and easy to grasp and almost too goddamn simple to believe. After Neecey had left and I'd gone back up to my room, it struck me that what I'd experienced beneath the kitchen-sink window was definitely *not* one of those moments. If I'd learned anything new from overhearing Neecey's conversation with Cynthia, it wasn't all that much, and what little I'd learned didn't seem very different from the little I'd known before.

It *was* different, though; e*verything* was different. And as I began to hash it all out, I realized it was a hell of a lot worse than I'd ever imagined. I'd already known that Neecey had changed—her behavior, her choice of friends, her absence from home, her sniveling stool pigeon complicity with mom. But what I hadn't known was that

181

she'd changed *because of Darren.* Not only had she acted as his mes-
senger after he'd stolen my bike, but now she also did what he told
her to do, so he wouldn't "cut her off." It gave me an empty, gnawing
feeling in the pit of my stomach because I knew Marlowe had
already seen the same damn thing in *Farewell, My Lovely:* in between
real and false sightings of the mountainous Moose Malloy and getting sapped in the back of the head like four or five times, Marlowe
had found Marriott's killer by delving into the shadowy realms of
juju, tea, American hashish, marijuana—"the stuff." And, as was
almost always the case for some screwed-up head case of a gorgeous
chick in Marlowe's investigations, it was a trail that ended in tears.

Yeah, I knew the whole damn story like the back of my own hand,
and I should've seen it coming from the very first play. Fucking Darren had lured Neecey away from Gary to draw her into his sordid
world of drugs and crime. She was probably hooked by now, close to
full-blown addiction, and because Darren had gotten her pinned so
tightly under his thumb, he'd started using her as a mule. I was
so pissed off at Neecey that I wanted to drag her up and down the
stairs by her hair and beat some fucking sense back into her. But she
was still my sister, and she must've been strung out something awful
to let herself get used like that. Shit, she probably spent most of her
time wandering around in a drug-induced stupor, drinking beer in
the mornings to dull the edge and lighting up again at night, being
forced to run packages for a scummy dope lord, and maybe being
forced to do other things, too.

I fought to stay calm. I sat Thrash on my desk chair and noticed
how different his face looked now. His eyes were fixed and glistening, his smile was fiendish and determined, and although his tongue
just hung there like it always did, it almost looked like he was licking
his lips. I felt it, too; I was finally on the right track. I took my key
chain out of my pocket, unlocked the side drawer of my desk, took
out my journal, and flipped through the pages. There it was: Darren
had said that he'd been with *most* of the crew on Saturday night at

the church, meaning that some of the other members had been *somewhere else*.

I felt unsteady, so I sat down on the edge of my bed with my journal in my lap. I knew it was only a matter of time before we'd lose Neecey completely to the ruinous clutches of the underworld, and it was up to me to bring her back. My head shook side to side as I heaved a long, heavy sigh. I couldn't help it. I felt bad for Neecey and really down about where she was headed. I realized she must've been reading my journal to find out what I knew about the case so she could keep Darren a step ahead of my investigation and make sure that it never got off the ground. Yeah, that was totally fucking pathetic, but that was just a sign of how far it'd gone, what she'd been reduced to.

I had to keep reminding myself that that wasn't my sister—it was the drugs. And as bad as that was, and it was pretty goddamn bad, the same exact thing could happen to just about anyone who didn't say no the first time and every time, or who didn't know when to say when was when. Shit, it'd happened to Sherlock Holmes—he went on long cocaine binges, closed all the curtains at 221B Baker Street, shot himself up with a seven percent solution of the white, and freaked out for days on his violin. No, that wasn't any kind of way for a man of his substance to live, but in a way, it'd happened to Marlowe, too. Christ, now that I thought about it, Marlowe spent so much time with a bottle that sometimes you'd think he was still teething.

Whatever. Everybody knew there was nothing rougher or harder to stomach than being a detective. Most of the time you just wound up finding out the most goddamn terrible things, things you'd never wanted to think or know about in the first place. But it came with the territory, that was the job, and now that I was a detective, I'd have to start getting used to it, too. My only hope was that it wasn't too late for Neecey, that there was something left of her to save, that dickless Darren hadn't already turned her all the way into a junkie slut.

The rain finally came in the late afternoon, exploding from the sky like a downward stream. Fat blasts of lightning dazzled the blackened clouds, a low mean thunder rumbled through town like herds of rhinos stampeding across sheet metal, and the raindrops themselves were so big and solid and round that they bounced like marbles off the street. The wind whipped and gusted for hours on end, gutters flooded, trees swayed and groaned, and I was confined to indoors for the rest of the day.

But that was fine by me because I needed every minute to come up with a plan. Neecey had let it slip that she and Cynthia were going somewhere around eight tonight to deliver the stuff and set up, and that they wanted to look hot when they got there. That meant a party, and since Darren had told me that his parents were out of town this week, the party would most likely be at his place, on the reservoir. So what I had to do wasn't exactly the same as putting a tail on Neecey, it was more like beating her to the spot and cutting her off at the pass.

Not like it was going to be some kind of cakewalk either. The fastest way to Darren's lair was to take the trail at the southeast corner of the mall parking lot, which led uphill to a barbed-wire fence that separated mall property from the big, undeveloped chunk of woods on the western edge of the reservoir. Once I got through the woods, I'd have to hang a right and walk along the banks until I got to Darren's, then stealth up through the trees and bushes in his backyard until I got close enough to his house, find a good place to conceal myself (maybe in the shrubs near the pool), stake the joint out, wait for the right moment, grab hold of Neecey, and drag her out of there, kicking and screaming if I had to.

The hard part would be getting her alone at a high-school party, because she'd be mingling, talking, drinking, dancing, or whatever else, and I didn't want to draw attention to myself, because I wasn't invited, and there'd be at least a couple people there who meant me nothing but harm and might take my crashing their party as an opportunity to give me some. Plus, I'd be out of my territory, out-manned, outnumbered, and if everything hung together the way I thought it would, there was a good chance that I could run up against the kind of high-school football players who were nasty and violent and known for dangling smaller kids by their ankles, just so they could laugh when their faces turned red and then gave them black eyes and bruised ribs by way of thanks for the entertainment.

No doubt about it, the situation was gonna be fraught with all manner of peril, but I knew I could do it if I had the right plan. And I already knew I'd have a few things working in my favor. The first was the element of surprise. Nobody in the entire world would ever expect me to crash a kegger on a Wednesday night. Not Neecey, not Darren, not nobody. Second, I'd had plenty of practice hiding where no one could see me, laying low, keeping quiet, and just watching things unfold, thanks to Manning the Lookout, and I had more than enough guidance on how to run a stakeout from the detective books I'd read. When Marlowe went on a stakeout or cased a joint, he walked you through it, step-by-step, like the layout of the place, where he hid and why, how to get a good view of things, or how to open a door latch or window lock with a penknife, or how to circle back to make sure you weren't being followed, and all the rest. The pointers I needed from him weren't all in one place, though, but spread out across his books, so I spent a couple of hours combing through each of Marlowe's cases, finding what was helpful, taking notes, and studying up to get myself as ready for any and everything as I possibly could.

And then there was the last thing I had working in my favor. I could go off. The fuse was fast and the package small, but the blast-radius was enormous. All I had to do was guide and control it. No, it probably wasn't enough to take on two high-school football players *and* seven graffiti-dropping stoners and tap-dance on all of their noses, but it might just be enough to get Neecey and me out of a tight scrape. That was, if it even came to that. I might not be able to get her alone or creep up close enough to snatch her out of there, and I had no intention of throwing myself into a meat grinder if she and I weren't guaranteed of coming out clean and whole on the other end.

No, the most important thing was to keep a watch on her—what she did, how she did it, who she talked to, whether anything changed hands between her and someone else—because if I didn't get my chance and couldn't get through to her tonight, then I wanted to have as much detail as possible when I handed the evidence over to mom tomorrow. Yeah, it would suck all ass to have to drop dime on my own older sister, but this was serious, and I guessed there were times when you just *had* to rat, to serve the greater good.

So that was my plan. And it was a pretty good one—simple, straightforward, and not as risky as it could've been. All I really had to do was get where I was going and control myself. Not because grandma had made me promise to, but because the case itself had left me no choice.

What I needed now was something to wear. I couldn't go with the white shorts and light blue T-shirt I had on, because I wouldn't be able to sneak up on a blind kid if I looked like the Boo-Berry Ghost flitting hauntingly through the night. But I had something else in mind. For Halloween last year I'd gone as a ninja assassin, and I still had the black drawstring pants and matching long-sleeved shirt hanging in the back of my closet. I got some scissors and cut the pants just under the knees to long shorts (it was summer after all), but I cut the sleeves to one-quarter length for a different reason. With all the push-ups and pull-ups I'd been doing, my arms had gotten knotty and hard, and it wasn't a bad idea to dangle them for whoever I might bump into, and maybe flex them a little for them to see, so they'd realize that I was not only crazy enough, which everybody already knew, but now also strong enough to do some serious fucking damage. I needed every edge I could get, and brandishing the guns during a standoff might be one of them.

All right, so the guns were .22's and not .45's, but there was nothing I could do about that, and I'd need to sport them anyway, because tonight I'd be all on my own. I'd be running, climbing, slinking, scurrying—maybe even rappelling, shit, who knew—and with all that constant movement, I couldn't afford to weigh myself down with any excess bulk, or allow the rustle of a backpack to broadcast my every change of direction. I had to go in clean, slick, unencumbered, and that meant Thrash had to stay home. I didn't know how to break it to him, but I knew it wouldn't be easy. He lived for shit like this.

Thrash wouldn't be the only one taking the night off. If I could get to Neecey and pull her out of there, the Cruiser would really come in handy in helping us make swift tracks. Only thing was, there was nowhere to park it while I'd be trying to fetch her. There was no way in hell I could leave the Cruiser in the mall parking lot unattended at night, not even for a few minutes, let alone a couple of hours, and the fence around the reservoir was like the Bermuda Triangle of bikes— sure, you could take one in there and lock it up to the post, but that's the last you'd ever see of it. No, whatever happened, I couldn't take a chance on losing the Cruiser, so tonight it would be the shoe leather express or nothing. That way, if I ever made it back to this place, there'd be at least one thing worth coming back to.

Downstairs in the toolbox there was a tiny screwdriver, the kind used for fixing eyeglasses, which I rummaged for and pulled out. It was just long and thin enough to jimmy a window latch between the panes or to depress the catch of a locked doorknob, and I might have to do one or the other or both, so it was coming with me. We also had a pocket flashlight, really more of a penlight, and I got fresh AA batteries from the refrigerator, put them in, and made sure the penlight worked, because you never knew when you'd need to see something in the dark.

I went upstairs to the hall closet, where we kept the towels and some of the outdoor stuff, and got the travel-sized bug spray. I'd be by the water, near the woods, not too long after dusk; it had rained a lot today, and it was still August, so that meant mosquitoes, probably swarms of them. I put everything in my pockets—the tiny screwdriver, the penlight, the bug spray—and found that the ten-dollar bill mom had left on the kitchen counter for pizza had somehow gotten in there.

I didn't remember taking it, but I put it in the top drawer of my desk with the other one. Yeah, I'd doubled my loot, but I'd also doubled my duty—the safety of grandma and Neecey depended on me earning every single cent in that drawer, all on my own, without any aid or help. But that's what being a detective was all about. I turned and searched the back of my closet for the sneakers mom had bought me a few months ago, the ones I'd hidden away and hoped we'd both forget about. They were the worst knock-off indoor soccer shoes you'd ever seen, so cheap and crappy that they looked like they'd come from a sale of irregular goods at the ninety-nine-cent store. I'd had no intention of ever wearing them, because you had to draw the line somewhere. But they were black, and with black sneakers, black shorts, and a black shirt I'd be so perfectly camouflaged for a night by the woods that I wouldn't even be able to see myself. So I laced them up.

Now came the hard part. Thrash was in my desk chair as usual, while I was sitting on the bed. I stood up and switched places with him. I didn't know why, it just seemed like the thing to do. I propped him up on the bed pillows and took a seat in the chair, staring down at my ankles and the laces on my sneakers. This was a big moment for us. I exhaled and raised my head to look at him. His eyes were small and beady, his smile was bitter and hostile, and with the way his skinny green arms were folded across his round yellow belly, he kind of resembled a gargoyle, or a demon.

"You can't just wish me good luck, right?" I said.

Thrash was quiet. I didn't like the sound of that. A thin line of sweat broke out on my forehead.

"C'mon, no final words of advice?" Nothing. I rubbed my hands back and forth on my knees; my heart swelled and shrank. Still nothing. He was giving me the silent treatment—my punishment for leaving him behind. Of all the things I hated, he knew I hated that the most.

"Fucking *say* something."

I waited. Thrash's eyes were fixed, immobile, as if he were looking beyond or through me. I started shaking and sweating, and I suddenly felt like tearing his little green ass to littler green shreds. But I didn't have the time to spare. My neck felt heavy and stiff. I couldn't take it anymore.

"Eat shit," I said. I stood up, grabbed Thrash by the shoulders, whipped him around, and slammed him facedown into the pillows.

That didn't take as long as I'd thought, but it was somehow worse than I'd expected. I stumbled into the bathroom, turned on the water in the sink, and threw cold water on my face. My insides felt sticky and black. Nobody was on my side; nobody believed in me, nobody cared, not even Thrash.

I could've killed a couple more minutes, but I couldn't wait anymore. I went downstairs, checked all the window and door locks, and took the biggest and deepest breath I'd ever taken. Nah, I wasn't anywhere near being on the jazz like Hannibal from *The A-Team;* I was jumpy and jittery and just barely keeping it together. Calm. I had to stay calm. I exhaled, let it all out, shook the stiffness from my arms and legs, rolled my neck, cracked my knuckles, and set myself. It was time. Before I left, I took the kitchen phone off the hook, in case mom called from work, so she wouldn't be able to tell that I wasn't where I'd promised her I'd be.

I walked out the front door, said no good-byes, and didn't look back.

FIFTEEN

A watch would've been a good idea, to keep track of time and all. But I didn't own one and never wore one, so the thought hadn't crossed my mind. All I had was the heavens to let me know the hour, and that didn't work out so well because I'd gotten a later start than I'd expected, and by the time I'd crossed the Circle, trekked to the southeast corner of the deserted mall parking lot, and made it up the dirt trail that led to the fence, it was already good and dark.

It had turned out to be a warm, clear night with the kind of slight, pleasant breeze whispering through the treetops that gave you goose bumps after a day of pounding thunderstorms. A few dim stars were blinking to life in the violet-black sky, and on the other side of the fence, a solemn thicket of woods and underbrush was the only thing standing between the reservoir and me.

There was a syrupy overripe smell oozing through the air and the rotting remains of four abused bikes locked helplessly to the fencepost. I sized up the ten-foot barbed-wire fence in front of me; everything was spooky and still. I could still turn around, I thought, go back to my room, look Thrash in the eye and try to explain to him how I'd punked out, report to grandma tomorrow that the case was too much for me and give the money back, wash my hands of Neecey as she became the black sheep of the family for a change, and then bitch and moan about it in my journal for everyone else in the house and the goddamn world to read. Or I could climb that fence, land on the ground with both feet, take none of the paths diverging in the woods because there weren't any, forge my own, and let the chips scatter and fall wherever they goddamn felt like it. Because once I'd passed this point, there'd be no turning back.

I clawed my way up the fence until I was near the top, then stretched one arm after the other over the three rows of barbed wire and clung tight to the top pole. I did what amounted to a dip up so my torso wouldn't get snagged or cut, and flung my legs up and over to the right like a gymnast—swinging them upward, bending at the waist, twisting over the barbs, readjusting my hands in midair—but as soon as my feet hit the other side of the fence, they didn't catch the links, but slipped straight down. I lost my grip, fell backward, landed with a soft splash of mud on my ankles and shins, and directly onto my butt, which instantly felt cold and wet.

I realized pretty much immediately that I hadn't put on underwear when I'd changed my clothes earlier, and I was not happy about the discovery. It wasn't like me to forget something as important as that, but it gave me an idea. If I ever got out of this, I'd start a new, top-secret journal, which I'd keep in a booby-trapped safe, and I'd compile my own list of pointers or rules that other detectives never told you. And my first rule would be: If you were going out to the woods in homemade ninja shorts after a day of hard rain, you *always* had to wear underwear, just in case you fell on your butt, because having to deal with swamp ass for the rest of the night totally sucked. That was a solid first principle—*Keep your ass dry*—and I wished I'd thought of it earlier, because it didn't do me a damn bit of good now.

But I'd made it up the trail, over the fence, and into the woods, and from this point on it was all downhill. The hillside wasn't too steep, but the ground sloped and rolled all the way from here to the reservoir bed, and if it weren't for the jungle of vegetation before me, it would've made for a nice, easy stroll. I couldn't even pretend to know what half the crap was called, because Thoreau was the naturalist, not me. But it didn't matter. I was going through anyway.

I took the penlight out of my pocket, turned it on, and probably would've laughed out loud if I hadn't needed it to be slightly more effective. The light was pale and weak and sputtering, and if the rays stretched a foot, then they stretched twenty-three miles. I'd been counting on that light to help me find my way, or at least to keep me from tangling my feet up and falling on my face. Fuck.

Well, at least I knew the direction I needed to go, diagonally southeast. I put my back to the mall so I was facing south, turned my shoulders forty-five degrees to the left to point myself southeast, and set off. My feet squished on wet earth and leaves with every step as I groped my way through the damp, furry darkness. Up ahead, the green-yellow glow of fireflies flared and darted through the trees like small, swirling eyes. The sudden wing-flap of a bird sounded somewhere in the branches above. I kept walking. The shushing of the breeze was muted and eerie, like the signal for an ambush. I froze. I felt watched, surrounded, as if I were being followed on all flanks and flushed into a trap. I knew it was just my imagination, but I couldn't shake the feeling that something hungry and sinister was awaiting me in the shadows. I breathed quietly, turned slowly, and saw all around me exactly what I'd expected to see—nothing. I exhaled and wiped the sweat off my face.

I tried to speed up, following the downward slope of the ground, plowing forward as quickly as I could through the thick maze of blackened trunks and undergrowth. My eyes had adjusted; I could see a dense grove of trees choked with bushes up ahead. When I reached it, I plunged my hands into the weave of branches like I was parting a crunchy curtain and wiggled my way through, as twigs snapped and needled my skin. It felt like I was going through the rollers in a car wash. But I pressed forward, and when I pushed through to the other side of the grove, I was covered head to toe with dewy rain, and the trees and shrubbery spread apart and the ground leveled out completely, so that the forest floor was flat in every direction.

All of a sudden I felt lost, but I kept going. After another fifteen paces or so the ground started to rise upward, which meant I was definitely heading in the wrong direction, because the reservoir was at the *bottom* of the hillside. I turned around and went back the way I'd come, or so I thought, but I must've veered off course a bit, because the grove I'd just pushed through was gone.

Without that landmark I couldn't tell which way I'd come in or how to get out. I stood there wet and nervous. I felt stuck. I wanted out, fast, and I knew I had to get moving, because the longer I stood there, the more nervous I'd get, until I couldn't move at all. I started walking; I didn't care which direction. I kept hiking over knotted, uneven terrain for what seemed like miles, until I came across a small clearing with a bumpy rock in it and decided to sit down. The rock was large, mossy, and slick, but my ass was wet anyway, so I took a seat. A bright half-moon was just visible through the parted treetops, and it shone down on me like the smile of the Cheshire cat.

A mob of crickets chirped back and forth all around me in the darkness. In different circumstances, I probably wouldn't have noticed them or paid them any mind. But I was trying to get my thoughts together and decide what to do next, and the noise was throwing me off. It seemed to grow louder and louder as I sat there—*reet, reet, reet*—like the knife thrusts during the shower scene in *Psycho*. I breathed deeply and tried to shake it off. I knew something as little as that shouldn't have bothered me, but it did, and it made me think of Thrash. The woods were his world, his niche, and many species of frog either hunted or mated nocturnally, so he probably could've gotten me where I needed to go, no problem at all, plus rustled up a snack of some sort, and maybe a slippery frog chick for me to cuddle up to, if that's what I wanted. Yeah, I could've used him now, and I was totally sorry I'd left him at home.

But I also thought of Thoreau, and how he could walk from town back to Walden in the dark, letting his feet and other senses guide him, while anybody else who tried the same wound up stranded in the middle of nowhere, just like me. Thrash, Thoreau, it didn't really matter, though. What I needed was a glow-in-the-dark compass, a scout, or a guide, like that poet that Orlando had told me about— what the hell was his name?—who was born on my birthday.

Shit. Getting to the party was supposed to be the *easy* part of my plan. I leaned over, rested my head in my hands, and tried to think. I needed to concentrate, figure out what the hell I was doing and which way to go, but the crickets were making such a goddamn racket that I couldn't. For a second, I pictured Thrash gobbling those pests like popcorn shrimp in barbecue sauce, but that didn't scare them off. I covered my ears and tried to focus again. My chin dropped to my chest. I felt completely down on myself, like I'd made a serious mistake, maybe a fatal one, and that I honestly might not get out of this, when I noticed that the crickets had gone quiet.

There was a faint sound, kind of like running water, just over my shoulder to the right. I stood up and ran toward it. Suddenly, a square, manicured hedge sprang up a few yards ahead of me and was coming on fast. But the ground was muddy and I had on shitty sneakers—no brakes and no time to put them on anyway—so by the time I thought to stop, I couldn't. My shins, arms, and face were whipped, stung, and cut up by the branches I hit on the way through, but at least I managed to tumble into a dive roll on the other side and come up on my feet. I shook off the dousing I'd gotten from the bushes, checked to make sure I still had everything in my pockets, and took a glance around to figure out where the hell I was.

The yard was enormous, bordered on both sides by hedges and trees, and flooded with half-moon light. Like most of the waterfront properties around the reservoir, the backyard was about thirty-five yards wide and maybe two hundred and fifty to three hundred yards long, sloping up from the water to whatever two-, three-, or four-story pile was overlooking it from the front. About fifteen yards to my right, the grass rose slightly and then burst up into large, irregular-shaped rocks, which leveled out to a small, natural-looking deck made of slate and pebbled concrete that blended seamlessly into the rippling surface of a kidney-shaped pool, which was lit from below by underwater lights. As the pool curved at the back, there were short all-weather palm trees and an exotic mound of earth, rock, and colorful flowers that rose gradually over the far edge of the water, kind of the way an oven range hooked over a stove. And from the creases in the rocks at the top of that mound, sheets of water cascaded down to the pool below, creating a nook or grotto about eight feet wide and eight feet deep.

I guess that was the running water I'd heard. But I knew that pool, just like I knew the first story of the house to my right was this concrete, steel, and high-glass affair that jutted out maybe twenty feet over the lawn beneath it, four or five feet aboveground, without struts or supports, so it hovered there like a weightless rectangle. It had massive glass walls and sliding doors that opened onto winding slate slabs acting as stairs, but which had no handrails or casings, so they looked like they were suspended in midair, and which drifted slowly down to the slate-and-pebble walkway that led through the grass to the pool. I also knew that inside there were four or five low, square-shaped chairs upholstered in this grainy fabric—some red, some white, others black—a tan sofa of the same style, hardwood floors, amoeba throw rugs, glass tables with thin metal frames, a few high-tech bookshelves and lamp stands, and these dark, almost dagger-shaped African masks hanging on the inner concrete wall. I knew all that because I'd been here before. Just that once, but it wasn't the sort of place you'd forget.

I was in Orlando's backyard, and I felt an overwhelming sense of relief at knowing where I was. But it didn't last long: just as instantly I felt this desperate urge to run over to that oversized aquarium and pound on the glass until Orlando came swimming down. But it didn't look like anybody was home, and he wasn't allowed to talk to me anyway, even if he'd wanted to.

In a couple more months it'd be three years since Orlando had given me *Walden,* and in all that time I'd never had a chance to talk to him about it. Nobody had ever given me a book before that, not even grandma yet, but I was excited as all hell to get a birthday present and couldn't wait to read it, which I did right away.

It sucked. Like I said, the book was hard and didn't have a plot, and at first it seemed as if the whole thing was nothing more than some uppity egghead spouting off about what he thought was essential for life, offering his opinions on every goddamn thing, as if anybody else could be paid to give a shit what he said. Not exactly a page-turner. In fact, it bored me so far off my ass every time I picked it up that I would've rather gone to the dentist and had my teeth drilled without novocaine than bother with the rest. But I didn't want to tell Orlando that, because he'd said it was one of his favorites, and I was worried he wouldn't want to be friends anymore when he realized I didn't like it or understand it.

I didn't know what to do. But when he asked me about it at school, I said I hadn't had time to read it because of junior peewee practice and homework and stuff, although I'd always finished my assignments in class and never had a minute of homework in my life. Yeah, I lied to his face to cover for myself, and I did it more than once, and each time I did, I knew it was a totally shitty thing to do to a friend. He seemed to buy it, though, and let it drop until football season ended. But he started up again in mid-November, asking me if I'd read it and if I liked it and what I thought and all these other questions, and I told him we should talk about it after Thanksgiving break, because I was still just getting into it.

That bought me more time, but after Thanksgiving break I stalled him again, and it wasn't until months later, after I'd read most of the detective books, that I'd finally tried *Walden* again and had better luck. But by then it was too late. I'd already clobbered Ms. Wither-spoon, got suspended, and been banned from speaking to Orlando about the book or anything else.

I'd always felt bad about that, really bad, and I still did. Since my suspension, I'd read the book closely, over and over, and made dozens of trips to the library to learn as much about Thoreau as I could. Shit, I probably knew enough about Thoreau to fill twenty book reports by now, but mostly it just seemed like wasted effort: I still wasn't a hundred percent sure what *Walden* was about, and I still had that feel-ing—like Orlando had given me a gift, and I'd given him the finger.

But Orlando was no dummy, and if he'd figured out what I'd done, then I didn't know how the hell I'd patch it up with him. I guess I was banking on getting my chance at the first official football practice: he'd get all stuttered up trying to explain what'd happened at tryouts, and I'd cut him off all cool and shit, and tell him I knew he never would've pasted me like that if Razor hadn't put him over a barrel, that it just wasn't like him, and that I'd figured it all out and didn't blame him and still wanted to be friends. And the more I thought about it, the more I realized a hell of a lot more was riding on the case than I'd expected. It wasn't just to stick up for grandma and the other old-timers, or to save Neecey from the danger she'd put herself in through her own idiot choices, as if that weren't enough. No, it was to clear Orlando's name, too, and it was my job to come through for all of us.

I was wet, cut up, covered in mud, and for some reason shivering, and while only a few minutes could've passed, it seemed as if I'd been loitering in Orlando's backyard for a long time now with nothing to show for it. But I'd gotten the grip on myself that I needed, so I was okay with the delay and the misdemeanor. I still didn't know what time it was, but I knew where to find the reservoir—just a couple hundred yards away, down the gently sloping grass to my left.

SIXTEEN

At the bottom of the hill the ground dropped another four or five feet straight down, just before the banks of the lake bed. On my right, there were wooden steps leading from Orlando's back-yard to the shoreline, but I positioned myself at the edge of the drop and jumped. My feet made a muffled slap as I landed and the backs of my heels sank an inch or so into dense, wet ground.

Everything was quiet on the shore; even the tiny ripples licking the grit and pebbles at my feet hardly made a sound. The breeze was much higher in the canopy now, so the air down here was moist and perfectly still, just like the water, and the reservoir stretched out smooth and sparkling before me like a small captured sky. I'd never seen the reservoir at night before, and the play of moon and starlight flickering on the surface made it seem larger than it was in the day-time, as if there were somehow more to see in the dark.

But there wasn't. There wasn't anything vast or mysterious about it, and it wasn't the small captured sky that it appeared to be, or the earth's eye, like Thoreau said. In fact, it wasn't even a reservoir. I'd looked it up. A reservoir was a man-made lake, or a deposit of fresh potable water (I'd looked up *potable,* too), which was used to serve the purposes of a community. But this wasn't either of those, because it wasn't man-made, and it wasn't potable because the salt minerals in the water made it unfit to drink. So, when you got right to it, it wasn't a reservoir at all. It was just a large pond or a small lake encircled by big hilly lawns with pricey houses at the top.

It hit me that Thoreau might've cared about that, because he was a stickler for words and names and stuff, and he'd put a lot of effort into figuring out why the pond was called Walden while he was there. I knew people used the wrong names for things all the time because they were too stupid to know better or just said what everybody else said or really didn't give a shit one way or the other. Not a major news flash. But I somehow got the feeling that if Thoreau had been from these parts instead of Concord, Massachusetts, he never would've tried to investigate the names or nature of things or to live deep and suck the marrow out of life, not here anyway, because all he would've been left with was a salty taste in his mouth and not a damn thing to write about. No, if he were with me now and saw this place today, Thoreau wouldn't conduct any experiments or build any cabins or plant any bean fields, but run the other way as fast as he could and never look back. Because today the reservoir was just like the kids who lived by it—spoiled through and through.

But it was still water, and because I was sweaty and dirty, my skin was mud-caked and rank, my clothes were filthy, my ass was damp and itchy, there was only one answer for all of it: I was going in.

I took off my clothes and sneakers, laid them on a rock, and dove into the reservoir's warm black water. My cuts stung a little as I went underneath, but they were getting cleaned out and the pain didn't last long. I hit a few chilly spots as the water got deeper and had the taste of salt and silt in my mouth. When I came up, I breaststroked for a while, gliding silently along the surface toward the center, then I turned onto my back and pedaled my feet. I was out alone after dark, far later than I was allowed to be or had ever been before, skinny-dipping off somebody else's property under the clearest of star- and moonlit skies. I had a case to crack, a sibling to save, and maybe some demons to wrestle, but there was nothing and nobody on my back for a change. And if anybody wanted to say that was wrong, then they could go ahead and say it, because it sure as hell didn't feel wrong to me.

I swam back to the shore, and as I rose up out of the reservoir, I felt water rushing down my skin, mud squishing between my toes, and saw the black-on-black shadow of myself breaking up in ripples. I went over to the rock, got dressed, and reapplied the bug spray. I couldn't find the screwdriver or the penlight, so I wrote them off. I teased my hair in case there was any gel left in it, and took a quick inventory: me, my cut-off ninja shorts and sleeveless shirt, house keys, bug spray, a mission to complete, a plan to complete it, and about damn time that I did it. That was all I had and all I needed. I was a detective on a case; nothing else mattered.

With the reservoir on my left, the banks on my right, the half-moon and its reflection brightening my way, getting to Darren's couldn't have been easier. The shore itself was a mixture of sand, fine pebbles, and mud that dampened the sound of my footsteps; the downward drop at the bank's edge provided cover from the houses up the lawns to my right; and the bug spray protected me from the few clouds of mosquitoes lingering here and there, hoping for a late-night snack.

I was flying solo through the darkness—sleek, undercover, low to the ground—just like I'd thought I would, which meant at least some of this was going exactly to plan, *my* plan. Now I only had to get to Darren's property, come up through the bushes and trees in his back-yard, find a good place to conceal myself, maybe in the evergreens and flower bushes by the pool, watch undetected for the right moment, get the drop on Neecey, and save the day.

A tall, rectangular hedgerow vaulted up from the edge of the drop-off on my right and marched in a thick rigid column up the grassy slope, while a finger of bushy shoreline poked ten or fifteen yards into the reservoir to my left. I'd finally reached the edge of Darren's property. I crept along the bushes and shrubs sprouting on the peninsula, staying low, keeping quiet, and wishing I knew more about nighttime sounds. The breeze was still high up in the treetops, swishing away; there were some crickets too, but further off so they weren't a menace; there were mournful twitters of what could've been sparrows or ravens or bats; the faint lapping of the reservoir shifting in its bed; a few spiked voices and the barely audible throb of a bass line wafting down from the party; the distant squelch of a frog or two; and this other sound that went *plunk,* then *slap,* very softly from somewhere around the bend. All the other sounds were more or less accounted for, but I didn't recognize that last one and had to make my mind up about it fast, because I was heading that way, and *had* to go that way, because I'd left myself no other route to carry out my plan. And if I was doing anything at this point, I was sticking to my plan.

I stopped where I was, squatted on my haunches, pricked up my ears, and listened again. There it was, but this time it was more of a *plip* than a *plunk,* followed by *slap-slap.* It wasn't coming from the dock at the bottom of Darren's property, because although the dock was made of wood planks, it was solid and moored, and there wasn't enough movement in the reservoir for the water to rise up and touch it. It could've been a small boat tied to the dock, but I didn't know if Darren even had one, and if he did, it would make more of a *tunk* or *thud* than a *plip,* so that wasn't it either. Besides, that wouldn't explain the *slap* sound. So my best guess was a fish: a tiny fish jumping or thrashing around in the shallows as it swam, or maybe a bigger fish that had accidentally beached itself and was flopping around, struggling to get free.

I heard the slaps again, with no *plunk* or *plip* this time. Yeah, a fish, definitely—that was its tail smacking against the shore as it tried to save itself from suffocating. What kind of fish could it be, though, if the reservoir had traces of salt in it? Jesus, I sure as hell didn't know the answer to that. What if it was something else? Christ. It was a fish, that's all there was to it, a hearty fish, something that was tough enough to live and breathe almost anywhere, ate whatever the hell it happened to find, and was making that sound again now—*slap, plip, slap.* Fuck it. I was gonna turn that corner, walk down the peninsula, find the fish, and throw it back so it would live to see a better day. I stood up. I was going. It was only a fish, or an eel, or a poisonous water snake—*aw, fuck!* Screw it. I had to go. I turned the corner anyway.

I saw what it was and stopped dead in my tracks.

It wasn't a fish, or an eel, or a snake. It was a *girl.* A girl maybe fifteen yards away wearing what looked like flat open-toed sandals or flip-flops; a few rubber and sparkly anklets at the bottommost V of each calf; a short, tight patterned skirt of either stretchy cotton or some other clingy material; a tube top and a button-down blouse, the latter of which had the sleeves cut off, the collar up, and was open all the way but tied at the waist; and she was sitting on a big gray rock, hunched over with her arms stiff and straight, bracelets on her wrists, rings on her fingers, her palms pressed next to her knees, head down, black hair covering her face, surrounded by distant shadows and drenched in moonlight, as if she'd just stepped out of a dream, or a music video.

No, it sure as hell wasn't any scaly fish, slimy eel, or snake, although I would've been more relieved to find myself in a pit of water moccasins, alligators, crocodiles, and great white sharks at feeding time than to come across this. Because bumping into Stacy Sanders at night on the shores of the reservoir—the two of us all alone with the view, the dark, and ourselves—was definitely *not* part of my plan.

She must not have heard me, because she didn't look up, so I covered my mouth, tried to keep my eyes from popping out of my head, crept back around the bushes at the peninsula's tip as quickly and quietly as I could, squatted down again, and tried to catch my breath. I wouldn't call it panic, but my palms were sweating, my stomach was gone, I might've been hyperventilating, and my mouth felt like I'd just finished a seven-course meal of nothing but paste. Shit, this was terrible, truly fucking terrible. Well, seeing Stacy wasn't all that terrible, but what it meant for my plan was.

Thing was, the trees, shrubs, and bushes that I'd intended to use for cover as I snuck up Darren's backyard to the pool area were on the *opposite* side of the property from where I was freaking out now. In order to get there, I'd have to pass right in front of her, and there was no way in hell I could do it without her seeing me. *Shit*. Worse than that, if I tried to follow the hedgerow on this side and wriggle between its branches somewhere further up, I'd not only make a buttload of noise breaking through, but the ruckus I made would also announce my presence to any- and everyone within a good fifty yards in all directions, even with the music on. *Shit*.

It had *never once* occurred to me that someone might be down here by the water, blocking my way.

I had to stay calm. My head and stomach were reeling, I was having trouble breathing, and I would've licked the condensation off a garbage truck's exhaust pipe just to wet my whistle, but I had to stay *calm*. I had to come up with my next move and execute it. Right now my biggest problem was Stacy. What could I do about her? She was alone, so I could go in hard and fast, leaving no witnesses, and bump her off without so much as ever having said hello to her. Yeah, right, that plan *sucked*. What else? I could create a diversion, like throw a rock or something so she'd turn her head at the moment I slipped by. Maybe, but if I threw a rock into the water, it'd only make her lift her head up so she'd be looking right at me. I could throw one into the woods behind her, sure, but would the slight sound of something clicking in trees and bushes attract her attention long enough for me to jet past? I was fast, sure, but not that fast. No one was.

I was stuck. I realized that with Stacy blocking my path, I'd come to a dead end, but it struck me that I hadn't heard the *plip* or *plunk-slap* sound for a while. Maybe she'd just walked away; it was a party after all, and down here was far away from all the action. I crab-walked in the mud to the edge of the bushes, peeked my head around, and saw Stacy sitting on the rock, just like before, only she was bouncing her heels against it now, and taking a swig out of what looked like a glass soda bottle, but fatter at the neck. *Shit, shit, shit!* I crept back, squatted on my haunches, and heard the *ploop-slap-slap* sound again.

What the hell was she doing here? Okay, I got that one. Stacy might not have been the prettiest girl in town, but she had that *thing* and it was *hot*—scorching—and everybody knew it, and even though it was a high-school party and she was just going into junior high like I was, one of the older scavengers buzzing around her had probably asked her to go, and she'd said what she always said, which was "Okay," only he'd gone to do a keg-stand or a bong hit or some shit and left her alone and she'd wandered down here to be on her own, because she was like that.

Wait a minute—that was it! The word I'd heard Stacy say more than any other was *okay;* she was *always* saying it, no matter the situation. So if I just walked around the bushes, down the peninsula, over to where she was sitting, and said, *Hey, what up,* real deep-voiced and suave, nodding my chin at her, and then told her not to tell anyone she'd seen me as I went on my way, chances were she'd say *okay!* What else would she say? *Nuh-uh, that's your ass, dickhead, I'm telling everybody,* and scream? No, I couldn't see that happening, Stacy was too laid-back for that. So all I had to do was play it cool, act chill, take my time, and it might just work.

Then again, it might not. But I couldn't come up with anything else, and I sure as hell wasn't going to let a *girl* scare me off the case, or keep me from saving my sister. All I had to do was go over and *try* to talk to her for the very first time in my life, whether I wanted to or not, because there was no other choice. I cleaned my hands off in the reservoir, patted some water quietly on my face, straightened my clothes as best I could, tried to fix my hair, sighed heavily, gave up on it, and walked around the bushes so I could totally destroy any chance I'd ever have with Stacy. Nobody ever said being a detective was easy, and I was glad nobody ever said that, because this was the hardest thing I'd ever tried to do.

SEVENTEEN

On my way down the other side of the peninsula, I figured out the second rule for my new top-secret detective manual: never attempt to strut—you know, put a little swagger and tilt in your walk—if your legs are shaking uncontrollably. You shouldn't even *think* about trying it, because you'd just wind up lumbering through the night like Frankenstein or the Creature from the Black Lagoon toward the chick who drove you nuts, and the first time she lifted her head and caught sight of you, she'd flinch, jerk back, and tense up, ready to bolt, like a cat sprayed with a garden hose, and that was *not* the reaction you wanted when you were trying to make a cool entrance, or a good first impression. No, it sure as hell wasn't, but that's what happened, and there was nothing I could do about it, so I kept stiff-legging it toward her.

When I was about ten or so feet from the rock, Stacy whispered, "Genie?"

The sound of *my* name in *her* high, soft voice caused my heart to sizzle from my chest and burst in the nighttime sky like fireworks. There was only one problem—that wasn't my name anymore. But if

I'd learned anything from being surrounded by three females all my life, it was that chicks *never* liked to be contradicted, especially when they were wrong, so I whispered back, "Yeah?"

"Ohmigod," she sighed heavily. "It's Stacy, Stacy Sanders, from sixth grade? You like totally scared me for a second."

"Sorry, I didn't me-uh-ahn to." *No!* That squeaky, gasping sound could *not* have been my voice. I felt the blood rising in my face. I wanted to die.

"That's okay," she said.

It was okay; everything was *okay;* the sky lit up again. I was getting closer, and Stacy was still seated on the rock, the same way as before, but her head was up now and slightly tilted, like it usually was, and she was looking at *me,* with her black bangs hanging to one side while the rest of her face was lit by moonlight, her hazel eyes widening, her nose bunching, and smiling, so that the little gap between her front teeth showed like two slightly parted knees. *Liquefied* was probably the closest word for what I felt, and I stopped to catch my breath.

"You wanna sit down," Stacy whispered, still smiling, tilting her head, and slapping the rock with her left palm, "and keep me company?"

I could hardly believe it—she'd invited me into her bubble, *holy shit*—but that didn't mean it was part of my plan. I was supposed to walk by—cool, real cool—tell her not to tell anyone she'd seen me, and get on with it. On the other hand, I'd made a promise to grandma that I'd be a gentleman, and a gentleman always obliged.

"Okay," I said, in what was far closer to my normal voice. But my throat was so dry at this point that sooner or later it would split open and I'd bleed to death all over her.

"Cool," she peeped as she tossed a small pebble from a pile on her right into the reservoir *(plip),* and then swatted her legs three times in rapid succession *(slap, slap, slap).* "The mosquitoes are totally killer, though," she warned.

As I sat down on the rock next to Stacy, I felt the warmth of her next to my frantic limbs, the lumps in my pockets pressing against my thighs, and then I remembered.

"I have some bug spray," I said, and felt, for a second, as if I ruled the world.

"Ohmigod! You're like an Eagle Scout. That's so cool!"

No, I wasn't any goddamn Cub or Boy or Eagle Scout or fucking Weeblo either; I was a *detective on a case,* goddamn it, but I didn't want to blow my cover, so I tried to play it cool.

She took the cap off the bug spray and squirted it on her arms, neck, and collarbones, then *untied her shirt, took it off, and handed it to me,* so she was wearing nothing but her yellow tube top, and sprayed the rest of her shoulders and stomach. I looked at the stars, the half-moon, the water, the dock, the faraway trees on the other shore, the mud and pebbles well below our feet, but the only thing I saw was Stacy rubbing bug spray on her stomach. I almost wiped my drool with her shirt, blouse, or whatever it was, but I turned my head and used my wrist instead. Not like that made me any more composed when she bent forward and sprayed her feet and ankles, one at a time, going around the straps of her flip-flops and her anklets, then the front of her tanned shins, knees, and thighs, up to the edge of her too-short, too-tight, orange-and-yellow tie-dyed skirt.

I felt fluttery and warm, pressed my eyes shut to stem the giddiness in my head, and the next thing I knew I was on my feet, facing Darren's lawn, with my back turned to Stacy. I could've told myself that I'd stood up because I was still on the job and that I'd taken the opportunity to case the joint while she was occupied. But that would've been a lie. Maybe it was instinct that got me off that rock, or a reflex, like when the doctor tapped you in the knee with a rubber mallet and your leg jerked forward automatically, no matter how hard you tried to keep it from moving. Whatever it was, I'd put a couple of feet between us, wiped the sweat off my palms, steadied my breathing, and shifted my gaze toward the party.

With the way the ground sloped upward, the white-yellow glow from the back of Darren's home was visible maybe fifteen yards above my head but two hundred and fifty or more yards away. The music was a bit clearer now, because I heard some treble and guitar licks along with the bass (although I couldn't make out the song); there were sounds of splashing in the pool to the left, as well as shouts, hollers, and blips of elevated voices throughout; and the tiny backlit forms of maybe a hundred teenagers could be seen darting everywhere to and fro—dancing, standing, running, diving, tumbling, embracing.

"Hey, Genie," Stacy beckoned, snapping me out of it, "could you like put some bug spray on my back?"

She was facing me when I turned around, and her hazel eyes glowed above her cheeks like a lynx's in the night. Not that I'd ever seen one. She handed me the bug spray and our fingers touched, just for an instant, like a single brush of a hummingbird's wing. She turned around, and I exhaled shakily but deeply, getting it all out, pumping the bug spray dispenser with my index finger toward her upper back, and then wiping the burning metallic mist from the corner of my mouth. I should probably point it at *her*, I thought, and tried again. *Pshhht, pshhht,* it went across her shoulder blades as I held her white blouse in my left hand and tried to think of cold and distant places with no hot chicks in them, like Vermont or Maine. Somehow, I didn't know how, but somehow I managed to spray her lower back without fainting, which was a major accomplishment.

"The back of my legs, too?"

The back of her legs, too? The question almost didn't make sense at first, but I was a gentleman, so I was obliging. The only problem was that Stacy had stood up, leaned slightly forward, bent over a little, and presented before my gaping mouth and disbelieving eyes a heart-shaped miracle in orange-and-yellow candy wrap. Steady, boy, steady. I had to play it cool, like it was no big thing—no big thing at all, just round and tight and shimmering and perfect and close enough to touch. *Aw, Christ!* She shouldn't be *allowed* outside with something like that for *everyone* to see! Why the hell wasn't she home with a babysitter or something? Shit, why wasn't *I?* No, Stacy was independent, she did her own thing, and she probably didn't listen to her mom either; she was a bad girl who'd snuck out at night, and what bad girls needed more than anything else was a good spanking. I was sick, perverted and sick, and I was going to jail or the asylum, simple as that.

"*Hur-ry,* the mosquitoes are way brutal."

Duty called, and I rallied to it despite my mental illness. I turned my head to the left as I squatted down, looking at the shore and glistening black water, until I'd safely cleared the source of all temptation, then turned my head back to see what I was doing and sprayed bug spray on the backs of Stacy's priceless knees and calves. I didn't touch them or anything else, though, because I hadn't been invited to and it was wrong to touch without asking or being asked, so I didn't. Then I stood up and realized that I'd done it, *I'd really done it,* without making an ass out of myself, passing out, or committing a crime. I felt great. My whole body was trembling and I'd collapse any second, but I felt great.

Stacy plopped back on the rock, took her shirt from me, put it back on, tied it at the bottom, and said, "Thanks, Genie; that totally saved me."

I was a hero; a *superhero*—Bug Man—and she'd said as much herself.

"Don't you wanna sit anymore?"

I'd done it, I was doing it; *I was talking to Stacy!* Well, *she* was talking to *me,* but it was time to break it down for her anyway.

"Huge," I said, and sat down beside her on the rock again.

"What?" She looked at me with that slow, puzzled look of hers.

"My name's Huge," I repeated, trying not to melt.

"Okay," she said. "Then why does everybody call you Genie?"

"Because they don't know me."

She squinted her eyes again and said, "Like *everybody* knows you; you're Genie Smalls, the meanest kid in our whole school. You decked Ms. Witherspoon with one punch, got left back, and busted Stevie Thurgood's face for like no reason at all. Everybody knows who you are, Genie, *everybody*. You're totally bad news."

I felt tight and tensed. Not so much for what she'd said, but for bringing up old shit. I did deck Ms. Witherspoon with one punch and got left back for it, but everybody knew that already—it was ancient history, over and done. And I might've been the meanest kid in the whole school, but I'd never tried to be; it just sort of came naturally. But only a couple of people might've seen me bust Stevie Thurgood's face on the last day of school, and that was something I'd rather forget.

Stevie hadn't said or done anything wrong to me, except get my awards at the assembly, and I knew even then that it wasn't *his* fault; our teachers were to blame. And, no, I'd never had anything against him, either; he was a pretty smart kid and got straight A's like I did, only I was smarter and my A's were higher and he had to work to get his. But he was kind of friendly and cheerful, so kids didn't hold his being a bookworm against him, and he had some friends and was popular and a few girls said he was cute, and he was standing near the bike rack after school on the very last day, with all the awards and a small group of kids around him signing the yearbooks they'd made us, and after they'd cleared off, I walked over to him from the bike rack, looked him in his happy brown eyes, heard Thrash whisper from my backpack, *Yeah, do it, you know you want to, go ahead,* as I cocked my right fist, shot it forward, and punched him in the mouth as hard as I could, saw his head whip back and him stumble a little, and watched the smile on his face crumble to confusion, pain, and fear.

I got on the Cruiser and rode off, like nothing had happened, but his bottom lip followed me home, or the image of it anyway—how it had popped and burst open and looked like a thousand bloody worms squirming out of his mouth. I got to my place and had to sweat it out for a few days, waiting for the ax to fall, but it never did; Stevie didn't tell on me—not to our teachers, his parents, or older cousins or friends who could've paid me in kind, like I deserved—and I got away with it scot-free. I felt down and sick to my stomach for the next few days, though, and couldn't talk to Thrash at all, and mom thought it was because of the awards assembly, so that's what I told her, and then she said how would I like to take the Cruiser down the Shore on my own, because she couldn't have me moping around the house with nothing to do all day, every day, all summer long, and that I deserved it as a reward for my grades and good behavior. She couldn't have been further off, but I jumped at the chance, went to the beach, felt a lot better when I was there, and never looked back—until now.

"Why'd you hit him, anyway?" Stacy asked.

I didn't know. I didn't even feel angry at the time; I just walked up and hit him, simple as that. It wasn't like I was proud of myself for it either, not in the least. I knew I owed Stevie Thurgood an apology just like I owed Cynthia one, which he'd probably get right after she'd gotten hers—never.

I shrugged my shoulders at Stacy. "Dunno," I said.

"So are you totally crazy like people say or just evil?"

Anybody else would've gotten a taste of both for asking me that. But Stacy had never seemed all that smart in school, so she probably wasn't trying to get smart now, and she was looking into my eyes with her mouth slightly open, her teeth peeking out, and that curious look of hers, and I could tell it was just a question, and that she only wanted to know the answer. So I gave it a shot.

"No, I just lose it sometimes."

"Why?"

Okay, I could do this. I'd been not-answering questions like these from counselors since third grade.

"I'm angry," I said, and found it easier to say than I'd expected.

"About what?"

"Everything all the time." That was good, too.

"But why?"

I had to wait for a second, just so I could check. Nope, I was fresh out of answers. "Can we talk about something else?"

"Okay."

I was crazy about that word, I really and truly was.

Stacy reached behind her with her right hand (I was sitting on her left side), raised the glass bottle to her lips, and took a sip. I rolled my tongue off the ground and back into my mouth. Not for what she'd done, but because Stacy had something to *drink,* and I was dying of thirst. Literally. I'd be dead any second, and I knew it.

"Want some?" she asked, and offered it to me.

Did I want some? I tried not to bark out a laugh, but I might've grunted some out anyway. She could've handed me a bottle of Liquid Drano and I would've downed the whole thing, which was just what I did, without stopping to think. Yeah, it was rude, and not very gentlemanly, and the beverage was sweet at first, too sweet, like overripe strawberries, and then bitter and hot in my throat.

"Whoa! You must really like wine coolers," Stacy said as I handed the empty bottle back to her.

Wine coolers? I'd just chugged *half* a wine cooler? Great. Now, on top of everything else, I was a wino, too.

"Sorry," I said.

"It's okay," Stacy purred as she dropped the bottle in the sandy mud at our feet. "I stole two more from the party."

She'd been to a high-school party, stolen from it, and then left to come down here and be by herself. Yeah, this was the girl for me.

"So what do you want to talk about," Stacy asked, "because you

214

never talk at school. Hey, where's that lizard you always have with you?"

Didn't *anybody* in this goddamn town know what a *frog* looked like? I didn't say that, though. I said, "I gave him the night off."

"Why? Doesn't he like skinny-dipping?" The smile Stacy flashed was secretive, devious. She leaned her shoulder against mine—what were the chances we'd *both* be wearing sleeveless shirts?—so I could feel her *skin,* and she whispered, "I saw you," before pulling away, ducking her head, and giggling behind her bangs.

You could've fried eggs on my face. But just as quickly it hit me that I'd been maybe a half-mile away in the dark, and that she couldn't have *seen* anything, not the Lookout at least, so all she'd seen was me swimming, and the rest was just a guess, or teasing. I could handle that.

"Don't worry." She lifted her head up, the same mischievous smile on her face. "I won't *tell* anyone, because then you'd *hate me* even more than you do now."

Wait. Hold on. I had to back up. I missed something. "What?"

"You hate me." Stacy pouted. "And I've never—" She stopped for a second before going on. "And you *shouldn't* hate me. I don't *want* you to."

I didn't know what the hell she was talking about or where this was coming from and I felt nervous—real, stiff-spined nervous. She had it all fucking wrong. A soft "No, I don't" was the best I could do.

"Yes, you *do.*" She was looking at me again, but her eyes and face were tighter now. That hurt; that hurt a lot. "You always look at me in school—I've seen you doing it a buh-gillion times, at the pool, too, on your bike—but you never say anything. And when people look at you like that but don't say anything, it means they're mad at you, because my dad used to do that to my mom and then they broke up. So it's like you're always mad at me, and if you're *always mad* at someone, then you *hate* them, the way you hate me."

Whoa. Stacy-logic was strange but sort of compelling. I didn't know what to say. I had no clue. I could hear cymbals and drums now, along with treble, guitar, and bass, longer snippets of louder voices carrying down, more splashing around, the feigned screams of girls looking for attention and the deep chug-chants of witless guys, like the party was all of a sudden closer or really cranking up. Maybe I was just getting used to being here, on the shores of the reservoir, because if you had enough time, you could get used to anything, and Christ knew I'd been here long enough, so maybe I was used to it now, and that's why I was hearing things.

I still didn't know what to say to Stacy, though, or how to get used to her, or being near her, or how to set her straight without saying something I didn't want to say and wasn't ready to, because I should've been hiding in the bushes by Darren's pool, helping my sister, finishing the case, and not like baring my heart to the girl I'd had a massive crush on for two years but had *never* spoken to before tonight. It was too much for me, way too much, and my plan was going to shit.

But there she was, *Stacy Sanders,* in the flesh, staring at *me,* with a troubled, questioning look, waiting for me to say something, anything, and it was getting late, real late, tight, nerve-racking, like I had to make a choice between one or the other—her or the case. The case was way up there, and she was down here, right next to me, warm, probably soft, practically touching, turning her back for a second to twist the cap off another wine cooler, while the moon was right and the water was right and the temperature was right and the darkness was right and the rock was just right, and she took a sip and was looking at me again, with almost pleading in her eyes, as if to say, *Why, why don't you like me,* and I did, I already did, I really did, but *she* didn't think so, and I didn't know how to tell her or what to say or how to say it, and I just wanted to go, I *had* to go, but I couldn't go, not now, not like this, confused and aching and torn, because here we were, up close, alone, and my heart was pounding and I *had* to go, but I *had* to stay, because this was my chance, my shot to make her understand and set things straight, and I grabbed the bottle and took a swig and wiped my mouth and still felt thirsty and looked at her the way she was looking at me, and something moved and shifted and broke or clicked but I didn't know what, and I heard myself whisper, "I don't hate you, Stacy, I *like* you, I've *always* liked you," and *could not believe* I'd said that and wanted to curl up into a ball or run and hide and take it all back, but I leaned over and kissed her instead and she kissed back and I was done, I was gone, I was lost and taken and somewhere else and totally fucked and there was no way back, out, or through. *I'd kissed Stacy Sanders right on the lips*—and my plan and my case and maybe even my sister were totally finished; *everything* I knew had come to an end.

"Cool, because I like you, too."

No, I didn't even cry.

"Are you cold?" she asked.

"W-w-why?" My teeth might've been chattering a little.

"Because you're like totally shivering, doofus."

That was good, it was funny and right, I was a doofus, and I didn't mind hearing it from her. "M-m-my clothes are damp," I said.

"If you take your shirt off, I'll rub your back and warm you up."

I wasn't a gentleman anymore, never had been, but I was obliging all the same. The shirt came off.

"You're like almost buffed, Genie."

First thing to do tomorrow, if it ever came: sit down and write a long letter to Herschel Walker, thanking him from the bottom of my heart.

"Huge," I reminded her.

"Oh, yeah. Okay . . . Huge."

Wow, that word, my name, and Stacy Sanders's cold little hand, rings, and bracelets rubbing up and down my shirtless back. I could die now, you could kill me; it wasn't *ever* getting any better than this.

Well, except for when she pressed her sticky lips against my neck and gave me a quick peck.

"How come you never talk?" she asked.

My mind was muddled and spinning, my stomach was somewhere under China, and I took a long pull of wine cooler to settle down. It tasted terrible and didn't work. But the answer to that one was easy, so I said, "I don't have anything to say."

She pulled her face back while resting her palm on the bottom of my spine. "But you're like wicked smart."

"Maybe, I don't know." I shrugged. "But it hasn't helped me any."

Stacy's face darkened for a second, then her eyes widened and she said, "*Oh*, I get it. You're like complicated, right?"

Yeah, I was complicated; I was all fucked up. I had goose bumps everywhere, and I would've strangled an entire convent of nuns for a shawl or a throw blanket. "Nah, I'm not. I'm not anything yet," I said, and spooked the living shit out of myself by saying it.

"Yeah, you are." Stacy smiled. "You're *bad*. Really, really bad, and totally sweet, and completely cute."

Okay, I got it. She was tipsy, maybe even hammered; she *had* to be. Why else would she say that to me, right now, with the state I was in? But I *knew* that being a stone-cold badass would work with chicks someday, not *acting* like one, but *being* one. *I knew it*. Chicks loved it; they couldn't get enough, like fat kids with ice cream. And maybe, just maybe, someday was today.

Stacy put the bottle down, wrapped her hands around my waist, leaned in close, placed her chin in the crook of my neck and her lips against my ear. "You smell like mud," she said. "You *were* skinny-dipping, weren't you?"

Jesus, she had detective skills, too. "What do you do in those note-books anyway?" I asked, because I really had to change the subject.

"My notebooks?" Stacy lifted her head, her smile half-hidden by uneven bangs. "From school?"

"Yeah."

"I draw clothes in them."

"Clothes?"

"Yeah, I design clothes—skirts, dresses, blouses, shorts—like sketch them in my notebook, draw patterns for them at home, then cut those out and make them, with like material and sewing and stuff. It's way fun, and that's what I want to do when I grow up, so, yeah." She stood up, and while I was saddened by the fact, it was a relief. "What do you think?" She spread her arms and spun around. "I made this outfit myself."

That explained why she'd been practically naked since about April—she'd been making her own clothes. But that seemed like a different thing to be into, and the outfit she had on was pretty sweet—the colors matched, the fabrics flowed, the style was in; okay, everything was too short, too tight, too revealing, and *maybe* a bit trashy, but I wasn't complaining.

"You look *awesome*," I blurted, blushed instantly, and felt like ripping my tongue out for betraying me.

Stacy dropped her head, and if I didn't know any better, which I didn't, I would've said she was blushing, too. Then, out of nowhere, she flexed her knees, reared back, and dove—literally dove—at me, into my lap, kissed me, and sat beside me again, with her arms around my waist. *Un-fucking-believable!* And rule number three of my classified detective manual would be: always compliment the girl of your dreams, because she just might kiss you—*again*. Yeah, my rules stomped all ass; they were everything you ever needed to know. My plan, on the other hand, was garbage, yesterday's trash, and I knew it. But for some reason, that didn't really bother me.

Stacy was rubbing my shoulder blades with her palm. Her skirt had hitched a little higher up because she'd thrown her far knee over mine while fastening her lips to my neck. Meanwhile, I pondered the reservoir's flickering surface, struggling not to let on how much it tickled, or to leap up and break into song. I tried to think nautical thoughts— endless waved horizons; infinite oceans in all directions; tranquil seas; water, water everywhere, and I couldn't remember the rest—but the Lookout was certain he'd spied land in the distance and was standing tall, craning his neck to see it. Where the *hell* had that wine cooler gone? Ah, there it was, so I swigged it, and it tasted awful—again—but I had to do something, *anything*, to get my mind off what was going on. Then Stacy kissed me again, long, slow, sticky, moist, and completely on purpose. Her skin was soft and smooth and smelled like hot tea with milk and sugar, and I realized that I had no words for this—the feelings, the textures, the taste, the smell—except that I was a goner, a total goner. The skin all over my body was alive and quivering, but she could've set me ablaze with a flamethrower and I wouldn't have noticed, cared, or moved an inch away. I kissed her back—what else could I do?—and wrapped my arms around her waist, and held on tight, so I wouldn't drift away, or drown.

Stacy pulled back, shook her head side to side, and smiled; her pupils were small and her cheeks were flushed. "Whoa," she thrummed.

Yeah, I knew *exactly* how she felt.

We were quiet for a minute, or a day, or a week, just sitting there in the dark, watching the stars and moon twinkle on the water, holding on tight, hearing the breeze in the treetops, the party gurgling in the distance, but then Stacy shifted a little, her knee went too far up and struck something, just barely, but I had to say ouch because it was something that couldn't be so much as brushed by a knee without smarting.

"Sorry, did I hurt you?" Stacy asked, looking down as she shifted her knee back toward mine. When she looked up, she was smiling that devious smile again, and said, "That's not more bug spray, is it?"

No, it wasn't bug spray. The Lookout, ever vigilant, was roaring a loud *Land Ho!* that no one could hear but *anyone* could see, especially if she was practically sitting in your lap. A lightning bolt of embarrassment crackled through me, and searing heat rose from my neck and ears. But there wasn't a damn thing I could do about it, and I knew it, so I tried to breathe deep and relax. Because if the Lookout was anything, he was committed to his work, and right now *he* was on the job.

I tried to cross my legs, out of sheer good manners, but my stomach muscles were stiff, knotted, and taut, which made it hard to lift my knee, and Stacy's hand was pressed down on my knee, to begin with, which kept me from moving it, and which made everything harder than it needed to be.

"Can I see it?" she whispered.

I wasn't sure I'd caught that; even though Stacy was looking me square in the face as she'd said it, and I saw her lips form the words as I heard them, so I had a pretty good idea of *exactly* what she'd said, and what she was asking, and just what it meant. When it finally sank in, the dilemma before me was all too clear. This was way too much for me, too new, too fast, too good to be true, and the *only* word I wanted to say was *yes!* But it also hit me that if I said yes, and showed her, then she would've seen *everything* there was to see, on top of the fact that I'd already told her everything there was to tell, or at least far more than I'd ever told anyone else, and then I'd be left with nothing she hadn't seen or heard, nothing to hide, no secrets; I'd be wide open, exposed, vulnerable, and *naked in front of a girl*. What if she didn't like it, any of it, or me, or worse, what if something went wrong? Because if I'd learned anything in life, I'd learned nothing was ever too good to be true, but something always went wrong—especially if you got caught with your pants down. So what was I supposed to do?

"*Plee-ease?*" Stacy sang. "You don't have to if you don't want to, but I *swear* I won't *tell* anyone."

Goddamn, she was persuasive when she wanted to be! But could I trust her, when I knew I couldn't trust anyone else? I gulped air, or tried to, but missed, and coughed. My legs might've been fidgeting. My breath was shallow, my hands were cold, my heart was racing, and my shirt was already off. How would I know whether or not I could trust her if I didn't *try?* The worst she could do was laugh. Aw, shit, that would totally destroy me. But if she did, we were right on the water, so I could just dive in and get it over with and never have to worry about anything ever again. So there was always that. But she wouldn't laugh, she couldn't; she'd asked me, she wanted to see it, and she'd sworn she wouldn't tell, she'd *sworn* it. It would be our secret, not hers, not mine, but ours. Would she keep it, though? I didn't know. How could I know if I didn't try? But what if I tried and something went wrong, like it always did? I had the feeling I could ask the same questions over and over, maybe forever, and never get anywhere. Fuck it. I was going with the flow; the shorts were coming down.

"You *promise* you won't tell?"

"I promise." Stacy nodded, and kissed me on the cheek.

"Okay," I relented as I untied the drawstring, lifted my hips, slid my shorts to my knees, and felt how warm and dry the rock was beneath my butt. First rule: keep your ass dry. Check.

"Holy shit, Genie, you got some big-ass balls!"

So I'd been told. But somehow I was ready to hear that, so it didn't really freak me out or embarrass me at all. "Huge," I reminded her.

"Well, they're a little big, but not like mega or anything." Stacy smirked at me. "So don't let it go to your head."

"No, my name," I said. "My name's Huge." Couldn't anyone get that straight?

"Omigod, yeah, sorry." Stacy blushed and covered her mouth with both hands. "I didn't *mean* . . ." She fumbled, cut herself off, and stopped.

This was awesome, truly awesome. She'd made the mistake; she was embarrassed, while I was calmer, cooler, more excited, nervous, riled up, and petrified—all at the same time—than I'd ever been before in my whole stupid life. I was in new territory, out of my depth, had my shorts around my ankles, with *Stacy Sanders* sitting next to me, and I was in control of myself, totally in control. Shit like this did not happen every day; no fucking way, not to me.

Stacy had pulled herself together; it looked like she was flowing with it, too. "I mean, uh, what I meant was . . . it's nice. It's . . . *pretty*."

Okay, so maybe I wasn't totally in control; maybe I wasn't so calm, maybe I wasn't all that ready. Because never—with all the dictionaries in the history of the world at my disposal and a million years to work through them—*never* would I have come up with that word to describe the Lookout. Never. It just wasn't possible; I could *not* have said that on my own. But somehow Stacy made it work; it fit. I was *naked*, she was *looking* at me, and she could've laughed or insulted me or mocked me or cried out and ran and destroyed me completely, but she went easy on me, she said something nice: *pretty*. Yeah, I was more grateful than I'd ever been and just totally fucking floored.

Not quite as floored, though, as when I felt her touch.

No, she didn't ask, and it was wrong to touch without asking or being asked, but I'd practically dared her to by pulling my shorts down in the first place. Besides, the Lookout seemed rather eager to make Stacy's acquaintance, and if he was okay with it, then I was, too.

"Is that okay?"

"Uh-huh," I squeaked.

"Cool, Huge. I really like you."

She could say that over and over and over again if she wanted to and it would never get old. As for me, I couldn't say anything. Not a word. I wanted to, but I couldn't—everything was just so . . . *different*. Same motion, same mechanics, practically same size fingers and hand, and I'd done it a thousand, ten thousand, or a hundred thousand times in the last year alone, but this was something else, someone else, a girl, *Stacy Sanders, holy shit*, and it was *not* the same at all. No way. It was different, meaning better, way better, as if I'd left some small detail out and had been doing it wrong all along. It was like all I'd ever been touching was skin—okay, sure, buzzing, sensitive, tickly skin, but still just skin—because that's all the Lookout was: skin and spongy tissue and blood. But Stacy was touching all that and something else, too, something more. It was tender and achy and hurting, but it felt good, really good, like a bowl of hot soup on a cold winter's day, and it spread out and spilled and warmed and lifted and startled and hurt and felt good again and even better and better still, and I wanted to tell her what she was doing, what she'd found and was touching, that I'd never felt it before, hadn't even known it was there, that there was *more* to me than I'd thought, but it was *there* now, right *now*, because *she* was doing it.

But I couldn't speak, my tongue was wooden, I had no voice; my mouth was slammed shut, just like my eyes, my limbs hardened, my chest steamed, my heart frothed, my brain went dry, so I had no words and nothing to say, but I wanted to, I *wanted* to anyway, to say something funny or nice, to make her smile or blush, to tell her something she'd like, to thank her, make promises, find in her what she'd found in me, and give it back, share it, but I couldn't, I couldn't; I was soaring and shaking and thrilled and lost and frightened and coming apart, and the best I could do was *warn* her.

"Look out!"

EIGHTEEN

I felt tingly, dizzy, and cold, almost as if—almost as if I'd done something wrong. I stood from the rock, hitched up my shorts, tied them, and turned around to look for Stacy. She was further inland, squatting down and washing her hands in the stream that crept its way through the lower part of Darren's property. The light from the party seemed harsher now, eerie; the tiny backlit figures I'd seen earlier were blurred and creepy, and the only sound I heard was blood flushing in my ears. Maybe it was all the wine cooler I'd slugged, maybe I was buzzed or drunk, because everything seemed a little slow, or tilted, like I couldn't get my balance—like something was off.

"I hate that part," Stacy said.

"I tried to warn you," I blushed. Wait a minute. *What?*

"It's okay," she chirped.

It was okay; everything was okay. *That part?*

Stacy stood up, shook the water off her hands, and then dried them on her skirt. She faced me, tilted her head, and smiled. "What?" she asked.

"Nothing," I said, staring, blinking. My brain was gluey; I was stuck on "that part." How could she know it had parts, or one that she hated?

"Wha-aat? Tell me, please?"

"You hate that part," I whispered, almost begging.

"Don't worry, it's okay."

Sure, everything was okay. *How could she know it had parts if she'd never done it before?*

"Seriously, it's okay," Stacy reassured me, and went on, "At least you didn't try to lick it off my hand like—" She clamped both palms over her mouth before she could finish. Her eyes were startled, questioning. She'd slipped, and was looking to see if I'd caught it.

Yeah, I'd caught it. Everything was *not* okay. She *had* done it before; it was my first time, but not hers. She'd done that with someone else, to someone else, for someone else, someone that—aw, gross! That was totally fucking gross! Who would do shit like that?

"Like *who*, Stacy?" I asked, although I had the dread feeling I already knew.

"Who what? N-n-nothing. N-n-no one." She looked up, down, left, right—anywhere but at me. "I mean, at least *you* didn't, like, because that would be . . ."

"Stop lying, Stacy." My voice was blunter and flatter than I'd expected, and it hit her hard.

"I'm not, I can't—" She stopped. It was sinking in to her now; she was nervous. Up went her hands to her mouth again, only there was more alarm in her eyes this time.

I was freezing, swaying, and queasy, but I could feel it starting to build. She'd done that with someone else. *Aw, Christ! Aw, shit!* I wasn't her first; she was mine, but I wasn't hers. She'd seen someone else the way she'd seen me, she'd touched someone else the way she'd touched me, she'd kissed someone else—*aw, fuck!* I'd fucking *kissed* her! I felt sick; I wanted to spit. I did.

"Did you promise him, too?" I growled. "Did you swear to Razor the way you swore to me?" My voice was nasty and biting, and I didn't know where this was going, only that it was going to get worse, much worse.

Stacy straightened up a little. "No, I never promised Razor, I didn't—Oh, shit!" She punched herself in the thigh and stomped her flip-flop in the grass.

Jesus! Could she suck any more at this? And I was going to trust her? I'd *already* trusted her? Mistake—big fucking mistake. "If you didn't swear to Razor, Stacy, then why can't you say it?" That practically stung as it left my mouth.

"I'm, I'm not supposed to—"

"You're not supposed to what? You're not supposed to go around jacking everybody off?"

"No! Don't *say* that! I don't! I'm not—"

"You're not what? You're not a liar? You're not a person who swears and then breaks her promise the first chance she gets? What? You're not what? Go on, say it."

"Please, Genie, stop. Please."

"Don't call me Genie! My name's Huge! Fucking Huge! Got it?"

"Okay, Huge."

"*Okay?* Jesus Christ, Stacy! Is that all you can say? No, you can say more; you have more to say. So say it."

"But I'm not supposed to—"

"Yeah, I've heard that one before. You're not supposed to what?"

"I'm not supposed to *tell*."

A backbreaking chill rattled down my spine. My lungs were hot and full, my veins flooded and throbbed, and blood or waves or bass drums thundered in my ears. I didn't want to think it. I couldn't. I wouldn't be able to take it. I was slipping already; I knew it. It was coming on fast and it wouldn't take much . . . or long.

"Can't we just drop it? Please, Huge? Like forget it and sit back down? *Please?*"

Stacy had clasped her hands beneath her chin, pleading, shaking, and I closed my eyes so I wouldn't have to see her face. But it was too late, way too late, and with my eyes closed I saw it anyway: *Stacy and Razor alone in the dark, up close . . . touching.*

I wasn't by the reservoir anymore. I was standing on the edge of a muddy, mile-high cliff in the dark, and the ground beneath my feet was starting to give way. I was ruined, devastated. I was wrong about her, totally wrong, and starting to fall. I wasn't thinking, I couldn't, but I heard the question—why'd you do it, Stacy, why, with *him*?—in the weakest and most pathetic voice I ever could've spoken.

Stacy took a half-step backward, then froze in her tracks; a shaft of moonlight illumined her face. Her eyes were squinted and a touch too spread out; her cheeks were a little too high and a little too sharp; there was nothing wrong with her nose except it was always bunched up; she had gapped front teeth, a slight under bite, and a mouth too wide by a fraction; there were three popped-zit scars on her forehead and one on her chin; her hair was dyed cheaply black and poorly cut; she was short and scrawny and dressed like a tart; and *she* was the girl, the thirteen-year-old girl, who'd just broken my heart. She'd killed me, but she was afraid now, very afraid. I saw it in her sad hazel eyes.

I looked down, swallowed hard, and said, "Why, Stacy? Why with him? Tell me the truth."

She wrapped her arms around herself and looked lost and alone. She dropped her face and kicked the ground.

"Why, Stacy?"

"But I'm not supposed to—"

"We've covered that already. Why?"

Stacy shifted her feet, still holding herself, and sighed a heavy, defeated sigh. She raised her head, looked at me finally, and said, "He *made* me do it."

"*What?*"

"Razor made me do it," she repeated. She wasn't looking down or away or anywhere else but at me.

"What do you mean, he *made* you do it?" I was getting hotter around the neck and face again. "How?"

"He said he'd *tell* if I didn't do it."

"Tell? Tell what?"

"What he wanted me to do with him, and more—things that I didn't do, things that I wouldn't do—but he said he'd tell *everyone* that I'd done them anyway, and tell them to tell everyone else, and they'd believe him and he'd do it, too, but he wouldn't if I . . ."

The moon was distant now and dim; it seemed much darker. Something inside me was wounded, crawling, dying, but I'd already come this far, so I had to press on. "But why?"

"Because he's a baby and a coward and a liar and he tells you he really likes you and wants to be boyfriend and girlfriend and gets all horny and grabs at you and just like whines and begs and won't stop until you feel sorry and do what he wants and I *hate* him." Stacy's cheeks were flushed; she was still holding herself, but she'd balled her hands into fists. "I hate him. I wish I'd never met him or talked to him or . . ."

She seemed to be telling the truth, but it wasn't what I wanted to know. "No, Stacy, why'd you go with him in the first place?" That was the best I could do; anything more and I didn't know what would happen.

Her cheeks were crimson, her eyes were wet, and her shoulders dropped just a little. "Because . . . he asked me to."

"And you said okay?!" I felt like hanging myself. It was so obvious, so ridiculous; it was almost funny. Suddenly I wasn't too fond of that word anymore, *okay*.

"Uh-huh." She nodded. "What was I supposed to say?"

"How about *fucking no*? Did you ever think of that?"

"But he told me he liked me and was begging and whining and crying—I didn't know what to do!"

"So you just said okay, what the hell, and whack, whack, whacked away?"

There was acid in that, hot blistering acid, but the way it came out almost made me laugh. Not like a good laugh, though. No, there were no gags or punch lines or answers here. It all meant nothing; I could see that now. If you asked her for it, she just handed it over, gave it up. What we'd done meant nothing. What I was after meant nothing. The case meant nothing. All of it was nothing. And that was funny, not like hilarious, but a different kind of funny; bitter and hollow and dead, but funny all the same. I should not have been the least bit surprised. Nah, I'd *always* been shit, I'd always been a joke, I'd always been nothing, and Stacy was exactly the confirmation I needed.

There was just one more thing I needed to ask.

"Stacy," I said, "are you a slut?" I just felt like I *had* to know.

She recoiled, as if I'd slapped her. "What?"

"Are you a slut? It's a simple fucking question."

"But why—" She faltered and stepped back. "He *begged*—"

"Yeah, we covered that already. He whined, he begged, he cried. Fine. The kid's a baby and a pussy and a liar and a bully. He manipulated you till you said okay, and then he leaned on you and pushed you around and intimidated you and threatened you and got you between a rock and a hard place and made you do something you didn't want to do. I get that; I get all of that. But that *still* doesn't answer my question."

Stacy looked confused; it might've been a little too much for her, maybe because she really wasn't all that smart. But I wanted an answer, and I was going to get it. "It's a simple question. Yes or no. *Are you a slut?*"

Her face plunged. She backed up again, tripped over her heels, and fell on her butt into the grass near the steps leading to Darren's lawn. She sat there, legs splayed, crumbling, breaking up. I stepped forward and she flinched, covered herself. She had to be scared; she had to. I had problems, I was violent, I'd punched a woman in the face, knocked her out cold, and everybody knew it. So why wouldn't

I beat the piss out of a girl? I was standing over her, fuming, pressing down, losing control, she could see it; I *had* to know, and she *would* tell me.

"Answer me."

"I, I, I—"

I was straddling her knees, bending forward, my fingers curling slowly to fists. *"Are . . . you . . . a . . . SLUT?"*

"P-p-please, Huge, *don't.*"

"I'm not going to *hurt you,*" I said, but wasn't convincing. "Just answer. Yes or no. Are you a slut?"

"I . . . *I don't know.*"

It stopped me breathless and cold. I might've been able to take one or the other, but I couldn't take *that:* Stacy didn't *know* what she was; she wasn't anything yet, just like me.

Stacy's eyes flooded, her mouth wrenched down, she pulled her hands to her face, and she wept: she sobbed and heaved and shook and folded and moaned and the ground was gone, totally gone, and I was pitching forward, plummeting, toppling end over end, losing it, all of it, completely, everything, all of me—gone, nothing, destroyed. I'd made her suffer, I was *watching* her suffer, right here, up close, and I was less, far less, than I'd ever been before, less than shit or negative numbers. I was filth, scum, a mad dog in need of putting down. And I *felt* it. Not for me, though, I didn't feel for me, there was nothing there, nobody home, but for her, I felt for her, how I was wronging her and how she'd been wronged, no matter what she'd done or with whom. Just the threat of a single fucking word had nailed her down, ripped her apart, and skinned her alive, like their words had done to me. But I wasn't thinking about me, I wasn't, I was going, I was gone. I leaned over—panting, trembling, crazed—pressed my lips to Stacy's forehead and whispered, "I'm sorry, Stacy, I am. It's not you, that's not you, you're *beautiful,* you are." And I *meant* it, more than anything I'd ever said.

Because it wasn't her. It was *him, them.* What *he'd* done, what *he'd* said; what *they'd* do and say in turn, and what they'd *all* believe. It didn't matter if it was right, if it fit, was an error, a mistake, or a bald-faced fucking lie; if enough people said it, and enough went along, then *everyone* would believe it—it would count, it would stick, it'd be *true*. And she'd have to *live* with that; we'd *all* have to live with that, and that was *retarted,* truly fucking *retarted*—and that wasn't even a word.

But we *all* did it; we *all* were *retarted.* I was, I did it, I'd just done it, I could see that now, although now was too late. I'd come too far, burned the bridges, razed the ground, and there was nothing left behind me and nothing waiting ahead, so I had to run and keep on running because, no matter what I would or would not do, I could not turn back.

I was bolting up the wooden steps, slashing my way up the slope, with nothing in me, before me, or holding me back. I was gone, totally fucking gone.

But I knew where *they* were.

NINETEEN

I tore through the backyard at a speed that didn't seem possible—two hundred and fifty to three hundred yards of frantic acceleration, all of it uphill; whipping the extra horses, inventing new gears, seventh gear, eighth gear, ninth gear, faster and faster, leaning forward, digging down, wanting more, stretching for it, tenth gear, eleventh gear, finding more speed, more velocity, but still not enough, never enough, pressing forward, craving more, needing more—racing, crying, and screaming out loud.

It all flashed into view and blurred by so quickly that most of it didn't register, but what really stuck with me was how everyone just watched. They saw and heard, turned with puzzlement or alarm, snapped to, shook it off, and stepped back or aside. Other than that, they did nothing. A foot, a hand, an elbow, a hip, a knee, a feint step—*anything* would've knocked me off stride and sent me crashing down, but nothing came. I couldn't blame them. They were just the small-town teenagers of small-town parents, minding their own business and having a good time. Maybe they were confused. Maybe they felt like they were missing something, something important that explained everything and made it all okay. But the many eyes that caught mine seemed to know the danger was real, and just looked on and did nothing.

Maybe I'd missed something, too. Not just at the moment because I was blazing forward, out of control, eyes clouded by tears, and baying like a banshee. No, maybe I'd missed something on one of the many steps I'd taken to get here. Shit, maybe I'd missed a lot of things. Then again, I couldn't tell, and wouldn't have stopped anyway.

The first thing I saw as I approached the broad, flat area to the right of Darren's yard was little furry Chakha over to my far left, at the edge of the swimming pool, with a play-fighting Cynthia on his shoulder as he dove them into the water. I remembered overhearing that Cynthia wanted to hook up, and Neecey busting on her about it, and I guessed this was why, because Chakha wasn't good looking. Then, just before I dashed through the revelers on the lawn, I caught a quick glimpse of the wood decking at the back of the house, with its crepe paper decorations, citronella candles, patio chairs and lounges, umbrella-ed tables with plastic plates, cups, and napkins on them, the trash can for the keg, one for the wine coolers, and one for the trash, all of which had poster-board signs taped to them, in large, handwritten, Magic Marker bubble script that I recognized and knew as Neecey's.

That's when I realized Neecey could've gone into my desk just to get my Magic Markers, and that she could've overturned the key to the side drawer without even noticing it. And I knew I could've made a mistake there, and that I *still* could've been missing something, maybe something important, and that maybe it had to do with what I saw when the partiers had finished splitting before me— Razor, Neecey, and Darren standing to the right of the barbecue pit, a few feet into the grass, near the hedge and ground lights, away from everyone else, talking.

The music was loud, driving, and jumbled all the way through, and although it was sizzling speed for a kid my age, it still must've taken me thirty-five or forty seconds to cover all that ground, enough time for me to realize that I should've paused to ask a few more questions before I did what I was going to do. But I was screeching forward, furious and wild, with a hollow heart and a *target* in sight, lined up and ready to go, which was all I needed and exactly what I got.

Well, sort of.

Left to right, it was Razor, Darren, and Neecey huddled in a semi-circle by the hedge, all of them three-quarter lit from below by the ground lights. Neecey saw me first. Her hair was up, her skin was Shake-N-Bake tan; she had on thin hoop earrings, a white tank top, and her hands were on her hips. She looked pretty, she looked great; she always did. When she saw me—I was maybe twenty yards out and closing fast—her dark eyes flashed wide and thick with fear. Almost instantly, though, her face changed; her eyes sank, her mouth frowned, she looked resigned, worried, defeated, like mom's face when I'd done something wrong, terribly, terribly wrong. It seemed like she was shaking her head no, or started to and stopped, I couldn't tell which. She stepped back, though, she definitely stepped back: two big steps.

Darren was next. He was standing beside Neecey with his shaggy orange hair, slow brown eyes, pukka bead choker, red Hawaiian shirt, and arms folded on his chest. His face was turned toward Razor and his lips were slightly pursed, like he was skeptical or smelled something bad. But he turned his head a little just as Neecey moved back and caught sight of me out of the corner of his eye—ten yards now and counting—and he looked baffled at first, just like he would. But then he changed, too, right away. His eyes glinted, his mouth turned upward, and he seemed to *smile* as he unfolded his arms and rubbed his hands together.

I didn't know exactly what to make of that, and as much as I wanted to crack Darren's face wide open and watch his brains spill out, his turn would have to wait, because Razor was first on the list. He was on my left, with his flattop hair, tight face, thin brow, narrow eyes, cruddy braces, and a dark blue Jim McMahon football jersey, cut off at the shoulders to show his long bony arms, which he was waving and flapping around, palms up, like he was asking or begging for something. Oh, *he was,* but he was focused on Neecey and Darren, so he didn't look up or see me coming at all.

I heard that cracking shrill voice of his in the split second before it happened, and I realized Razor was just some spoiled, candy-assed kid who played quarterback and bullied people and had rich parents who never said no, and that he'd been given all he ever wanted but still held his breath, stomped his feet, cried, yelled, and threw fits until everybody coughed up more.

I pitied him for that, being spineless and weak, but I was too filled with hate to stop myself. Yeah, *hate,* for everything and everyone. I hated Razor and kids like him, bullies and babies and everyone like that; I hated the kids at the party, kids at school, teachers, counselors, coaches, cops, priests, principals, and mall security; I hated the old man for leaving, mom for working so hard, Neecey for growing up, grandma for growing old; I hated all the old-timers and their smelly old folks' homes, the misers who ran them, owned them, made money off them; I hated bigots and pushovers, people who watched, people who helped, people who believed and did what they were told, people who went to church and people who didn't, people who lied and schemed and broke rules and hurt others and got away with it, and people who tried to catch and punish them. And I hated the Circle and the mall and the reservoir and the town and the whole fucking world for being petty and pointless and cruel, and I hated myself for being a part of it, the smallest, meanest part, and *exactly the same as everyone else.*

I dropped the pedal again, one last time, went faster still, disgustingly fast, put everything I had into it and packed my fist and wound it tight and pulled it back and lashed it forward with all of my body, hurling it like a javelin at the moon. But it had rained all day and it was wet and slick and muddy and my sneakers sucked shit and my left foot slipped and slid forward as it planted; my balance lurched and shifted, but I caught it quick, just in time, and snapped my right leg around, got my foot down, whipped my hips and shoulder through, and chucked my fist, myself, full-bodied and flying, right at Razor's sternum. But I was off. I slipped and came up short. My fist missed its target by about twelve inches, due south. I'd come blasting out of the woods in homemade ninja shorts, shirtless, screaming and crying, going Mach 10, had wound everything up to throw a punch, a murderous punch, slid forward, lost my balance, caught myself, readjusted, launched it, and then landed it, but *not anywhere near* the spot I'd aimed at or expected. With all that momentum, all that I had, *I punched Ray "the Razor" Tuffalo right in the nuts.*

Nah, you were *never, ever* supposed to do that, and every single guy who'd ever lived knew it. Razor's eyes bulged and his mouth dropped open and he tried to grab his stomach but I was still moving forward, the momentum carrying me through, and I crashed into him, onto my hands and knees, with my face in his crotch. He bent forward, over my shoulders, and as I tried to get to my feet, the pain must've started catching up with him, because when you got hit in the nuts, it took a second or two for the pain to flower and bloom, and then he pitched forward, groaning, sucking air, and fell on top of me. He was long and bony and heavy and right on my back, pressing me into the ground, grass, and mud, which oozed between my lips onto my tongue, but when I squirmed free a little and was able to push him away, he rolled over like a dirty diaper, because that's all he was, filthy and flimsy, and he'd just gotten totally clobbered in the balls, so he was pretty much helpless, too.

I got to my feet, wiped my mouth, and stood over him, ready to bash his ear through the other side of his skull, rearing my fist back to do it, when I just glimpsed, coming at me, a guy I hadn't thought to look for but should have. Because if Razor was there, then Tommy Sharpe would be with him, and he was bigger and meaner and broad and solid and gigantic as all hell and was maybe two feet away, letting his massive fist fly, BLAM, and my world lit up from within, all white, blinding white, then pale yellow, then this wavy blue, and then black and red checkers, and my eyes came open and somehow I didn't go down, although I should've gone down and wanted to, because the second one was on its way already and I had no time to move or think, and BLAM, I got it again, and that one hurt, *that really fucking hurt,* like getting clubbed with a cinder block, and my neck whipped back and I felt myself falling and the left side of my head cracking open and I went down, straight down, right on top of Razor.

I was down but not out—exactly how, I had *no* earthly clue—and I'd somehow fallen on my back, so I was lying on top of Razor, who was starting to stir, maybe recover, while I was facing up, watching the light show fade in front of my eyes, and then looking into the kind, forgiving face of Tommy Sharpe, who was leaning over me, locked and loaded, and I knew the next one would kill me—it was gonna rock my left eye socket again, the one he'd just bashed twice, but it'd smash clean through this time, sending his fist and shards of bone straight into my brain, and I'd be dead.

But I wasn't afraid, I was too rabid, loopy, and punch drunk to be afraid. No, I was curious. I wanted to see if he could do it, I wanted to see if he had the guts to pulverize someone weaker and smaller to death. So I kept my eyes open; I wanted to *watch.*

Tommy's pale blue eyes were steady and glistening, his giant fist was drawn all the way back and holding firm, and everything about him said he had the physical strength and the steely stomach and that, yeah, he was going to do it.

Out of nowhere, the fist shot across from my right like a bullet into the left side of Tommy's jaw—*thwack*—and before Tommy had a chance to do anything, even straighten his head—which had been totally whipped, snapped, and clocked—the next punch was already in his stomach—*whoomp!* Razor was pushing at my back now, trying to get to his feet, and the shouts of *Fight! Fight!* were growing, pouring in; I made myself as heavy as I could and pinned my arms and legs down to keep Razor where he was. The next one wasn't a punch, but a short, brutal kick to the side of Tommy's knee, buckling it, so he stumbled, and then no more kicks or punches; he was behind Tommy now, twisting Tommy's wrist back to his shoulder blade, driving him forward, riding him down, pushing his face into the ground.

Razor grunted, surged, and finally threw me off; I flew forward onto my hands and knees and, for the first time, tasted the blood. Razor got to his feet, but he was too late and outnumbered. Everyone from the party had gathered around, and the crew were circled in closest—Sticky, Burger, Squat, Roni, Lyle, Chakha—looking *extremely* perturbed and decidedly *unfriendly* should something, *anything* befall their leader as he knelt on Tommy Sharpe's back.

"Dude, you want more?" Darren panted. "Because I got some if you want it."

"No, D, chill," Tommy grunted.

"I *so* can't hear you, dude," Darren taunted, "so like speak up and tell me what you want."

"No more, D, no more."

"Can I let you up, dude? You cool?"

"Yeah, I'm cool. I'm done."

I began lifting myself off the ground and turned my head to watch.

Darren got up slowly, putting plenty of distance between him and Tommy Sharpe, just like a pro. Tommy got to his feet, stood up straight, and started brushing himself off. He was six or seven inches taller than Darren and fifty or sixty pounds heavier, easily, but Darren had kicked his ass like nothing, like he wasn't even there.

I was on all fours with my head tilted, so everything was skewed, but even I could tell that Darren actually seemed mad. And that didn't add up. Instantly, though, the bullshit con artist faker in him kicked in and he started acting cool, as if he'd already pulled himself together. Then again, everyone else was watching, too.

"What the fuck, dude, seriously?" Darren asked. "We're like trying to have a party—a few brews, some tunes, chill out—but you gotta come in here and like shit all over it. What's your fucking damage?"

There must've been fifty or sixty teenagers standing around, four or five heads deep in every direction, but it was quiet, very quiet. Somebody must've turned the music off.

Tommy pointed at me. "That little shit—"

"No, dude, don't try blaming *him*, he's just a *kid*. He's like not even in *junior high* yet."

As soon as I heard him say that, I had a feeling I knew what Darren was up to. He was tying up the loose ends, cutting Razor and Tommy—his hired thugs—off in public for everyone to see, so that nobody would ever think about linking them back to him.

"But *he* started it, D," Tommy countered, still pointing at me, "he did! You *saw* him, dude—"

"No way," Darren cut him off again, "I didn't see *shit*. All I saw was *you* like pounding a twelve-year-old kid at *my* party. *My* party, dude, and now he's fucking *bleeding*."

That part was true. My nose was pretty much gushing.

"But you *saw* him clock Razor in the nuts," Tommy griped. "You *saw* him. *Everybody* fucking saw him! What was I supposed to do?"

Darren was a half-step ahead, though, like he always seemed to be when he wasn't high. "Dude, save it, all right? Everybody knows how you and your bud Razor try to act all hard with younger kids, so don't even *try* to tell me Razor didn't start this shit, and that the little dude here wasn't just sticking up for himself. Don't even run that shit, because nobody's buying it."

I shifted my eyes to Razor along with everybody else. He was standing there, a few feet away from Tommy, looking pinched and muddy and sullen, but not saying anything. He couldn't; he had too much to lose. Contradicting Darren would mean antagonizing the whole crew, and seven against two was clearly suicidal odds, even to a nitwit. Besides, if it got out that he'd tried to lick what he'd tried to lick off Stacy's hand, then the other jocks would label him a fag, whether it was true or prejudiced or not, and they'd never let up on him and tear him apart and that would be that. And if it got out that he'd coerced Stacy by threatening to lie about what she'd done with him and trying to brand her a slut without her being one, then no girl in high school would ever look at him again, let alone talk to him, or whatever else. So whether or not Razor knew that I myself would be more than willing to supply the above information to all the interested parties in our immediate vicinity, he at least seemed to realize that he was screwed coming and going. And although I still thought he was stupid and spoiled and weak, he seemed to have just enough sense to keep his mouth shut. I had to give it to him for that, because if he'd said *anything*, he only would've made things worse for himself. Instead, he just put his hands in his short pockets and shrugged, leaving Tommy Sharpe—his friend—to take the brunt of it. Yeah, real class act.

"See?" Darren started up again. "Razor's not even denying it. You two dudes, man . . . shit." Darren shook his head. "And you *made* me hit you for *that*? Jesus, dude, you know I'm like *so* not into violence, and now I'm feeling all totally low and down on myself for clocking you. That's *so* bogus, dude, it's like afflicting my self-esteem."

Tommy had just been whipped twice over, and he seemed to realize it. "Sorry, D. I mean it, man. Sorry."

I had to give it to Darren; Tommy *made* him kick his ass, which upset him, so Tommy had to apologize for it—in front of everyone. Nice touch.

"No, dude, you know what? *I'm* the sorry one"—Darren changed his tune without skipping a beat—"stomping on you and like dressing you down in front of everybody and shit. That's wrong—severe and wrong. That's totally my bad. C'mon, dude, let's make it up."

Darren stuck out his hand and, with his false apology hanging in the air and everyone watching, Tommy had no choice but to take it. I guess that's when I realized that Tommy and Razor might've been big guys, and maybe tough guys (well, at least one was), but they were still *younger* than Darren, and he was letting them know it.

"Is it squashed?" Darren asked.

"Yeah, D, it's squashed," Tommy agreed.

"Cool." Darren smiled. "And this ain't against you, dude, because that shit between us is like dead and buried already." He looked up at all the other teenagers gathered round, raised his voice, and said, "Dudes, everybody knows this is *my* party and *my* house and like *my* rules, and the first rule is just totally *no fighting*, like never, and that's all for shit now tonight. So thanks for kicking it with the crew, and we'll live to jam another day, but this one's *so* over for me that it's *done*."

There was an outburst of groans and nos and come-ons and chill-outs, but Darren stood his ground. "Sorry, dudes, no dice. This party's totally over, so everyone clear out, and don't make me like call the cops or anything, because that's just too fucking beat. *Hasta*."

Darren turned, wedged through the crowd, walked across the deck, went inside, closed the sliding glass door behind him, and turned off some but not all of the outdoor lights. And he probably did all that just because he could.

It was Darren's house and Darren's rules and Darren's story, made up on the spot, but with plenty of kids to see it, and no one to contradict it, even though Tommy Sharpe had tried. So, chances were people would believe it. After all, it was just what kids had come to expect from Darren—just another expert job pulled off by the most popular, most partying, good-guy outlaw in town, tagged and signed *in person* this time by no less than the man himself.

Darren was in charge; everybody around here knew it and accepted it.

Yeah, I'd been right all along.

TWENTY

During the commotion of kids starting to leave,
Neecey took me inside Darren's house, to the half bathroom between
the kitchen and the back den. She stopped up my nosebleed with
some toilet paper, put a cold washcloth on the back of my neck, and
cleaned the blood off my face, chest, and hands. Then she led me
into the kitchen, got a frozen hamburger patty out of the freezer,
used a kitchen towel to tie it in place over my left eye, and then gave
me a frozen hot dog to press against the left side of my nose, which
was swelling badly, too. She sat me on one of the stools at the breakfast bar in the center of the kitchen, got me some aspirins and apple
juice to drink, and then went back outside to the deck. And she did
all of that without saying a word.

It would've been a golden opportunity to inspect her for the
symptoms of drug abuse or to lay hold of her before she left, but I
was in too much pain to try to do anything. The left side of my face
felt crushed, my entire head was thumping, and my neck and shoulders felt like I'd been whiplashed from behind at ninety miles an
hour. I had to give it to Tommy; as far as mindless overgrown brutes

went, that kid could really throw a punch. Detective manual rule number four: never fuck around with Tommy Sharpe.

I massaged the back of my neck with my free hand just long enough for the ringing in my ears to soften to a dizzying buzz, and checked to see if anyone was around. Then I stood up slowly from the bar stool and trod gingerly into the back den. There wasn't a place on me that didn't seem to yowl as I moved, but it wasn't over yet, so I couldn't let that stop me.

Inside the den there was a plush red throw rug in the middle of the floor, two black leather sofas facing each other from across the room, black lacquer cabinets and shelves along the walls, a four-stack stereo console, a big TV with a Betamax and a VCR directly underneath, and a small lamp in the far corner emitting a dim light. Behind the sofa to my left were some built-in window seats with fluffy red throw pillows, and above them were the back windows. They were the kind that opened in and out instead of up and down, and since we didn't have windows like that at home, it took me a couple of seconds to draw that conclusion and find a handle. I cranked one open as far as it would go, put the hot dog in my pocket to free up both my hands, and removed the screen, which I hid behind the curtain on the right-hand side of the window seat. Then I took a step back to inspect my handiwork. It would be a tight fit, but our escape route was all set up and ready to go. Now all I had to do was get both Neecey and me through it and out to safety. Right, no problem at all.

I hoisted the frozen hot dog out of my pocket and held it against my aching nose. Then I checked to make sure that the frozen hamburger tied to my eye was securely in place, so nothing would look amiss as I sat at the bar stool in the kitchen playing wounded possum, waiting for a shot to spirit Neecey and me the hell out of there. I leaned my back against the wall by the doorway that led to the kitchen and listened to the sound of a few stragglers moping through the house and out the front door. I heard a voice calling my name. It was Neecey's voice, and it was moving closer, but I couldn't call out to her because I didn't know if she was alone. I slinked back around the sofa to the window seats, wrapped myself in the curtain where I'd hidden the screen, and waited. My heart galloped. This might be my only chance to shanghai my sister back to the semblance of a normal life, and while I was barely standing on my own steam, I still had to try to make the most of it.

A backlit form appeared in the doorway, but I couldn't tell who it belonged to because I only had one good eye to look with and the curtain blocked most of its view. The form came closer, crossed the threshold, and stopped. I steeled myself to make a quick dive out the window and book it for all I was worth.

"Genie?" Neecey called. "You in there?"

Exactly what I'd hoped to hear. "Yeah, Neece," I whispered, "I'm over here."

"Where?" She paused. "Genie, um, what the hell are you doing hiding behind the curtains like that?"

I'd answer that one later. Right now it was time to put my plan into action. "Come over here," I said, stepping out. "I want to show you something."

Neecey walked around the back of the nearest sofa and over to the window seats. "What do you want to show me? You need to be like totally sitting down after the pounding you took."

"Here, look." I pointed through the open window, and when Neecey leaned over toward the sill, I dropped the hot dog, squatted down, jammed my palms under her butt, and pushed her upward with whatever force I could muster.

"Genie! What the fuck?!"

Neecey was either lighter than I'd expected, or I was having one of those surges of superhuman strength that people got in life-or-death situations, because just like that, I'd lifted her off the ground and wedged her torso out the window. Now all I had to do was shove her hips and legs through and we'd be gone.

"Stop, Genie! Stop!" she shrieked. Worse still, she started kicking her legs like a whipped giraffe so I couldn't get hold of them.

"Quiet, Neecey," I said, panting. "They'll hear you!"

"Yo . . . what the—*Holy shit!*" Darren's voice hitched, then quickened sharply from the doorway. "Little dude! Like back off. *Release!*"

Next thing I knew, Darren's orange hair and red Hawaiian shirt were beside me, and his tanned forearms and hands were reaching out to grab Neecey by the hips and pull her back in. I pushed harder, but one of Neecey's flailing feet caught me in the chest and knocked me back. Darren slid into the space I'd just vacated, gripped hold of Neecey more securely, and began to guide her back in.

Fucking Darren. That was it; I'd had it with him. I felt this piercing sensation ignite in my belly and my hands shaking wildly as everything before me flashed a dark, blinding red. "Get your filthy fucking hands off my goddamn sister!" I screamed—and lunged.

No, it probably wasn't a good idea. Darren had already proven that he was a much better scrapper than I'd ever given him credit for, while I'd just taken the whooping of a lifetime and was in no shape for a double bill. He must've turned just in time as I'd charged him, and crashed a swift uppercut flush under my nostrils that rammed the bridge of my nose into my brain and killed me, because all of a sudden everything was quiet and still, like a slow-motion sequence with no sound, and I felt as if I were sailing gently through the air, or maybe floating outside my own body. Then I was resting comfortably on my back, landing and sinking into big, soft cushions. For a split second it felt like all the tension and violence inside of me were somehow gone, and now that they were, there was no way they'd ever come back.

But all that changed as soon as I realized I wasn't dead, and that Darren had just worked some kind of flip or toss on me that had sent me flying onto the nearest sofa, where I'd landed safely and was lying stretched out on my back. And when I felt the seat of his shorts pressing down on my chest and stomach, I was glad my rage hadn't vanished for good, because I needed every ounce of it to throw punches and buck and jerk around and howl like a goddamn lunatic for him to get off.

"Chill, little dude, *chill*," Darren ordered. "You gotta like simmer down and maintain yourself before I'll even *think* of letting you up."

I kept struggling as fiercely as I could, reaching up to slap or grab at his nose, his hair, his ear—anything I could lay a hand to—but he was too tall for me to reach that high.

"Genie, seriously! *What the fuck* is your damage?"

Neecey's cheeks were bright red, her eyes were blazing, and I could see it all pretty clearly because she was standing right over me. *Goddamn it*. My rescue attempt had been shot to shit and I'd fallen into enemy clutches to boot, and I realized that unless I pulled it together somehow, I could be stuck with Neecey screeching into my face while Darren rested his ass on my chest all night.

I closed my eyes, tried to relax and take deep breaths, but it wasn't exactly easy with a 160-pound dildo perched atop my rib cage.

"You settled, little dude?" Darren asked. "Or are you stoked to be a La-Z-Boy for a while, because this is like way relaxing."

"No," I lied, "I'm settled."

"Swear it, Genie," Neecey insisted.

"Okay," I coughed, "I swear."

Darren hopped off me, and I continued to lie there on the sofa as the two of them hovered cautiously and stared. They didn't say anything and neither did I, and after a minute or two of all of us doing our best amateur mime routines, I decided I'd composed myself enough to sit up.

"You see, little dude, you just needed to steady some from all the upheaval," Darren said, placing his hand on my shoulder.

"Get your fucking hand *off* me," I snapped at him.

"Jesus Christ, Genie! What is your *deal* already? Are you like completely bat shit? God only knows what you're doing here, or like why in the hell you were trying to push me out the window, but Darren just fully saved your pathetic little life, and you're still acting like a total *asshole*."

"I was trying to *save you,* Neecey," I told her. "And stop defending *him.* You're *always* fucking defending him. I have eyes, you know. I can see. And I know *exactly* what kind of low-down dirty bullshit he's up to, even if *you* don't."

Neecey started to say something, but Darren took hold of her hand and muzzled her, proving beyond all doubt who was driving that bus.

"We better like hear him out and shit," he said, raising an eyebrow at Neecey in a way that seemed to be signaling something. "Sounds like he's got the goods on me, and I need to know if he does."

I didn't know what the hell kind of code he was using, but it was obvious he knew I was serious.

"No, I don't have 'the goods' on you, D," I said, nice and easy, "I got 'the stuff.' Yeah, that's right, 'the stuff' you had Neecey smuggle over here tonight and the same *stuff* you lured her away from Gary to mule around town. I know how you get the money to pay for it, and the web of crimes you've been spinning to throw the coppers off your scent. You can bank on it, painter boy, I know *all* of it, and I have *proof*."

Darren squeezed Neecey's hand again to clam her up. "Ah-ight, little dude, this is the moment you've been waiting for. Let's see what you got." There was a glint of craft in his eyes, the twinkle of a career criminal who only showed emotion while walking the tightrope of being had.

"I'll be more than happy to give it," I said. "But I'm not stupid enough to spill my guts in front of both of you so I can get double-teamed by a pair of professional bullshitters. No fucking way. Before I say anything, one of you has to go."

"That's like completely fine," Neecey said, glaring. "Because I *so* totally have a few things to say to you, too."

Darren turned toward the door.

"No," I said. "*He* stays, *you* go."

Darren and Neecey both spun on their heels and stared at each other.

"It's cool, Neece." Darren winked at her.

Neecey looked stunned and lost but relented anyway, rolling her eyes. "*Whatever*. But if your little pissing contest lasts like more than fifteen minutes, then I'm totally coming back in." She pulled the door closed behind her when she left.

"*You got what* you wanted, little dude, so spill."

"I'd say stop me when I'm getting cold, but since that ain't gonna happen . . ." I trailed off, letting him get used to the noose I was about to tighten, before starting again. "Remember the other day when you told me that *most* of the crew had been tagging the church with you on Saturday night?"

"Yeah, at the arcade." Darren shrugged. "What of it?"

"Nothing really, except you forgot to add that the *rest* of the crew had been at the retirement home, dropping a wank tag on the sign out front, making it look like amateur bullshit *on purpose*."

Darren's lips curled dismissively.

"Yeah, I have to give it to you," I went on, "it was a brilliant plan. Pulling two jobs at different places across town from each other on the same night, one that you'd intended to claim as your *own* work, and one that you'd intended to pass off as *somebody else's*. That way nobody would ever *dream* of linking the two, nobody would connect the dots and figure out that the tag on the church was just a *decoy*, an alibi that seemed to place you guys somewhere else. And although nobody *saw* your hit on the church, you sure as hell made a point of *telling* everybody about it."

Darren slowly folded his arms across his chest. "Ah-ight, you got my full-on attention, little dude. What else?"

I could tell he was playing the role of the underworld crime boss like a salty old veteran, and that I had to match him stride for stride without letting it rattle me. "I'll tell you what else," I snarled. "How about the reason you guys needed that alibi in the first place?"

He nodded.

"Not only the church, but the whole goddamn kaboodle of tags you and the crew have been dropping this summer have *all* just been a cover to divert attention away from the *real* crimes you've been committing, crimes that've been going on at the retirement home for over a month now."

"What crimes?"

"That's the sixty-four-thousand-dollar question, isn't it?" I'd cleared him back a couple of steps and was pacing in front of the sofa now. "The *real* crime was swiping cash from old folks at the retirement home, weak and harmless seniors who'd forgotten to lock their windows at night."

"Someone's been jacking the retirement home?" For a second Darren's concern almost seemed genuine.

"Don't act so shocked, okay?" I fired back. "You already know *all* about it." I was still hurting and wobbly, but it felt like the cobwebs were clearing from my head and the whole plot was laid out before me now, down to the smallest details. "Once you and your buds had broken in the first time and seen how easy it was, you realized you'd struck the mother lode of free loot and wanted to draw from the well again and again. But you knew you couldn't get away with it forever, unless you played it smart, and by planting a fake tag on the sign at the scene of the burglaries, you'd made it look like there were some *other* vandals on the loose in town, to shift suspicion away from yourselves and throw the authorities off your trail."

I was picking up steam now; I felt it. "Yeah, you'd *thought* your plan had worked and steered everybody away from what you were *really* up to, even the cops who'd come to your house on Sunday morning to hassle you about it. But since you're better than David Copperfield when it comes to deceiving people, you lied to the fuzz, dodged the heat, and *thought* you were in the clear. Then *I* showed up at the arcade on Monday and questioned you about the sign at the retirement home, too, and you started to *think again*."

Darren's face had stiffened and his eyes were squinting.

"But that's when you remembered that you're the leader of a gang, the kind of arch criminal who has the clout and the connections to hire a couple of toughs like Razor and Tommy to rub someone out of the picture if he wanted to. And that someone was *me*."

"I know, I'm like all fiendish and shit," Darren jibed, cracking a smile. "But riddle me this, McScruff. If Razor and Tommy are like my hit squad and all, then why did I just totally waste one of them while I was getting your back?"

"Because you *weren't* getting my back. You just jumped at the chance to make it *look like you were,* to put a wall of distance between you and your henchmen for everyone to see."

Darren smiled wider and nodded his head.

"And with Razor and Tommy out of the picture, nobody would be able to trace *any* of their deeds back to *you.* No fucking way. Not the sweet lullaby you'd sent me at football tryouts, or having ordered Razor over to our house to try to root out what Neecey knew about me being on to you, just in case she needed a little roughing-up, too. And when that didn't work, you'd opted for a more direct route and convinced Neecey to read my journal, to see exactly how close I was getting."

I put my hand up, cutting Darren off before he could speak. "Yeah, I know how you got my sister strung out on drugs and alcohol and took complete advantage and were using the shit out of her. That's why I followed her here tonight—I came to get her *away* from you and all your bullshit." I sighed loudly, slowly shaking my head. "Even the stupidest pushers know that nobody ever suspects a hot chick, and that's *exactly* what makes hot chicks perfect to cart contraband or payoffs wherever they need to go. Jesus, it was a foul, nasty business, coldly calculated from beginning to end, but that's *all* you ever wanted her for."

"Sounds like you got the angles all figured out."

"You can bet your ass I do, and it all starts with the simple fact that somewhere along the line *you lost control*. You went from being a petty vandal and small-time toker to a full-blown addict with a monkey on your back, so you had to start selling what little weed you didn't burn to make ends meet. But your habit was too big by then and too expensive and you couldn't pay off your suppliers and you had to turn to more serious forms of crime to get yourself out of their debt. So you tapped Neecey as your beard and carrier and started stealing from the retirement home and then dropped a shitty-ass tag on the front sign to try to cover it up. Drugs and money and sex—that's what all of this was about. Then again, that's what it's *always* about."

Darren, still smiling, flipped his hair back and sat down on the sofa on the opposite side of the room. "Proof, little dude. You said you had proof."

"I do. One of the perpetrators dropped a black rubber bracelet by the sign at the retirement home, and I have it."

"Oh, yeah? Where?"

"Don't worry," I said, "it's in a safe place. And when I hand it over to the cops tomorrow and they find out that the fingerprints on it belong to you, or one of your boys, you're gonna be in a dickload of trouble."

The room went quiet—cemetery quiet. Now was the time for him to break down and confess, so I stood there stony silent and waited for it.

Finally, Darren shrugged and said, "Yeah, maybe. Except for when the cops find out that the bracelet doesn't belong to any of us, little dude, 'cause none of us were there."

I'd expected a lowlife like Darren to try to lie his way out of it, but it was the way he'd said it, relaxed, unconcerned, that threw me off. But I wasn't gonna let that or a blatant fucking falsehood stand in my way.

"Oh, that's right, what the hell was I thinking?" I poured it on. "If you *say* you're innocent, then you *must* be. Jesus Christ! What kind of *chump* do you take me for?"

"Seriously, little dude." He spoke calmly, his brown eyes steady on me. "Me and most of the crew hit the church on Saturday night, just like I told you, nothing else. And I said 'most' of us because Roni stayed home to babysit his little sis. We been totally raggin' on him about it since then, too."

He still seemed so unfazed that what he'd just said didn't even sound like a lie. I started to feel unsteady, confused, as if the after-shock of the head blows I'd suffered were kicking in. I knew Roni had a younger sister, two grades below me, and that the crew mocked him all the time for treating her like a princess. I began to think maybe I'd shown my hand too soon, and that it might be better to play along for a second so I could hit him from another direction.

"All right, let's just *pretend* you guys *didn't* tag the sign at the retirement home. Fine, we're pretending. But if you didn't do it, then *who did?*"

"Like I told you the other day, little dude, I don't *know* who did it."

"Horseshit."

"Sincerely," he insisted. "It's like I got an *idea* who did it, but—"

"Oh, you have a *suspect?* Why didn't you just say so? Who?"

"Well, the smart money's on Razor, bro-ski. I totally thought you'd fingered him for the perp yourself, and that's why you bum-rushed his package like you did."

"*Razor?*" It was so preposterous I almost laughed. But it only went to prove what I already suspected, that Darren was trying to play me for a chump. That was his game, but I wasn't gonna let on that I knew it just yet. "That doesn't make *any* sense," I said, still pretend-ing. "He's never been a tagger before, so why would he try to be one now?"

"Anybody's guess," he prevaricated. "But in the past few weeks he's been more amped and aggro than ever. Sticky says there's a rumor going around that he's been copping cycles with Tommy for when football starts next week, which would totally explain it and shit—"

"Wait. Cycles? What's that?" I asked.

"Juice, little dude."

"Juice?"

"Shee-it." He sucked his teeth and shook his head. "You need to get out more. Juice is steroids, mini man."

"*Steroids?*" I'd heard the whispers in town about steroids before— how they made you bigger, stronger, faster, hornier than a dump truck full of toads, and prone to fits of uncontrollable rage. And those whispers only got louder and more specific when it came to starters on the high-school football team, especially star players like Chuck and Easy. "Tommy Sharpe does steroids?" I asked.

Darren pulled his face back a little, staring at me quizzically. "Dude, tell me you didn't get a look at him while he was thumping your skull? Nobody goes from being the Pillsbury Doughboy to like the One Man Gang in two months without juice. Nobody."

I'd gotten a good look at Tommy Sharpe all right, more of him than I'd ever wanted to see in fact, and the kid was pretty much a monster. But I'd gotten several good looks at Razor, too, and he was just as bony as ever. "If Razor's taking steroids like Tommy, then why the hell is he still so skinny?"

"No clue. They work faster for some people than for others, and you're supposed to pump crazy iron to get the max results and shit. Tommy's been doing weight training with the team all summer, but Razor hasn't because he's been too busy talking smack about how he's gonna quit and all. So maybe that's it. Or maybe he hasn't been taking them as long."

I wondered what the hell made Darren such an authority on steroids; then again, if there was one thing he knew about, it was drugs. "So you're telling me that Razor tagged the sign at the retirement home because he's on steroids?" The question sounded stupid even as it came out of my mouth.

"Like I said, little dude, I can't say for sure. But maybe he's the one boosting cash from the home, too, to front for his juice and shit, and he tagged the sign to make it look like *we'd* been doing it."

This wasn't the way it was supposed to go. There was too much new information, too many unforeseen twists to the story. Worse still, some of it was actually starting to make sense. I held my ground, though, and pushed back in the other direction. "Well, that's it, then. Razor tagged the sign at the retirement home to conceal the fact that he's been stealing money from there to pay for the steroids he's taking that have had *no visible effect* on him whatsoever. While you're at it, why don't you try to sell me a bridge in the desert, because I'm not buying that shit either."

"You can like buy it or not, I'm just telling you what I heard." Darren paused, fingering his pukka bead choker. "All's I know is that ever since he figured out he'd be surfing pine this season, Razor's been telling everybody he's gonna quit the team and acting like full-on assness to everyone. That kid's always been twisted," he added, "but throw a little juice into that mix and he'd be bringing the chaos for real."

"Like I really give two shits about Razor's behavioral history," I said.

"Like who does? I'm just trying to tell you why I think he did it and shit."

"It's called a *motive*," I specified, "and if you're gonna conjure one up for Razor out of thin air, then you damn well better dazzle me with it."

"Conjure?" Darren laughed. "Dude, no matter how much Razor *says* he's gonna quit football, he totally *can't*. He's roughed up too many younger brothers and sisters of kids in high school, and he'll be dead meat on his own without his jock buds getting his back. Nobody rocks the mic solo in the big HS and lives to tell about it, little dude," he declared. "You gotta roll deep twenty-four-seven, or your ass is destined for toast. It's like a natural law and shit."

"So you really expect me to believe that Razor's become this out-of-control menace because he's a confused, unlikable kid who doesn't know where or how to fit in? That is the *weakest* shit I have *ever* fucking heard."

"Stow that mess, little dude. People've told *you* the same thing like a million times and shit."

Okay, maybe they had. But I knew we were talking about Razor, not me, so I wasn't gonna let him befuddle me into thinking otherwise. From what I knew about the hit at the retirement home, however, I could see that it wouldn't necessarily take two people to pull it off, if the one person who'd done it happened to have a moped, like Razor did. All he'd have to do is stand on top of the seat, commit the crime, and then crank the engine and be gone. Worse still, a different picture of *all* the crimes was rapidly forming in my punch-addled head, a picture that had a spoiled and desperate Razor stealing money from the home to pay for steroids to up his chances on the football team, tagging the front sign to try to steer the blame toward Darren and the crew, coercing Stacy into easing his supercharged hormones, and breaking the window at the black church because he was a sleazy, bigoted juice-hound who was losing every single bit of his perverse and feeble mind.

Then again, I wasn't certain about any of it. The only thing I knew for sure was that I was starting to doubt some of the conclusions I'd drawn. "So what if Razor did it?" I shifted ground. "He's still working for *you* anyway."

"Sorry to disappoint, little dude, but that's a negative, too. Me and the crew have zero tolerance for buzz assassins like Tommy and Razor. Besides, ever since Razor dropped by your *casa* the other day to try to press up on your sis, he and I have had beef."

Maybe that's why Neecey had stonewalled me; it was *exactly* the kind of thing that would've set me off. The tables were turning hard and fast. I had to try to swing them back in my favor. "All right, if all that's true, and you're not lying to me, then why the hell didn't you do anything about it? And if you have such beef with him, then what were Razor and Tommy doing at your party tonight?"

"Dude, I said I *thought* Razor did it, but that I didn't *know* for sure. And since nobody actually saw him do it or can like prove it or anything, there's nothing anybody can do about it. You can't just go *accusing* people because you don't *like* them and shit."

I realized Darren had aimed that last part at me, but it hit the mark anyway.

"And I didn't invite them to the soiree either, little dude," he went on, "they just bogarted it. But since they did, me and your sis were getting in Razor's eye, like putting the heat on him and getting some payback for trespassing and trying to take liberties and all. But that's when you came jetting in and dive-bombed his gonads and shit. By the way, that was fucking *awesome*," Darren laughed. "Beyond bitchin', little dude. Seriously."

He leaned forward as far as he could from his seat on the sofa and stretched his hand toward me for a high five. I must've had a concussion or something, because I actually found myself starting to lean in that direction when the sound of Neecey's voice snapped me back.

"Don't you even *dare*, Genie! And what are you like high-fiving him for, Darren?"

Darren seemed every bit as shocked to discover that Neecey had been eavesdropping on our conversation from the other side of the door as I was. "I told you it was cool, Neece," he said, frowning. "You didn't have to go all dippin'."

"Well, he's *my* brother, and I'm like so glad I did or I never would've heard all the totally wrong and heinous things he just said about us."

I was pissed and worried that Neecey had heard everything, but she'd given me an opening, maybe my last, so I jumped on it. "Oh, yeah? If they were so heinous and goddamn wrong, then why don't you tell me about 'the stuff'? I *heard* you talking about it on the phone *myself*, and how Darren would cut you off if you didn't bring it. And you haven't even *tried* to deny it."

"Du-uu-ude," Darren groaned, "*don't*. Trust me."

"You can*not* be serious," Neecey hissed. "'The stuff' you think I was supposed to be all smuggling or whatever was *party decorations*."

No, that was *not* the answer I'd been looking for. I shifted my eyes nervously to Darren.

He shrugged again, almost apologetically this time. "Yeah, little dude, it's not a righteous party without the favors. And since you guys live closer to the supermarket, I fronted Neecey some ducats to pick the stuff up and bring it over, while me and the crew were out cashing in some solids to land the beverages."

"The stuff was party decorations?" I asked meekly.

"To like ease your mind and shit," Darren offered, "I score the cheeba from my cousin in Holmdel, totally free of charge. He grows it under a black light in his closet—"

"*Darren.*"

"Steady, Neece, it's not like an invitation or anything. I'm just saying, is all."

"Well, don't, not in front of *him*. He's only *twelve*."

"Nuh-unh," I mumbled, "I'm almost thirteen."

"*Duh!*" Neecey sniped. "Almost thirteen *is* twelve, Genie. And you're like only twelve years old but you're already a complete psycho who's been left back for decking a teacher, and now you're turning into this way scary stalker who eavesdrops on people and totally follows them, too. And that's not funny, Genie, that's *serious*."

I didn't say anything to that, mostly because I was trying to figure out just how serious this was going to get.

"I'm not trying to butt in or whatever . . ." Darren hesitated.

"*But* . . ." Neecey rolled her eyes.

"It's just, if the little dude earnestly thought you were jeopardizing your person or whatever, like he said, then you can't majorly ream him for what he did. Dude junior just showed some extra vigilance and follow-through is all, like a badass younger bro's supposed to."

"How would *you* know what a younger brother is supposed to do,

Darren? You're an *only child*. And why are you like sticking up for him? Didn't you hear—"

"Chill, Neece. I totally heard what he said, but I'm like sticking up for him anyway."

"But why?" Neecey asked, looking genuinely baffled.

"Because the little dude's either all on his own or you and your moms got him so blanketed that he can't like move and shit, so like who else is gonna do it?"

I guess Neecey wasn't expecting Darren to say that—shit, neither was I—because a lot of the tension seemed to drain out of her and she didn't say anything in return.

"I'm just saying there's like another way to look at it that doesn't chop the little dude down so much, is all. And for the record," Darren addressed me while standing up, "I know you been grudging on me since I took your old bike, and that you're totally against me seeing your sis because of it. I'm full-on sorry about that, little dude, because things should be way more copacetic between you and me. But I'm not wiggin' on you for what you said and shit. Earnestly. It was a most wicked story you told, and I was way into hearing it."

Fucking Darren. He was making it harder and harder for me to keep hating him.

"Where are you going?" Neecey asked as Darren made for the door.

"I gotta check on the damage the crew is wreaking on the homestead. But I can grab a fresh meat patch for the little dude's eye jammy while I'm out there if you want."

It was about then that I finally noticed the raw juices streaming down my face. "I don't know where the hot dog got to," I informed Neecey, "but he's right. This thing is pretty much thawed. I'm not sure it's doing much good, though, so don't bother."

"You know you need to put steak on a black eye so it'll heal, Genie," Neecey nagged.

"Yeah, but this is a hamburger, not a steak."

"That's chopped Black Angus sirloin you got on your mug, little dude," Darren cut in, "the only thing my pops'll grill. And sirloin is total steak, trust me."

"But it's *made* into a hamburger," I said, "so it might not work the right way."

"Genie, you don't know what the hell you're talking about," Neecey proclaimed. "Darren's getting you another one and you're gonna wear it whether you want to or not."

TWENTY-ONE

Darren's departure had left Neecey and me alone, all to ourselves, which was the absolute last place I wanted to be. Yeah, I'd fucked up royally this time, and with the way her eyes were burning holes in my face from across the room, it didn't look like she was going to pass on the opportunity to tell me *all* about it. I couldn't say I blamed her, but that wasn't gonna make what was coming my way any easier to take, and any second now she was going to let me have it.

So I got ready for it. But it didn't come. Instead, she sat down next to me on the sofa and put her arm around my shoulder. Then she said, "Close your eyes."

"Why?" I didn't know where she was going with this, and that made me nervous.

"Just do it."

I did.

"Eyes closed?"

"Yeah."

"Now, I want you to do me a favor."

"What?" I gulped.

"I want you to clear your mind and try to imagine what it's like for me to have a brother like *you*."

I couldn't be sure where she'd learned that trick, but it was one of the nastiest she'd ever pulled on me, and I hadn't been expecting it. *A brother like you.* Yeah, I'd heard her whining about what it was like so many times that I knew the litany by heart: how she'd been forced to babysit me for the past three years; how we were chained together at the hip, so she could hardly go anywhere or do anything without bringing me along; how she had to look out for me and clean up after me and make sure I had something to eat for dinner and that I brushed my teeth before I went to bed; and especially how mom held her responsible for me when she was at work, so when I got into trouble or a fight, Neecey always got yelled at and grounded, too. I knew all that, just like I knew I was draining every second of joy out of her otherwise carefree adolescence. But for some reason it stuck with me this time—*a brother like you*—and I had to swallow hard to keep from choking up.

"Tell me something, Genie."

"W-what," I croaked.

"Where are you supposed to be?"

She'd changed directions on me, and I was having trouble following. "What?"

"It's an easy question. Where are you supposed to be?"

"Home."

"Right. And who's supposed to be watching you?"

"No one. I'm supposed to be watching myself."

"Okay, so tell me, *genius*, if you're supposed to be home watching yourself, then how are you going to explain that gnarly shiner of yours to mom?"

Cold shivers of panic ripped all the way through me, because I hadn't thought of that yet, and I had *no idea* how I'd pull it off.

"Stop frowning, Genie, it makes you look simple." Neecey sighed heavily and continued, "I so can't even *try* to help you this time. Mom's going to slaughter you, completely slaughter you, and if I try to get involved I'll be stuck babysitting you until I graduate, and there's *nothing* I can do about like *any* of it."

The gravity of it was sinking in fast; I'd hung us both. "So what are we going to tell her?" I asked.

"*We* aren't going to tell her anything, Genie—*you are. You* broke your promise to mom, not me, so you're going to have to like face her *all by yourself.*"

I nodded. But just because I knew I'd have to face mom alone didn't mean I was looking forward to it.

"You took the whole fucking cake this time, Genie," she went on. "You realize that, don't you?"

I guess I had.

"And you're a totally untrusting piece of shit—you know that, too, right?"

I declined to respond.

"A dope-smuggling slut? Is that what you *really* think of me? And you even accused me of reading your journal? You know, sometimes you *really* suck."

"But if you didn't read it," I braved the waters, "then how did you know about Stacy?"

"I met Stacy at the pool with Cynthia this summer, nimrod, and she totally asked me about you, so I just put like two and two together."

Okay, I felt stupid for not having thought of that, because Cynthia lived at Sunnybrook, too, and took Neecey to the pool there all the time. But at least it made me hold off on asking her whether she'd ratted me out to mom—it seemed her list of charges against me was long enough already.

Neecey dropped her chin and exhaled harshly, but tried to be calmer when she spoke again. "Sure, mom and I are totally curious about what you write in your journal because you've been like all dedicated for nearly a year now, but your counselor said we're not even supposed to like *ask* you about it until you come to us and tell us you're ready to share, which we figure will be like *never*."

"That's not true, Neecey," I tried to protest, "I will—"

"No you *won't*, Genie, because you're completely warped and think nobody really cares about you and that everybody's out to get you."

That stung more than it should have, and the lump in my throat started to tighten again when the door creaked open and a blast of music and light flooded the room. Darren peeked his head around the door and for a second I was almost glad to see him.

"Dudes, one burger bandage, coming up." He smiled.

Neecey stood up from the sofa, walked over to Darren, and retrieved it from him. Then she came over to me, removed the towel and the lump of soggy meat from my face, and fastened a fresh, ice-cold chopped sirloin patty in its place.

"There," she said. "With a little luck, you won't look *exactly* like the Elephant Man for the next two weeks. You totally don't deserve my help, though, or Darren's either." Neecey paused—a little too maliciously, I thought. "You have something you want to say to him, *don't you*, Genie?"

She'd just pushed a fresh hot plate of crow under my nose and it was time for me to dig in. I stood up and looked straight at Darren with my free eye. I knew I didn't have any choice in the matter, so I bit the bullet and said, "Thanks, D, you know for—"

He put his hand up, waving me off. "No sweat, little dude. I promised your sis I'd look out for you and you gave me a prime chance to come through. So we're square." Then he flipped his hair back and said, "Check it, Neece, the crew cranked up the after party and it's totally choice. How 'bout we go kick it and get the little dude some eats? He's gotta be full-on ravenous."

"I don't know, Darren, I'm so totally pissed at him."

"Ah-ight, I totally get it, the little dude pissed you off severely and you're still sore at him. But it's like you got all the time you need to be pissed and sore tomorrow. Right now there's a total fiesta goin' on, and the little dude's my guest, so I'm obliged to show him some hospitality and shit."

Neecey folded her arms across her chest while she mulled it over. "All right," she finally said to Darren, "I guess he's allowed to eat." Then she pointed at me and said, "But don't think you're getting off easy, Genie, because I am *so not* done with you."

Funny, I'd never thought she was.

"Hear that, little dude?" Darren beamed. "Official party reprieve, effective most pronto."

Fucking Darren. I'd always pegged him as the villain, but here he was, saving my ass again.

The three of us walked out of the back den and into the kitchen, where the crew and a handful of girls were drinking and dancing and laughing and having what looked like an awesome time. Darren called for everyone's attention and introduced me to them as the new paperweight champion of the world, and they all whooped and whistled and cheered. Then he sat me at the breakfast bar in the center of the kitchen and gave me a hamburger, a cooked one, with cheese and a toasted bun and ketchup and everything, and after I'd scarfed that down, he got me another. Then Squat came over and handed me half a cup of foamy beer, and just like that it was official—I was partying for the very first time in my life, and not minding it at all.

Darren had cranked the stereo and was dancing around with Burger and Squat—popping and whopping and moon-walking on the kitchen's white tile floor in socks they'd fetched from upstairs—and once in a while Squat would shout "D-break!" and they'd go into this crazy kick-boxing routine right on rhythm. They were lauding Darren's triumph over Tommy Sharpe, all three of them, reenacting it to song—bragging and boasting and having a blast—and they were funny as hell to watch. Through my right eye, the one that wasn't covered, I just glimpsed Roni sneaking into the den with a blonde in a tight red dress that left little about her figure to speculation, closing the door behind them. Chakha and Cynthia were still in their swimsuits, and every few minutes they darted into the kitchen or back outside, like Captain Caveman after one of the Teen Angels. They were both sopping wet, giggling, and blushing the whole time. I didn't see Lyle, because he was outside at the barbecue pit manning the grill, but I saw the short, curvy brunette and the wispy redhead who were supplying him with various meats and fixings from the refrigerator and freezer. And Sticky, the pipe-cleaner klepto, had his dark hair slicked back and was wearing mirrored sunglasses, long white coveralls with a zipper down the front that was open to his waist, and about half a wheelbarrow of fake gold chains across his bird chest. He was drinking keg beer from a bucket-sized brandy snifter and entertaining not one, or two, but *three* dark-haired honeys with Elvis impersonations, flipping up his collar, saying, "Hey, baby, don't make the King smack ass," and tossing fake karate moves into the air so they all fell out laughing.

I was mostly watching, taking in the sights and sounds of it all, and mowing down whatever edible thing chanced within my reach. I had to give it to him, Lyle could hook the grub up with the best of them, and if this was all the crew was really up to, it wasn't anywhere near as despicable as I'd thought. Yeah, a teenage party like this was probably every parent's worst nightmare, but it seemed Darren and the crew were just out for good times, and that they'd gotten pretty skilled at getting them.

After a little while, Sticky sidled up next to me at the breakfast bar and said, "You *totally* should've seen yourself pillaging Razor's nutsack, little dude, like all berserk and out of nowhere. You're hardcore sinister, for real."

Darren came around the other side of me and said, "Totally.

You've kicked a teacher's ass and fronted a deuce of high-school football players all by yourself—and you haven't even started seventh grade yet. Once we get the word out, you're gonna be the most feared kid in the history of junior high."

"You're gonna be a legend, little dude," Burger agreed from behind the refrigerator door. "Total legend."

I didn't know if they were right about that and I didn't really care. I'd never done anything to try to be popular, and I didn't think I wanted to be, especially on the back of some watered-down bullshit like that. But if kids passed the story around and gave me less trouble because of it, then I knew I probably wouldn't bother correcting them. That was one thing I could definitely use more of—less trouble—and letting people believe what they wanted to believe didn't seem like the worst way to get it.

I had to admit it, being at the after party and getting congratulated by everybody was a lot of fun, and I was having a good time. But I still felt out of place. Maybe it was because I still didn't know what had happened with the sign or who had really done it, or because I'd proven beyond all reasonable doubt that I was the worst fucking detective the world had ever seen. Shit, Marlowe would not have appreciated my skills the tiniest little bit, and now that I thought about it, neither would my client. So maybe it felt like something was off because I'd been wrong about most everything and everyone over the past few days, and probably much longer than that. Or maybe because I realized I'd not only humiliated my sister in front of her friends by throwing another fit in public, but I'd embarrassed myself, too. Or maybe I was just having trouble accepting that people around here were being friendly to me, because they'd never been that way before. Then again, I couldn't put my finger on it, and I was in no position to judge. Maybe I wasn't out of place. Maybe nothing was off. Maybe all of it was just in my head.

I'd lost track of Neecey for a while but caught sight of her as she was coming inside from the deck, telling Darren it was almost eleven-thirty and that they had to get me home. When I heard that, I stood up from my stool at the breakfast bar, finished the few dollops of froth left in my beer, and removed the chopped sirloin patty from my eye. Darren set off to round up Sticky and get the show on the road, and I headed for the bathroom to wash my face. Just as I got to the door, I felt a small, cold hand slip into mine. Yeah, I was taken by surprise because I thought she'd be long gone by now, and because I couldn't bring myself to look at her yet because of what I'd done. But she leaned her head against my shoulder and just stayed where she was, holding my hand.

"Thanks," she whispered.

No, I didn't understand Stacy. I couldn't figure out what she'd be thanking *me* for, or the way her mind worked, and I knew right then it would probably take me ages to grasp the littlest bit of it. But I was happy that she was standing beside me, and I was willing to take my time.

TWENTY-TWO

Either Sticky was drunk or he was a rotten driver or he was paying too much attention to the tape deck instead of the road, because we were going too fast, veering and swerving all over the place, but he somehow managed to keep "We Are the Champions" by Queen blasting on a continuous loop throughout the entire ride. Besides Sticky, it was Darren, Neecey, Cynthia, Chakha, Stacy, and me, and the top was off Sticky's Jeep and we were crammed together and the music was blaring and we were all singing along at the top of our lungs, as if we'd taken the party with us instead of having left it. Sticky was in the driver's seat, Darren was in the passenger seat with Neecey in his lap, and to my left, Chakha's and Cynthia's arms and legs were so tangled up that it was hard to tell who was sitting on whom. You didn't have to be Dr. Ruth to know that I'd never be Manning the Lookout again. No fucking way. But with Stacy sitting on my lap, it was kind of difficult for me to shed a tear at its passing.

The plan was to drop Stacy off, then me, then the others would return to Darren's for a little while, although I didn't ask what for, and then they'd all get in the Jeep again later and drop Neecey and Cynthia at Cynthia's place, where they were staying tonight. It seemed like too much driving and too many trips and too much backtracking, but I had Stacy's butt cheeks bouncing around on my thighs and we were all belting out "No time for losers, 'cause we are the chaaaaamp-yons" as loud as we could, so I just sat back and sponged it all in while it lasted.

We pulled up in front of Stacy's apartment, and she hopped off me, over the side of the Jeep, and onto the pavement, practically before we'd even stopped. I still hadn't said anything to her since we'd met up in the kitchen, and I didn't know what to do, so I just kind of sat there, twiddling my thumbs. Sticky looked over his shoulder from the driver's seat, lifted his sunglasses, and said, "Little dude, you have to like walk her to the door, or she'll think you got no chivalry and whatnot," and he nodded his chin at me to get out. So that's what I did.

Stacy was standing at the curb, waiting for me, and as soon as I'd reached her, she took my hand again. It was a short walk to her apartment, maybe twelve yards, but I was nervous all the way. Everything was quiet, until Sticky howled, "Lit-tle duuu-uuuu-uuuude!" into the night, and the others hit and punched him and told him to shut up, and I felt myself blushing. My heart started pounding as we got to her door, because I still didn't know what to say, but Stacy turned to me, gave me a quick kiss, slipped something into my hand, and bolted inside and out of sight before I had a chance to catch my breath or blink.

I looked down into my palm, steadied it with my other hand for a second, then unfolded the piece of paper and saw her name written out in big, loopy cursive and her phone number underneath it. Yeah, I got the digits, and it felt like I'd won the lottery and Super Bowl MVP, both at the same time, only a million times better. And I noticed something else, a tiny detail that really jumped out: Stacy didn't spell her name with a *y* at the end, the way our teachers spelled it and the way I'd always written it in my journal. No, she spelled it with an *i*—Staci—and for some reason that one letter seemed to change everything. Sure, I knew I still had a lot to feel bad about, but right now I couldn't help feeling happier and more excited than I'd ever thought possible. Then again, maybe it had nothing to do with the *i* at the end of Staci's name. Maybe it was the heart she'd used to dot it.

I probably should've known everything was going way too well and that I was due for a fall, most likely a catastrophic one, around the next corner. Sure enough, as we pulled up to our house, we saw mom's car parked at the curb and all the houselights on.

"Holy fuck," Neecey whispered, and then asked Darren what time it was.

It was about midnight, but only just, he said, which meant mom shouldn't have been home for at least another hour on a Wednesday.

Neecey turned to look at me from the passenger seat. "We are so totally and utterly and forever fucked, Genie, I'm *not* even kidding."

I had to agree, but I thought there was a chance that *we* didn't have to be, so I said, "Just let me out and you guys beat it, and I won't tell her I was with you."

"See, the little dude is chilly to the bone," Sticky said. "My younger bro wouldn't do that for me."

"Dude," Darren chimed in, "you saw how he ransacked Razor's jewels; little dude fears no fear."

They were wrong, dead wrong, both of them. I just thought Neecey deserved a pass if she could get it, and I'd give her one if I could.

But she said, "Genie, get a clue, okay? She's waiting for you and she's already seen the Jeep, trust me."

I said I'd tell mom that I got a ride from someone, and Neecey laughed in my face before I'd even finished.

"Who?" she asked. "*Who* would you get a ride from, Genie, or *where* would you be at this hour, because you don't have *any* friends."

Sticky, Darren, Cynthia, and Chakha all protested—*Hey, whoa, back off, way harsh, we're his friends*—but Neecey was right. If I had a friend, she was either sitting on top of Darren in the passenger seat telling me the truth, or she was home in her apartment right now, and I'd just made that friend tonight and didn't know if she even owned a bicycle, let alone a car.

"We're going in together," Neecey ordered, "and if you say like even *one word* before she gets it all out of her system, then I won't have to kill you tomorrow because she'll murder you tonight, got that?"

I nodded.

"This is serious, Genie, so like don't fuck it up, I'm totally begging you."

I nodded again.

Neecey said good-bye to everyone and that she'd see them around the end of October or early November when she wasn't grounded anymore. I said good-bye, too, and thanks for the ride and everything else and that I'd had fun, because I did. They all said good-bye and waved back, and somebody, most likely Darren, said, "Go on, little dude, show your *madre* what you're made of," and I appreciated the encouragement, but that was *exactly* what I feared.

From the outside of the house, things looked bad. Inside the house, they looked even worse. As soon as we opened the door we smelled smoke, cigarette smoke, and mom only ever smoked when she was at what she called her "wit's end," and the air was so thick and stale that she must've been witless for a while now. Neecey and I looked at each other before we went into the kitchen to face the music, and it was somehow reassuring to see that I wasn't the only one terrified out of my skin.

Not reassuring enough, though. When we got into the kitchen, mom was still wearing the black T-shirt and jeans she wore to work at the bar, her hair was down and badly mussed, she was drinking back an entire cigarette, and her mascara had run from her eyes, which were glaring rather nastily at us. Instantly, I felt panicked, and had this overwhelming urge to say something to her—to apologize, confess, beg, plead, whatever—anything to calm her down and bring her back to earth. But just as I was about to open my mouth, Neecey reached out and grabbed my hand, steadying me and reminding me to shut the hell up, which I did. Mom stood up from the chair at the kitchen table, mashed out her cigarette, and proceeded to make us feel as if we'd both made a big mistake by being born.

Having a bad temper kind of ran in the family, and Neecey and I had been expecting things to get hot. But mom was madder than I'd ever seen her before—scalding, cursing, scary mad—so mad that I honestly thought she was going to lose control and start swinging, although she'd never hit either of us before. Not that I could've blamed her if she'd made an exception just this once. She had every right to rip my arms off and beat me over the head with them if she wanted to, because I'd not only lied to her and disobeyed her and generally screwed the pooch every which way from Sunday, but I'd worried her to the point where she'd actually feared for my life. Yeah, I did, and even guys on death row knew that worrying a mom on top of making her angry was just about as capital a crime as you could ever commit.

Thing was, she'd called to check up on me this evening and found the line busy because I'd left it off the hook. No, I could not have made a more dumb-fuck amateur move if I'd tried. Because once mom called and got a busy signal, which of course she would, she'd call back a few minutes later, which of course she did, and she'd get a busy signal again, and then she'd keep at it until she realized that the phone had been busy for nearly an hour. This would confuse and disturb mom for basically the same reason Neecey had just brought up in the Jeep: who the *hell* could I *possibly* be talking to, when I didn't have *any* friends? Okay, I might've overlooked that line of thought earlier, when I'd taken the phone off the hook before leaving the house. It was possible.

So mom called the operator to make an emergency breakthrough, and found that the line was out of service. Yup, now she was worried. She called the retirement home to see if I was there by some chance, they told her I wasn't, and then she started to panic. She called Cynthia's mom and asked for Neecey, but Neecey and Cynthia were already out, so she asked Mrs. Murdock where they'd gone and she said she didn't know—they were out with friends and they'd be back later. So mom called our house again, got another busy signal, and said, *That's it,* and left work, right in the middle of her shift, leaving only one person to cover the whole bar. Bad news, very bad news. And when she got here, she found nobody home, the phone off the hook, the Cruiser locked to the back porch, and, worse still, Thrash facedown on the bed in my room. Mom said seeing him like that actually damaged something in her brain. I'd *never* left him that way before, but there he was, my tiny plush sidekick and best friend, all alone with his face in the pillow and his backside up in the air, while I was *nowhere* to be found, and she said the sight of that was just so creepy and chilling that she knew, she just *knew,* that I'd been abducted, sexually abused, dismembered, and dumped on the roadside hours ago, and she sort of lost it.

I had to give it to mom, though, because as soon as we'd walked into the kitchen, she seemed to find whatever it was she'd lost, gathered it up, gave *all* of it to me, and still had enough left over to rope Neecey into the fire so she wouldn't feel left out in the cold. And if you've ever had your mother mad at you like that—inside out, beside herself, head melting, skin splitting open, serpents and fire shooting out of her mouth—then you already knew it was the absolute worst experience you could *ever* possibly have, and the only thing you wanted to do was pretend it wasn't happening, or disappear, but you couldn't do either, so you just wound up feeling like a worthless piece of shit and bawling like a helpless two-year-old that hadn't been fed, changed, or held for weeks.

It was a solid thirty minutes of screaming and angry tears before mom had burned off all her excess fuel and had to sit back down to recharge with three more cigarettes. Thanks to Neecey, we'd both managed to stay quiet and not make it any worse for ourselves than it already was. Mom sat smoking at the kitchen table, and we stood exactly where we were—rigid, cowering, chins on our chests—for a few more minutes of tense and painful silence.

Then mom stood up, came over to me, and said, "Come here, let me take a look at that eye." She held my head with both hands, inspected me, and sucked her teeth. "Where's your shirt? Or should I be afraid to ask?"

Come to think of it, I had no idea where it was. As mom turned her back and went to the refrigerator, I took a quick look at Neecey; she shook her head no, so I didn't answer the question.

"We're all out of steak," mom went on, "so you'll have to settle for hamburger."

This time it was Neecey who stole a peek at me, quickly shooting out her tongue, as if to say, *I told you so,* and for some reason she and I couldn't help snickering. Nah, that was not a smart move on our part when we were still in grave and immediate danger, and mom turned around to ask what was so goddamn funny. I didn't want to break the silence first, so I waited for Neecey to speak.

"It's just, Genie doesn't think hamburger will work on a black eye. He thinks you need like a steak."

Maybe that caught mom off guard a little, because she shrugged and said, "It doesn't really matter what kind of meat you use; it's more important to have a dense mold for the eye socket, so the cold and pressure are even enough to reduce the swelling."

"So a chopped sirloin patty," I worked up the nerve to say, "if it was like frozen solid, wouldn't be as good as, say, a really cold rump?"

Mom shrugged again. "No, probably not, especially since a frozen patty won't come in contact with most of the wound."

I smirked at Neecey, I couldn't help it, and mom saw that, too. Then, out of nowhere, she said, "Not that you'd ever want a really cold rump pressed against your face."

We all burst out laughing.

Yeah, it was a stupid joke, and not the kind mom would usually make, but we laughed anyway. It showed me that no matter how angry mom was, she was doing her best to go easy on us. That helped a lot. She was still upset and wanted to know what had happened, but she was much calmer, more composed, and it made Neecey and me feel more relaxed and easy about what was coming. We still had to go through the chore of giving her a flimsy cocka-mamie bullshit story and waiting for her to mete out justice, but we all knew the routine, so we just got to it.

And the only things mom learned from us that she didn't know already were that I *had* taken grandma up on the case, lied to her about it, heard Neecey talking to Cynthia on the phone, followed them tonight, and then got into a fight with a kid who'd tried to pick on me. That was it. There was nothing about Darren or the crew, hardly any names, no mention of the church or Razor or Staci or drugs of any kind or Tommy Sharpe or, when you got right to it, really *any* of the important details at all. It was just a story about me doing exactly what mom and Neecey had been trying forever to keep me from doing, without most of the stuff I'd gone through to do it; except, of course, the lying and promise-breaking, sneaking out of the house, and getting into a fight, all of which pretty much had to be admitted and paid for. Mom wasn't ecstatic about any of it, but she didn't seem surprised either, and maybe that's why she didn't ask for specifics. Besides, the only proof she needed was written all over the left side of my face.

So we cut off the tiniest sliver of what'd happened and chewed it over with mom for a while, and she was pretty cool about it, all things considered. When we were finished, she said, "You realize, Genie, this is probably the *worst* thing you've ever done, even worse than hitting that teacher, because I honestly and sincerely believe in my heart that you didn't *mean* to do that. God, I *have* to believe that. But you *meant* to do this, you even *lied to my face* so you could, and that, Genie, deserves the *worst* punishment you've ever had."

Thing was, mom wasn't even mad when she said it, and that's what really scared me. I realized I was looking at being grounded forever—I was looking at *life*.

"Honestly," she went on, "I don't even know *what* I'm going to do with you this time, because *nothing* seems to work."

Yeah, I'd heard that one before, too, but this time was different. This time I *felt* it, and goddamn it, it *hurt*. My own mother was on the brink of thinking I was hopeless, and everything was starting to look bleak—when Neecey jumped in. She told mom to blame her instead, or that they should blame themselves, because they both had some idea of what I might do and could've talked to me about it, but they didn't. Mom held steady, though, and asked Neecey if she thought I would've listened.

"No, he never listens, but we still didn't try, so that's like partly our fault."

But I *was* listening this time; I was standing right there.

"Do you really think we should be having this discussion in front of him now?"

"Probably not, mom," Neecey replied, "but if we don't have it in front of him like sooner or later, he'll never know and he'll keep doing the same things over and over again."

I guess that's when it hit me that mom was responsible for all three of us, but *both* of them were responsible for *me,* and it took *everything* they had working *together* to handle the job. I wanted to jump in and tell them that I got it now and that I'd try to do better, but they were starting to argue about what they should do and what was best for me, and I didn't want to get in the middle of it any more than I already was.

Eventually, mom said, "What am I supposed to do, Neecey? He *has* to be punished."

Neecey paused. "But you *can't* punish him this time."

"Oh, no? Why not?" Mom's smile was more like a dare.

Then Neecey dropped the bombshell. "Because he met a girl tonight and he likes her and she likes him, and if you punish him now, he'll lose the best shot at having a real friend that he's had in like three years, so you *can't*."

Mom was *not* expecting that—shit, neither was I—and it took a second to sink in. "A girl? What *girl*? A *high-school* girl?"

"No, mom, she's going into seventh grade, like Genie."

"Then what's she doing at a high-school party?"

"Chill, mom. She just like crashed it, and nobody even knew she was there or we would've made her leave. But all she did was like sit down by the reservoir and talk to Genie, and you know what? Now they completely *like* each other, so we totally have to think about that."

Mom looked at me and I could tell the new information was causing her some doubt, maybe even hesitation, so I ran with it, and showed her the piece of paper with Staci's name and number on it. Mom made this face like she'd just gotten a big tax return *and* a notice of audit from the IRS at the same time, so I was having trouble reading it. She handed the paper back to me and slouched a little.

"Is this true?"

"Yeah, mom, it's true."

Mom sighed and looked back at Neecey. "Well, if she *really* likes him, she'll be waiting for him when school starts in two weeks."

Denied.

But Neecey didn't give in. "No, mom, she like totally *won't* and we both know it. If he doesn't go after her tomorrow or like the next day, she won't even remember his *name* in two weeks, or that she ever liked him in the first place." Mom tried to object, but Neecey kept going. "You were thirteen once, mom, and maybe because I'm younger I like remember it better or whatever, but we both totally know that in two weeks she'll have a crush on someone else who isn't completely grounded for life and Genie will miss his chance. But this is his chance, mom. It *is*. And she's a sweet girl, I swear, she's *really* nice, and you're totally going to *love* her. Come on, mom, please, *don't do this to him*. Please, mom, *please*."

Jesus, Neecey was making my plight seem goddamn desperate and she was laying everything on the line to break mom down. At that moment, no matter how it turned out, I knew I had my big sister back for good.

Mom raked her hands over her face and sighed heavily, almost groaning. It was obvious that she was having a conflict, a deep one, between my high crimes and loneliness, and which was more important—justice being done or the possibility of me having a friend. It was eating her up as we all stood there in the kitchen, and it showed, *every bit* of it showed. But then mom shook it off, straightened up, and wiped her eyes. "I almost don't know what to do with you anymore, Genie, that's how far you've gone. And there isn't a single reason I can think of for me to trust you."

No, that wasn't the answer I was looking for.

"But I'm just about at the end of my rope, so maybe it's time to try something new." Mom paused. This was it; my whole future hung in the balance. "Maybe *you* should tell *me* what your punishment should be."

Suddenly there was a ray of light through the darkness. I knew the answer right away, but I had to play it cool, give it some time, and make it look like a struggle or she'd think I was letting myself off easy and I'd blow it. I fidgeted around a little, wrung my hands, dropped my head, and drew circles on the floor with my foot. Both mom and Neecey were quiet, waiting. It was working.

"First," I said, "I'm going to paint the sign tomorrow, so it'll be fixed."

Mom folded her arms and nodded her head in a way that meant what I'd just said was not even close to being good enough. "Okay . . . what else?"

"I, um, I probably shouldn't get any allowance for like a month, maybe two, and I'll have to do extra chores."

Mom nodded again.

Now for my medicine. "We'll have to call Pauline to watch me when you and Neecey are out." Yuck. I felt sick before the words had even left my mouth. But these were desperate times, sacrifices had to be made, and if I didn't know any better, I would've sworn that mom was fighting off a smile, a real one. She seemed to soften up. The moment felt right. It was time to go for broke. "Well, it's not really a punishment, but I'm going to tell both of you about some of the things in my journal, because it's probably time you knew."

All of a sudden I had four dark brown eyes staring at me in total disbelief, the wet and quivering eyes of my mother and sister, then their arms all around me, their lips on my forehead and cheeks, their tears mixing with mine, and I knew the worst was over. Everything wasn't fixed and nothing was perfect, but it seemed as if a new horizon was opening before us out of the shitstorm I'd created. No, I'd never really listened to them before, but tonight I'd paid attention. And I guess I understood a bit more about what they wanted from me, how far they were willing to go to get it, and how little it'd take to meet them halfway.

Sure, I'd gotten out of the worst thing I'd ever done by making up my own punishment, comprised of things I'd *already* decided to do, or that were coming to me anyway. So you could say I got off easy. Fine. But I'd also been up against the wall and found a way to snatch this one back from the edge of dread and despair, and I was still offering something back to mom and Neecey for everything they'd done for me. Yeah, all right, I'd gotten myself off the hook. But I was home, too.

TWENTY-THREE

It was strange. I slept soundly that night but awoke the next morning certain that the ax would fall. I mean, I couldn't just get away with it. I couldn't break promises to my mother and grandmother, lie, disobey, think all the scummy things I'd thought about my sister, sneak out of the house after dark, trespass, make out with the girl I was crazy about, then insult and threaten her, wallop some kid in the scrotum, have my face flattened, get caught red-handed on the back end, and then sweep it all under the rug with a "punishment" that was about as hard to take as using the "Get Out of Jail Free" card in Monopoly. No, I couldn't *possibly* get away with all that. Nothing in life was ever that easy. There were consequences; there were *always* consequences.

Yeah, I looked like shit because my eye was all greenish-purple and puffy, but even that wasn't as bad as it could've been, thanks, I guess, to the healing properties of cows. And I knew it'd get better in a week or so, because I'd had plenty of black eyes before. Some kids collected baseball cards, some hoarded mint-condition coins, others stamps; I collected shiners. It was a hobby of mine; I was good at it. Damn good.

I jumped out of bed, carefully rolled the stiffness out of my neck, skipped my exercises, went to the bathroom, brushed my teeth, and then headed downstairs to have some breakfast. The phone rang as I arrived in the kitchen, and when I picked it up, the ax finally fell. Well, it didn't actually fall; it was more like I just got it. On the line was Mr. Dunbar, assistant coach of the junior-high football team, and he told me that he and Coach Rose had talked it over, and while I'd been the fastest kid at tryouts and had good hands, the other guys were a lot bigger than I was and much stronger, too, and after seeing what'd happened to me during the punt return, they figured I'd only wind up getting hurt. So they thought it best if I sat this season out, and if I got taller and put on a few pounds by next August, I was more than welcome to try out again then.

That was it. I was cut. I'd gotten cut from the junior-high football team quicker than one of Jerry's Kids, and I'd been cut even though everyone with cleats, shoulder pads, and a cup knew for a fact that I could play, because Coach Rose had had it in for me way before I'd ever stepped on the field. That was the *only* reason for it, and it was total bullshit. Mr. Dunbar said I shouldn't feel too bad about it, because there was always next year, and because both he and Coach Rose were very sorry about the decision. Yeah, they were sorry all right. But not as sorry as they'd be when I rammed that goddamn whistle all the way up Coach Rose's ass.

I hung up the phone feeling angry and disappointed. Not just because I'd been shafted and didn't make the team, but because I realized nothing had really changed. I was still the same scorned and unwanted kid with a black mark against his name, I still had the same violent history pinned to my sleeve, and no matter what I did or did not do, people around here would never let me forget it. I'd learned more in the past few days than I'd learned in my whole stupid life, but none of that seemed to matter to anyone else. They already knew more about me than they'd ever need to know, and there was no way in hell they'd ever let me be some kind of local legend like Darren and the others said, because you couldn't be a legend if you were still just a loser.

Sure, I now realized I couldn't claim to know much, but I knew just enough to be sure that the world I lived in hadn't changed a bit: it was still a small, crappy town populated by people who were smaller and crappier. And at the top of that petty shit heap was Orlando, or whoever the hell he was now; he'd changed a lot, and everything was all his fault. He'd hit me at tryouts *on purpose,* sucker punched the shit out of me, knocked me out cold, then led me to blame it on somebody else, but he'd done it *all* on his own. Nobody had put him up to it or forced him to do it, and it didn't have anything to do with Razor or the sign or anything else; it just happened on the same damn day, and taking Orlando at his word, believing in him, and dreaming up excuses for what he'd done was where I'd gone wrong. I guess I'd figured it out when I'd stumbled into his backyard last night, but the damned honest truth was that I didn't want to think about it at the time, or to ask the question later, because *I didn't want to know.* I didn't want to know, didn't want it to be *true,* and I must've supposed the best course of action was to just keep avoiding it. But I couldn't keep avoiding it. *Orlando had done that to me;* it was a *fact,* it was *true,* and I *knew* it.

And knowing that hurt. It hurt in every possible way. Not just physically, or because for a long time Orlando had been the only friend I'd ever had, or because he'd fucked me all up on the case, or because the little show he'd put on had given Coach Rose the excuse he'd been looking for to cut me from the team. No, it hurt even more because he'd *betrayed* me; he'd *really* betrayed me, like nothing about our friendship had ever been real, like it'd never meant anything to him, as if we'd never known each other at all. And that meant there was no going back to being friends.

Fuck it. I didn't give a shit. I didn't give a shit about Orlando or his depressive, deceitful, backstabbing, friendless, sorry-assed, book-wormy self, or if I'd ever see or talk to him again. For all I cared, he could go fucking rot. I didn't need him anymore. Darren and the crew had all said they liked me last night, and more than that, I now had the phone number of someone else who did.

I got Staci's number from upstairs in my room, came back down, took a deep breath, and punched in the digits. She picked up on the first ring, which surprised me, but she said that her mother worked nights and she was sleeping now and she didn't want the phone to wake her. I told Staci to get dressed because I was coming to pick her up in about half an hour. She said okay, and, yeah, I was already starting to like that word again.

I treated myself to a long, overdue scrubbing in the shower. Then I dried off, got dressed, gelled and spiked my hair, and left. When I pulled up in front of Staci's apartment on the Cruiser, she was already waiting outside. She was wearing white denim cutoffs (although nowhere near as short as the ones she'd worn Monday), a red tank top, three thousand bracelets and anklets, white-and-red tube socks pushed all the way down, and black Converse low-tops. She kind of looked like a candy cane, but everyone who ever met me knew I had a sweet tooth, so that was right up my alley. She stood up from the front steps as I approached, waved, tilted her head, and smiled that gap-toothed smile, while the morning sun shone crisp and warm in the cloudless sky above. It looked, felt, and even smelled as if a beautiful day was dawning.

Staci hopped on behind me, and it hit me that, for once, I'd made a good decision without knowing it at the time. I'd always thought the Cruiser just *had* to have a banana seat for the way it would look—it seemed *right*, matched the style I'd had in mind—and there had never been *any* question of settling for something else. But now I could see my banana seat had another advantage; it was the perfect size for the three of us to sit on—me, Staci, and her precious rear cargo—and I felt thankful and proud as all hell for having trusted my vision.

I popped the kickstand and we rolled out. I asked Staci if she'd eaten breakfast. She said no and I smiled to myself. Our first stop was McDonald's. I ordered a sausage-and-cheese biscuit, hash browns, and orange juice, and Staci ordered the same, only with an Egg McMuffin instead, but told me she didn't have any money before she did. I smiled again, whipped a ten out of my pocket, and told her it was on me. When we got to the window, I slapped the bill down on the counter like it was burning my hand, grabbed the bag, handed it to Staci, asked her to check the order, counted my change, and pedaled off like a pro. Just like that, I'd taken Staci out to eat, like a real date. And of course I used the drive-through.

We pulled up to the retirement home, I chained the Cruiser to the NO PARKING sign out front, and then Staci and I sat down on the curb. I was about to dig in when I felt her looking at me.

"What's wrong?" I asked.

"Nothing." She paused. "It's just, what are we doing here?"

"My grandma lives here. She's old and going senile, but she's still my grandma. There's something I have to tell her real fast, and then we can book it and do something else."

Staci's face drew back a little, and her eyes widened as if she'd just been told to go sit in the corner. Maybe she didn't like old people or being around them, but just as quickly her face relaxed and she nodded her head. Then she scooted closer to me so that our knees were touching, bit into her McMuffin, and somehow made it clear that she understood. No, it didn't last all that long, but it was easily the best McDonald's breakfast I'd ever had, and everybody on solid food knew that Mickey D's breakfasts were the best you could get.

After we'd finished, I grabbed all our trash, wadded it into a ball, stood up, said come on to Staci, gave her my hand to help her up, and kept hold of her as we walked in. Kathy was at the desk, looking as ridiculously hot as ever in her sandals and short skirt and tight top and jaw-dropping cleavage and big hair, but her pretty face flashed hard and fast with mixed emotions when she saw us come in. She got up quickly, rushed over from behind the desk, started rubbing my cheeks, neck, and head, looked totally worried, and asked me what happened. Before I could get a word in, Staci said, "He beat up this high-school guy that was mean and bothering me."

That was only sort of true, but it didn't seem like the right time to make an issue out of it, because Kathy's green eyes got all round and big and she pulled her head back some and just kind of looked at me, and then at Staci, and then at me again and smiled. Yeah, I smiled, too. After a few seconds of us all grinning at one another like morons, Kathy said, "If you beat him up, then what happened to your eye?"

"Well, she never said I beat up his friend, too."

We laughed.

"I guess not," Kathy said. "So are you going to introduce me to your girlfriend, or what?"

Girlfriend? Whoa.

"Hi, I'm Staci," Staci cut in, as if I had no say in the matter whatsoever.

"Hi, Staci, I'm Kathy. Nice to meet you."

The introductions were over, and I'd just been informed that Staci was my girlfriend. I said it before, and I'll say it again: whoa.

"So what are you guys up to? Going to see Toots?"

"Yeah, for a minute. Where's Pencil Neck?"

"He's out of the office today, why?"

I was considering trying to have a man-to-man with him about what was really going on in, or out of, Livia's room. But he wasn't around, so it would have to wait. Then again, it wouldn't be so easy having a man-to-man with Bryan when I knew one of us didn't qualify.

"No reason," I answered, thinking that *everything* seemed to be going my way.

"Hey, K-kathy?" Staci stammered quietly at her feet.

"Yeah, hon?"

"The sign out front? Why isn't it fixed yet?"

"Oh, *tell* me about it, Staci," Kathy dished.

"Can *we* do it?" Staci asked her, and then looked at me. "*Can* we?"

For some reason the idea hadn't even crossed my mind. I'd planned to repaint the sign by myself sometime later in the day, after we were done hanging out, just like I'd told mom I would last night. I'd never thought about asking Staci to help me, maybe because painting the front sign at an old folks' home wasn't exactly the coolest thing to ask a chick to do on a first date and all. But since she suggested it, and I had to do it anyway, I was more than inclined to agree.

"You really *want* to?" Kathy asked.

Staci nodded; I followed suit.

"Okay. I don't see why not."

Kathy circled behind the desk, made a call, and in a few minutes two of the home's janitors came out with a large can of white paint, one of black, four brushes, stencil letters, a level, a T square, a yardstick, four or five sharpened pencils, and two six-foot fold-up ladders. I felt like screaming, *If you already had the goddamn stuff, then why haven't you fixed the fucking sign yet?*, but Staci was there and Kathy was still smiling in this really pleased and knowing way, so I just swallowed it and got ready to get to work. Grandma would just have to wait.

It turned into a major event; then again, almost anything that ever happened at the retirement home was an event of some magnitude to the inmates. Staci and I set up the ladders on the island, next to the sign, and covered the tag with two coats of white paint. While we waited for them to dry, the parade of onlookers began. The old-timers shuffled across the parking lot in groups of two, three, or four, Cuthbert Stansted and Livia and all the rest, in their loud outfits and sweaters and heavy shoes, with their walkers and wheelchairs, to see what we were doing and to ask the question—over and over—what are you doing, what are you doing, what are you doing? We told them their sign needed repainting and we'd volunteered to do it, and they seemed to buy it because they told us what good kids we were. Yeah, right.

In the meantime, it started getting warm out, so it only took a little while for both base coats to dry, and when they did, Staci and I got started on the hard part—the lettering. We had to use the yardstick and the level to draw pencil guidelines first, so the letters wouldn't slant up or down or a mixture of both, because that would look like shit. But since there were two of us—one to hold the yardstick with the level on top and the other to run a pencil along the bottom—it was no problem at all. No, I couldn't have done it all by myself, and I would've made a total mess of it if I'd tried. But Staci seemed to have a knack for that kind of work, which she said probably came from making all those patterns for clothes, because she was always tracing the outlines of things. I didn't know where she'd gotten it from, but she was about six or seven grades better than I was, at the stenciling, too, so I tried to hold my own and not make a klutz of myself in front of all the old men and women circling our knees and ankles.

They were all still coming out and watching in turn, especially the ones who knew every damn thing about every kind of job ever performed in the history of human endeavors and whose sole purpose in life was to share that information with everyone all the time, whether they were asked for it or not. Luckily, old farts like that were outnumbered by sweet grandma and grandpa types who told them to pipe down and quit bothering us because we were doing a wonderful job. Shit, for them we could've done the sign in crayon and left-handed and they would've said it was the most beautiful craftsmanship they'd ever beheld.

It took a while, but we got through it okay, and we'd finished the measuring, lining, and stenciling by lunchtime. Most of the crowd dispersed to the cafeteria for grub. I asked Staci if she was hungry and she said not yet, so we switched paint and brushes and started on the letters. Grandma still hadn't come out. I could see her room from where we were, and I saw that the curtains were opened and that she was sitting in her chair watching us from a distance, but she hadn't come outside to say hello or to see what we were doing. I took that for what it was, a bad omen. Maybe mom had called her this morning and told her everything that'd happened, and grandma was either sulking about it because she'd gotten blamed or was pissed off at me because I'd fucked it all up. Either way, she wouldn't be in too great a mood when we went to see her later on, and I was glad as hell I hadn't gone to see her first. As soon as she got me alone, she was going to lower the whole goddamn boom on me and more, and suddenly I was dreading it.

If I wanted my ass all in one piece, which I did, then I'd have to come up with a plan. I couldn't think about it too much, though, because staying within the lines of stenciled letters with a paintbrush took more concentration than I'd expected, and I was focusing my attention on that. I must've had my tongue sticking out of the corner of my mouth, like I sometimes did when I was concentrating intently, because Staci asked me if I was okay.

"I'm cool," I said, "how you doing?"

"I'm okay."

Yeah, she *was* okay. After a few more minutes of working in silence, Staci laughed.

"What's so funny?" I asked.

"Oh, I was just thinking."

"What?"

"Nothing."

"Come on, you can tell me."

"It's nothing, really."

"C'mon, Staci, *please?*"

"It's just, I mean . . ."

"What?"

"I was laughing because I was thinking how much easier it is to do this on a ladder."

It took me a few seconds to realize what she meant, but when I did, it was like a pair of icy cold hands had torn through my abdomen and ripped out my spleen. The tips of my ears sizzled, my mind raced, and just like that I could see it all too clearly. If you had a brand-new moped to stand on, you wouldn't *need* two people to pull the job off, but that didn't mean *only one* had done it.

Jesus H. Christ, that *so* fucking figured, didn't it? How in the shit-smeared world did I *not* see that coming? How the hell could I be such a *sucker*? *Goddamn it!* Why didn't *anybody* tell me? But did anyone else even *know*, like Neecey or Darren or someone else? No, they *couldn't* have known. But if they couldn't have known, then why were Darren's words from the arcade thundering back to me, telling me all I'd needed to know, right from the very beginning: *wank, hand painted, hand job*. Maybe because my life was a *joke*, that's why—a dirty fucking joke.

Sure, everybody knew, why not? They fucking *had* to. Shit, they *all* knew what'd really happened, *everybody except me*, and they'd *all* been laughing their asses off about it behind my back. But why didn't somebody *say something* last night? Why was I the *only one* left in the dark? What the hell was so goddamn *wrong* with me that everybody *always* had to treat me like a fucking *chump*?

I felt empty and all alone, and I was gripping the wooden rails of the ladder so hard that it seemed as if they'd splinter through my palms.

"Hey, your face is like all red. You okay?"

I wasn't. I really wasn't. I didn't know what I was, or what the hell I was supposed to be. Worse still, I didn't know a goddamn thing about anyone else. I didn't know if Neecey, Darren, and the others hadn't told me last night because they didn't know, or thought I knew already, or for some other reason. Maybe that's why I'd wondered about them acting all friendly and nice to me, because something about it just didn't seem right. Maybe it *wasn't* all in my head, maybe they'd just been *pretending* to like me to serve their ulterior motives. But *why*? What had I *ever* done to *them*? Why would they play me like that? Did they think I was some kind of wild, piece-of-shit, vicious asshole of a menace who needed to be lied to and dicked around and handled with kid gloves like . . . *like Razor?* Was that *why?*

Jesus, the idea of being lumped together with that scumbag just totally and completely sucked, and there was *no way* I could tell if that's what people around here really thought of me. I sure as hell hoped not, because I didn't think I deserved it. But I honestly didn't know, and that made everything seem even worse. Yeah, I'd had my doubts about Darren and the crew and I thought I'd gotten over them, but I still couldn't tell if everything they'd said to me was *true,* or if the way they'd treated me was *real.*

And I couldn't tell about Staci either. She must've thought I already knew, she *must have,* because she'd asked me why I'd brought her here in the first place, she'd been casual about admitting what she'd done, and she didn't seem to be hiding anything. But she *was* hiding something, wasn't she? She'd been hiding things all along. She'd been hiding what she'd done with Razor, and that she'd been *here, with him, at the sign.* She'd *done it, she* was to blame; *that's* what she'd been hiding, and *that's* why she'd been so goddamn eager to repaint the sign, *to hide it all over again.*

Okay, sure, maybe Razor had forced her to do that, too, but even if she'd been forced to do some of it, she hadn't been forced to do *all* of it, and none of that would ever change the fact that she'd just copped to being the *perpetrator,* and that's something she would *always* be. That counted for something; there were consequences for that.

It was happening all over again. I was back by the reservoir in the dark, standing on the edge of a cliff, and the ground was giving way. All the heartache and madness were back, fresh and painful as ever. It was like I'd never left, like I'd never escaped, like wherever I went or whatever I did, they'd be right on my tail and I'd never get away. I closed my eyes and tried to steady myself, but all I could see was Staci painting the sign while standing on Razor's moped, one of her black rubber bracelets falling to the ground without her noticing, the two of them alone together, kissing, touching. It made me feel hateful and sick. And it made me realize I wasn't the blond Satan I'd thought I was, because at the end of the book Sam Spade refused to play the sap. But that's exactly what I was doing: I *was* playing the fucking sap, *covering up a crime for the sake of a guilty chick.*

Goddamn it. Knowing, really *knowing* where I stood and what I was doing was a hell of a lot worse than any punishment I could've ever dreamed up for myself. I felt foolish, shamed, humiliated, used, and I knew if I didn't make a stand and part ways with Staci right now, then I'd not only play the sap, but I'd be guilty, too. I'd be an *accessory after the fact,* and that would rope me in with the rest of them, with all their lies and petty crimes, all their cliques and false friendships, and I'd be just like everyone else. It seemed too high a price to pay for what I'd done, too harsh a sentence, a sentence I'd be reminded of each time I looked at Staci's face. And that would ruin *everything,* like a stain, or a wound that wouldn't heal. Unless I cut her loose, there'd be no escaping it, and not much hope that it would *ever* go away.

Those were the facts of the case, *my* case, and they said I was screwed. I'd either have to get used to being a pussy-whipped pushover chump, or go right back to where I'd started, as a violent half-crazed loner, only now with a broken heart, too.

Then it hit me there was another way to look at things, another set of facts standing side by side that told the same story with a different slant. True, I didn't know Staci all that well, and I didn't know how far I could trust her. But I *liked* her anyway. I'd liked her before I'd met her and I liked her even more now. She'd earned it. She'd forgiven me for the way I'd acted at the reservoir, how I'd scared her, hurt her feelings, made her cry, and she *still* wanted to hang out with me and have Kathy call her my girlfriend and fix the sign with me and tell people that I'd *defended* her. So she was either the biggest idiot in the entire tristate area, or she really liked me, too.

Either way, I figured we were made for each other. She was coming to me with enough baggage to open her own luggage kiosk at the mall, but I wasn't exactly a saint, and while she might not be all that smart, I wasn't any kind of genius either. No, I wasn't. Other people had always said that and they had *always* been wrong. I was just a mixed-up kid hanging out with the girl he liked, trying to do something right and good for a change.

Those were facts, too, and I could see my case both ways, the good way and the shitty way, and how I couldn't have the one without taking some of the other. So maybe that was three ways. Whatever. None of them told me what to do or which way to go; they were just facts, there for anyone to see. Then again, maybe how you saw things wasn't always what mattered most. Maybe everything depended on how much shit you were willing to take. Fuck it. I made my decision.

I took a deep breath, rolled my neck out, and got right to the point. As calmly as I could, I asked her why she'd painted "arted" over "irement," although I used different words and grammar when I put the question to her.

Staci looked over at me and told me that the night they'd been together, Razor had picked her up on his moped and brought her here, and even though it'd seemed a weird place to hang out, she hadn't thought much of it. Not too long after he'd coerced her into doing the first thing, he said he had one more thing for her to do, and told her to get up on the moped seat with the paint can and brush (that were in the backpack he'd worn) and paint something on the sign. She took the things and stood on top of the seat, but when she got up there, she didn't know what to do, or what to paint. So she asked Razor, and he said, "I don't know, paint anything," and she said, "God, you're retarded," but he was too busy being nervous and looking over both shoulders and hiding in the bushes to pay attention to what she was saying, so he replied, "Yeah, that's good, paint that, whatever, just hurry." Staci looked back at the sign, realized some of the letters were already there, left the first three as they were, blacked out the end of the word in a few quick strokes, slopped the rest out as fast as should could, jumped down, handed everything to Razor, and begged him to hurry packing up so they could leave. And she kept looking me right in the eye the whole time she was telling me about it.

I nodded and took another breath. "Did Razor force you to do that, too?"

"Not really, I guess." Staci looked confused. "But it was right afterward."

"Then why did you do it?"

She shrugged. "I didn't think about it. I was upset and I thought Razor would leave me alone if I did, so I did it."

"But what the hell made Razor decide on this sign in the first place? You know, what was the point? What was he trying to prove?"

"Oh . . ." Staci replied hesitantly, maybe because it was too many questions at once. "I dunno. I thought he was biting off Darren and the crew to try to be popular, like everybody else does, but that he was too chicken to go through with it. I didn't ask him, though, so I don't know for sure."

"You didn't *ask* him?"

"Why would I? I was feeling all bad about everything and what he'd say to everyone and thinking how much I hated him and how much he sucked. I just really wanted to go home."

Staci had a point there. Razor did suck. "So you didn't mean anything by it?"

She tilted her head and frowned. "What, you mean like ranking on the old folks or something?"

"Yeah." I shrugged. "I guess."

"Ohmigod, I like never even thought about that," she cringed. "So you hate me now, don't you? Because your grandmother's like, uh, because she like lives here and all?"

"No, Staci, I don't hate you," I said, "I really don't. I was just asking." I paused, struggling for something to say. "By the way, you know you spell *retarded* with a *d* and not two *t*s, right?"

"Really? Whoa, maybe that's why everybody thinks I'm so dumb." Her face reddened and she tried to laugh. It didn't work. "I'm not dumb, though. I just don't like school, and I'm not a good speller."

I had to give it to her: if Staci was anything, she was honest. It was hard not to like her for that, and I knew right then it'd be even harder to let her go. So I wasn't going to.

"I'm not crazy about school either," I said, "but I can pretty much spell my ass off. I can help you if you want."

"That's sweet." She smiled. "Yeah, sure, okay."

That was it. Seriously. I'd asked, she'd answered, and it was done. I wasn't exactly clicking my heels together with glee or anything, but I wasn't beside myself with rage about it either. I knew what'd happened and I'd found out who'd done it, but there wasn't much I could do about any of it. I'd already punched the sleazebag most responsible square in the nuts—in public, for everyone to see, no less—so if I'd had a hankering for revenge, I figured I'd satisfied it already. Then again, as much as I couldn't stand Razor, I'd learned he wasn't the only guilty party involved. Staci was *kind of* guilty for what she'd done, and now I was, too.

We finished repainting the sign and cleaned up when we were through. Yeah, I'd covered up the crime I'd been paid to solve. I was a chump; I'd played the sap. And I knew for a fact I'd do it again. Case closed.

I knocked once on the door to grandma's room and pushed it open like I always did, and she was sitting in her chair by the window with it turned to face the door, as if she'd been expecting me. Her wig was a little bit crooked, but both of her eyebrows matched, and her teeth were in, so she looked fine. But the expression on her face said it all. Her brow was furrowed, her eyes were narrowed and sharp, her lips bunched, and everything about her said she was more disappointed in me than she'd ever been before. I'd always tried my best to do everything she asked or told me to do. But I'd failed on the case and I knew it, I'd broken my promise to her and I knew it, I'd failed *her* and I knew it. It was all too clear that she knew it, too, and she was letting me know through the look in her eyes.

That hurt me more than anything else I'd been through, and it would've been unbearable, broken me down to tears on the spot, if I hadn't seen it coming and had the presence of mind to stop by the front desk beforehand and arrange for some backup. Kathy nudged me aside from the threshold and pushed Staci by the shoulders into grandma's room, then introduced her to grandma as my girlfriend. Everything about grandma changed instantly; she sat up a little straighter, she tilted her head, flashed her eyes, flung her hands out toward Staci, smiled as big and happily as she could, and told Staci to come over and give her a kiss, and Staci smiled back and said okay and did. It was the closest thing to a miracle I'd ever witnessed, and yeah, it got me *totally* off the hook. Well, at least for the time being.

But it was awesome. Kathy and Staci got my back and then grandma picked up the ball and ran with it; she treated Staci like an old friend or a member of the family, and sat her down next to her and patted her knees and played with her hair and paid her compliments and offered her shitty candy and made Staci tell her all about herself, as if I weren't even there. Ordinarily, that would've made me jealous and crazy, because she was *my* grandma and she was supposed to be paying attention to me, but for some reason, it seemed better to share her at the moment, and Staci and grandma seemed to be enjoying it, too. Yeah, I loved that woman, and I was going to miss everything about her when she was gone. But that was sorrow for another day. Today she was here and with me and talking and laughing and all on my side every step of the way, and I—I was overjoyed.

It was about three-thirty when we left, after we'd kissed grandma good-bye maybe fourteen times apiece. When we finally got out of

.there, I asked Staci what she wanted to eat. She asked if we could have pizza, and I said we could have pterodactyl if she wanted, and she said no thanks, she'd never tried that before. Okay, she didn't get the joke, and it was hard for me to tell if she was dumb or not, but I knew where the good pizza joint was, so that's where we went. I locked the Cruiser to the bike stand out front, went to the counter, ordered a small pie and a Cherry Coke for her, because that's what she wanted, and a vanilla milkshake for me, while she went to the back and got us a booth. That's what you called the division of labor, and it seemed like a pretty good racket.

When I brought our drinks over, she asked how come I wasn't having soda, too, because it went better with pizza than a milkshake. I said she was right, and it wasn't like I had anything against soda, but I had to have my daily quotient of dairy; it built strong bones and teeth and helped you grow, and if I wanted anything in life, I wanted to reach my full height. As soon as I'd said it, I got the feeling I'd heard it before, or maybe read it somewhere. I couldn't remember where, though, so I wasn't sure if those were my words or someone else's, but I realized they had nothing to do with inches. Staci smiled and said I shouldn't worry. She liked it that we were both the same size; it was like we were a pair, like we matched.

We were at the pizza parlor for maybe an hour and a half, just talking, hanging out, stuffing our faces, and having a great time. Then we got back on the Cruiser and I took Staci to her place. She asked me if I wanted to come up to meet her mom, because it was a little after five and she'd be awake, but I told her I'd have to take a rain check, because I was grounded and had to get home to do my chores. I'd pressed my luck with mom far enough, so I intended to hold up my end of our bargain. I didn't mention anything about Pauline to Staci, though, because having a babysitter for the foreseeable future made me feel, well, it made me feel like a baby. I guessed I'd have to tell her sooner or later, but I thought it could wait for some other time.

Instead, I asked her what she was doing tomorrow, and she said we could do whatever if it rained, or go to the pool together if it was nice. I said cool and kissed her good-bye and felt a bittersweet pang as I watched Staci and her butt and all the rest of her disappear through the door. I was about halfway home before I realized that as a detective I'd gotten everything wrong or backward. *Everything.* Shit, I didn't even get the girl in the end. The girl got me.

TWENTY-FOUR

Early the next morning I was on my hands and knees in the upstairs bathroom, gloved to my elbows, scrub brush in hand, bucket of sudsy disinfectant by my side, scouring the tub, toilet, and tiles like some kind of galley slave, when I heard the phone ring. I booked it downstairs, peeling off the gloves, taking two steps at a time, because I thought it was Staci. It was. She said hi and asked if she'd woken me up and I told her I'd gotten up extra early to get all my chores done this morning so we could spend the whole day together, but that it'd be about an hour before I was finished. She said that was okay, because the pool didn't open until ten, so we had plenty of time. I told her I'd be at her place at ten o'clock sharp, and she said okay. Then I said, come to think of it, I might want to shower first, so make that ten-oh-three. She said okay. Well, better make it five after, I said, just to be on the safe side. She said okay. Hey, Staci, I said. What, she asked. Nothing, I said. She said okay. I said good-bye, hung up the phone, and nearly fell on the floor laughing. I couldn't help it. Everything was just so goddamn *okay*.

Well, maybe everything wasn't okay, but as I got back to cleaning the bathroom, I realized everything felt different. Sure, it probably wouldn't matter to most people in town that I'd had a change of heart, or that I'd finally gotten myself a real friend—more than a friend, a *girl*friend, which everybody knew was totally cool—because people were assholes, so sooner or later they'd find a way to shit on that, too. I could practically hear the kids at junior high now: "Psst, check out the half-slut and the lunatic," or "Hey, Dopey and Crazy, where are the others?" Christ, I'd have to be a goddamn idiot to think for one second that crap like that would ever go away, and I might've been a sucker, a sap, a psycho, and a fool, but I wasn't an idiot. I knew that kind of nonsense would be coming down the pike one way or another, but even the thought of more mocking bullshit like that just didn't seem as important anymore.

I finished my chores, took a fast shower, went into my room, and threw on a swimsuit, a white tank top, and my canvas sneakers. Thrash was still seated in my wooden desk chair, where he'd been for the past couple of days. We hadn't spoken since he'd shut me out on Wednesday night, but I'd gone to bed without him both the past nights for the first time in almost five years and still slept like a baby. We'd been through so much over the years that I didn't want to leave things in a bad way between us, but when I tried to explain to him everything that'd gone down, I realized I just couldn't. I guess I *could* have, but I knew Thrash would *never* understand. He'd get some of it, like the plots and counterplots, the scheming and anger, the violence, fighting, and revenge, but all the rest, all the real important parts, would sail right over his little green head. So I didn't bother telling him anything. I just lifted him up from the chair, took one last look at his wide plastic eyes, his goofy grin, his dangling pink tongue, said my good-byes, placed him in the back corner of my closet, and closed the door. I didn't drag it out, or get all teary-eyed and mushy either, because I didn't know if it was good-bye forever or only good-bye for a while. It was just good-bye, see you later, time to move on.

I hopped on the Cruiser and tried to set a new land-speed record on my way over to Staci's. She was waiting at the curb for me when I got there, wearing flip-flops, denim cutoffs, and a pink bikini top, with a plastic beach bag slung over her shoulder. Yeah, she was skinnier than a Pick Up Stick, flatter than old soda, and not all that pretty, but she still looked great to me. She hopped on the Cruiser; I drove us to the pool, locked my ride to the bike stand in front, and grinned from ear to ear as Staci flashed her member's and guest badges to the lifeguard. I was finally inside the Sunnybrook Pool Club—with Staci Sanders on my arm no less—and it'd just opened its gates like two seconds ago, so nobody else was there yet. We pulled two chairs over and dropped our stuff in the far right corner where she usually sat, then I stripped down and headed straight in. I didn't wait for Staci; I wanted to be first. It seemed like a good idea to be up to my chest in water by the time she'd finally wriggled out of those shorts, to camouflage the sight of my periscope going up, which it was pretty much bound to do. What could I say? The Lookout had a mind of his own, and it was one-track all the way.

Whatever. I did a one-and-a-half off the high board and Staci dove in after me. We swam around together and did handstands and backward somersaults in the low end, had a friendly splash fight, pretended we were gonna dunk each other, fake-wrestled a little, and during our breath-holding contest, she cheated and kissed me underwater, so I cracked up, blew bubbles, and lost. Yeah, there was all this cutesy, cuddly, corny-assed kid shit going on all over the goddamn place, and I knew I should've excused myself for a second and kicked my own ass for acting like such a lovesick, sissified dork, but for some reason I didn't. Christ, I wasn't even thirteen yet, and I was already going soft.

But somehow I wasn't having a blast either, and that didn't make *any* sense. Sure, it might've been completely sappy and all kinds of gay, but this was *exactly* what I'd *always* wanted, what I'd hoped and dreamed for, and no matter how it looked to anyone else, I should've been having *fun*. Shit, I should've been having the goddamn time of my life. But I wasn't. It was like I was there, but not really. Part of me was holding hands with Staci while we lay on lounge chairs by the pool, enjoying being with her and getting to know her and eating it all up, and part of me just wasn't. That other part of me couldn't have been further away; it was on the other side of the globe, and my mind was somewhere else.

I knew what it was. I was thinking about Orlando. I thought that was all over and done with, that I'd cut the ties clean, but it was still gnawing at me. I sighed and looked upward as I lay on my back, and saw that the sky above me was mixed; it was partly sunny or partly cloudy, whatever you wanted to say. It was the kind of midmorning that might clear up in a few minutes or bring down a storm, but that hadn't really decided what kind of day it wanted to be yet.

I sat up all of a sudden, got dressed quickly, told Staci I was sorry but I'd forgotten to do something that I absolutely *had* to do, that couldn't wait, and that I'd try to meet her at the pool later. She was obviously surprised and disappointed that I was cutting our date short, but she tried to be a trouper about it; she smiled, nodded her head, and said okay anyway. Man, oh, man, she was *great*.

I was already on the Cruiser and more than halfway home before it hit me that I'd just bolted out on Staci and left her *completely* hanging. More than that, I'd just *lied* to her, too. Jesus, I really must've been some kind of goddamn idiot to risk hurting her feelings again, and maybe even losing her over it this time, too. But I just *had* to know; it was eating away at me, tearing me up inside, and if I didn't do something, I'd never get over it, never let go.

I got home, parked the Cruiser round back, and ran up to my room. It was better to settle it now, right now, to find out whatever the hell I could, deal with it as it came, and then put it to bed. I wanted to get over it. I wanted it *done*. I wanted to move on. All I needed was an *excuse,* you know, some trivial, half-assed reason that gave me permission to do what I was going to do anyway. We all had excuses for everything we did, and we used them all the time; I knew what my excuse was, what it would be, and I was tearing my room apart to find it. There it was; it had fallen behind my desk. I tossed *Walden* into my backpack, hurdled down the stairs, slammed the back door, jumped on the Cruiser, and was off again.

I raced to Orlando's place like his house was burning down. I felt this mad crush of urgency, of trouble, dire trouble, like Orlando was in danger. I didn't know why I felt that way, but I did. Maybe it was because he lived by someone like Razor, or because he'd been team-mates with Razor and Tommy Sharpe last year, or because they were the kind of guys that wouldn't think twice about forcing Orlando into something awful, something he couldn't get himself out of. Yeah, it occurred to me all of that might be more bullshit; that I just wanted to *think* Orlando was in danger in some way so I could pre-tend to be a hero again, or believe I was trying to help.

I jumped off at the curb huffing and sweating, walked the Cruiser up to the front of Orlando's house, and dropped the kickstand. I had no idea what the hell I was doing, or what I was after. I didn't know if Orlando even liked me anymore, if he had *ever* liked me, if we'd really been friends, or if somewhere along the line he'd real-ized that I'd lied to him and strung him out and never talked to him about the book he'd given me, was hurt by that, and then we'd never spoken again, and that's what he'd been left with—nothing, a painful, empty nothing—and it stuck with him, gnawed at him, and tore him up, till it all turned bitter and raw. I didn't know if that's how he felt, or if it was just another excuse. I didn't know if he'd hit me at tryouts on purpose, if it had been an accident, or what he'd meant to say before I'd cut him off: if he'd meant to apologize, to explain, or to lie to cover it up. I didn't know any of it. And I didn't know what would happen when I knocked on his front door, if any-one was home, if his mom would answer and chase me away with a bat, or if he'd open it, take one look at me, and start swinging himself.

All I knew was that it was time for me to return his book. He'd given it to me almost three years ago, and now I was giving it back. I didn't have much use for it anyway, because I never really understood it. It'd just confused me into thinking that I was different, that I could rely on myself, that I didn't need anything or anyone, and that I could try to go it alone. But I couldn't. As cruel and pointless as other people were, I *needed* them, I couldn't move an inch without them and all of their shit, because when you got right to it, I was puny and frightened and weak, same as everyone else. I thought I could hear someone rustling inside, but I didn't know who it was, or what would happen. I took a breath to ready myself; I was standing there wide open and vulnerable, but I was getting on with it, trying something new.

I was sick and fucking tired of being the smallest and meanest kid in a small and meaningless town. I wanted to be bigger than I was, better, more grown up. I didn't know if that was too much to want, or too little, or if there was a single chance in hell that I'd *ever* be able to get it. But I really didn't give a shit, because I *wanted* it anyway.

I wanted the world and everyone in it to be huge—like me.

ACKNOWLEDGMENTS

I would like to thank Julian Pavia, Tina Constable, and the rest of the stellar team at Crown for all their hard work and enthusiasm; Joe Regal at Regal Literary for his guidance and savvy; Lauren Pearson in the London office for her insight and support; and Markus "the Hammer" Hoffmann for all his patience and toil, all the edits, critiques, suggestions, reading and rereading, late-night phone conversations, drinks, football matches, and friendship. Any writer who has brutal but sympathetic readers of the early drafts is truly fortunate, so I must thank Hartford Gongaware for his hand in the Savannah Symposium, the perfect steaks, the Southern swamps (both real and imagined), Duke's, and nearly twenty years of kinship, and Alison Kinney, who is in all things nigh incomparable. Finally, I would like to thank Ellen Victoria Holloman for everything, everything.